CURSED DARKNESS

ANGELS OF FATE - BOOK 2

C.S. WILDE

~

"We are the monsters."

~

Cover image by Mirella Santana

Edited by Christina Walker and Sara Mack

An Exclusive Serial Featuring Liam

Join the Wildlings at subscribepage.com/liam to keep up to date with the latest on C.S. Wilde and participate in amazing giveaways. Also, you'll get an exclusive short-story featuring Liam.

LIAM

$\mathscr{L}$iam rushed through cold streets. His heavy footsteps hit concrete and splashed across puddles, soaking the bottom of his jeans, but he didn't slow down.

It had rained before he'd left the Legion, and by the fresh dewy scent hanging in the air and the dark-gray clouds rumbling above, it would rain again soon.

Fuck Jal and the rest of the Legion. He needed to be alone, and he needed out of that godsdamned mansion.

A danger to others, they said.

He scoffed. Liam was a Selfless, or at least he used to be. He could never harm an innocent.

A cruel laugh akin to his own rumbled from deep within his essence. This was why Jal and the others didn't trust him: the darkness. It took over newly turned demons with a vice; a mad juggernaut that infected Liam's essence and taunted him constantly.

"Shut up," he told the void inside him.

The mocking laugh rumbled louder as he ran. It roared in his eardrums, and when it was done, the sheer power that mocked, challenged, and punished him every single second of every single day whispered, *Fool.*

Maybe the darkness used Liam's voice because it was also a part of him. He couldn't tell for sure; this entire mess didn't make any sense.

"Fuck you," he growled at the darkness—no, at himself. They were one now.

Chilly wind whipped against his body, but the cold didn't bother him. Underneath his skin, he was burning. His legs hurt and the night air pricked his lungs, but he didn't stop.

The darkness silenced when he ran; Hells knew why. So Liam kept at it.

He regretted becoming a demon the moment he came back from the dead. As soon as he'd regained consciousness, a swarm of darkness swallowed him whole, piercing in and out of him, gutting all that made Liam who he was. That was the funny, if not cruel, thing about the darkness: it took his greatest fears and insecurities and slammed them against him, driving Liam to the edge of madness.

No wonder third-tier demons, or baby demons as Jal called him, often lost their minds.

"What doesn't kill you makes you stronger," Jal once said with a shrug.

Bullshit.

The darkness feasted on Liam. If this was a battle with himself, he was losing. And Jal, Jophiel, and Lilith, they couldn't do shit about it.

The priests and priestesses of the Gray tried meditating with him, but how could they teach Liam to dominate a monster they had never faced? After ten minutes he had to leave the room, because the darkness threatened to burst out of him and engulf them all.

The chaotic force spinning inside him was impatient, but so was he.

Weren't they the same in the end?

Right now he could barely sense the darkness, so running definitely helped.

His lungs felt like sandpaper, maybe from exhaustion, maybe from the storm raging inside him. Maybe both. He wiped sweat off his forehead and kept going.

He couldn't understand why in all the Hells he'd chosen to become a demon. Temporary insanity was his best guess.

You know why, the darkness whispered from somewhere bottomless inside him.

"I don't," he grumbled.

The darkness didn't reply or argue. This thing inside him wasn't forthcoming or particularly clear.

Liam kept running, pushing himself until he couldn't anymore. He heaved one last desperate breath before his legs buckled and he fell chest-down in an alley.

He grunted as he rolled over and laid on his back, watching the low clouds looming over the buildings that resembled black monoliths. His shirt was soaked with sweat, but it had already started drying—the perks of blessed fabric. *Or was it damned?* He couldn't tell the difference anymore.

His frantic breathing was the only sound he could hear, which meant a lot considering this city never slept.

What was that thing Jal had told him?

Make the darkness what you want it to be.

As if that was easy.

"It's why demons are a lot tougher than angels. Well, those of us who don't succumb to the darkness that is," Jal told him on a gloomy Sunday morning. "The dark rewards the strong, punishes the weak. If you control it, its gifts will go far beyond your imagination."

Liam knew an empty promise when he heard one, but he didn't have many options.

All we had is gone, the darkness crooned, its tentacles

squeezing and poisoning everything that made Liam who he was.

This time, it was right. The entire Nine-five had been slaughtered; the Cap, too. And Archie was nowhere to be found. Kev had been assigned to a new precinct, but the kid was a double agent for the Legion now. He came to visit Liam once, but when Kev saw the cloud of buzzing darkness that swarmed around him and heard Liam's desperate cries, he left.

Liam recalled hearing a croaked, "I failed you, mate," but he couldn't be sure. The memories of his first days as a demon were a blurry mess.

He touched the tips of his pointed teeth. Hells, he became a monster.

"For what?" he bellowed.

You know, the darkness answered.

"For fuck's sake!" He rubbed the bridge of his nose.

A part of him was glad Ava hadn't come to see him, even if her absence hurt.

She doesn't care about us, the darkness whispered with Liam's own voice. *She's mated to the Messenger, the angel she has loved from the beginning. It's always been him. We were an indulgence.*

Swarms of darkness clouded his thoughts.

She never loved us. She was never ours.

Liam crouched on the ground, smacking his forehead against the wet concrete as he clawed at his face. "Shut up!" he bellowed.

Gabriel flashed in his mind. He held a woman's severed head. His pitch-black eyes glinted, his saw-teeth sharp as blades. "You're one of us now, brother."

"No!" Liam shouted, pressing his skull harder on the ground. Maybe his forehead would crack and that would be the end of it, but a demon's body wasn't easy to maim.

His mind spun and he thought he would hurl, but he never did. The darkness was cruel in that way: even if his body tried to get rid of it, it couldn't.

I'm not leaving. I've always been here.

"Liam?"

He froze, falling within himself. He looked up to see Ava, standing before him, her features too sharp, too pointy, and yet fogged on the edges. Like she was a dream or a memory.

"You're not real," he told himself. Or her. Maybe both.

"I can't be with you," Ava continued. "You're of the dark now. I'm light, and so is Ezra."

The Messenger materialized beside her. He had one hand wrapped around her waist and a smug look stamped on his face. They both flung their heads back as they laughed ice daggers.

The darkness could be a cruel asshole sometimes— scratch that.

All the time.

"It's not real," Liam muttered, but he wasn't so sure anymore.

"Be patient," Jal's words rang in his mind. "You used to be an Archangel. The transition to demon will hit you like a wrecking ball."

It certainly did.

Ava and the Messenger disappeared. The Captain now crouched before him, her empty eye sockets crying wine-red blood. "The dark has always been strong in you. With your father, too." Her grin spread unnaturally wide, more a monster in a nightmare than the Cap he used to know. "Give in, Liam."

"You're not real!" he bellowed, spit forming at the corners of his mouth.

Furious flames spilled from his skin, but they didn't burn him. His demonic fire was just as hard to control as the darkness, but at least it was soothing—a fiery breeze that danced all around him.

He was lucky Jal had given him these blessed, *damned*, black shirt and jeans. Every time Liam's flames surfaced, he burned all the clothes he wore to ashes. Eventually, Jal handed him a pile of garments and grumbled, "Here you go. Watching your dick literally on fire isn't my favorite pastime."

Liam chuckled at the memory, and the flames sunk back into his skin.

When he lifted his head to face the Cap, she was gone, replaced by an old lady with a pink hat who stood at the entrance of the alley. Worry and fear took turns on her face.

Was she real?

"A-are you all right, sir?" She gave a fearful step forward. "I called 911. You were burning not a moment ago." She kept approaching, but when she saw his face, she screamed in horror and almost stumbled back.

Liam growled a beastly sound that rolled up in his chest, a snarl all darkness and nothing like him. Well, maybe a little like him.

The old lady made the sign of the cross before hurrying out of the alley.

A laugh rumbled in Liam's ribcage, he and the darkness aligned. At least *that* had been fun.

He peeked at a rain puddle to his left, and a demon stared back at him. Black, beady eyes, pale skin, and saw-sharp teeth. His once kempt hair now reached the lower side of his ears, almost curtaining his eyes.

This was him now. Lost. A monster.

A mess.

Liam was tired; so freaking tired of fighting this void, this madness, through every waking moment. Perhaps he should give in and become one of those third-tier demons he abhorred so much. *A monster possessed by the dark.*

Would he become a fog of darkness or turn into a toad-monster?

"You fucking sissy," a voice grumbled from the mouth of the alley.

Liam didn't need to turn; he knew Jal stood there. Somehow, he was sure the demon wasn't a figment of his imagination.

"Leave me alone," he barked, pressing his forehead against the cold ground. His heated skin hissed against the rain water.

"Baby demons are worse than teenagers. Everything is a Shakespearian drama with you." Jal's steps tapped on the concrete until he halted by Liam's side. His black boots almost mingled with the darkness of the alley. "Come on. Off we go."

A furnace burned inside Liam's ribcage, an unending fire that craved to scorch everything in its path. His flames rose from his core and whipped at Jal like angry fire snakes.

Make me, the darkness challenged.

"I'll remind you that I'm a Drakar, the evolution of the puny Terror you are now." The demon raised his hand which quickly became a torch. "Kicking your ass, on the other hand, has become one of my favorite sports, so I'm game."

We're alone, the darkness whispered in Liam's ears. *He's no friend of ours.*

A cry broke through his throat. "Stop!"

Jal rolled his eyes, unfazed. "You chose to become a demon to face the dark, but now it's consuming you." He shook his head and crossed his arms. "It's about time you got over it."

The words echoed through Liam's essence, a command

he forced himself to follow. Slowly, the fire waned, settling back underneath his skin and bones.

He glared at his own hand. It looked ashy and pale, but at least it wasn't burning.

For the first time, Liam sensed a quiet hollow inside him, an abyss he couldn't quite access. Yet it was there, quiet, peaceful. *Inviting.*

"That's the true darkness," Jal said, clearly guessing what Liam felt. "Everything else is bullshit your body comes up with." He pointed at Liam's head. "Think of it as an autoimmune system. The fact that you were an Archangel once doesn't help, of course."

"What do you mean?"

He shrugged. "I've been through what you're going through, but my transition wasn't as bad. My guess is that whatever is left of your angelic essence is rejecting your new demonic side."

As if on cue, the darkness showed him Archie shaking his head in disappointment, followed by the Cap's lifeless corpse forever gaping at him with missing eyes. Then flashes of Ava and Ezra tangled in bed. The Messenger thrusted inside her, and Ava moaned the way she'd moaned underneath Liam.

He slammed both hands on his head and screamed as he tried to push the darkness away. "Let me breathe!"

Our Guardian abandoned us. Our father, too.

The darkness silenced immediately, almost as if it knew it had gone too far.

One deep breath, then another. "Is Ava really in love with Ezraphael?"

Jal winced and clicked his tongue. "This is how we got here, remember? Thinking about Ava isn't helping."

"Is she with him?" Liam barked, the darkness pulsing in unison with his burning heart.

"Yes, of course she is! You knew she would be from the

start, you idiot!" Jal flung his arms up. "You were okay with it!"

"I didn't think she would become his mate," Liam croaked. "She's in love with him, always has been."

"Maybe. But she did kill another angel for you. Literally chopped his head off." He let the words hang there for a moment, just enough to make Liam feel guilty. "If we had lost Ezraphael, we would've lost the entire Order. Ava knew that, I knew that, everyone knew that except you. You have to get over this, otherwise your pointless penitence will never end." Jal ran a hand through the long silky hair which cascaded down his shoulders. "Ava has a duty. You both do."

"A duty? To the fucking Messenger?" Liam snorted. "To the Gods?"

Jal stepped forward and crouched before him. "To yourselves." He poked Liam's chest, right on the spot where his heart drummed. "This is the only faith you need, remember?"

Yeah. It's how he'd gotten in this mess.

Sirens wailed from a distance, and Jal let out an exasperated sigh. "The human police will soon be here. You're not exactly being discreet."

Liam gritted his teeth, accidentally biting his bottom lip and drawing blood. "I need to see her."

"You can't." Jal rested his elbows on his knees. "So, what else do you want to do?"

"I-I don't know." His voice was more of a whisper. "I don't know who I am anymore, or what to think …"

Jal scrubbed his hand down his face, looking tired all of a sudden. "Yeah, I assumed this would be the case." He nodded to someone behind Liam. "Jophiel let me call in the cavalry."

At the entrance of the alley stood a demon hidden by the darkness, his draconian wings coiled behind his back.

A second-tier, like Jal.

He stepped closer, and his features came to view under

the faint city lights. Liam noticed a squared chin and tousled sandy hair. A dark-blond stubble peppered his jaw, and his kind gray eyes glinted with a mix of worry and sorrow.

Liam gaped, unable to think or even breathe. Without meaning to, he cried. Tears streamed down his face, and he couldn't make them stop.

"You're here," he mumbled.

Archie smiled down at him. "Hey, kid."

2

AVA

*A*va peered into Justine's brown irises as they sat cross-legged and facing each other. The training room's padded white floor might be softer than hard ground, but they'd been here for so long that Ava couldn't feel her bottom anymore.

Beads of sweat bloomed from her friend's forehead, but instead of giving up, Justine shot Ava a victorious smile. "You'll eventually cave, you know."

Invisible hands brushed Ava's mental wall, teasing, *prodding.* None too surprising, since Justine was a powerful Erudite. Ava didn't doubt her friend would ascend to Virtue sooner than expected.

"You've been trying to break my barrier for a whole hour now." Her lips twitched into a smug grin. "You said we'd be done in ten minutes?"

"Can't let a Guardian beat me at my own game, can I? Ugh, sorry. I meant *Dominion*. I keep forgetting you're not a Guardian anymore." Justine nodded to Ava's wings, which hung from her back like sleeping willow branches and sprawled on the floor behind her. "Look, you're not a daughter of the God of Knowledge and Logic. You shouldn't have such a strong mental wall." This with a certain bitterness in her tone. "It's a matter of honor now."

Ava rolled her shoulders. "All I hear are excuses."

"Oh, give me time, dear. I broke it once, didn't I?"

Ava's concentration wavered. "Only because I had returned after …" She didn't need to complete the sentence. *After Liam's death.* "I hadn't expected my best friend to invade my privacy and learn about the Legion. I know better now."

Justine gave her an exasperated sigh. "I was worried, Ava. You came back different. It wasn't just the Dominion change; you were harsher, less—"

"—amiable?"

Justine shrugged. "Patient, I'd say. But yes, that too."

Ava had wanted to run away the minute she stepped back in the Order. She couldn't wait to be in Liam's arms again. But Ezra needed her and so did the Order, so much so that she hadn't had time to visit the Legion or the man—well, the *demon*—she loved.

Ava grumbled deep in her throat. She was certain her selflessness would someday be her doom.

Justine took advantage of her distraction and increased the mental pressure on Ava's wall, but she reinforced it just in time.

"It's normal, you know," Justine said carelessly. "You've been through a lot. I'd be worried if you were the same angel."

"True." A cold shiver spread down Ava's spine. "Sometimes I look at myself in the mirror and I don't know who or what I'm seeing." It scared her, glaring into the unknown beyond her own eyes, but Ava kept this to herself.

Justine leaned forward and laid a hand on hers. "You went through severe trauma. Watching Liam die, killing an Archangel … Just give yourself time to adapt, okay?"

Yes, time. That's all Ava needed. *It had to be.*

Justine straightened her posture, fixing herself in a perfect meditational position. Her mental drill kept trying to pierce Ava's wall. "So, when are you taking me to the Legion?"

"Once I'm able to get there myself." She blew air through her lips and leaned back on her hands, looking at the ceiling in a clear cue for a time-out. Justine's mental drill stopped. "Being Ezra's mate is—"

"—a stupid idea?" She gave Ava a knowing smile.

"*Demanding.* Assisting him with the Order and helping him recover takes all of my time. I assumed I would have been able to see Liam by now." Her fingers pressed the bridge of her nose. "I hate that I haven't."

As one of the three heads of the Order, Ezra had to attend endless meetings. Ava stood by his side through them all, because that's what mates were expected to do—support their companions. Not only that, but throughout their days, Ava constantly reminded Ezra of the angel he used to be.

Slowly, Talahel's cruel ideas and crippling doubt began receding within the Messenger the way a virus leaves its host.

"Do you think Ezra is ready to learn about the Legion?" Justine asked.

"Soon." Pride swelled in Ava's chest. "All he needed was a push in the right direction. He's doing remarkably well."

She rejoiced at the memory of Ezra, at his wide smile and peaceful blue eyes. The kindest angel she knew was coming back from the madness that had nearly engulfed him.

Justine frowned at her. Her friend could always read her expressions like a book.

Ava cleared her throat, sensing Justine's unspoken question. "I'm proud of him, that's all."

"Hmm, sure." Justine squinted at her. "I suppose it's no

surprise Mr. Do Good recovered so quickly, especially with his dear Ava by his side."

"Who's this Mr. Do Good you speak of?" Ezra's playful tone came from the entrance.

He was leaning on the door frame with his arms crossed and a charming grin stamped on his face.

The Messenger wore his usual silver bodysuit and white kilt. Today his hair was wrapped in a high bun that complimented the hard lines of his features. His sleeveless clothing revealed thick biceps and strong muscles that tapered down to corded forearms.

Standing this way, he reminded Ava of a silver panther about to prowl.

Talahel's wickedness had devoured Ezra from his edges, but after the last couple of weeks, he began recovering. He didn't resemble a sickly skeleton anymore, and the dark circles under his eyes had disappeared. All because Ava showed Ezra how *she* saw him—kind, merciful. Honorable.

Gradually, he became the Messenger he used to be, the man Ava had loved for one hundred years.

"Oh, no one in particular." Justine smiled at Ava as she stood up, fixing her light-gray kilt. "If you'll excuse me, I'll go check on the Captain."

A sting pierced Ava's chest. "Could you tell her I said hello?"

"I will, like every other time." She gave Ava a tight-lipped nod. "Let's hope she's responsive today."

Ava stood and trapped Justine in a grateful hug. "Thank you, my friend." She leaned closer to Justine's ear and whispered, "Being here without you wouldn't have been easy."

Justine stepped away and grabbed her chin gently, looking up at Ava. "Even the best of Dominions need to be watched over, too."

"Excuse me!" An angry voice blasted from the entrance.

Its owner hurried past Ezra without noticing him. "What is an Erudite doing in a room reserved for ascended angels?"

The man had a bland complexion and bland frame. His hair and eyes were a dull gray-brown. *Dominion Hawke.* A stuck-up angel who followed the Order's rules to the letter.

Ava ground her teeth but forced herself to calm down. "Dominion Hawke, Erudite Dubois was under my supervision—"

"I do not care, Dominion Lightway," the angel snapped. "The rules are clear, and—"

"The rules can be broken if the Messenger says so." Ezra stepped forward, his tone placid as water and hard as stone. "Do remember, Dominion Hawke, that as a child of the Goddess of Love and Life, you answer to me. And that the angel standing before you is my mate."

The Dominion blinked at Ezra. "My Messenger, you are known for your kindness, but also for ignoring rules that should not be broken." He waved at Ava. "When Dominion Lightway was a Guardian, she reported directly to you. That's blasphemous enough. Now she's bringing lower angels into ascended space? That's preposterous!"

Ezra stepped forward, looming over Hawke. "I will remind you again that I am your chief angel, and that I could send you to any of the Order's offices in the entire world. Aiding humans in areas stricken by war, famine, and cruelty is a noble job that can destroy an angel. I've watched many of my peers go mad from all the desperation and pain ..."

Hawke shrank under Ezra's towering presence. "M-my Messenger, I could never—"

"So I ask again. Will you allow," Ezra sneered because Hawke was in no position to allow anything, "Erudite Dubois to train with Dominion Lightway?"

"Of course." Hawke swallowed dryly. "But even your mate must abide by the Order's rules."

Something inside Ava cracked. She closed her fists so hard that her nails bit her palm. Being diplomatic, an important skill for a high-angel's mate, was becoming harder with each passing day.

Run. She wanted to run away from here.

"Do not forget you were a third-tier once, Dominion Hawke," Ava argued instead of punching him, even if the latter felt much more compelling. "We're all children of the Gods, regardless of how the Order deems us."

Ezra shot her a stern look. "Anger is oozing from you in fiery waves, my mate. Control it. Set the example."

"But I *want* Dominion Hawke to know how his lack of kindness angers me," she countered, her vision turning red. "A second-tier is no better than a third-tier. Lower angels, ascended, we're all the same."

"We are not the same. The rules are clear," Dominion Hawke snapped. "Respect the institution!"

"Enough!" She barked and took one furious step forward.

Heavens, she would smack a punch on his face and she wouldn't regret it. Not even a bit.

Hawke stepped back, now glaring between her and Ezra, a silent plea for the Messenger to intervene. But Ezra did nothing. His attention was trapped on Ava, his blue eyes shooting disappointment at her.

Well, Gods forgive her for not being as composed and perfect as Ezra. Ava was truly sorry she had abandoned Liam and the Legion to be here, arguing with a blind, stuck-up Dominion who didn't know right from wrong in this crooked Order. And she was sorry if her anger disappointed Ezra. No, in fact, she wasn't sorry at all.

She simply didn't care.

Justine stepped in her way and cupped her cheeks. "There are times when amicability and patience can be a virtue, dear." She turned to Dominion Hawke. "We'll be sure to abide by the rules." With that, Justine winked at Ava and left the room.

"I must train with my mate," Ezra stated dryly. "Unless you also have an issue with that, Hawke?"

"No, my Messenger," Hawke countered, resembling a scared deer more than a man. "Thank you, my Messenger." And with that, he bowed and left, closing the glass door behind him.

"This was insubordination." Ava pointed at the entrance. "You should punish him."

Ezra watched her with a pained expression as if her words physically hurt him. "I'm not that kind of commander, Ava, and you're not that kind of angel. Just breathe."

Gods, he was right. Ava inhaled and exhaled deeply, but her fury didn't wane.

"Besides, Hawke isn't wrong." Ezra shrugged. Loose strands of light silver hair escaped from his high-bun and graced his face. "We do tend to disobey the rules, don't we?"

"The rules are nonsense!" she shouted, still trying to control her breathing.

He scanned her with calculating eyes. "You say I should be more like Talahel? Subjugate those under my command to my every will?"

This silenced the turmoil inside her at once, leaving her mind awfully empty.

"No. I just ..." She blew an exasperated breath. "It's not fair. No wonder Talahel introduced his wickedness into the Order. Our ways are not of the Gods, Ezra. They never have been."

Erudites, Guardians, and Warriors received little support from the Order and so did the Selfless precincts. Ascended angels, however, had everything they needed.

What made it worse was that lower angels were content in their misery, like Ava had once been. They didn't know how badly they were treated because they didn't have access to the world of Dominions, Virtues, and Archangels. They couldn't demand justice if they were unaware of the inequalities.

But Ava had ascended. Now she *knew*, and not being able to change things killed her.

"It isn't fair," Ezra said, stepping closer to her. "But it's the way. It always has been. I've tried to change it, but I can't do it alone. The Sword and the Throne need to agree, and yet the Throne is trapped in the old ways. The Sword ... well, from what you've told me, he's a monster Hells-bent on destroying mankind and the In-Betweens." He lifted her chin gently. "One battle at a time, Ava."

For a split second, she lost herself in Ezra's calm blue eyes. They brought her peace; the antithesis of Liam's fire.

Her former partner flashed in her mind: those piercing green eyes, his boyish grin. Sorrow stung her from inside because Ava had failed him as his Guardian. As his friend and lover, too.

She shook her head and pulled back from Ezra's grip.

"So many battles to fight ..." Ava rubbed her forehead and sighed dispiritedly.

"One day, once we've handled Talahel, we'll change the Order. I promise." Ezra shot her a charming grin. "You're stubborn enough to do it."

"I came here to defeat Talahel, but there's so much more that needs fixing." She worried her bottom lip. "Sometimes I feel as if I'm going nowhere, no matter how hard I try."

The last few weeks had passed in a blur of hearings with angels who disagreed with this or that, Archangels who demanded more funds, outraged Virtues complaining about books' missing pages, and Guardians who wanted to help more humans—or better yet, the Dominions in charge of them voiced the Guardians' demands since lower angels weren't allowed in the hearings.

Meanwhile, Talahel was still free to smite the In-Betweens without mercy, the Legion still needed all the help it could get, and Liam was still a demon.

Suddenly, breathing became very hard.

"Do you remember the first time we met?" Ezra asked as he cupped her cheeks. He inhaled deeply, a cue for her to do the same.

She inhaled and held her breath, then exhaled.

Ezra's soothing stare helped. His peace, the peace she was here to help save, wrapped around her completely.

It felt like a victim saving the savior, but this was one of Ezra's beauties; his capacity to care beyond himself, to help a drowning man even if it meant taking his place.

Ezra had set the example Ava followed through her entire life as a Guardian. And for a moment that passed all too quickly, she wondered if this was the true reason she was here— so Ezra could save her as much as she saved him.

"Yes," she said quietly. "I remember."

THE FIRST TIME Ava stepped into the Order's main hall, she couldn't believe her eyes.

"There really are three Gods," she muttered as she stared at the marbled statues carved on the enormous wall before her.

Her mentor, Dominion Vera Evestar, a thin, short woman who wore her chocolate hair always in a high bun, turned back to Ava. "Well, you're standing here, reborn as a Guardian." Vera's brown wings wiggled as if to point out that she was also an angel. "None of us has ever seen the Gods though, so maybe there's only one. Maybe there's a thousand. Who knows? It's all the same principle in the end, isn't it?" She waved her hand dismissively. "Be kind to thy neighbor, blah, blah, blah."

Ava giggled. Vera didn't look or act like the angels she'd read about in the holy books.

As they crossed the gargantuan hall made of white marbled walls peppered by golden vines, Ava muttered, "Is this the gateway to Heaven?" She gasped. "I mean, the Heavens?"

Plural. She had to become accustomed to that.

Vera shrugged. "It's the closest you and I will ever get to them."

Memories of Ava's past life swirled in her mind. She wanted to perform the Gods work, to help humans in pain, but she missed the children from the orphanage. Letting go of her life proved harder than she assumed, but Ava didn't wish to complain. It didn't seem a very angelic thing to do.

Lost in those thoughts, she bumped against a hard surface.

A strong chest.

"My apologies," she started before losing her speech to the most beautiful creature she'd ever seen.

His hair was moonlight silver, his kind eyes the color of the sky, and when he smiled down at her with perfect white teeth framed by a squared jaw, Ava's knees wobbled.

Ezra kept his attention locked on Ava as he handed some papers to Vera. "A new assignment," he said, his piercing blue gaze still trapped on Ava's. He bowed his head slightly. "Welcome, Guardian." He gave her his strong hand. "I'm Ezraphael, the Messenger."

"And my boss," Vera added, her arms crossed. "Even though I trained the bastard."

He frowned at her with a grin. "You could've ascended to Messenger a long time ago, esteemed mentor."

Vera waved her hand in the air. "You know I'm not made for that. I prefer instructing the newbies. It's a lot more fun."

"I-I'm Ava," she broke their interaction, her voice a shy whisper as she shook Ezraphael's hand.

"A beautiful name." His curious frown told Ava she intrigued him, but perhaps she was mistaken. This must be how he looked at all the new angels. "It's fine to miss your old life, by the way."

Not her old life, just the children from the orphanage. She hadn't seen little boy Charlie since her death. Was he well fed and healthy? Were they all? And her mother, Gods … Longing and sadness crashed against Ava at once. Without meaning to, she began to cry.

Vera had told her that unless the people she had known were assigned to her, they shouldn't be a concern. But Ava couldn't stop thinking and worrying about them. Wasn't this why she became a Guardian in the first place? To help and care for others?

Within seconds Ezra had Ava in his strong arms, warmth pulsing from him as he laid a hand on the back of her head. "It will get better, this I promise you." Golden wisps of light coated his words, seeping into Ava's skin, and slowly her tears waned. A sense of fulfillment and purpose coursed through her.

Vera cleared her throat. "I'm taking her to initiation now."

"Let your pain give you strength." Ezra kissed Ava's forehead. "Let your light shine, Guardian. I'm here for you, and Vera is the best mentor you could have. You will be fine."

Vera rolled her eyes. "Ever the charmer, Ezzie."

He gave Vera a chiding glance before letting Ava go.

She prayed he would hold her again, but instead, Ezra stepped aside and showed them the way.

As they walked away, Ava glanced back at him, her heart

beating madly and her skin flushing. The encouraging smile Ezra gave her beamed with love and care.

"Be careful, girl," Vera said. "That smile can cause wars."

But the Messenger kept his promise. As the days passed, Ezra looked after Ava, and it didn't take long for her to become the best Guardian in the Order under his and Vera's guidance.

Eventually, Ezra requested that Ava report to him directly.

When she informed Vera during one of their tea breaks, she expected her mentor to be upset. Instead, Vera smirked in that knowing way of hers, a wise owl trapped inside her delicate features. "Of course I'm not upset. I gave him the idea."

Ava frowned. "Why? Did I disappoint you, esteemed mentor?"

Vera tapped her cheek gently. "Far from that, Ava. But a lower angel reporting directly to the Messenger?" Her eyes glinted with mischief. "It's a wonderful thing and something only our Ezzie could achieve. The Order desperately needs this." Vera must've sensed Ava's confusion because she added, "Once you ascend, you'll understand."

EZRA'S HANDS still cupped Ava's cheeks, his gaze trapping hers. "I'm here for you, as I was on that day. I'll always fight with and for you."

She chuckled. "That is a very Messenger thing to say."

"I had a good teacher." He winked at her. "I like to think I earned the name?"

"You absolutely did." She laid her hands atop his. "Thank you. I needed this, my friend."

He winced at the word and released her as if Ava's skin had burnt him.

What Ezra wanted, Ava could not give. And he accepted that, agreeing they would become mates even though she would never be with him in a romantic way.

Ava loved Ezra, she truly did. But she couldn't love him the way he wanted her to.

Because now there was Liam.

"Feels like so long ago since I first walked into the Order's hall," she muttered, glancing at the training room's glassed wall.

The wonder and awe which had been there during her journey as a Guardian now had been replaced by disapproval and disgust.

Ava wanted to save the Order desperately because there were things to be saved; pure things like the angelic devotion to mankind, or the advances and sciences used by the Order which were then carefully introduced into the world of men.

The Order might be crooked, but it still focused on helping humans and improving the world. For that alone, it was worth saving.

"That day when I saw you," Ezra said, "it was as if the light in me echoed with yours. I can't explain it."

"Your light also soothed me. Always did." Her words shook Ava to her bones, as if there was an answer to an unknown question hidden in them.

The image of Liam, bloodied and dying, flashed in her mind. Shadows wrapped around him, pulling him away from her and into a darkness beyond.

She held the need to scream.

Ezra must've sensed her agony because he stepped back with a confused frown. Before Ava could attempt to explain, he said, "Let's see if we can get those wings of yours working, shall we?"

3

LIAM

*S*unlight peered through the barred window of Liam's cell. The irony of a Selfless sleeping in jail wasn't lost on him, but then again, he wasn't part of the supernatural police anymore.

Liam grumbled and turned on his bed, facing the sandstone wall. He pulled the blanket over his head.

He could've picked any room in the Legion. Jophiel had said so himself, but Liam didn't want to be near others, especially the priests of the Gray. Humans were frailer than demons and the In-Betweens. He didn't doubt a few of the Gray could kick his ass on any given day, but they were still human. If he had a demonic fit, they might be harmed.

So the dungeons became his new home, though his cell was never locked.

The place wasn't all that bad. The sandstone walls and barred windows which opened to ground level took in light well. Fresh air coursed through the corridors, coming from the windows and natural ventilation tubes that cut through the stone.

The sound of water dripping in the distance made for

constant background noise, and the scent of wet iron wafted through the place. It added a sour tang to the air, but Liam had gotten used to the smell and the noise by now.

A curtain to block the sunlight would've been nice, though.

On his first day here, Liam asked Jal why there weren't any prisoners.

"We can't afford to take any," he'd said, remorse all over him. "Not as things are at the moment."

Liam rolled in bed, left then right, until he gave up and kicked the blanket away.

Guess sleeping time was over.

Not that he had much sleep anyway. Last night's events replayed in his mind nonstop. Archie looked at least twenty years younger, and he also had navy dragon-wings attached to his back.

Why did the old man wait so long to show himself?

Archie had begun to apologize, but Liam got up and walked back to the Legion. At some point Jal and his father stopped calling after him.

The darkness hadn't bothered Liam during the way back, and it had stayed quiet throughout the night. Maybe it pitied him; maybe he pitied himself.

Hells, he was really losing his mind.

He sat up and rubbed his forehead. The scent of brimstone mixed with something spicy came from the cell's entrance. Like cinnamon burning on lava.

Do not listen, the dark whispered in his ears, lazily waking up. *He left us.*

Liam raised one eyebrow at Archie, who stood by the cell's half-open door. He got up and went to him only to slam the bars closed on his father's face.

The darkness spread through the edges of Liam's

consciousness, shadow tentacles that wrapped around his thoughts and words, dragging him down to an endless deep.

Where were you when we died, Father?

Liam paced around the room, his breathing ragged as he fought the waking darkness that told him he was alone and that he shouldn't trust Archie or any of those motherfuckers in the Legion—no, in the entire world. There was only the darkness and Liam, and this was how it would always be.

Archie stood outside, his hands gripping the bars. "You gotta let me in, kid."

If guilt had a tone, it was his.

"It's not locked," Liam barked without looking at him, his attention on the barred window. Sunlight stung his eyes, but it felt better than staring at Archie.

Ava left us. So did Father.

Shut the fuck up, he thought back.

The rusty iron door squeaked and steps clicked on the stone floor. Liam kept his back to Archie, but the darkness in him pulsed like a sonar. He didn't see, but he *felt* the old man sitting on the stone bench opposite his bed. His father's face and movements thrummed in the darkness inside him, around him, everywhere.

"We have a lot to talk about," Archie said. His tone was ragged and tired. It belonged to old man Archie, not this forty-year-old demon in Liam's cell, this stranger who had abandoned him.

Liam's breathing echoed inside his eardrums as he pushed the tentacles of darkness away. It didn't work, of course. If anything, they gripped him harder.

Without turning to Archie, he said through gritted teeth, "You left me."

"I had to, kid. It was too dangerous."

"You should've told me," Liam snapped. "You raised me. I'm not just your partner, I'm your son!" He spun around and pointed to the day outside. "It was always you and me against the world. We were a team!"

A moment of silence and then, "I know."

"That's not good enough."

"You are my son and always will be." Archie stood and pointed at him in the same dominant manner. Heck, it was scary how much he'd taken from his father, even if they weren't biologically related. "But I had to deal with my own darkness. It was imperative that I take on my current mission. As you've seen for yourself, the darkness isn't easy to control; it's a part of us we never explored before. It took me some time to find myself again."

He observed Archie's navy wings wrapped over his shoulders like a cape, and for a split second the old man reminded him of a giant bat or a vampire. Not the real ones but those from the old horror movies.

A hint of sunlight brushed upon the scales and made them gleam a deep blue.

Liam nodded at the wings. "Why are they on display, Archie? Show off or fight?" His answer was silence, so Liam continued. "You ascended quickly. Or is it descended, since we're all going one floor down?" He scratched his cheeks as a mad laugh burst from his throat, but Liam hadn't meant to laugh.

The darkness did.

"I had to go on an undercover mission," Archie explained. "All the shit that's happening, it hangs on how well my undercover work plays out. That's why I wasn't here when you arrived and why I didn't contact you before."

"A mission?" Liam frowned. "You abandoned me for a fucking mission?"

Hurt gleamed in Archie's eyes. His throat bobbed, and he sniffed back tears. He opened his mouth once, twice, but nothing came out. Finally, he managed, "We slay monsters,

Liam. We protect the weak and save the world, no matter the cost."

Liam scoffed, but he understood where Archie was coming from. His father wouldn't be his hero if he weren't the type of man who'd sacrifice anything for the greater good.

Still, the darkness wanted Archie to suffer, so the words rushed out of Liam's throat before he could stop them. "Yeah, tell that to the Cap. She was collateral in your fight for the greater good. We both were."

Archie bit his lip and looked away. His hero, the unshakable wall who raised him, seemed smaller somehow.

"You think leaving all of you was easy?" he croaked.

Liam slammed a hand on his forehead. A massive hangover had to feel better than this. "I'm sorry. The dark takes over sometimes."

"It's not *the* dark, it's *your* dark, kid." Archie shoved his hands in his black jeans pockets. "Look, you want to join me in this mission? It would be undercover work just like old times. Maybe it will be good for you. And for me too, you know, to have my boy around after so long."

A beastly growl bubbled in Liam's throat. "Old times are gone."

"Clearly." Archie waved at his own face.

The gray of his hair had become a dirty blonde, and so had his ashen stubble. The deep wrinkles that once marred his face were completely gone.

"Your dark isn't bad, kid," Archie continued. "It's relentless, but it makes you stronger if you overcome it. Insecurity, anger, it's all part of the package. The good news is that I went through the exact same shit, so I can show you how to control it." Archie angled his head and observed him. "Do you trust me?"

Liam stood there, pondering what to say. Finally, he nodded.

Archie's movements were fast, and Liam might've tried to dodge the oncoming attack if he believed Archie would actually punch him.

The old man's fist crashed against his face, sending him back a couple of steps.

Liam leaned on the wall, resting a hand over his throbbing left cheek. "What in all the Hells!"

"You're a Terror," Archie said casually, as if hitting Liam had been no big deal. "This means you get extraordinary speed and the power of fire, all from that wild darkness within you. Let's dig those powers up. What do you say?"

"And fighting will help me control the dark? How?"

Archie shrugged. "Worked for me."

Liam snorted. *Good enough, then.*

He sprinted toward his father, a scream erupting from his throat. He kicked Archie's stomach with the plant of his foot, sending the old man slamming against the opposite wall.

Bits of stone and dust fell over Archie's wings. Shadows covered them and then the wings disappeared in a fog of darkness. The dust fell on Archie's black sweater, peppering his black pants.

Fitting clothing for a demon.

"You don't want to fight anymore?" Liam asked.

"I can take you without them, kid." Archie brushed off the dirt from his clothes as if Liam's attack had been nothing. "How's that voice inside your head?"

Liam skipped a breath because the darkness had silenced. He glared at his hands and feet, feeling for the first time like himself again.

The old man smiled. "Good."

They walked in circles until Archie charged and punched, but Liam dodged just in time. Archie's fist met the wall inches from Liam's face, leaving the deep imprint of his knuckles in the stone.

Liam glared at it. "When did you get so strong?"

Archie cracked his neck left and right, then shrugged. "I'm a Behemoth. Strength is one of our main skills. So is shapeshifting, but let's leave that for another time." He raised one finger. "Now, I truly want you to consider joining me. My mission required I infiltrate a demonic faction, and to be here with you, I had to leave my duties. If I brought in a new recruit, I'd get extra points. Also, I'd be able to work with my partner, my *son*, again. It's two birds with one stone, really."

Archie went for a punch but stopped midway and tripped Liam with his leg instead. Damned old man; he caught him off guard.

Liam's back slammed on the uneven ground, all breath fleeing his lungs. "So …" He coughed. "You assumed I'd say yes to this mission. After all I've been through?"

Archie's gaze softened. "I know you, Liam. Always have." He motioned to the cell as if there were no walls around them. "You're stronger than this. How's the darkness?"

Liam scanned his own mind. "Quiet."

"Excellent."

Archie raised his foot to slam it down on Liam's chest, but Liam rolled out of the way just in time, quickly jumping to his feet.

He raised his fists and shifted his weight, ready to fight.

He felt the darkness inside, but it was razor-focused on Archie. Instead of working against him, the darkness worked *with* him, making Liam's instincts sharper, his movements quicker.

He could get used to this.

"Why didn't you trust me?" Liam asked as he nailed two punches on the old man's face.

Archie spun, then glared at him in surprise.

"You could've let me know you were okay." Liam hit another punch straight into his jaw. "Hells, have Jophiel tell me, since you couldn't escape your precious *demonic duties*." A jab to his stomach. The old man bent over, failing to put up a fight. "But no, you just treated me like a child. You always do."

Something broke inside Archie. Liam could see it through those light-gray eyes that had watched him his entire life. And from the pit where Liam's darkness lived, his own voice hissed, *we went too far.*

Archie's eyes glistened as he straightened up. Had Liam's attacks done nothing to him? "I trust you with my life, kid. Always have, always will. I just wanted a way out for you."

Liam snorted. "Look how well it turned out."

"Yeah." His voice cracked. "But I'll make it up to you." He charged and punched Liam's stomach.

They clashed against each other, a fury of never-ending attacks. Soon enough, the left side of Liam's face felt swollen, and his arms and legs hurt. His trunk pulsed where Archie had hit him.

After one calculated strike, he broke the old man's nose. Before he could jump around and celebrate, a dark fog surged from Archie's pores, enveloping the wound. After a moment, his nose was healed.

Just like that.

"Hey! Not fair!"

Archie grinned. "Who said anything about fair?"

They kept fighting, and even though Liam's entire body hurt and he was certain he'd broken a limb or two, he felt free—free in a way he hadn't been in a long time.

Archie knew he would, of course. The old man spoke "Liam" fluently.

With a kick, Archie slammed him against the left stone

wall. A cloud of dirt and debris enveloped Liam, dirt sticking to his skin and clothes.

He barely felt his body as he forced himself to stand straight—actually, it was a miracle he was still standing.

It didn't last long, though. He fell with his knees on the ground, the piercing sting of bone hitting stone coursing through his kneecaps. Liam broke into violent coughs that splattered blood all over the sandstone.

A cloud of darkness shot from Archie's fingers and enveloped him. It felt cold to the touch as it wrapped around his ribs, then pushed inside his mouth. Yet Liam could breathe normally, if not for the coughs that threatened to choke him.

Within a moment, all his wounds had healed—inside and outside.

Liam watched his arms, now free of any bruises. "Oh, you will show me how to do this, old man." He stood and inhaled deeply, feeling better than before.

"It's a skill you'll get as soon as you ascend to a Drakar," Archie explained.

"Isn't that what Jal is?"

The old man chuckled. "He said you're besties now because you're the same type of demon, only with different ascension levels."

A smile hooked up on the left side of Liam's cheek.

"He also told me about Ava." Archie wrapped his hands behind his back. "She was important to you, wasn't she?"

"She *is*," Liam muttered.

The darkness rushed to surface with the fury of a geyser, ripping Liam apart.

She's nothing!

His entire body cramped from inside as the dark urged him to end Ava, Archie, the godsdamned Legion, and they would burn down the Order, too. They would burn down the entire fucking world.

She left us!

Liam clawed at his temples as a piercing pain impaled his skull. A low groan escaped his lips, a sound half-man and half-beast.

"Fight it!" Archie yelled from a distance.

Liam couldn't see him. He could barely open his eyes from all the pain. "I can't!"

The darkness coursed inside him, burning his veins, sinking into his bones.

She's nothing!

She's everything!

"Liam!" He barely registered Archie's muffled screams.

The darkness spread inside him, and Liam fell on his knees. The deep dark swallowed his jail cell, leaving Liam alone in an unending void that gnawed at him.

It was eerily quiet now.

He looked around. Cold sweat coated his skin, but at least he could think straight.

"Archie? You there?"

Nothing.

A thousand voices hissed across the pitch-black, then gathered into one tone: Ava's. In the void, she whispered, "We are the monsters."

Liam screamed if only to drown her voice with his own, to destroy the truth she spoke. The truth he couldn't understand but already hated.

He screamed until he couldn't feel his throat anymore.

4

AVA

*T*he training room was set to a sunny mountain weather. Alps peppered with snow decorated the horizon, and a clear blue sky graced the landscape.

Ava inhaled the fresh mountain air as unseen cows mooed in the distance. This virtual setting was so real, she could swear she stood outdoors.

The room was seven stories high, which was why Ezra flew carelessly above. Meanwhile, back in the precincts, the training rooms resembled public school gymnasiums. Lower angels weren't much better off.

The differences between angelic classes were gargantuan.

Ava's wings itched and wiggled. The stubborn things never obeyed her commands. Making them disappear into her essence was nearly impossible. Ezra had often used his light to help, but then her wings would pop out at the most inconvenient of times. Like when Ava was giving a lecture to newly formed Guardians and her wings flashed to life, spreading wide. Which would've been fine if most wings flashed randomly, but usually angels and demons only revealed their wings if they wanted to fly, show off, fight, or

… *fuck*. The giggling that followed told Ava exactly what her students assumed.

Her wings also failed at their main purpose. Every time she tried to fly, the naughty things would flap in an uncoordinated mess, crashing Ava mightily to the floor. Thank the Gods for her Dominion's shield, otherwise she would've broken more bones than she could afford.

Ava stared up at Ezra as he hovered in the air, his nearly-white wings with gold tipped feathers beating in perfect synchrony. With his silver hair and bodysuit, he reminded her of the moon hanging in the sky.

"Show off," she grumbled.

"Are you doing the back exercises I taught you?"

Ava wiped sweat off her forehead with the back of her hand. They had battled for two hours, which was why Ezra had removed the upper part of his bodysuit and tied it around his waist, leaving his chest bare. Sweat contoured his defined muscles, amplifying his musky and metallic scent.

They had started with sword fighting, then proceeded with hand-to-hand combat, where Ezra mercilessly defeated Ava. She'd won one battle out of six, but the victory felt bitter-sweet. Liam had taught her how to move swiftly, how to overpower an enemy. And he wasn't here.

The base of her throat tingled. "I do the exercises every day!"

According to Ezra, her back muscles needed to be strong to maintain movement mid-flight. Ava did her exercises religiously, but they had been futile. All she was left with was sore muscles and rebel wings.

Ezra raised one dark-silver eyebrow. "Doesn't look like you're doing them."

She grumbled a curse as her wings flapped awkwardly behind her. Ava looked back at them pointedly. "How do you control these damned things?"

"They're a part of you, but you're seeing them as something separate." He tapped his chin and angled his head. "Also, your back muscles need to be stronger."

She rolled her eyes, then watched her hands. She moved her fingers, tracing the sensation back to some part of her brain.

If she could only replicate that with her wings ...

At once, they flapped in unison. *Once, twice.* Ava glared back at them from her shoulder, a smile creasing her lips.

They flapped again and boosted her up.

Fingers moving. That's all it was.

She focused on Ezra, and her wings pushed her up, following the beats of her heart, taking her higher and higher.

It worked!

She was about to reach the Messenger, who had his hand outstretched to hers, waiting.

A warm, giddy sensation spread inside Ava as she focused on his wide, proud grin. A gentle pull, a memory of the pull she'd felt with Liam, tugged at her. This sensation wasn't simple lust, and it wasn't simple care. This was complicated and intricate, like ...

Love. The love she once felt for Ezra before she met Liam. The love that was coming to surface, and yes, it was more memory than feeling, but it was still there.

And it terrified her.

Ava's wings disappeared in a flash. Her body felt lighter for a split second before gravity grabbed her with a vice.

Ava's heart leapt to her throat as she free-fell to the ground.

Her golden shield spread atop her skin in an instant, and she braced herself for impact. But before she crashed, Ezra had her in his arms, his naked, sweaty chest firm against her body.

He landed softly, his gaze locked onto Ava's as the shield vanished from her skin.

They were so close that she could feel his heart beating.

"Careful," he murmured. "And focus. Why did your wings disappear?"

"I don't know," she lied.

Ezra gave her a mocking glance that came out too charming. "You can do better than that."

Ava sighed, rubbing her forehead. "I guess they reacted to …" *Fear of feeling something for you.* "Insecurity," she said instead, clearing her throat. "I thought I'd fall."

"And so you did," Ezra countered, his arms a stone bed beneath her. "Control your emotions, and you control your wings."

She swallowed dryly, unable to break free from his loving glance. "Hopefully they'll only come back once I summon them."

He nudged his nose with hers. "Or maybe they'll pop up whenever you feel …"

As if on cue, her wings flashed behind her.

Ava blushed furiously at Ezra's naughty grin. She slapped his chest. "My wings come and go as they wish. It doesn't mean I'm in any way aroused!"

"Oh, really?" He leaned forward, and against all common sense, Ava didn't move away. "Shall we test your theory?" His voice was a sultry enchantment that froze all of her.

Ava caught herself lost in his musky, metallic scent and his warm, perfect body against hers. An aching sensation pooled in her most intimate parts.

Giving herself to Ezra could be so easy …the soft skin of his lips had almost reached hers, his breath mingling with Ava's.

She immediately snapped out of whatever trance had

taken hold of her and jumped to the ground, stepping away from him.

He frowned. "Why do you walk away from this? From us?"

"There's no us," she said through gritted teeth. Shame wrapped her with cold, sharp fingers.

"You loved me once, Ava." He slammed both hands on his waist. "You still do. You might be a powerful Dominion, but I'm a high angel. Your feelings are so clear. Why do you fight them?"

"You're seeing what you want to see." A knot clogged her throat, and tears stung her eyes because there was truth to what he said. "Of course I love you, Ezra. As a friend."

"I'm more than that," he countered, his voice failing at the end. "I have to be."

She didn't want to hurt him. Their connection went deep but not in the way Ezra wanted it to. Not in the way Ava herself had once desired a long time ago, before Liam entered her life.

"I can't give you what you want, Ezra. I've told you this from the beginning."

The time for her and Ezra had passed, and he would have to come to terms with it. So would she, apparently.

Ezra looked at the door, biting his own teeth. "But you feel something …" He scoffed. "Never mind."

She hugged herself, avoiding his stare.

The silence between them was a brick wall she hoped he wouldn't break. She felt his gaze upon her, pressing for answers she didn't have and didn't want to give. Answers she couldn't face.

Ezra let out a long breath. He shook his head as he studied his own boots. "Fine. We should get ready, then. After all, today is judgement day."

~

AVA OBSERVED the glassed dome and the blue sky beyond it. Light poured through the surface and spilled over the courtroom ahead, highlighting the white marbled floor, stands, and visitors' gallery. The vast courtroom felt empty in the way of cathedrals or maybe arenas. Ava couldn't decide which.

Her steps tapped on the marbled floor and echoed around the place, breaking the silence.

A cathedral. Definitely a cathedral.

She placed herself on the white witness stand and nodded to the angel sitting higher up beside her, the woman who held her fate in her hands.

Agathe, the Throne.

Her judge.

"Welcome, Dominion Lightway," Agathe said from her judge's stand.

Ava bowed her head. "Thank you, my Throne."

Ezra sat on the right-hand side of the visitors' gallery, pointedly ignoring the angel who occupied the opposite edge.

His cold-shoulder treatment didn't seem to bother Talahel. The Sword's predatory hazel eyes were fixed on Ava.

Talahel's orange hair was tied in a long braid, the sides of his temples shaved. Swirling tribal tattoos decorated his skin on both sides of his head. With his wine-red bodysuit that neared on black, he reminded Ava of a man dressed in blood.

She lifted her chin slightly, looking down her nose. A silent message that said she didn't fear him.

He smirked.

"Dominion Lightway?" Agathe peered at Ava with obsidian irises that matched the slick raven hair cascading down her shoulders. Aligned with her black bodysuit, the high angel made a blatant contrast to the whiteness of the room.

Something scratched Ava's mind the way a cat stretches out its claws.

Testing, warning.

The Throne was the head of all Erudites and Virtues, which meant her telepathic and telekinetic skills were unmatched in the entire Order. Her bodysuit was black, but her kilt silver, the opposite of the uniform used by her Virtues.

Ava swallowed and stared directly into those black irises, her words a whisper only judge and defendant could hear. "I believe, my Throne, that withdrawing information from an angel's mind is against the will of the Gods?"

Heavens, if Agathe found out about the Legion ...

"It certainly is." The Throne angled her head, curiosity clear in her expression. "I'm surprised you have such a strong mental wall. Usually only Virtues can raise one such as yours." She pointed a black-nailed finger at her. "Then again, compared to mine, it is a weak, puny wall."

Ava couldn't tell if Agathe had tried to offend her or state a simple fact.

"My Erudite sister has taught me how to raise one," she explained.

The Throne studied her. "I suppose the light works in strange ways. I know you will speak the truth, Ava Lightway. I never peer into an angel's mind, for I trust the Gods' servants blindly."

Well, perhaps she shouldn't.

Talahel's defense attorney, assigned by Agathe herself, occupied the council's table on the left side. The desk on the right, where Ava's defense should've been, was empty.

As if on cue, the wooden door slammed open, and a Dominion with brown wings and hair tied up in a bun entered. She carried paper folders and wore a white bodysuit with a silver kilt equal to Ava's.

The only difference between a Guardian and a Dominion, aside from status and power, was the color of their kilts. A Guardian's was white, a Dominion's was gray.

Once Vera reached her desk, she winked at Ava, who gave her a quick wave.

Vera dropped on her seat, spreading her wings wide—clearly showing off. She casually threw her folders on the marbled table.

Agathe's raven wings flashed behind her, obsidian black and majestic in the way only crowns or precious jewels could be. They were at least twice the size of Vera's, and they were also a statement.

The Throne smiled at Vera, who countered with an easy, playful grin in return. In a flash of light, their wings disappeared.

"You're late, Dominion Evestar," Agathe noted.

The old owl shrugged in her chair, tying both hands over her stomach. "My apologies, my Throne."

Agathe waited for Vera to continue, but no further explanation came. The Throne let out an exasperated sigh, then slammed her hand on the judge's stand, using her strong palm as the gavel. "We shall commence."

Talahel's defense, Virtue Lisle, rose from his desk and fixed his glasses. He walked toward Ava's stand. "Dominion Lightway, is it true you murdered an entire troop of Warriors?"

Ava's fists clenched, and she pressed her lips tight. She wished she could tell everyone about Talahel, but she had no proof of his involvement with Gabriel's deeds. Even worse, Talahel was the head of the Order's army. Archangels and Warriors worshipped him, which meant fighting the Sword was reckless at best and stupid at worst.

Ava might be angry, but she wasn't a fool. If she was to defeat Talahel, she would need concrete, damning proof that could shatter his people's faith in him.

From the visitors' gallery, Talahel gave her a defiant grin. The freckles on his skin made him look innocent and jovial.

Ava turned to the Virtue. "I was given the sword of revelation, and it freed the light of my essence in a way I couldn't control." She wore a mask of composure, avoiding yes or no answers like Vera had instructed her the week before. "It pains me to have hurt my brothers and sisters in the process, but that was never my intention."

A lie. Those villains had deserved to die, and Ava was glad she'd done it even if unintentionally.

Virtue Lisle raised his brow. "You do understand that what happened makes you a danger to everyone around you?"

Ezra stood at once. "My Throne, Dominion Lightway's explosive burst only happened because I gave her the sword of revelation. It has remained dormant since. Such an event will never happen again."

She could only hope.

"Excuse me, my Throne." Vera leaned back in her chair, that old, wise owl trapped inside her piercing stare. "Virtue Lisle's comment is irrelevant. I motion for dismissal."

Agathe nodded. "Dismissed."

Ava frowned at them, not knowing what had happened. By his befuddled expression, neither did Lisle.

"The light can behave in strange ways, especially when it comes to Dominion Lightway," Agathe explained like a patient parent. "Her essence has been under control since the event, and she's been thoroughly examined. I see no reason to tag her as a danger to the Order. Stick to the questioning at hand, Lisle."

The Virtue glanced at Agathe and then Vera, back and forth, his mouth open in confusion and shock.

Agathe motioned for him to go on, so he shook his head and cleared his throat. "Tell us the events of September thirteenth, when you killed Archangel Gabriel."

"Before the *Messenger* killed him," Ava corrected.

Vera didn't look up from the papers she was casually reading. "Objection, my Throne. The counselor is misleading the witness."

"Taken," Agatha said.

Lisle's cheeks flushed red, but he kept a composed demeanor.

As far as the Order knew, Ezra had killed Gabriel. After all, her essence's explosion disintegrated a troop of Warriors. If the Order suspected Ava had also killed an Archangel, she would've faced her final death by now.

Virtue Lisle wrapped his hands behind his back and strolled across the room. "Indeed, the Messenger killed Gabriel because he had murdered Captain Shelly Abernathy and Selfless Liam Striker."

"And Selfless Archibald Brennan," Ava added.

The Virtue quickly addressed Agathe. "No proof was ever found of that, my Throne."

"Defendant's statement dismissed," she agreed.

Ava exhaled slowly, trying to keep her anger at bay. Blood pounded under her skull, and her heart thumped in her ears. She hated that she sat here being questioned while Talahel was right there, utterly powerful.

Utterly free.

She wanted to tear his larynx from his throat, but without proof of his evil, she would start a civil war within the strongest branch of the Order. After that, all others around the world would likely fall.

No. Ava's war had to be silent and unseen.

The Virtue walked back and checked some papers on his desk. Without turning to her, he said, "According to your statement, Archangel Gabriel talked about eliminating humans and In-Betweens to create a world of angels and demons."

"Indeed."

And Talahel was the mastermind behind it all. *He's sitting right there!*

One deep breath. Then another.

Patience.

The Virtue nodded as if satisfied with her answer. "Scheming such evil might be possible for a human, but angels are the purest creatures the Gods created. Gabriel could've never—"

"Enough, Lisle," Agathe said from the judge's stand, her attention locked on Ava. "Dominion Lightway, your story matches the Messenger's perfectly, though to no surprise since you're mates."

"That doesn't compromise my testimony in any way," she stated.

From her desk, Vera winced. Ava must've said something wrong.

The Throne snorted as if she was remembering a past life long forgotten. "Many human lawmakers would disagree with you. So would I, once. But the Order is different from human courts. The light of the Gods is strong within us." She slammed her hand on her marbled desk, and the dry thump swam across the room. "I'm ready to make a judgement."

"But my Throne," Lisle stammered.

Agathe raised one eyebrow at him, and the Virtue shrank beneath her stare.

"Talahel," she said. "Gabriel murdered Captain Shelly Abernathy. His fingerprints were all over the body, especially her eye sockets. It was a cruel death. I believe the Messenger when he says Gabriel also murdered Selfless Liam Striker, though his body was never found." She slammed her hand on the marbled surface twice, each thump as loud as an iron hammer. "You will make sure none of your Warriors or Archangels behave in such despicable manner again. If they do, you're hereby ordered to grant them the final death."

Talahel stood from his bench and bowed his head to her. "I shall, my Throne. However, we do not know what this Captain did to deserve such fate."

Agathe's lips twitched in horror. "You say it was her fault that Gabriel tortured her before ending her life?"

"I do not excuse Gabriel's actions; I simply say he wasn't a madman. The reactions reported in this court do not seem like him."

A storm whirled inside Ava, her very bones shaking with fury. She opened her mouth to argue, but Ezra's glare stopped her. It begged her to wait.

Losing her temper might be exactly what Talahel wanted.

"There's a reason why our courts are guided by evidence, my Sword," Agathe said dryly.

"Indeed." Talahel wrapped both hands behind his back. "I shall make sure none of mine behave in such despicable way again. However, Dominion Lightway has murdered an entire troop, either by accident or sheer will. I demand retribution."

"Dominion Lightway." Agathe turned to her. "You're hereby declared innocent of the events of September thirteenth. Keep doing the Gods' work." She raised one thin eyebrow at Talahel. "Revenge is not the way of the Gods, brother. You should pray for forgiveness. Teach yours by example, my Sword."

He bowed to her and placed a hand on his chest. "Yes, my Throne. It's been a difficult time for me."

"To us all." She slammed her hand twice on the desk. "Now, we shall discuss the matter of the In-Betweens. The

Messenger's statement is quite alarming. If demons are behind the increase of In-Between attacks on humans, they must be stopped."

"This is nonsense, my Throne," Talahel said, leaving the visitors' gallery to enter the center of the courtroom. "Demons can't articulate on such a level. The In-Betweens lie. And even if this were true, what do we owe those who didn't choose the light?"

"They didn't choose the dark, either." Agathe frowned at him. "And we owe them mercy if their attacks are the result of desperation."

"Their depositions aren't valid to the Order," Talahel argued. "We cannot rely on In-Betweens to tell the truth, and we never have. This is simply their attempt to harm humans without receiving the adequate punishment."

"That might as well be," Agathe said. "Dominion Evestar, however, had an excellent idea." She nodded at Vera, who in turn smirked at Talahel. "We will build a task force."

Talahel blew air through his lips. "A task force? That's completely unnecessary. If it will make my brothers and sisters happy, I will ask my angels to—"

Agathe raised her hand. "I appreciate the offering, brother. But the arm of the Order should not investigate this alone. You already have so much on your shoulders."

The Throne actually meant this. There was no inch of irony in her words. She truly wished to help that animal. Ava could feel her compassion and kindness flowing in soft clouds around her.

"I shall assign two of my most trusted Virtues," the Throne continued. "You will assign two of your Archangels, and Ezrapahel two of his Dominions. They shall dig deeper into this matter and report directly to us. In the meantime, we will continue to smite In-Betweens who threaten humans, even if they're being forced to do it."

"I choose Vera," Ezra said as he entered the center of the courtroom, standing beside Talahel and yet paying him no attention. "I also choose Dominion Phillae."

Talahel's hands balled into fists, but he kept a poised expression. "Sithrael and Monahe." He glanced at Ava, a threat hidden within his soulless eyes.

"Very well," Agathe said. "I choose Virtue Moon and Lisle."

Lisle bowed to her. "I shall make you proud, my Throne."

"I know you will," she said without looking at him. "Well then, now that this matter has been settled, I'm needed in another hearing."

With that, she vanished in a cloud of smoke as dark as her hair. Every high angel had a special power unique to themselves, and Agathe's was teleportation.

"Pointless, really, for her to have wings," Virtue Lisle said as he walked to his desk and gathered his papers.

Vera gathered her own folders. "In this world, nothing is ever pointless." She went to him and tapped his shoulder. "Come. Let me buy you a coffee. You played a fair game."

He chuckled. "You can be nice when you're not being a bitch, you know."

"Why, Lisle, I'm always a bitch."

As soon as they walked out of the room, the tension between Ezra and Talahel became invisible thunder cracking in the air.

"I'm deeply sorry about Gabriel's fate." Ezra's composed demeanor revealed nothing. "But he spoke of an alliance with demons to eradicate In-Betweens. Such horrible crimes can't go unpunished, don't you think, brother?"

"That is indeed terrible." Talahel frowned, feigning disgust.

Oh, what an actor he was.

"I'm glad you stopped him before it was too late," he went

on. "However, I simply can't imagine Gabriel killing innocents in such manner."

Ava left the witness stand and went to Ezra's side. "His fingerprints were on the Captain's body."

"Were they?" Talahel raised his shoulders.

"Oh, you're good." She bared her teeth at him. "But I'm better."

She would tie him to the demonic activity, and she would have him locked up for genocide.

Nowadays, the In-Betweens weren't taken captive, nor did they have a right to trial. They were simply killed because they had attacked the Order. Their basic rights were annulled on that same day, thanks to the Sword.

Hatred grew strong among angels, tainting everything the Order fought for. All because of demons—all because of Talahel.

Ava would end him with her bare hands; the threat sizzled on the tip of her tongue.

Ezra softly pressed her forearm in a silent message that said, *"Careful."*

"I'm a high angel, Dominion Lightway. You stand no chance against me." Talahel clicked his tongue and surveyed her wings. "I wonder how you got those beautiful snow-white feathers." He frowned at Ezra. "They're as white as Michael's, are they not?"

Ezra ignored his provocation. "A remarkable coincidence indeed."

"Hmm." Talahel shrugged. "I suppose yours comes close, being light silver and gold and all." He tapped Ezra's shoulder. "It's truly a pity. I loved Gabriel, as I love all of them." He turned to Ava. "Remember, Dominion Lightway, that you have murdered an entire troop of my Warriors. If you didn't have the protection of the Messenger, you'd be dead by now."

With that, he went to the door.

"I will remind you again, brother," Ezra said through gritted teeth. "That revenge is not the way of the Gods."

"Indeed." Talahel glared back at them from over his shoulder. A cruel grin cut across his lips. "But perhaps it is *my* way."

5

LIAM

*L*iam watched the training room's ceiling spin. His shallow breaths dragged in his ears, and he felt drunk even though he hadn't taken a drop of alcohol. He tried to focus, but the ceiling still whirled above him.

The metallic taste of blood spread in his mouth. At some point in the last hour, he must've cut his tongue with his sharp teeth.

His muscles hurt. No, his damned bones hurt. He doubted he'd ever get up again.

"Come on!" Jal's voice came from afar, and Liam scowled. "We don't have all day."

He felt someone kick his calf. Drowsily, he grumbled, "Fucking demon."

After the darkness receded and Liam returned to his own mind, Archie ordered a strict training schedule for him. When he wasn't fighting the old man, he was fighting Jal. And when he wasn't fighting either, Liam was too tired to even breathe.

Today, he'd battled Jal through the entire morning.

Striking the demon proved harder than he expected. Jal was stronger and faster, and when he slammed an ear clap near his temples, Liam lost his balance and thundered to the ground like a falling tree.

"I assumed you were the good cop in Archie's routine," Liam said as he tried to sit straight. The room span furiously, so he laid back again. "You were supposed to go easy on me, right?"

"I let you hit me once. That counts."

Yeah, and Liam's punch didn't leave a tiny blotch on the demon's face.

Asshole.

Archie and Jal trained Liam so hard that they would often carry him to his cell—sometimes Liam was awake, sometimes unconscious. If he had trained with Archie, he was probably not only comatose but barely breathing.

The next day, however, he woke perfectly healed from his battle wounds.

And then it all started again.

Ava was his trigger; that much was clear. Every time he thought of her, the darkness went berserk.

Archie said no one could tell exactly why, but Jal had a theory of his own.

"The dark *is* you, dumbass," he said this morning before they'd begun. "No one watches your back more than yourself, capisce?"

"No. Not at all."

"Look, missing Ava hurts, right? So the darkness is trying to protect you. Every time you think of her, it goes berserk so that you stop thinking about her."

He'd chortled. "Protect me? The fucking thing doesn't give me a moment of peace. It's always driving me mad, not only when I think of Ava."

Jal leaned forward and whispered as if he was about to tell Liam a big secret. "Yeah, but when you think of her it goes crazier than usual, doesn't it?"

Well, he couldn't argue with that.

In any case, Archie and Jal's training worked. The darkness stopped fighting against Liam to fight *with* him and soon enough, he became used to it. So when mad ideas and visions bubbled to surface, he found that razor sharp determination that took ahold of him when he fought.

Boom, alignment.

The darkness was no fool, though.

Liam was constantly on edge, constantly fighting, and sometimes he got tired. The darkness often took advantage of these moments and swallowed him entirely, showing him images of the Legion piled with corpses, assuring Liam it had been his fault.

Once, it showed him Jal's beheaded corpse, and another time it was Jophiel hanging from a cross. This thing inside took his fears to a whole new level.

Eventually, Liam controlled these fits on his own. But when he imagined Ava making love to the Messenger, he lost it so bad that Archie had to punch him unconscious.

"Are you getting up or not?" Jal asked from a distance, his voice now clearer in Liam's ears.

The ceiling had finally stopped moving.

"You suck," Liam grunted as he pushed himself up.

Jal was dabbing a towel over his naked torso, drying his sweat. He grabbed another towel from the bench next to them and shot it at Liam, who began drying his bare chest.

Lilith watched them from the bench. She drank from a wine glass filled with thick, dark liquid that sure as Hells hadn't come from grapes.

"My, oh my, what a show, gentlemen." She licked her lips,

her cheeks flushed. Her eyes gleamed with predatory glee. "Do let me know the next time you'll be training, yes?"

Liam rolled his eyes, but Jal puffed up his chest like a peacock in heat. A flirty grin crossed the demon's squared jaw, and Lilith grinned at him in return, a spark of lust breaking the air between them.

Today, the vampire queen wore her red hair in a high bun with a few loose curls framing the sides of her face. Instead of her typical corseted dress, she had a very business-like black suit and skirt which contoured her curves all too well.

Especially her plump chest.

"Much as I loved my corseted dress, I suppose I must keep up with the times," she said, clearly enjoying the attention she received. "Don't you think, Liam?"

"I don't care," he snapped, looking away.

If Lilith were anyone else, Liam would say she was beautiful, tantalizing even. Then again, the vampire queen had glamoured him. She had also said he and Ava were soulmates.

Lilith might be pretty, but she was also a liar.

He draped his towel over his shoulder. "Well, I'm done for the day."

The vampire queen drank her glass empty, then leaned back on the bench. "You've had some rough weeks. If you need help relaxing, just let me know." She winked at him. "I can send some of my girls for you."

He glared at Jal, silently asking him to intervene, but the demon simply shrugged and added, "Sex could help blow off some steam. And Lilith's girls have experience with … things."

"I don't need to pay for sex, thanks," he grumbled.

"Who said anything about paying?" Lilith frowned. "I do not run a brothel, you idiot. My girls enjoy activities of the sexual kind. Pleasure is what both sides get from this deal. And something tells me you aim to please." She analyzed her own nails. "Carmelita and Annabelle have already made themselves available, should you so wish."

He couldn't remember what Carmelita and Anabelle looked like, but he must've walked past them in the Legion's corridors.

The fact he hadn't noticed them, or any woman really, showed him how far gone he was. How completely Ava owned him.

His thoughts rushed back to his Guardian, naked and underneath him, and his groin reacted to her.

He took a deep, steadying breath. "I'm fine, thanks."

Liam turned to leave, aching for the coldest shower he could get.

"Wait a sec there, baby demon." Jal caught up to him. "I have to take you somewhere. Let's shower and then get rolling."

Hmm, odd. Archie had ordered Liam to stay at the Legion and never leave without him.

Jal must've read the question in his face. "It's Archie-approved, all right?" He tapped Liam's shoulder playfully, but sensed his hesitation. "Okay, fine. He has no clue. But I wouldn't be a demon if I didn't break the rules every now and then."

JAL AND LIAM crossed the park in silence, following a dimly lit path lined by lamp posts that belonged to the previous century. Car honks, shouting, and sirens—typical city noise —rang faintly in the distance, almost as if the park could absorb sound.

They both wore tight black shirts and dark blue jeans. Jal had lent a good deal of his damned and fire resistant clothes to Liam, which meant they often dressed the same. The smartass comments from Lilith about them being Tweedledee and Tweedledum had been endless. Still were, actually.

"What do you know about the current state of things?" Jal asked as they walked.

Liam shrugged. "Ava is in the Order, trying to imprison Talahel and help Ezraphael."

The mention of her name stirred the darkness a little. He harnessed the focus he'd learned during his battles and surprisingly, the beast went back to sleep.

"Yes," Jal said. "Ava's mission is vital to our success. You have to know that. She didn't leave you for nothing."

True.

Still, Liam forced himself not to dwell on her sweet smile, her lavender scent, her soft curves …

"Without the Order," Jal continued, "the Legion won't have enough power to save the In-Betweens, humans, and even angels themselves. See, right now the Order is more castle of glass than mighty hand of the Gods. Ava is trying to save it from the inside, and none of us can help her … at least not in any significant way."

"So, what's the Legion doing?"

"Mostly?" Jal scratched his chin. "We're protecting the In-Betweens while Jophiel comes up with a way to join our forces with the Order."

Liam snorted. "The Legion considers the In-Betweens equal to angels. Humans, too. I don't see the Order accepting that anytime soon."

"Baby steps, yeah?"

Two pretty brunettes passed by them in jogging suits.

They smiled at Jal and he whistled at them, watching the women go.

"The transition Jophiel wants is complicated," he went on once they turned a corner. "Especially since angels hate werewolves and vampires for their attack on the Order." He grunted to the night sky. "Thanks a lot, Lothar."

"He's not there," Liam muttered, shoving his hands on his jean's pockets.

The werewolf lord was dead. As a supernatural, he was simply gone. No Heavens for him. No Hells, either.

Just oblivion.

"Anyway," Jal shrugged as he walked, "amid this mess, we can't forget our true enemy: the demons who force the shift on werewolves and steal legal blood supplies from the vamps."

"We don't have enough manpower to protect the In-Betweens from Talahel and stop these demons, do we?"

"See, I knew you weren't just a pretty face." He punched Liam lightly on his shoulder, then joined his own hands. "As I said, Order plus Legion equals victory. It's the only way."

Liam considered this for a moment. "So, what are we doing here?"

"Well …" Jal scratched the back of his neck. "Remember the 'we need all the help we can get' part?"

Liam nodded.

"After Lothar's death, werewolves deserted the Legion. We have a couple of rogue tail-swingers but not nearly enough." He raised his index finger. "That's where I step in."

Right ahead, a group of humans sat in a circle under a willow tree. It was new moon today, so the figures blended perfectly with the darkness.

"They can't hear or smell us from here." Jal held Liam's shoulder, stopping him. "After Lothar's death, his birth son Suther ordered all packs to leave the Legion."

Liam gaped at him. "Lothar had a birth son? Sure, vamps and dogs call anyone they turn their children, but can they actually procreate?"

"None of us can, knucklehead. Suther is Lothar's actual son from when he was human. Daddy died and became a werewolf. Decades passed, his son aged, and when it was Suther's turn to go, he became a werewolf too." Jal watched the group with a certain sadness. "It would be heartwarming if it wasn't so tragic."

The story sunk into Liam, piercing his chest. He understood how painful losing a father could be, blood related or not. Even if Archie was fine now, he would never forget the sound of the old man's heart monitor flatlining.

"Follow my lead," Jal said.

The dogs raised their heads, catching their scent as they approached. It worked both ways. The stench of wet fur invaded Liam's nostrils, too.

The men and women showed them their sharp canines but didn't stand.

A first warning.

These weren't weak werewolves or newly born, either. The size of their canines and their muscular build told Liam these were pack leaders.

Alphas.

The head of the group sat cross-legged atop a square rock. He might not be the biggest of them, but his proud straight posture denoted that here he was king.

"Always look them in the eyes," Jal muttered.

"Not my first encounter with a bunch of Alphas, demon."

"Then freaking look them straight in the eyes, *demon.*"

Liam wasn't used to being called a demon yet, and the insult stung. He'd have to get used to it at some point, though.

Might as well be now.

As they approached, the man on the rock growled at them. *A final warning.*

Jal halted, so did Liam.

The man was actually young. Even though he resembled a bodybuilder and seemed to be taller than Liam, his face said he couldn't be older than twenty. He had Lothar's hazel eyes and the same straight nose, but his hair was longer and slightly curled. Liam bet that under the sun, it would turn a honey-gold like his father's.

"Leave, demons." Suther bared his teeth at Liam and Jal. "Leave before we rip you apart."

Jal raised his hands. "We come in peace."

"I have nothing to discuss with you." Suther barked at them and it was strange, seeing a man-shaped creature make that beastly sound. "Your Legion failed my father. You failed all In-Betweens. I'm surprised Lilith still stands by you."

Jal's forehead crinkled. "Well, she's not a fucking cowa—"

Liam stepped forward and pushed Jal back, silencing him just in time. So much for following that asshole's lead.

"We're sorry about Lothar," he said in a diplomatic tone that felt odd in his mouth. "I was there when—"

Suther jumped to his feet, the muscles in his arms bulging as he fisted his hands. "I *wasn't* there! Do you know why?" He stomped toward him, but Liam didn't flinch or step back. "Father imprisoned me until it was done. I couldn't fight beside him one last time." Suther's minted breath washed against Liam's face. "When I was released, I discovered my father's head had been severed by angelic hands, and I had inherited his packs. All of them! Do you think that's fair, demon? That I was left with such humongous responsibility and couldn't afford to avenge my father? Do you doubt I'd give my life to end his murderer?"

Oh, Liam wished he would. Lothar's murderer was none other than Ava's mate, Ezraphael himself.

He didn't need to add wood to a burning fire, though, even if a part of him desperately wanted to.

"Lothar knew the risks and the outcomes," he said matter-of-factly.

"Yes, he did. And so do I. You'll do well to stay away from my people." Before Liam could reply, Suther sniffed the air over his head, wincing as if he stank of old eggs. "Why do you smell of both angel and demon?"

Forget that; how could Suther *smell* it?

"He used to be of the light," Jal explained with a bored demeanor, ignoring the surprise in Suther's young face. "Look, we've all sacrificed a lot to be here. Your father's death," Jal shook his head, "it hurt us, too. Lothar used brute force to make his point, but the Legion stands for a peaceful transition. We could've never supported his attack, even if we wanted to save him."

Suther's fury now focused on Jal. "The Order has searched for a reason to smite the In-Betweens for centuries. My father gave them motive, yes, but if the Legion had aided him, this ongoing genocide of my people, of Lilith's people, could have been avoided. And my father would still be standing here."

"If the Legion had aided Lothar, it would've perished with him," Jal countered, his tone mournful.

Suther barked once, a sound that reverberated throughout the park. Immediately, all pack leaders stood and growled at Liam and Jal.

They took a step back. This could go really bad, really fast.

"Stay away from us," the werewolf lord growled, then walked away.

His pack leaders followed.

Liam let out a relieved breath once they were gone. "That went well."

He expected a witty remark from Jal, but the demon's typical playfulness had vanished. This scared Liam more than the pack of angry Alphas.

"We're at war," Jal said, his voice a whisper. "And we're losing."

6

AVA

*T*he view from Ava's new quarters was breathtaking. Unlike her old room, which faced a decadent building, she now looked over the entire city, a profusion of blinking towers drenched in the soft pink and orange that preceded sunrise.

Ava watched the skyline as an invisible force squeezed her chest. She wanted to visit the Legion and drown in Liam's arms. She had to apologize for not seeing him sooner; for choosing to be here with Ezra. But Liam would understand this was all for the greater good. If anything, he understood the importance of duty.

Her wings spread and flapped without coordination, first the left followed by the right. They too wanted to go to him.

"If you did your job," Ava grumbled at the feathery slumps behind her, "then we could've flown to Liam a long time ago and no one would have noticed."

Her wings recoiled. Ava got the distinct sensation they'd been offended.

She rubbed the bridge of her nose and sighed. This was

silly, of course. Her wings weren't a dog in need of training. They were a part of her, like her light and darkness.

A soft breeze made the white linen curtains flutter. The cold marble floor numbed the soles of her feet.

Everything was cold in this room.

She missed the carpeted floor of her old quarters and even the internal airing system—the windows were always kept shut in the lower floors, where the third-tiers lived.

This room's marbled walls and arched windows, the sheer size of it, felt more similar to a palace than to an angel's quarters. It might be bigger, better, but it was also unfamiliar.

Everything felt more detached the higher she went within the Order.

When Ava was a Guardian, the compassion and kindness of the light had consumed her completely, blinding her to the evil around her. The evil within the Order.

To kill Gabriel, she had to free a beast that had been asleep inside her. And maybe that beast of darkness made her less amicable and compliant, but it also helped Ava see clearer than ever before. She never felt more real—more herself—than right now.

A knock came from inside her mind as if there was a backdoor at the base of her skull. Ava frowned, wondering if she had gone temporarily insane.

Then came a second knock.

A presence waited before her mental wall; she could sense it standing there, right on the edge of her consciousness. She closed her eyes and sunk into herself, immersed in a profound void.

Ava opened her eyes and watched the golden rift in her essence. *A waterfall of light.* And inside it, behind the sparkling brilliance, lied the new beast she had freed.

Her light purred in the way of a pleased feline, but the darkness ingrained within sat still and quiet.

Watching.

She turned in the opposite direction toward her mind wall. It appeared to be a never ending line made of either marble or bone. Then again, the wall wasn't material, and neither was the waterfall. She had no clue why they looked that way.

Mysteries of the mind, she supposed.

She lowered the wall into the void around her, and an old man stepped forward.

He had a white beard with hair to match. His chocolate skin almost mingled with the darkness around him, highlighting his sky-blue eyes. He wore a white T-shirt with golden letters that spelled "ABBA."

This was odd. Jophiel usually wore heavy-metal or rock band shirts.

It didn't matter. He was here!

A smile bloomed on Ava's lips as she ran to him. She hadn't known the Seraph for long, but his Legion was merciful and inclusive—exactly what the Order should've been.

The sight of Jophiel brought a warm and giddy sensation to her core, not only because she missed the Seraph, but also for what he represented.

A new hope.

They hugged in the darkness for a while, neither of them uttering a word, neither really wanting to let go. Ava held a rush of tears that pushed for freedom. Instead of letting them out, she took a deep breath and stepped back.

"How is he?" She didn't need to explain who "he" was.

"He's …" Jophiel hissed through his teeth. "It's hard, Ava. Liam's doing well, but he has a long way to go. I'd say he's fine, all things considered."

"I wanted to go see him, I—"

He raised his palm. "Your mission here is of utmost

importance. You saved Ezraphael, and with him you can also save the Order. Be proud of what you're accomplishing."

She was, but at the same time, helping those in need and focusing on the greater good ... it wasn't enough.

What about her and Liam's happiness?

A pang of shame swam down her spine. For the first time, Ava missed the compassionate angel she used to be.

Her rift rumbled with a growl.

Jophiel stared beyond her, at the rift where her beasts resided. A frown of either worry or curiosity creased his forehead.

"Jophiel?"

"Hmm?" He blinked and looked down at her. "Ah, yes. Bring Ezraphael to me when you're ready. The time has come, but be careful with his feelings. They're fragile, and a broken heart could still push him to the wrong side."

"Ezra's stronger than you give him credit for." She crossed her arms. "And I can't pretend to love him. It's not fair to him or me."

He raised an eyebrow. "You don't need to pretend. You do love him, child, perhaps not the way you love Liam, but he *is* in your heart. I'm surprised you haven't noticed it yet. As a daughter of the Goddess of Love and Life, emotions should be your specialty."

The words were a sledgehammer and a wrecking ball that hit her at once. She cleared her throat. "I love Ezra as a friend."

He rolled his eyes as if he knew Ava was lying to herself.

But she wasn't.

She couldn't be.

Ava scratched the back of her neck, hoping to change the course of this conversation. "I've been training."

Jophiel gave her a pleased grin. "I've noticed. Your wall is stronger."

"It is, but if I'm to spend time in Agathe's presence, I need your—"

"No mental wall you raise will ever stop her. Be glad she's known for respecting the Order's laws and an angel's privacy."

Ava nodded. "I also tried moving heavy objects with my mind. Justine was there to help, but it didn't work."

"*That* I can help you with. Once Ezraphael knows about us, training you will be easier. As the Messenger, he can cover for you."

"I will bring him to the Legion as soon as possible." When realization dawned on Ava, a spark of excitement burned in her chest.

If she went to the Legion, she would see Liam again!

Jophiel raised his attention to the rift behind her, narrowing his eyes. "How are you feeling?"

"Fine." She rolled her shoulders. "Though I've grown more impatient. Reckless, I'd say. Especially when it comes to facing the inequalities in the Order."

"As I expected." He still watched the rift. "As a Guardian, you had too much light. Now, you've unlocked that which will bring you balance. There's nothing wrong with it, but balance will come with a price, as most things often do."

"How can I find this balance? And what's the price I'll pay?"

"You're already paying it." He raised his head like a wolf catching a scent. "I must go now." Jophiel's image began fading before her. "Bring him to me."

And with that he was gone.

Ava opened her eyes and watched the city ahead. She mulled over Jophiel's words but still couldn't understand their meaning.

What price was she paying?

Eventually she gave up and headed to her bed. She

grabbed the white bodysuit and gray kilt laying on the mattress. Her silk nightgown pooled at her feet, and then she put on the comfortable fabric that stretched and adapted to her forms.

At least wearing clothes wasn't as impossible as before—her bodysuits had slits on the back to fit her wings.

The damned things knew what to do now, which Ava counted as a victory. It had taken them a day or two to learn to act as second arms, though. If only they would vanish into her light, they could make things much easier. Being able to fly without free-falling into a nasty crash would be nice, too.

Her wings wiggled in a silent complaint.

By the time a soft knock came from the door, Ava had already zipped the bodysuit shut and fixed the kilt around her waist.

"Come in," she said.

Ezra entered, wearing a bodysuit that clung to his tight muscles, his white linen kilt placed around his waist. His uniform differed from Ava's on technicalities: while his suit was silver, hers was white, and though his kilt was white, hers was gray.

His hair was tied in a low braid that cascaded down the right side of his chest. When he gave Ava that picture-perfect smile, she wondered if he was real or a vision.

Admiring him felt wrong, though. So she looked away.

"Today we're teaching your wings to go into your light, or my name isn't Ezraphael Stormglow." He walked to her and smoothed out the frame of her wings. "Also, let's see if we can get them to fly again. I feel we're almost there."

Ava gave him a discouraged grin, so Ezra nudged her with his shoulder. "Is everything all right?"

"Yes," she lied. "I just hate falling."

She went to the window and crossed her arms, watching

the view. Every day since Liam's death, Ava was choosing duty over love.

And for what?

Ezra stepped beside her, pointing at the landscape. "It's wonderful, isn't it?"

She nodded mindlessly.

"You're thinking about him," he said, his words a statement more than a question.

How did he know? Her mental wall was strongly in place and besides, Ezra couldn't read thoughts, only feel her emotions.

Perhaps they had been enough.

"He's one of us," she countered quietly.

"It's more than that. You love Liam," he said, even though she had never told him the truth out of fear it could push him to Talahel's side.

"Ezra, I …"

"Have you ever wondered if your Guardian instincts got mixed with your real feelings? A lot changed for you in a very short time, and Liam became your only safe haven." He studied his own silver boots. "Maybe what you feel for him isn't love. Maybe you clung to him because he was the only one you could trust. He became home to you, the home I used to be." He swallowed dryly. "I'll never forgive myself for letting you down, Ava."

She clenched her teeth and focused on the landscape ahead, taking the time to process his words.

At first Ava wanted to slap Ezra and push him out of her room, but she couldn't do something that would hurt him, and this would. *Mightily.* He still had hope, and she couldn't kill that flicker.

Not yet.

So she settled with a quiet, "I didn't mistake my feelings for love."

Didn't she, though?

Hells, the seed was planted.

"You were his Guardian, and I assigned you to him," Ezra continued. "Do you understand the implications of your being in love with him?"

If the Throne discovered that Ava had been romantically involved with a charge, it could cost her everything she had given up to be here. Not to mention it would ruin her entire mission.

"You mean I can't be with Liam." The words corroded her vocal chords.

She refused to accept them.

"You shouldn't have been with Liam when he was human, and you shouldn't be with him now. He's a demon, Ava," Ezra said. "You need to let him go."

Ava's body felt heavy, and she wondered if her limbs had turned into stone. Breathing, thinking, functioning, it all became too difficult.

She wasn't ready to face that truth, so she rushed to the round desk near her window and grabbed some papers. She handed them to Ezra.

Before he could ask what they were, or why Ava had given them to him so abruptly, she explained, "We might not be able to denounce Talahel, but we can make his life harder."

Ezra read the papers and smiled. "You're denying him the shipments of holy guns and swords he requested."

"Well, *you* are." She pointed to the empty signature place-holders.

Ezra went to her desk, took a pen, and promptly signed them. "After our training, hand the documents to Virtue Chang from protocols."

"By the way," she said, "I know someone who can help us defeat Talahel."

Ezra frowned. "You do?"

"Yes, and I can take you to him."

Ezra watched her for a long while, his doubt forming a cloud of shaking gray against her Dominion's essence.

"If you think it's best," he finally said.

"It is. But you must keep an open mind. Promise me this."

He watched her with a mix of hurt and longing that pierced her chest. "For you, Ava, anything."

7

LIAM

*T*he darkness was always there, always a part of him. Sometimes it whispered, sometimes it bellowed, but through the darkness' furious fits, Liam learned to find himself.

Slowly.

It was all about control.

So when the dark told him that Ava was fucking the Messenger while Father beat him, Liam didn't stop moving, didn't let the darkness take over. Instead, he swiveled on his base and charged forward, slamming a punch on Archie's face that sent the old man three steps back.

Sweat beaded on Liam's forehead. His knuckles ached, his ribs too, but he didn't care. He had blocked the darkness and punched a second-tier demon.

Two things to be damn proud of.

Archie rubbed his jaw. "Not bad, kid."

Liam had missed this: the adrenaline, the anticipation. The focus. He couldn't wait to be out in the field again with the old man.

"I'm ready, Archie." He swayed from one foot to the other, his fists raised. "Let's bring down some demons."

"Ironic, since we're demons too." Archie unsheathed his sword and gave him a roguish grin. Shadows grew from the old man's back, revealing his wings.

Playtime was over.

Liam unsheathed his sword, a crappy weapon that hung on a black leather belt around his waist, occupying the sheath that used to belong to Michael's blade.

His blade.

This sword's hilt was too light. Even after three days, Liam hadn't adjusted to it. Compared to his old weapon, a mighty silver and blue beast, this thing felt like a scared little rat in his hands. But the Order had snagged Michael's sword after Liam's death, and there was no retrieving it.

Angelic hands tended to do that—steal things that belonged to him.

Archie charged, his steps silent against the training room's padded floor. Their blades clanged, once, twice.

Step back. Attack.

Liam held his defense, which was better than during their first sword fight. Back then, Archie slashed a deep cut on his thigh in less than a minute.

The darkness purred inside him, pleased with Liam's progress, *their progress*. It felt weird. The darkness might be many things, but supportive wasn't one of them.

Archie took advantage of his distraction and pushed Liam's blade away, slashing a diagonal cut across his stomach. Blood poured from the wound.

"Sunovabitch," Liam grumbled before dropping his sword and falling to his knees.

He stamped his hands on the deep gash in a futile attempt to stop the bleeding. His consciousness would slip away any moment now.

A pitch-black fog shot from Archie's hands and enveloped Liam's trunk. The fog seeped into his skin in icy tendrils that pierced his core.

The wound soon numbed. Blood stopped pouring. When the fog retreated back into Archie, Liam's deadly wound had been completely healed.

He wished his darkness could do that. Maybe someday it would.

He glanced at his fallen sword and snorted. *Useless.* He needed Michael's sword, his sword, because Liam was Michael. Or at least he used to be.

"Why can't we remember?" he asked quietly.

The old man stepped closer. "You mean our time as angels?"

He nodded.

"I don't know. Because this is a new life?" Archie sheathed his sword. "Michael and Acheron—that was my name by the way, or so I was told—their lives are gone. There's no use in mourning them." He dropped on the padded ground beside Liam. "We should look forward, not backward."

"I was forced to become a Selfless."

"You weren't forced to become a demon." Archie propped both elbows on his knees. "The darkness isn't good or evil; it just is. It crashes against you, like the light does in newborn angels. And I guess some part of you, the part that was still Michael, knew this."

Liam chortled. "Stupidest decision I ever made."

"I don't think so. You knew exactly what you were doing, even if it's not clear to you now. The light makes you softer, the darkness makes you harder, but you're still *you*. Make sense?"

He snorted. "Nothing does these days."

"True," Archie chuckled. After a moment of silence, he asked, "What do you know about how demons organize?"

"They don't. Demonic factions have always been scattered." Liam shrugged. "It's why demons were never able to stand against the Order."

"And now they're tampering with wolfsugar, stealing blood supplies right under the Order's nose, and making angels do the dirty work for them. What does that tell you?"

Liam gaped at him. "They're coordinating."

"Microscopically so," the old man added. "For the first time in millennia, demons are uniting under one goal. What it is exactly, I don't know. My gut feeling tells me it goes beyond exterminating the In-Betweens."

Liam's jaw clenched, and his heartbeats quickened. "How do we stop them?"

"By observing." Archie lifted his finger. "A snake is nothing without its head. We find the head, cut it off, and the whole thing ends."

"Is this why you went undercover?"

"Yes." Archie tapped his leg and stood. "We'll meet a demon today. The Legion, the Order, the entire world … they all hang on this mission, kid. *Our* mission."

Liam crossed his arms. "Gee, no pressure."

"That's how we roll, partner." Archie winked at him before walking to a gym bag he'd left near the corner. From inside, he pulled Liam's old black leather jacket.

Liam focused on the glassed walls, then on the floor. "I'm not a Selfless anymore."

"You're right." Archie stepped toward him and sat on his own heels. He pushed the jacket against Liam's chest, poking the spot where his heart was. "This is the only faith you need to follow. What does it tell you?"

Liam squinted at the jacket.

Look what good it did to us, his own voice whispered. Shadow tentacles brushed softly against his mind. *Greater good*, the darkness chortled. *The greater good took Ava from us.*

Liam slammed a hand on his forehead. "Shut the fuck up." He gritted his teeth as he pushed the tentacles away, but they stuck like glue.

Something nudged his chest again, and he looked down at his leather jacket. Archie wasn't taking no for an answer.

Worry formed soft wrinkles on the old man's face. "Are you with me, kid?"

Liam blinked and focused, pulling from his core that sharp determination which controlled the beast.

The darkness silenced.

"When wasn't I?" He took the damn jacket.

THE DEMON WAITED for them on an empty pier. He was scrawny and slightly shorter than Liam. If it weren't for the stench of sulfur and the darkness pulsing inside him, which tingled against Liam's own, he would have mistaken the creature for a normal human.

He had short copper hair and hazel eyes that neared orange. His skin was too pale, and it contrasted with the black makeup that contoured his feline eyelids. His mouth was painted black, a mirror to Archie's own.

Maybe the members of this gang were all goths.

"You bring me a new recruit, Archibald?" The man's voice was cracking boulders and rumbling clouds, a tone that didn't match his frail appearance. He snorted as he eyed Liam up and down. "You don't look very powerful."

"Neither do you," he countered.

Archie smacked the back of Liam's neck. "Kid's not very smart, Hauk."

The demon's wide grin spread through most of his jaw. "At least he's honest."

"And a Fallen, like me," Archie added.

"Hmm." He watched the old man with calculating eyes. Finally, Hauk clapped a hand on Archie's back with such strength his shoulder bones cracked. "Offer accepted!"

Not a hint of pain flashed on Archie's face. His black fog sprouted from his skin and enveloped the wound, popping bones back into place.

The old man had always been a tough fucker.

"I assume this is Liam Striker, your former partner?"

"Yeah," Archie said casually.

Hauk didn't know Liam was also Archie's son. It might come to their advantage someday.

"Ah, the Fury Boys." He licked his lips. "What a win for our side. Master will be pleased."

Master?

Liam shot a curious look at Archie, but the old man ignored him, his attention focused on Hauk.

The demon gave Liam a nonchalant shrug. "I'm glad to see you follow your partner wherever he goes, little demon."

"Little?" Liam eyed Hauk with contempt. "I'm bigger than you, asshole."

Archie shot him a glare filled with reproach, but Hauk mockingly stamped a hand on his chest and feigned shock. "Why, such language, little demon. Would your Gods approve of this?"

"Not my Gods anymore."

Renouncing them wasn't hard. Liam had never believed them in the first place. Maybe Michael did, but Liam had survived enough shit in his life to know that no one was watching.

No one cared.

Hauk studied him, then sniffed the air. The demon's nose crinkled, as if he'd smelled something rotten. "He might be Fallen, but his darkness is too haphazard. Just look at his beady eyes and sharp teeth. I have no use for youngsters who can't control the darkness."

After all Liam had gone through, it still wasn't enough?

Well, screw you too.

"He's almost there," Archie said. "Give me a couple of days. He'll be ready."

Hauk raised an eyebrow at the old man. "Oh, will he?"

A fog of darkness spread behind the demon to reveal enormous gray wings without any scales, the surface identical to shark skin.

Without warning, the talons of Hauk's right wing snatched Liam's shoulder and flung him some ten feet away like a freaking football.

Liam still hadn't crashed when Hauk boosted above him. The demon sucker-punched his stomach midair, and Liam's back crashed against the ground. His body dragged for a few feet before inertia let him go.

He bent over and gasped blood. His stomach ached, his muscles throbbed. Also, he might've thrown up a lung when Hauk punched him. Breathing hurt like the Hells.

If Liam was still a Selfless, he would be dead by now, but demonic bodies were tougher than human flesh.

Hauk's features changed as he strolled toward Liam. His wings snapped the way twigs break, then merged into his back. His bones cracked and shifted underneath his skin. Liam could swear the demon had grown taller.

Muscles bulged from Hauk's thin frame, close enough to rip his skin open. His eyes shifted color, from orange to clear green, but he kept focused on Liam as if the process didn't hurt at all. His skin grew some shades darker, and when he was done, Liam stared at a perfect copy of himself.

Well, not himself exactly. Hauk's version didn't share Liam's beady eyes and sharp teeth. This wasn't who he was now.

It was the man he used to be.

"What the fuck!" he bellowed.

Archie had told him that Behemoths had the ability to shapeshift, but he'd never seen a change. He never imagined it was so brutal.

Hauk smirked with perfectly square teeth, unlike Liam's pointy ones. That bastard had become everything he craved to be: himself again.

"Take off my face," he croaked, his voice weaker than he'd intended.

"It's not *your* face." Hauk chuckled and assessed him top to bottom. "Not anymore."

Liam forced himself up, every muscle aching. Flames sprouted from his skin and whipped around him.

From a distance behind Hauk, Archie shouted, "Let it go, kid. He's just teasing you."

The old man glared at him in a way that begged, *"Don't screw this up."*

Liam focused on Hauk. "Consider myself teased. Now take my face off."

"Why?" The demon stepped closer to Liam so they were eye-to-eye.

Liam balled his fists, and something sharp bit into his palm. He looked down to see his blazing hands had turned into draconian claws. Sharp, four fingered talons coated by night-dark scales.

Hauk's eyes almost popped out of their sockets. "Your Terror can shapeshift like a Beast, Archibald."

Liam's flaming hands—*claws*—shook as he remembered what Archie had told him. Terrors such as himself evolved into Drakars like Jal. Beasts evolved into Behemoths, like Hauk and Archie. And Obsessors evolved into Possessors.

Being a Terror, Liam shouldn't be able to shapeshift.

He glared at his flaming, beastly claws. His stomach

clenched, and he might as well throw up now.

"That's new," Archie said in the same tone he used when Liam was eight and decided to play tightrope on their balcony's ledge.

Liam took a deep breath, easing his nerves. His claws shifted slowly back into five fingers, cracking underneath scales that soon smoothed out to skin.

He didn't know how he'd done that, either.

At least shapeshifting didn't hurt, nor did it look as nasty as Hauk had made it seem.

Liam kept his flames burning, though. He bared his teeth at his opponent. "I asked you to take my—" He coughed and spat blood on Hauk's face.

Shit. His lungs weren't right after the last attack. But by the fury in the demon's eyes, Liam wouldn't survive the day anyway.

The darkness spread within him, tentacles of wrath filling his chest, stretching into his arms and legs, preparing him to battle. And beneath the darkness something burned, something close to lava. Or melted gold, he couldn't tell which.

Hauk charged with an angry howl. Liam dodged.

He was just as flabbergasted as his opponent—a lower demon couldn't possibly be faster than an ascended one.

He didn't have time to figure out any of this. The flames intensified over his right fist, enveloping his hand in a fire ball.

Hauk was still gaping when Liam jumped up and smashed his burning fist against the demon's face; the face that had once belonged to him.

Hauk's screams drowned the air, but Liam kept pushing his fist into the demon's forehead.

The bastard fell to his knees, bellowing in pain, half of his face melting and cracking under Liam's strike.

"Stop it!" Archie shouted.

But Liam didn't listen. He kept pressing. "It's my face!"

"Enough!" Archie showed up from nowhere. His knuckles smashed against Liam's jaw, sending him away from Hauk.

He watched as the old man bent down and shot a dark fog at Hauk's face. The demon swatted Archie away, and through what was left of Liam's semblance—a mess of melted and charred flesh—he grumbled, "I can heal myself."

Liam's legs buckled, and he fell to his knees. He coughed blood that spattered on the ground, the same blood that filled his lungs.

Archie ran toward him. "Hellsdamned, Liam!"

He kneeled on the floor and pressed a hand over Liam's chest. A cloud of darkness burst from Archie's hand, enveloping his torso in a gripping yet refreshing cold.

The pain vanished. After a moment, Liam inhaled deeply. His ribs and stomach didn't hurt anymore, and breathing got easier.

"You almost ruined it," Archie whispered through gritted teeth.

"It was me," Liam croaked, his voice cracking. "It's who I was. Who I'll never be."

"You're Liam Striker. *My* boy, no matter what you look like. Understand?" Archie's furious glare softened. "We can't afford mistakes, kid. There's a lot hanging on our shoulders."

Once he was done healing him, Archie helped Liam up.

He still ran his hands over Liam's chest, being the worried father that he was, scanning for further injuries.

Hauk stepped toward them, now in his original form. His jaw bent unnaturally to the left, and when he cracked it in place with a loud snap, Liam winced.

The demon watched them like a hungry lion. Finally, he smiled and pointed at Liam.

"You're valuable. Reckless, but valuable." He nodded at Archie. "Get him ready."

8

AVA

"It looks abandoned," Ezra said as he watched the mansion's decadent façade. He narrowed his eyes at the garden of blackened leafless trees with curling branches. "Are you sure someone who lives here can help us?"

Ava nudged him with her shoulder. "Have faith."

Ezra could sense her emotions, so she wrapped her blooming excitement somewhere deep inside, safe into her wall. There she allowed happiness to bubble, because today she might see Liam.

Feeling like a giddy schoolgirl felt wrong, though. There was so much at stake. The entire fate of the Order—and the Legion—depended on Ezra's acceptance of Jophiel as a Seraph. Only by uniting with the Legion could they stop Talahel.

On they went, crossing the stone path that cut through the garden. Dried bushes lined the way. In their silence, Ezra's words echoed in Ava's memory, bringing a sour taste to her tongue.

What if your Guardian instincts got mixed with your real feelings?

She observed him with annoyance as they moved on, trying to hide the tang of bitterness that swam across her.

In truth, Ava was angry with herself. Disappointed really, that Ezra had so easily infected her with doubt.

But did this mean she agreed with him? Had she truly taken advantage of Liam?

They reached the wooden door, and Ava opened it. A huge, golden chandelier hung from the ceiling, and a wine-colored carpet rested on the floor. The golden symbol of the Gods— the triangle within the circle—was woven into the tapestry.

She smiled at the sight of the Legion's main hall.

"Is this a place of the Order?" Ezra frowned at the symbol in the carpet.

"In a way."

Ahead, a row of stairs led left and right to an inner balcony and the second floor. Below the balcony stood a wooden door—the entrance to the Legion's training underground.

Ezra sniffed the air and stepped back, immediately unsheathing his sword and acquiring a defense position. "Vampires. Too many of them."

She gently pushed the blade down. "I know."

Ezra forced the sword up, shock and hurt swallowing his glare. "Ava, what have you done?"

"What I asked of her." Jophiel appeared from the top of the inner balcony, leaning on the railing.

Before Ezra could ask who in the Hells he was, Jophiel's light exploded from his essence in a golden sandstorm that smashed against them. The brightness should've blinded her, but Ava could see clearly. The whiteness engulfed the room, and golden lightning peppered it like veins.

Jophiel's heavenly light was a living, breathing thing.

Ezra stepped back from the force of it, and so did she. Their legs buckled under Jophiel's squashing light, a sun flare that burned through the room, through their very core. And yet, this unmerciful power was kind. It filled Ava's heart with the peace and love from the Gods.

Tears escaped her eyes as serenity spread inside her. She couldn't recall the last time she had felt so at peace.

This was only a small glimpse of Jophiel's power. She sensed the extent of his burning light stretching to an endless distance inside him.

By Ezra's gaping, he felt the same. His sword clanged on the ground, his jaw hanging open. His breaths came out ragged and shallow. "I-It can't be."

Ava put a hand on his shoulder. "It is."

Tears tracked down Ezra's cheeks as Jophiel descended the stairs, his golden essence still thrumming against theirs.

The Seraph stopped before them, his blue eyes shining with love and care. "Welcome."

Ezra opened his mouth to speak, but the words failed him.

His awe only lasted a moment, however. "You're a charlatan!" He bared his teeth at Jophiel. "How can you fake heavenly light on Earth? This is blasphemy!" Before Jophiel could reply, Ezra turned to Ava, his essence shooting anger and disappointment at her. "How could you be foolish enough to believe this lie?"

Jophiel watched him with an undecipherable expression. He then craned his neck left and peered at Ava. "You once asked me why I didn't reveal myself to the Order." He nodded at Ezra. "This is why. Ezraphael's heart is fairly open to my revelation. He has felt my power, and yet he denies it."

"Speak to *me*, charlatan! I'm standing right in front of you!" Ezra barked at Jophiel, his fists balled. "And you're not a Seraph! The mere fact you're here is proof. If a Seraph comes to Earth, he will shine as a thousand suns and destroy the entire planet."

Jophiel scratched his white beard while observing Ezra. "As the Messenger, you receive sensations and ideas from the Gods, correct?" Ezra didn't confirm or deny this, he simply stared at Jophiel with bloodthirsty fury. "Well then, we both know it's not the Gods you spoke to, but the king of the first Heaven. And he's been awfully quiet for the past few years, hasn't he?"

Ezra chortled. "You're not Jophiel. I would—"

"You prayed for me once." He took one step forward. Ezra didn't step back. "You asked for guidance because you loved someone underneath your ranking, and you feared declaring your feelings would bring the wrath of the Order upon her." Ezra's throat bobbed, but Jophiel kept speaking, almost as if his words were a series of attacks. "They wouldn't harm you, of course. You're a high angel, but she was a lower angel at the time. Practically defenseless, wasn't she?"

Ezra shook his head, his lips quivering, but no denial came out.

"I told you to remember the source of your Goddess' powers. The love for life. The love for others, which surpassed the love for oneself." He shot Ava a sorrowful glance, then focused on Ezra again. "And so, you said nothing to that angel for the longest time. Until your desperation grew, fueled by a dark influence, and you gave her the sword of revelation. This way, she would certainly ascend and you could finally be together."

Ava's throat dried. She couldn't tell if she was still breathing. "Is this true?"

Ezra's entire body shook. "Forgive me, Ava. I … I was lost."

Ava loved and hated him for sacrificing his feelings for

her for so long. Maybe if he had told her before, things would've been different.

Heavens. An entire century ...

Ezra might've done bad things under Talahel's influence —such as killing Lothar or lying to her. But Ava hadn't been near him to help; she hadn't seen how much he'd needed her. Desperation had consumed the best angel she knew, and Ava only realized it when it was too late.

This was why she stood beside Ezra now. Why she had agreed to become his mate.

Guilt.

And from the rift, her beasts whispered, *not only that.*

"There's nothing to be forgiven," she said, cupping his cheek. "The past is gone, and we all make mistakes."

"The light is strong in you, Ava," Jophiel remarked.

Ezra's attention snapped toward him, as if for a moment he had forgotten the Seraph was standing here. He dropped to the floor and bowed at Jophiel's feet. "Mighty king of the first Heaven, I am your servant, so long I exist in your infinite Glory, the Gods—"

"That's enough." Jophiel's thunderous voice boomed with a coating of love and kindness. "I'm not a God. Do not worship me like one, child."

Ezra obeyed his command and promptly stood.

"Welcome to the Legion, Ezraphael Stormglow." Jophiel rested both hands on his shoulders.

"Legion?" Ezra stuttered, then shook his head. "How can you even be standing here, my king? This is insane."

"It's a long story. One I'll gladly—"

Ezra sniffed the air and stepped back. When he bared his teeth at some point beyond Jophiel, Ava realized a tinge of sulfur had spread through the room.

Behind Jophiel stood Jal. The demon watched them with a mocking grin.

His long obsidian hair was tied in a low ponytail, his chest bare. He wore black training pants, and by the amount of sweat on his chest, he'd been doing exactly that.

"Jal!" Ava ran to him and wrapped the demon in a tight hug, ignoring the stickiness of his skin.

"Angel girl, I stink like a possum." His arms closed around her anyway.

"You always stink, demon," she said, her eyes stinging with tears.

He laid a gentle hand atop her head. "Are those assholes at the Order treating you right?" He snarled at some point behind her, and Ava didn't need to look back to know it had been at Ezra.

Her throat piled with words that refused to come out. Despair closed around Ava with a vengeance, and she let him go. "It's been difficult. But we're making progress."

A lie. But she couldn't bear to disappoint Jal.

"Nothing is easy nowadays." He watched her for a moment. "He's getting better, by the way."

Ava skipped a breath—or maybe several. "Can I see him?"

Jal shot Jophiel a worried glance. "Later. Liam is with Archie now. His darkness can be unstable at times, and you're a mighty trigger for him." He snarled lowly when he focused on Ezra. "So is the Messenger."

"I demand an explanation!" Ezra shouted from behind. "You harbor a demon! Jal of Jaipur, if I'm not mistaken."

A hint of pride took over Jal, and an arrogant grin spread on his face. "You've heard of me, Messenger?"

"Your fame precedes you, creature."

Ava turned back to see Ezra glaring at them.

"This demon saved Liam's life," she said. "He saved mine, too."

Ezra chortled in disbelief. "You're confused. This thing has clearly tainted a Seraph. He can't be underestimated."

"No." She observed the wooden walls around her. "For the first time, I'm seeing clearly. This is how the Order should be."

"I feared we might ask too much of you tonight, Messenger." Jophiel clapped his hands. "If I were in your position, I'd react the same way. Which is why I requested the help of an old friend."

A wooden door that blended perfectly with the timbered wall next to the right staircase opened, and Vera stepped into the room. She leaned on the doorframe, her arms crossed. "What a nice reunion."

Ava gasped, unable to hold the elation that wafted from her in warm, jittery waves.

The old owl winked at her, then stepped toward Ezra. His lips moved but the words vanished before he could utter them.

"I'm seeing things," he mumbled. "None of this makes sense."

"I know." Vera gave him her hand. She had never been the motherly type, but right now that's exactly how she seemed. "Do you want to understand, or do you want to deny it? You can do both, Ezzie, and no one here will judge you."

He considered this for a moment. When he stepped back, Ava's heart tightened.

Ezra must've sensed her disappointment, because his attention snapped toward her. Slowly, his shoulders relaxed. "I want to understand." He motioned to Vera. "If you and Ava believe this madness, then perhaps so should I."

Vera showed him the room behind her, a silent request for Ezra to follow, although it had seemed more of an order. Vera rarely *requested* anything.

"I'll catch up with you later," Jophiel said. "Right now, I must discuss certain matters with Ava."

Ezra took this news unhappily, that much was clear in his expression. Still, he told her, "You know where I am."

Something warm and giddy filled her chest. Ezra worried for her even when the world as he knew it had crumbled before him. The kindness and devotion in his core were magnificent.

As soon as he entered the room and Vera closed the door, Jophiel led Ava through the entrance below the balcony.

Jal waved goodbye before the door closed, then off they went.

They crossed the Legion's dark wooden corridors which were filled with vampires and members of the Gray. They gathered in rooms where they read, talked, or watched TV. Some vampires fed on volunteering priests and priestesses, since legal blood supplies were hard to come by these days, leaving them little choice—especially for newborns who didn't know how to hunt properly yet.

They were the easiest targets.

Some of the doors were closed, some half open to meetings and briefings. She found Lilith in a room yelling at a vampire, but before she could sense her presence, Ava had already hurried past the door.

Her heart drummed in her ears. If she were to work with the Legion, being close to that *bloodsucker* would prove to be a difficult task.

A thought flashed in her mind, stealing all her breath.

Had Lilith gotten close to Liam?

Gods, if she had, Ava would end her.

An angel with blue hair passed by them. *Erudite Lichtwind?* A friend of Justine's, if Ava recalled correctly.

He walked with a lean vampire female dressed in jeans and a white shirt. They flirted with each other, their lust forming velvety clouds around them.

Ava found it sweet, if not heart-warming.

Jophiel leaned closer and pointed at the distancing backs of the angel and the vampire. "You see, that is the purpose of my Legion. Good creatures, no matter their origin, together for what's best for mankind. Honor, love, kindness, they take different shapes; shapes that can be angelic or not." His lips twitched with a veiled grin. "Surprising shapes, don't you think?"

Ava was certain his words carried a double meaning but what it might be, she couldn't tell.

"How do you know that they're truly good?" she asked, her focus still on the distancing pair.

The principles at the Order were simpler: angels were good, humans were to be protected, In-Betweens must be controlled, and demons had to die.

"Our recruiting requirements are very strict." Jophiel tapped his forehead, perhaps to indicate that those strict requirements were in his mind. "Things at the Legion aren't as black and white as in the Order, but we don't allow those without goodness within to enter or to find out about us." He shrugged. "It has worked so far."

The wooden walls gave place to gray-painted plaster and LED lights. Soon they were walking past the Legion's many training rooms.

A long silence ensued between them until Ava had to break it. "Let me see him. He doesn't need to know I'm here. I just—" Her voice broke. "I just need to see him."

"In time." Jophiel frowned at her quizzically. "You don't want to hinder his recovery, do you?"

Of course not. She wanted what was best for Liam, always.

Oh, the Seraph was smart.

They passed one training room with four vampires who battled a couple of humans dressed in loose gray clothes.

The priests of the Gray moved swiftly, like river water or a breeze, their flannel clothing swooshing behind them.

Never in her hundred years had Ava seen humans move that way, more panthers than men and women.

"Remarkable, isn't it?" Jophiel said.

It truly was.

He tapped her shoulder, drawing her attention to an empty training room on the left. As they went inside, the room's padded floors sunk slightly underneath Ava's boots.

"You have an affinity with Erudite essence, and I presume Warrior essence," Jophiel said as he placed himself in front of her. "I want to know how far both go, if you'll allow me."

She frowned. "You mean I could potentially turn into a Virtue and an Archangel?"

"Indeed."

Ava chortled. "That's impossible."

"Is it?" That was his only reply.

She noticed thick concrete squares at the back of the room, at least ten of them, piling atop one another to shape a small pyramid.

"No, no, no." She swallowed. "I can never lift them on my own. Or with my mind."

She didn't have an Archangel's strength or a Virtue's telekinesis.

The Seraph shrugged. "Regardless, you will try."

Heavens, this would not end well.

To say that her training had been frustrating was a kindness. Ava had stared at the rocks fiercely, but her pitiful telekinesis only made them shake slightly.

Her head hurt and throbbed. Actually, her entire body felt as if it was made of shattering glass covered in ever-lengthening cracks—the price of simply trying to use a power that wasn't native to her essence.

A high cost for no return. The damned blocks hadn't moved an inch.

The silence didn't help. It reminded Ava that she had failed Liam, and that she was failing the In-Betweens and the Order by allowing Talahel to walk free. That she was failing Ezra too, because he loved her and she didn't love him back.

The light and the dark stirred inside her the way the ocean thrashes in a storm, a reflection of her own torments.

In a flash, her wings materialized behind her, flapping without any coordination.

"Let's try something else." Jophiel nodded at her wings. "Let's make them follow your commands."

"I've been trying for weeks," Ava grumbled.

"Well, you haven't tried it with me." Ava felt him piercing through her ivory mental wall as if it was made of paper.

She closed her eyes and looked within. In her essence's void, Jophiel pointed to the rift inside her. The home of her beasts.

"You're ignoring them," he said. "It's why you can't move the rocks and why you can't fly. You're afraid to set them free."

Ava hated that he spoke truths she didn't want to face.

"If I free them, how am I supposed to control them?"

"You don't." He shrugged. "You're not just light anymore. You're both, and they are you. It stopped being about control a while ago. Now it's about adaptation."

She opened her eyes and watched the training room with worry. "I don't know how to—"

"Don't worry. Just do."

Apparently, she didn't have much of a choice.

She pulled out a fraction of the powers inside her rift. Darkness and light flowed into her veins, dancing in streams that filled her body—no, her essence too. She watched the back of her arms glitter the way stars twinkle in the night sky.

"You're still afraid, but I suppose that's good enough for today," Jophiel said. "Now, shove your wings into your light and your darkness. Give them equal weight, Ava. *Balance*. It's all about balance."

With a thought, she pushed her wings into her essence. Her body felt lighter, and when she glared behind her shoulders, her wings were gone.

Her skin stopped shining.

"Heavens!" A laugh burst from her throat. "Did you see that?"

Before Jophiel could answer, she commanded her wings to move the way she would her arms or legs. They appeared behind her in a golden flash.

Limbs. Her wings were simply limbs she needed to move.

Ava pushed them back into her essence, and they disappeared. Then she made them reappear again, only to see them flash golden and vanish into the air.

This might not be as good as flying, but it was definitely progress.

Jophiel smiled. "There you go. Be proud of your achievement. But you're not here to control your wings, you're here to move those blocks." He pointed at them.

Jophiel could be a heartless and demanding teacher.

So back to the rocks it was.

Ava glared at the blocks for a long time, at some point even praying for them to move. The specks of light and dark she had freed balanced inside both her essence and her body. Sometimes, they twinkled underneath her skin.

Still nothing.

Her head hurt and her skin was covered in sweat, but the stones didn't move an inch.

In the past, Ava had managed to lift a wooden table while fighting with lower demons—she blamed it on adrenaline. But these cement blocks?

No chance in all the Heavens.

"Why did you become Ezraphael's mate?" Jophiel blurted.

She blinked at him, not understanding where the question had come from.

Jophiel stared at her in a way that said she had all the time in the world, but he expected an answer.

"I needed to save him from evil," she finally admitted. "It was for the good of the Order and himself. And a little bit for my own good." She studied her boots. "He helped me so many times … it was only fair."

"Yes, but you could've done all that without becoming his mate."

She threw her arms up in frustration. "You said I had to be kind to him or the truth could push Ezra to Talahel's side!"

"Yes, but I didn't tell you to become his mate."

An angry bark escaped her lips. She paced in a circle, wishing she could slap Jophiel in his smug face.

He flashed her an easy grin. "Oh, the dark in you is most amusing, Ava."

"Delightful." She crossed her arms. "How's that magnanimous Seraph's power working in your human body, by the way?"

A low blow. She knew it the moment the words left her mouth.

Before she could apologize, Jophiel raised his shoulders. "Can't use them much without coming close to my final death, so it's been hard. As you well know."

If Jophiel could use his powers without consequence, this silent war would've been over a lot sooner. If he did, however, he might not only destroy himself but the entire city.

Not being able to help as much as he wanted was a cruel torture. Ava *felt* the pain and distress seeping from his essence. And she had poked his wound without thinking twice.

Thank her darkness for that.

"I'm sorry," she whispered.

"I know." He watched her with complete kindness. "I'll admit yours is not a simple situation, Ava. You went through so much, and you discovered a side of yourself you didn't know existed. You're not who you used to be and not who you're supposed to be. You're midway." He caressed his beard as he always did when he was deep in thought. "If you and Liam were soulmates, your bond would've snapped in place by now. Why do you think this hasn't happened yet?"

"Maybe it takes longer with us." The beasts of dark and light snarled at Jophiel. Damned him for making her face all the things she tried hard to ignore. "What's so special about the soulmate bond anyway?"

"Oh." A cloud of longing and sadness bloomed inside him, but he quickly hid it from her. "It's something that must be felt, and it's glorious. You will know when it happens. If it happens."

She remembered the words Justine had read in the ancient books. *"When the bonding link snaps, thunder will crack. Essences will shatter before coming back to one piece, and thus, two will become one; one will become two."*

Who could possibly look forward to that?

"Answer me this," Jophiel continued. "How can you know who you love if you don't yet know who you are?"

The question was a blade to her chest.

"I …" She swallowed, sensing a surge of emotion coming. "I thought Liam completed me, but we're not soulmates.

Which means my Guardian feelings got mixed into the situation, and I failed him. I was his Guardian! I wasn't supposed to take advantage …" her voice cracked, and tears swelled in her eyes. "I used to be better than this. Sometimes I miss the old me. She had the entire world figured out."

"Your old self was lost in an illusion," Jophiel countered. "Now you're free."

If so, freedom wasn't that great.

She wiped her tears with the base of her palm. "It doesn't matter, does it? I abandoned him anyway. Like I abandoned Ezra."

"You demand too much of yourself." He stepped forward and cupped her cheek. "The way I see it, you and Liam need to become who you're supposed to be. Ezraphael, too. Only then will you all know the truth about yourselves and each other." He laid a hand on her shoulder. "You will never find balance until you face your feelings, Ava. The same applies to the wild powers within you. Never be afraid."

She felt the rift inside her and the beasts that purred within. This was her problem.

Ava wasn't scared of her feelings or of her light and dark.

She was terrified.

9

LIAM

*L*iam's punch smacked Archie's jawbone and sent the old man swiveling around the training room. While Archie recovered, Liam raised his fists and shifted his weight on both feet.

He would win this fight today; he could feel it.

The darkness still whispered to him, but he was focused enough to ignore the words that belittled, mocked, and challenged him. And because Liam learned to use the darkness, his movements became faster. *Smarter.*

Archie wiped the blood that poured from his lips. He studied his red-smudged hand and grinned. "We're getting there."

A black fog enveloped the cut, and his blood stopped flowing.

"When will I get another chance to impress Hauk?" Liam asked, eager to head back to the field.

A mission. A purpose. This is what he had needed to tame the darkness all along.

"Once we get you under control, okay?" Worry deepened the wrinkles on Archie's forehead. "Don't get too cocky. Your darkness is still haphazard and strong. It can catch you unprepared. Also, we need to understand why you shapeshifted. You're a Terror, kid. Your powers are fire and speed."

Liam shrugged. "Ava could tap into other angels' powers. Maybe I have the same skill."

He raised his hand and focused on it. His head thumped so hard it might explode. Soon enough, night-black fur grew on his skin, his fingers stretched into sharp claws, and when Liam's entire body felt as if it was shattering with pain, he stopped.

His upper arm resembled that of a werewolf. The black fur was remarkably shiny, the tips of his claws as sharp as a serpent's tooth.

Archie nodded at the sight, still in thought. "Tapping into different powers is … Hells, I would say rare, but I never heard of something similar to this before."

"I don't know what to tell you." Liam rolled his eyes, and the movement pricked his skull. He inhaled deeply through clenched teeth. "I can't explain it. We can only use it to our advantage. Whatever this is," he wiggled his furry claws, "it makes me valuable to Hauk."

"Oh, we will use it to our advantage," Archie assured. "We simply need to be careful."

Unable to keep this for much longer, Liam let go of the effort. The fur disappeared underneath his skin. His claws morphed back into fingers as the pressure on his entire body dimmed.

He studied his father for a moment. "What are you afraid of?"

Archie ran a hand through his sand-blond hair. "Your darkness is too wild. Undercover work, especially for the Hells' Gorge, can be … unpleasant."

Why did he always treat Liam like a child?

"I'm no stranger to undercover work, Archie."

Liam wanted to share the burden of this mission with him. Yes, he needed to occupy himself, but most of all, he wanted to watch over his father. Demons weren't known for their kindness and after meeting Hauk ... Hells be damned if he would let Archie get hurt again.

Liam stepped closer to him, holding the old man's gaze. "I'm your partner, I'm your son, and I'm ready."

Archie shook his head and raised a finger at him. "You're not ready. But I suppose you're ready enough."

"That's what I'm talking about." Liam fisted his own palm. "I can do this, old man. I can trick Hauk, and I can help us find whoever Master is."

Archie gave him that typical fatherly look, the one that oozed with pride and embarrassed Liam in front of his school friends. "I know you can."

He took advantage of Liam's relaxed stance and jolted toward him, slamming a kick on his stomach.

Liam lurched back. His belly muscles ached and a few breaths escaped him, but he was used to pain by now. He quickly regained his balance and raised his arms in defense.

"First lesson on demons, kid," Archie said. "They play dirty."

Liam sneered and ran toward his father, hungry for battle. Their attacks became hollow thuds against bones and flesh.

The darkness spread inside him, aligning with his movements. Liam became faster. Every punch drawn and every kick received invigorated him.

"Nice," Archie said as he dodged a punch. "Why don't we make this more fun, though?"

Archie's face puffed red as he hunched over. The old man grew like a flower in spring, his muscles bulging. The change happened too quickly: flesh and bone bent and stretched, swelling and growing.

When Archie was done, he had grown three times his original size.

His giant navy wings appeared in a fog of darkness behind him, spanning the length of a helicopter.

Liam's jaw dropped. "No fucking way."

Archie chortled, his arms crossed. "Lesson number two: expect the unexpected." His voice boomed louder and deeper than normal.

"Not cool, old man." Liam balled his fists, but a grin creased his lips.

He had no idea how to fight a giant demon, but he would have fun trying.

He reached for that burning force underneath his darkness, the source of his fire. In the past, the darkness might have hindered Liam by confusing him with smoke and mirrors and ghosts of his past. But this time, it was quiet.

Watching.

Liam had the darkness—no, himself—under control.

In the vast void of his essence, he heard a mocking laugh similar to his own. Still, flames bloomed on his skin and whipped around him, turning Liam into a human torch.

The darkness, ever aligning and contained, intertwined with his movements. Liam watched his own burning hands and smiled.

"I got this," he told himself, knowing that this time it was true.

A strange sensation brushed across his essence as softly as a spring breeze. It was soothing and good, but at the same time chaotic and hungry.

Light and dark.

He froze, his eyes wide. Liam's darkness had a way of showing him things, and right now, it showed him this energy, this force inside the Legion's walls. He couldn't pinpoint exactly where, but it was close.

Archie frowned at him. "Kid? You all right?"

The darkness spread inside him, trying to catch a clearer taste of that presence.

Familiar. So familiar ...

His breathing echoed inside his eardrums.

Light. It was her light he recognized, thrumming against his dark essence. He couldn't tell how or why he knew it, but the presence was Ava.

She was here.

His fire sunk back into his skin.

Archie stepped closer, concern swimming through his face. "Kid?"

"Ava," Liam muttered as he dropped his stance, focusing so he could find her exact location.

He snapped his head to the left, but the movement hadn't felt particularly his.

The darkness. It was ready to take over. It needed to be free to find his, *their*, princess.

Let me out, his own voice whispered. *She's here, and she's ours.*

"Kid!" Archie snapped his fingers in front of him, but he didn't really see it. His attention was locked on Ava's pulsing presence as if she were a fading song he strained to hear.

The old man slapped his face, but Liam barely felt it. The darkness had caught her scent, and it would find her.

Almost there ...

Archie's tone held fear. "Liam, listen to me. You need to control—"

He didn't catch what came next. Liam sprinted out of the training room, following the connection that blinked in and out, the path to the woman he loved.

It might not be exact, but he and the darkness were done waiting.

His Ava. His light.

She had finally come to him!

He and the darkness smiled as they sped through the corridor, leaving Archie behind and bellowing their name.

There were too many pathways, too many training rooms, but she was here, and Liam would find her.

He always would.

10

10

AVA

A strange tingling tickled Ava's essence, a sensation close to a soft caress.

Jophiel, who led the way out of the training room, stopped by the open door and turned back to her. "Is everything all right?"

"Hmm," she mumbled, focusing on the growing sensation which pulsed stronger by the second. It rushed toward Ava, unstoppable, unyielding, and so familiar.

She never felt this way this before, anxious and comfortable at the same time, except when—her stomach knotted and her heart soared.

Except when she was with Liam.

A void smashed into her, a power both mellow and angry that reverberated within Ava's bones. Every angel felt something similar when a demon approached, but this was different. This presence was her own doomsday, a force of nature born to consume and love her.

The scent of oak and earth invaded her nostrils, either a memory or the effect of the approaching presence.

Her mouth stretched in an incredulous grin.

Liam.

He was coming for her.

"This won't end well," Jophiel grumbled as a dark blur dashed through the open door.

Just like that, Liam stood before her, his chest heaving up and down, his beady eyes wide. His spine was straight, and his muscles clenched. Heavens, she'd forgotten how tall he was.

Liam's tanned skin had acquired a sickly pale shade, and his eyes weren't the same. Neither were his sharp teeth.

He must've read the shock in her face because he lowered his head. *Hiding.* A bitter cloud of disgust swirled around him.

"No," Ava croaked as she took one step forward. "Please don't be ashamed."

She wanted to jump at him and cover him with kisses, demonic features and all. But she had failed Liam in so many ways … guilt stapled her feet firmly to the ground.

"I'm so sorry," she whispered, her heart breaking. "This is all my fault."

Liam raised his head, his deep frown telling Ava she had offended him. "No. I *chose* to become a demon."

He stepped closer until he towered over her. His night-black hair brushed a corded neck atop broad shoulders, his body a sculpture of strength and pure temptation.

Liam's earthy fragrances mixed with the demonic scent of brimstone, and yet the oaky flavor was still there. He might be a demon, but he was still Liam.

His warm hand cupped her cheek. Gods, she missed his skin on hers, his scent, even if mingled with a demonic musk. He might belong to the dark now, but she would take him as he was.

"You came back, princess," he said quietly, his eyes hooded and his voice shallow.

She couldn't hold the whine that came after hearing her nickname, an odd mix of longing and happiness soaring inside her.

Princess.

The word had bothered her once, but not now. Not ever again.

He lifted her chin gently, staring into her as he bowed his head. He nudged her nose with his before his mouth crashed down on Ava's, drowning her in hungry kisses that set her depths on fire.

His sharp teeth cut her tongue, but Ava's light quickly healed the wounds. It made their breathless kisses painful and titillating at the same time, a new sensation she couldn't wait to explore.

With him. Always with him.

He pulled back, watching her with worry. "Am I hurting you?"

Ava could see her reflection in his dark irises. "Yes." She pulled his head down and possessed his mouth all to herself.

Liam's right hand clasped the side of her neck, the other dug into the curve of her waist and pulled her to him. She slammed against his strong chest—and the growing force underneath his pants.

Heavens, she didn't care that Jophiel was still in the room. She needed Liam, and she needed him now.

"What you do to me," he muttered, pressing his forehead on hers. He took a deep, centering breath. "Gods, I've missed you, Ava."

"I missed you too." She held back her tears. "I couldn't break free of my mate duties; there have been so many fires to put out, so many battles to fight. I'm sorry I didn't come sooner."

He blinked and stepped back, something cracking inside him.

"So it's true." His throat bobbed. "I thought …" He chortled. "I don't know what I thought."

Ava froze, her entire body sinking in itself. "I had to become Ezra's mate."

"You didn't *have* to," Jophiel countered from the entrance.

Ava glared at him with a mix of shock and outrage. She didn't know how to kill a nosy Seraph, but she would find a way.

"You love him?" Liam asked, despair and hurt woven into his words.

Gods, as a Dominion she could feel his pain.

Ava's heart shattered right then, and from her rift, mingled within her light, that dark beast she had set free whispered, *look what we've done.*

"Do you, Ava?" he barked, his dark hair falling over his temples.

"I don't!" She stepped forward, aching to hold him again, but flames sprouted from Liam's skin.

She gaped at the burning demon before her, the one who looked so much and nothing at all like her former partner.

"You're lying!" he bellowed.

He was right. Ava shouldn't lie to him. She couldn't fail him all over again. "I do love Ezra, but not the way I love you."

Liam's fire burned brighter. Thank Heavens for the blessed training room, or the padded floor would've caught on fire.

His black beads locked on her as he bared pointy teeth. "You don't seem awfully sure, *princess.*"

Her chest ached, but Ava stood her ground. Liam deserved her honesty, even if it pained them both.

"I'm not sure if my feelings for you got mixed with my Guardian instincts." The words were cracked glass scraping the walls of her throat. "I don't want to fail you again."

His fire vanished as he watched her with wide, pitch-black spheres, his jaw hanging open. "I've known from the moment I saw you …" He shook his head, a certain madness glinting on his eyes. He slammed a hand on his forehead. "Shut up!"

"Liam?"

He sneered like a man made of evil and chaos. "You fucked the Messenger, didn't you?"

This wasn't the Liam she knew. This was a demon through and through, a demon born because Ava had failed to protect her charge, her partner. Her *everything*.

She sniffed back tears. "I would never do that to you. I owe it to both of us to be sure," she said. "I owe it to Ezra, too. I caused you so much pain already! This is all my fault."

"You give yourself too much credit, princess," he spat, her nickname poison on his tongue. "You loved Ezraphael for what? A hundred years? I can't compete with that." His beady eyes widened, and he grinned in the way of a wolf about to eat its prey. "Or maybe I can."

His bones cracked underneath his skin, but Liam held her attention, as if breaking his own face didn't hurt. His nose thinned, his cheekbones got higher, and his skin lightened. His dark hair grew right before her eyes, its color turning into a silver that neared white. Even his irises changed until sky-blue eyes stared back at her.

Ava gasped and stepped back. Liam was still Liam from the neck down, but his face belonged to Ezra now. Her mate glared at her with a fury that felt wrong on his kind, serene features.

"Is this better?" Ezra, no, *Liam*, bellowed. "Will you want me now, Ava? Am I enough?" He bent over at his stomach and slammed both hands on his head. "Shut up!"

"Please stop," she croaked. Tears formed rivers down her cheeks. "By all the Gods, this isn't you, Liam."

"Clearly," he growled, glaring at her with Ezra's blue eyes.

His features cracked back into place until he was Liam once again. This time, though, he kept his green eyes and his square human teeth.

This vision hurt her the worst, because this was Liam as he used to be. The Liam she had failed. The Liam who had died so that this demon was born.

"Back to the way we were?" he asked with a cruel smirk.

Her chest pricked, and Ava barely managed to breathe. "I'm not sure that the angel you fell in love with still exists. I'm not her anymore, even though I wish I was." She reached for his hand, but he pulled back.

She wanted to tell him about the darkness inside her and how she had beheaded Gabriel without any mercy or guilt. How she had gotten her wings through fury and bloodthirst.

"I'm not the Guardian you used to know. You would be so disappointed in me now," she whispered.

"You're right," he growled. "You're not my Ava, you bitch."

His words hurt like physical blades that pierced her chest and ripped her soul.

Liam walked forward, a train of wrath and muscle about to run her over. Anger and contempt gushed from him, but by all the Gods, she would not fail him again.

She would not run.

"Please," she begged, shrinking before his looming form. "I won't fight you."

"Enough!" Jophiel boomed as he approached. "This is no good for either of you. Liam, you must understand that Ava's work with the Messenger is of extreme importance—"

Liam bellowed something raw and guttural, a cry that shook the room's glassed wall. Flames burst from his skin again.

"Perfect Ava with her perfect Messenger," he spat with revulsion.

"Control it," Jophiel warned.

Perfect? There was nothing perfect about her. How could he see her that way?

"Princess, princess, princess." He shook his head. "You're right. We're not who we used to be anymore."

He swiveled and punched Jophiel in his stomach, surprise giving Liam all the advantage he needed.

The Seraph flew across the room and into the window. His body slammed against the blessed surface, and it cracked.

The unbreakable window actually cracked.

Before Ava could react, Liam took momentum and boosted toward her, jabbing the side of her ribcage. The sheer power of his attack flung her onto the opposite wall.

Breath fled her lungs as her back hit concrete. Her entire body hurt, and she struggled to balance on her own feet. She vaguely recorded the scent of burnt flesh.

When she looked down, she noticed her white bodysuit had been vaporized over the wound. Dry, blackened skin formed a circle across half of her trunk.

Her healing took over, numbing the overwhelming pain, which wasn't greater than the pain of knowing who had inflicted it.

Let him give her the final peace.

Ava had failed Liam, and she deserved to be punished. No more light and dark, Order and Legion. No more Ezra and Liam.

Nothing but blissful oblivion.

He blinked and stepped back, glaring at his shaking, burning hands. "Ava, I'm so sorry." He turned to her, tears streaming down his face and turning to vapor because of the heat. "I slay monsters. I'm not one of them!" He bent over and clawed both hands on his head. "Shut the fuck up!"

Somehow she had fallen atop her ankle in a bad angle, so she limped toward him as her healing took care of it. "You can get through this." Tears blurred her vision. "You *will* get through this."

"We won't." The Liam she knew disappeared, replaced by the demon. He stomped toward her and raised his flaming hand.

Ava prepared for the strike and the burn. If this was her end, she would face it without fear.

But the flames vanished.

Instead of ending her, Liam caressed her cheek with his palm. It felt warm to the touch, warmer than human skin but not scorching.

"I will never hurt you again. I'm so sorry, Ava." His face crumpled in pain. He bit his teeth and closed his eyes. "Shut up!"

He stepped back, and fire bloomed over his body again, turning him into a human torch. He kept shaking his head as if a thousand bees were zinging around him. When Liam fell to his knees, bellowing his lungs out, Ava thought she had lost him forever.

She had failed to protect him, and now he was being consumed by darkness.

Well, she wouldn't make the same mistake again. To the Hells with duty, with the Order, and the Legion.

"I will be here for you," she promised. "I won't abandon you again."

He glared at her with absolute horror. "No, Ava! By the Gods, I can't hold it much longer!"

A blur of light grabbed Liam by his neck, lifting him off the ground. Golden light coursed through Jophiel's veins, glittering rivers underneath his dark skin.

The Seraph's light burned Liam so fiercely that the scent of singed flesh wafted throughout the room.

"Stop!" she yelled. "You're hurting him!"

"This will help him find his angelic light, Ava. It's there, drowned by the dark," Jophiel said simply, his attention on Liam. "It will be painful, but no one can heal him better than I."

Liam's cries filled the room, piercing her ears, her heart, everything.

"Stop!" She balled her fists.

Her golden shield spread atop her body in a thin, cold layer that tingled her skin. "Stop, or so help me Gods, I'll make you release him!"

Jophiel observed her from above his nose until finally he gave in. His skin stopped shining and he freed Liam, who slumped on the floor.

His breaths were a horrid wheezing sound that belonged to a dying man.

Ava threw herself at him, checking his burnt flesh. She shot her healing light into his body, and maybe she was going crazy, but she felt it connect with something underneath the darkness.

A shy, flickering light of Liam's own.

Her beast of dark watched from inside the rift, and Ava could swear she, *it*, waited for something. But what it was, she had no clue.

Liam raised his face, and Ava peered right through the demon, into the man he used to be.

He gave her a weak smile. "Your light, princess …" He closed his eyes, and his muscles relaxed under her touch.

"You better take her from here, Jo." A bulky demon with sandy hair leaned against the doorframe.

He was absurdly tall, and Ava blinked twice to make sure she hadn't gone mad.

She had to be hallucinating. The man was a giant, but then again, he wasn't exactly a man. His darkness was strong, and it thrummed against her essence, telling her what he really was: a second-tier demon.

His wings weren't on display, which meant he didn't mean to fight.

"Their light and dark are connected in a strange way," Jophiel told the demon. "Liam isn't strong enough yet, which is why his darkness reacts so violently to hers. Their powers want to connect but can't. I've never seen something similar to this."

"Well, we can't run any risks, not with everything that's at stake." He nudged his chin toward Ava as he walked inside the room. "My son has a mission. Being close to you clearly won't help. I'm sure you understand the sacrifices we must make in the name of duty."

Ava stared at him. "Archibald?"

That was all she could muster. Heavens, he seemed much younger than the picture on his file.

The man nodded. "Hello, Ava. I wish we'd met under different circumstances."

Jophiel went to her and kindly took Ava's hand, bringing her to her feet. "Let's go, dear." When he grabbed the sides of her arms with his strong hands, she realized this wasn't a request.

"I'm not leaving! Not again." She tried to break free of Jophiel's grip, but his fingers were iron and stone. "I abandoned him once, for duty, for the greater good, and look what happened."

She couldn't recognize her own voice. A deep sadness was carved into her tone, tattooed there forever.

"If you care for him, you must let him go." Jophiel pulled her away from Liam too easily, as if Ava were made of sticks and air.

She looked back at her partner, her charge, her lover, who now crouched on the ground, his forehead stamped on the padded floor, his body shaking.

"Go," Liam croaked, his voice almost muted.

Her legs faltered, but Jophiel kept his hold on her as he dragged her out of the training room.

She fought him with all the strength she could gather, and still, it wasn't enough.

They passed by the broad shouldered giant, and he laid a bulky hand on her shoulder. "Give him time," he said kindly. "Give it to yourself, too."

If she could speak, she would have begged him to let her stay.

"Liam needs to disperse his darkness," Jophiel told Archibald.

The demon let out a weary sigh and cracked his knuckles. "The boy has always been good at releasing steam. Should be no problem."

"What do you mean?" Ava managed.

Jophiel and Archibald exchanged a worried glance before he continued dragging her out of the room.

The giant demon closed the door behind them.

Soon screams gushed from inside; angry war cries that turned into beastly growls. And they belonged to Liam.

Jophiel kept dragging Ava, his arms tightly wrapped around her.

The windowed wall of the training room shook.

She fought the Seraph, but it was the same as trying to break free from a giant python tightly coiled around her. At some point, he held her so strongly that Ava could barely breathe.

"What's happening?" she demanded. "Please, let me go! He's hurting him!"

From the distance, Liam bellowed her name.

She cried his.

Jophiel didn't stop.

11

AVA

*M*emories of what happened crowded Ava's thoughts. She tossed and turned the entire night, and she cried—Gods, she sobbed.

"Will you want me now, Ava?"

Guilt, freezing and consuming, bolted through her nonstop. The doubt Ezra had planted grew stronger with each passing hour.

Had she truly mixed her feelings?

The Guardian Liam put on a pedestal was far from perfect. In all her kindness and devotion, she had gotten him killed. Also, that foolish angel had been certain she loved him, but maybe she was wrong. And in being wrong, she hurt him.

She hurt them both.

Getting out of bed the next day felt as easy as carrying a mountain on her shoulders, but eventually, Ava went on to perform all her duties as Ezra's mate.

She attended meetings with Dominions, Virtues, and the occasional Archangel. She also listened to their wishes and complaints, patiently telling them she would pass them on to the Messenger. Which she didn't, of course, since Ezra was avoiding her.

He should've attended at least four meetings but was nowhere to be found. He also ignored her messages.

Ava hoped he wasn't upset that she had left him at the Legion without explanation, but she knew better. Confronting him seemed like a bad idea in any case, so she gave him the time he needed.

The following days passed in a succession of neatly-timed events. Ava would get up and check the tablet on her dresser for all the meetings she had to attend. Ezra always planned the schedule beforehand, so they were never in the same space at the same time.

She would then go about her day, more automated robot than anything else. Ava fulfilled her duties, had lunch—whenever she managed to eat more than a forkful—and worked on ad hoc requests, such as running background checks on humans who would attend an upcoming political event.

Dominions Cheng and Luzacima handled the care of two key politicians in the matter, guiding them as Ava had once guided her charges.

She was glad to help with the research, but deep down, cold, gray jealousy filled her chest. While Cheng and Luzacima were out there helping others, Ava was stuck here, trying not to think of anything.

She missed fieldwork and helping those in need. But how could she watch over someone when she'd become romantically involved with her last charge? Maybe Liam would still be alive if they hadn't been together.

Back at the docks, she'd felt his life slipping through her fingers, and there had been nothing she could do.

What kind of angel did that make her?

This morning, she simply didn't get up. Ava lay there,

watching the ceiling of her room, stuck in a numb void and feeling that she failed everyone around her: the Legion, the Order, Ezra, Liam, and especially herself.

"Dominion Lightway," the robotic tune of her scheduler rang from the tablet. *"You are late for your ten o'clock meeting."*

As much as she would prefer it, Ava couldn't waste an entire day, not when she was the Messenger's mate. Her duties always came first.

Eventually, she got up.

At lunch time, hunched over the cafeteria table, she drew circles on her plate with her fork, avoiding the cold vegetables and chicken.

"Oh, Hells." The voice came from Ava's left, and when she raised her head, she saw Vera standing beside her.

The old owl sat across from her and leaned over the table, her words a whisper. "All this sadness and angst are nearly palpable to other Dominions. Hide them, Ava. They're no one's business but your own."

She blinked, taking longer than usual to digest her former mentor's words. Finally, she nodded and strengthened her mind wall, wrapping her essence around itself.

"Always keep *you* to yourself." Vera gave her an approving nod. "Hiding emotions is the greatest skill a Dominion can have."

Ava frowned. "Why?"

"We are the most powerful children of the Goddess of Love and Life." The old owl forked her food and ate quickly, speaking between swallows and mouthfuls. "We're supposed to inspire and take care of others. If everyone could see we don't have our shit together, our reputation would be ruined."

Ava chuckled at Vera's knack for telling things as they were, then pushed the vegetables around her plate with the fork. "Why didn't you tell me you were with the Legion?"

Vera peered at Ava, her mouth a flat line. "Does it matter?"

"I suppose it doesn't."

"Indeed." After a long pause, her former mentor sighed. "Still, I owe you the truth. I didn't tell you because you had a lot to handle. Besides, the last time we spoke you hadn't been assigned to that Selfless yet. And then the attack on the Order happened, and all Hells went loose."

Ava drew a deep breath. "Everything changed so fast."

"It did. But the world doesn't change, dear. Only we do. It's a reflection of our choices." Vera let her words hang between them as if she expected Ava to figure some hidden meaning woven into them.

Instead, Ava crossed her arms and looked away. "I just want to curl up in bed and sleep."

"A bit of advice?" Vera offered but left Ava no time to oppose. "The choices you made have consequences, and you must face them. Only then," she pointed at Ava's chest, "will the void inside you go away. And maybe, you might find the answers and the balance you so clearly crave."

"You sound a lot like a certain Seraph we know," Ava grumbled.

Vera shot her a proud grin. "Why, thank you." She clasped her hands on the table and leaned closer. "You know, Ezra is a worthy angel."

Ava narrowed her eyes at her, wondering where Vera was going with this.

"He always tried to break the stupid rules," she continued. "It was the good in him, Ava, shining through. He's important to the Legion and to the Order."

"You're stating the obvious," Ava countered dryly. "I wouldn't be here if that wasn't the case."

She raised one knowing eyebrow. "Wouldn't you?"

Ava couldn't say. She loved Ezra for his kindness and his

heart, and when he'd needed her, she didn't hesitate to stand beside him.

Loved. The word sat there, its mere presence making her uncomfortable.

"I would like you to see her," the old owl blurted. "When she's ready, of course."

"Who?"

"Shelaria." She tapped her own chin. "You used to know her as the Nine-five's Captain."

"She doesn't want to see anyone." Ava's voice was a dim sound. "Justine is taking care of her."

"Yes, but eventually the Captain will call for you. I'm the Dominion assigned to her emotional health, so I would know."

Of course. Justine might take care of the Captain's thoughts and memories, but Vera worked on her emotions. One was complementary to the other.

As far as Ava knew, turning into an angel after being a Selfless wasn't an easy process. Centuries of memories flooded their sense of self, mingling with the memories of their past human life. Many angels went mad in the process and required extensive help, sometimes for decades.

"She will also want to see Liam." Vera rubbed her forehead. "But we'll cross that bridge when we get to it."

Liam, Ezra, Shelaria. They all hung heavy on Ava's conscious. The sudden need to cry climbed up her throat, but she swallowed it back.

"I'm failing everyone I care about," she mumbled.

The old owl smirked and held Ava's hand. Love and compassion shot from her, feeding Ava's essence. "That's simply not possible, dear. You and Ezra are the best angels I ever trained."

Vera wasn't one to enjoy long displays of emotion, so she gave Ava a supportive nod before clearing her throat and leaning back on her chair, arms folded. "You're clearly done with your food." She looked side to side as if making sure they had enough privacy. "Let's walk. I need to discuss something with you."

They put their trays away and exited the cafeteria. Up here, in the levels exclusive to ascended angels, the corridors were wider and brighter than in the lower levels.

Nothing in the Order was fair.

Her dark and light beasts growled in unison. Ava couldn't stand the inequalities either, but she calmed the powers inside her. It was only a matter of time until she and Ezra changed things.

Or so she hoped.

They passed by a small fountain, then palm trees and blooming flowers, all peppering the vast, white marbled space. Big arched windows let in fresh air.

Too many angels milled about nearby, so Vera pointed to a corridor on the left. They followed it until it was so empty that Ava could hear their footsteps.

"As you might know, Ezra met with Jophiel after whatever happened between you and Liam," Vera said quietly, her mouth barely moving. "The Seraph didn't tell him anything, of course, but if I figured out something happened between you and demon boy, so did Ezra."

Ava swallowed. "He's been avoiding me."

"Talk to him. He might be the Messenger, but he's also a man in love, and men in love tend to do stupid things."

"I will," she said quietly.

"Good. Now, let me get you up to speed." Vera watched the empty way ahead. "There's only one way to bring down Talahel in a peaceful manner."

"Incriminating evidence."

She nodded. "The Legion is busy with demons and In-Betweens, trying to figure out who's behind all this. That's their problem. Ours is to remove Talahel from the high-angel council before he destroys the entire Order." Vera checked the space around them again. "My gut feeling tells me that Talahel isn't simply attacking uncontrolled In-Betweens or making an alliance with demons. He's working *for* them. But the bastard can cover his tracks and—" Vera snapped her lips shut.

Steps clicked from behind. They both turned to see a tall Archangel with short brown hair and cruelty hidden beneath a mask of kindness. A flash of light burst from his back, and moss-colored wings that faded to white at the bottom spread wide behind him.

"What's your intention, Sithrael?" Vera asked as she watched him the way a lion watches prey. "Show off or fight?"

He crossed his bare arms and eyed her up and down. "Maybe I want to fuck, Vera."

"Oh Gods no, dear." Pity filled the old owl's tone. "No one here wants to fuck you."

The Archangel shot her a smirk filled with anger. Ava could feel it, a slashing and burning sensation that built on itself.

Instead of acting on it, Sithrael bowed respectfully at them. "We request your opinion on a task-force matter. Finding you today was quite hard. Were you hiding by any chance?"

Vera rolled her eyes. "I don't appreciate being followed." She gave him a weary sigh. "Nevertheless, I shall be with you in a moment."

The man's gaze lingered on Ava, then on Vera, before he went away.

"That's Talahel's watchdog," Vera whispered once Sithrael left their sight. "He's jamming the investigation, throwing in false clues, and tampering with evidence. Lisle's on to him, so am I, but he's always three steps ahead."

Ava ground her teeth. "Talahel's goons are doing the dirty work for him like Gabriel once did. Which means that if they're caught, there will be no ties between their actions and the Sword."

"Indeed," she said. "Ava, this task force is going nowhere. Lisle and I are pushing as much as we can, but we need someone outside our jurisdiction to investigate."

Ava smiled as the idea came to her. The useless, powerless angel who had taken over her for the past week vanished, giving place to her usual self—not who she used to be, nor who she wanted to be, but who she was now.

She didn't believe in signs, but this must surely be the next best thing.

"I know the right angel for the job."

LIAM

*L*iam entered his cell after a long day training with Archie. They had started so early in the morning that the sky was still dark, and they had finished when the sun had lowered in the horizon.

His hair was damp from the shower he'd just had, his muscles sore. He threw his training bag on the floor and caught his reflection in the small mirror hanging above his bed.

A few days ago, Liam had used his shapeshifting abilities to morph into Ezraphael and then back to his old self again.

Since then, his eyes would sometimes look human and green, only to turn into dark beads shortly after. Sometimes he woke looking perfectly human, sometimes perfectly demonic.

Right now, his right eye was pitch-black while his left eye showed green irises streaked with hazel at the borders. His teeth remained saw-sharp, however.

"It's the darkness," Jal explained from beyond the bars, startling him. The demon could be sneaky as fuck. "You're getting used to it."

Was he?

Liam watched his arm. He could feel the darkness thrumming under his skin, but underneath that chaotic, cruel mass, there was light.

Whatever Jophiel had done to him, it had helped. Still, compared to his darkness, the light was nothing but a speck of dust.

Warm and shining but always hiding.

At least he controlled the darkness now. Except when Ava was near. Or when he thought about her for too long.

"She saw me as a demon," Liam said quietly as he wiped beads of sweat from his forehead. It would be a warm night. "I didn't want her to see me like that."

The right side of Liam's face was still swollen from one of Archie's punches. He touched the wound with the tips of his fingers only to wince in pain.

Archie would've healed him if he'd had the time, but Jophiel had summoned him at the last minute. The old man left faster than Liam could say goodbye.

He felt Jal's eyes rolling. He wasn't looking at the demon, but the darkness showed him Jal's movements, as did the shy light inside him. The light wasn't a new sensation, more like a distant memory Jophiel had unlocked.

"You're still conquering the darkness," Jal said. "There's nothing to be ashamed of. Next time, when you see her—"

"Will there be a next time?" Liam muttered, turning toward him. "Ava doesn't feel the way I do; she said so herself." He balled his fists and took a deep breath, forcing them open. "Her presence triggered my darkness. I can't understand why, but until I do, I won't see her again. It's not safe for her."

"For you, either." The demon shrugged. "Look, she's confused. So are you. You should both stop being drama queens and give yourselves some time. Have *faith*."

Liam chuckled. "Now you're just mocking me."

Jal gave him a playful wink.

"Maybe I could help." Lilith walked into view.

She moved in a sinuous way worthy of snakes, her hips performing a slow, sensual dance. She stopped beside Jal near the entrance and waved at Liam.

Jal licked his lips, his attention fully locked on Lilith's butt. The vamp wore a skin tight red dress down to her knees and black high-heeled shoes. Her crimson hair was tied in a high bun, her curls framing her face.

She gave Jal a lopsided grin that said she was perfectly aware of her effect on him.

If Liam weren't so appalled by Lilith, he would also think she was attractive. Heck, if he didn't need Ava like the air he breathed, and if Lilith hadn't glamoured him …

He rubbed the bridge of his nose. "How can you help, bloodsucker?"

"If experience has taught me anything, it's that one's frustrations can be appeased with a little …" She bit her bottom lip slowly, sensually. "Release."

Did she mean sex again?

Liam blinked, his mouth gaping open. "You have to be joking. I said I don't want your girls to—"

"What if you could be with Ava?"

Jal chuckled, and Lilith shot him a death glare. "What?" she snapped.

"Are you saying you want to have sex with him?"

"No. I said there's a way for him to be with her, you idiot." She stopped in thought. "But what if I *were* proposing sex? Am I forbidden to be lascivious just because I'm a woman? Am I a whore simply because I enjoy fucking, Jal of Jaipur?"

"You tell me," he said calmly, hands behind his back.

Lilith growled underneath her breath, her fangs on full

display. "You had sex with half of the supernatural world. Does that make you a whore?"

Jal showed his teeth in an elated grin. "Absolutely."

Lilith eyed him up and down with a mix of anger and lust. She waved him off and turned back to Liam. "It's just a harmless mind trick, baby demon. But it could help you."

"I'm not following." Liam frowned. "I can't be physically close to Ava."

As if to answer, Lilith's features changed, but not like Archie's or Hauk's. This change caught him by surprise. One moment she was the queen of the vamps, the next his Ava stood before him, occupying Lilith's place.

She wore a black leather jacket and jeans, the same clothes from when they were investigating Archie's murder.

His partner. His Ava.

No. Not his.

She spun in a circle. "Good enough?"

Heavens, it was Ava's voice. Liam couldn't speak, so he just nodded. He knew this was glamour, but he didn't want it to stop.

Lilith waltzed into the cell, every tilt of her hips a calculated move that oozed sex. It put him off. His princess didn't move like that. Ava had no clue of how beautiful she was, how perfect, which made her all more appealing.

Lilith had done an outstanding job, though. She'd nailed Ava's curvy waist, those legs that went on for days, her rosy lips, and her kind blue eyes.

She even smelled the same as Ava.

A knot twisted in his throat as Lilith—Ava—draped her arms over his shoulders.

Liam hugged her, taking in the lavender scent at the curve of her neck.

"How can you smell like her?" he muttered.

Ava said nothing. She just stayed this way, holding him, her hand slowly caressing the back of his neck.

He took a deep breath and stepped away. Tears piled in his eyes as he watched this fake doll that mimicked his Guardian. "I'm sorry I hit you."

Ava blinked at him, as if he had caught her by surprise. She shot Jal a worried glance, but the demon encouraged her to play along.

"You weren't yourself," Ava said. "I forgive you."

"You know what's worse? The real you did forgive me." He snorted. "She's the greatest angel I've ever met, and I don't deserve her. I've always known that. Maybe that's why I was so angry." Something in his chest shrunk. "Losing her was inevitable."

A certain peace washed over him, and he couldn't understand why.

This wacko therapy of Lilith's might be working.

"You need to forgive yourself, too," Ava said, planting the palms of her hands on his chest.

A sting of pain coursed through his body because that's what the real Ava would have said, or at least the Ava he used to know.

Was she truly gone?

He shoved his hands in his jeans pockets. "You fear that what you felt for me wasn't real. But I know it was, Ava. It had to be."

"And if I don't feel the same way about you anymore?" She cupped his cheek. "Will you still be all right?"

She leaned closer. Liam remembered faintly that this wasn't Ava, but she sounded and smelled like her. So he wrapped his arm around her waist, bringing her closer.

She stood on the tips of her toes, her nose almost nudging his.

Liam lowered his head and completed their kiss. He did it

slowly, gently, nibbling at her lips cautiously, the way he had done before they'd made love.

So long ago ...

He broke free from the kiss and pressed his forehead to hers. "I think I'll be fine."

"All right," Jal clapped his hands loudly, breaking Liam from whatever trance had taken hold of him. "Time out."

In his arms now stood Lilith, pity and sorrow carved in her pretty features.

Pretty.

That was the first time Liam saw her this way.

"Thank you," he muttered, still holding her in his arms.

"Anytime." She gave him a sad, tight-lipped grin. "I'm so sorry you're going through this."

"Don't be." That's all he could say. Because his loss, his sorrow, they weren't Lilith's to have.

They were all his.

"What's going on here?" Archie stepped into view, frowning at Liam and Lilith from outside the cell.

Jal cleared his throat. "Shock therapy?"

Archie wasn't buying it; Liam knew this expression well. It was the same one he had when Liam told him he'd been to the movies with friends, when actually he'd been making out with Rosie O'Connel in the parking lot.

The old man let out a weary sigh, then slammed both hands on his waist. "Suit up, kid. Time is of the essence." He nodded to Liam's jacket, which was sprawled on his bed. "We're infiltrating Hells' Gorge today."

13

LIAM

"I look like a jackass," Liam said as he watched his own reflection in a car window.

His eyes—both green this time—were outlined by charcoal eyeliner, his mouth painted with a deep black. He gritted his teeth and watched perfectly white squares appear in the reflection.

A smile bloomed on his lips. He might resemble an emo dude from the nineties, but at least he looked like a *human* emo dude.

Ever since Liam had become a demon, his hair had grown into an unkempt floppy mop that nearly touched his chin line. He should get a haircut, but Michael had long hair, and sometimes Liam felt him in that faint wisp of light inside, the one he was barely aware of most of the time.

It was strange, wanting to be a man he'd never met, and yet he was in this mess so that he wouldn't be like Michael. After all, the Archangel's darkness had once made him kill humans.

Was that why they had become a demon? To learn to control this raging juggernaut inside them?

There was a difference between having darkness within and letting it consume you. Michael had said so himself.

Liam watched his reflection again. He took an elastic band from his pocket—a gift from Jal, *"Because really Liam, not every man can pull off a long luscious mane"*—and tied his hair in a man-bun that only increased his douchbaggery. But at least he felt half-way between himself and Michael.

A pretty good compromise.

"If it helps, we both look like jackasses, kid," Archie said, pointing at his own panda eyes and black lips. The old man's sand-blond hair was combed back in a style that belonged in the fifties. Or a *Grease* musical. "It sucks, but the whole emo thing is the signature of the Gorge, and we have to follow it. You ready?"

Liam patted the two holy guns strapped in the shoulder holster underneath his jacket. Archie had cursed the bullets with his essence, so he supposed they were damned guns now. Liam then patted the sheathed sword attached to his belt. "Let's go fool some demons, old man."

Adrenaline pierced through his body. Liam had missed fieldwork, and a part of him still couldn't believe that the Fury Boys were back on the streets. An eager smile broke across his lips only to disappear as fast as it came.

The Fury Boys weren't here to protect. As gang members of the Gorge, he and Archie were here to wreak havoc.

They stopped before a brick warehouse with broken windows. Not long ago sector thirteen had been inhabited by vamp covens, but demons had "evicted" them.

Lilith told him that the darklings left two bloodsuckers alive to spread the word that this was now demonic territory. *Two out of hundreds.* Lilith had cried then, and that was the first time he saw a vampire's tears. They weren't dark-red as in most stories, just clear as a crystal. It made Lilith, with all her pearly skin, unnaturally blue irises and sharp fangs, look all too human.

Blood rolled faster in Liam's veins.

"You're unfocused, kid. If I can sense it, so will Hauk," Archie said, his attention on the upper floors of the façade. "You got your shit together?"

Liam took a deep breath, steadying his heartbeat and the storm in his darkness.

"Better." Archie scratched his own chin and clicked his tongue. This never preceded good news. "Look, you'll have to do things to earn their trust today. Things that will haunt you. *Change* you."

He scoffed. "Not my first rodeo, old man."

Archie gripped the back of Liam's neck and pressed his forehead against his. "You're strong, son. So much more than you think. And I'm here, okay? We're in this together."

"I know." Liam swallowed, fearing what awaited them for the first time. "The price we pay for the greater good, huh?"

Archie let him go and watched him with a certain longing. "I never did it for the greater good, kid. Just for you." He sighed deeply. "When all seems lost—and it will—remember we're not trying to save the whole world. Just those we care about."

Liam froze there, letting the words sink in.

"Whatever it takes," he said quietly.

Archie nodded. "Whatever it takes."

Inside the warehouse they went.

Fire flickered dimly in the center of the cavernous space, the only source of light in the darkness. Liam counted at least twenty demons talking with each other where the light hit, thirty more hidden in the shadows—the darkness showed them to him, their essences thrumming against Liam's own.

He straightened his posture and tensed his muscles. He knew pack psychology and that he had to assert himself. There was no place for the weak here.

The demons silenced as he and Archie approached the fire pit.

Hauk was watching the flames. They highlighted the red and orange in his hair, and for a moment, Liam wondered if his head was catching fire.

They stopped behind him, but Hauk didn't turn around.

"Is he truly ready, Archibald?"

"He is," the old man assured with complete confidence.

Hauk spun around and narrowed his eyes at Liam. "Remains to be seen."

He and Archie remained unfazed, their hands behind their backs, their chests puffed in perfect military fashion.

A shadow spread behind Hauk, revealing his gray, scale-less wings.

He's showing off, Liam thought. Like a peacock displaying his feathers. The comparison made Hauk a little less grand, a little more insecure in Liam's eyes.

Hauk craned his neck left, observing him. A shiver ran down Liam's spine. The demon was a Behemoth, so he couldn't read minds.

Could he?

"Let's begin," Hauk said, his expression revealing nothing.

Two bulky second-tier demons—Drakars like Jal, if the warmer way their essences felt was any indication—grabbed Liam by his arms and pushed him far from the fire, close to the edge of darkness in the warehouse.

Just when he thought they might start beating him, the demons released Liam and stepped away.

Hauk approached and halted beside him, watching the dark ahead.

"Come, pet," he ordered, his finger calling for whatever stood in the darkness. The rattling of chains ensued, then stopped. Hauk rolled his eyes. "Come forward, or I'll drag you out myself."

The rattling clanged closer, and then a figure stepped into the light.

Had Liam's guard been down, he would have gasped. But he wouldn't fail in his mission, and he wouldn't give that bastard Hauk the pleasure of seeing him shaken. So he faked complete nonchalance as he observed the Archangel before him.

A woman stumbled into the dim light. She had strawberry blonde hair a shade darker than Ava's, but that was the only thing they had in common. Her face was longer, harsher than his Guardian's, her eyes bleak and lost. She was also shorter and bulkier than Ava.

Her black armless bodysuit was cut all over by blades. Purple blotches peppered her exposed skin, including both of her cheeks. Her beige wings were in worse shape. The left one hung crooked behind her; the other had been chopped off at the first joint with a clean, long cut. A thick crust of blood coated the wound.

Why hadn't she healed herself?

She couldn't grow back her severed wing, but at least her bruises and broken bones could be fixed.

A low vibration caressed Liam's darkness, coming from the obsidian chains around her feet and wrists.

That's why.

The chains had been damned, which meant they could stop an angel's healing. The rest of their powers, too. They could also burn through angelic essence, which explained the circles of rotting flesh on the Archangel's wrists and ankles, where the chains touched her skin.

It was amazing the woman could even stand.

Blessed cuffs would've also neutralized her powers, but at least they wouldn't harm her upon touch. Using damned cuffs was needlessly cruel.

"You tortured an Archangel," Liam said matter-of-factly, his tone even.

Hauk chortled. "Obviously."

"I assumed they were helping us finish the In-Betweens?"

"Us? You mean me. You're not of the Gorge yet." Hauk growled at Archie, who had stepped by Liam's side. "I see your partner has shared too much information with you."

Archie shrugged as if he had no care in this world. "Liam will pass whatever test you throw at him."

"Will he?" A low growl rumbled deep within the demon's chest. He then stepped toward the prisoner. "We're all hungry snakes, eating each other up until there's only one left." Hauk took the woman's chin and almost squeezed her jawbone. She bravely held a whimper. "Which snake do you think will survive, angel?"

She glared at Hauk with defiance. "I know *you* won't."

"Neither will you." The demon let her go.

He then pivoted on his heel and kicked her right knee, sending her shrieking to the ground. Blood pooled where bone broke through skin.

The Archangel's screams slashed through Liam's ears, his chest, his very core, but he had to keep a composed demeanor. He had to control the urge to help her, control the raging fury that craved Hauk's death.

The demon returned to Liam's side with a bored look on his face.

"What did she do to be here?" Liam asked, his voice detached.

"She found out about my agreement with Talahel. She

was going to expose us to the Throne, but her brothers betrayed her." He waved at the whimpering Archangel kneeling in a pool of her own blood. "She needs to be eliminated. I figured you should have some fun with her before that."

All sounds became muffled. Liam clenched his jaw so tight he feared his teeth would crack.

This woman fought on his side. Unlike most Archangels under Talahel's command, she was *good*. For a moment, he saw Ava in her place, even if they weren't similar.

"So, you're Talahel's henchman now?" Liam chortled. "Kind of pathetic."

Hauk gave him a wide grin that engulfed the lower half of his face. "That's what I want Talahel to think."

"Why?"

"None of your business."

A void swirled in Liam's chest. He had to earn Hauk's trust, no matter what. The words cracked as they went up his throat, but when they came out, they were glued back together. "What do you want me to do with her?"

"I was going to have you torture her, but since you're so eager to enter the Gorge …" Hauk shrugged. "You know what to do."

"T-the Order will hear of this," the Archangel said, her voice rasping and weak.

"No, it won't. Talahel will make sure of that," Hauk assured her. "He plays right into Master's game."

Liam's eyes widened. "This is all Master's idea?"

"Everything is." Hauk tapped his shoulder. "Go on, now. We don't have time to waste."

Sacrifices. So many sacrifices …

"Wait." Archie stepped forward, fear stamped on his face. "Let me do it."

"Why?" Hauk frowned suspiciously. "You're already a part of the Gorge."

"Yes, but Liam has been recently turned. We have to ease him into our ways, don't you think?" The old man relaxed his posture slightly, but it was too late. Hauk's piercing stare said the bastard knew Archie was trying to protect him.

"I'm fine." Liam moved to unsheathe his sword before things got worse, but Hauk held his arm.

The demon stared straight at Archie as he ordered, "She dies by fire."

Archie's mouth dropped open. "But I'm a Behemoth. I can't kill her with fire."

"I know." Hauk showed Liam the Archangel. "What are you waiting for?"

Every part of him shook, but he clamped his muscles harder.

There was no escaping this, and now he had to fix Archie's mess. When one rides with wolves, one must learn to bite; the old man had taught this to Liam himself.

He should've known better than to let his fatherly instincts get the best of him.

"I'm not a child you need to protect," Liam told Archie, his tone rough and angry. "I'm a demon now."

Archie blinked, awareness shining in his eyes. He raised his hands in an apologetic manner. "Old habits die hard, I suppose."

"Just get it done," Hauk barked at Liam.

It hit him that this was it. There was no escaping what would come next. Hells, he had never killed an innocent, even when he went undercover.

"Please," the Archangel stuttered. "Michael, you were the best of us. We fought together!"

Liam felt as if he stood at the edge of a cliff. No. He was already falling.

Fuck, fuck, fuck.

"Michael is dead," he growled, faking a hatred he didn't have.

Sorry. He was so sorry.

He glanced at Archie, who watched him with worry. Liam wanted to run from here and take the Archangel with him, but he had to become a part of the Gorge today. It was either that or die as he and Archie fought some fifty demons.

Either way, that Archangel was dead. As much as it felt like the right thing, going down with her wouldn't help their cause.

The Archangel's lips trembled. "Help me. Stand with the Gods once again, brother."

"No," he said, the denial ripping him from inside out because all he wanted was to save her.

Archie must have known this would scar Liam forever. It was why he'd messed up trying to protect him.

"I'm done being on your side of the scale," he said. "I'm with them now." Liam pointed back to Hauk and the rest of the demons, causing murmurs of approval.

Fire burst from his skin, and an angry scream ripped through his throat. The demons probably thought he was furious at the Archangel, but no.

Only at himself.

Tears trickled down the Archangel's cheeks. The flames around Liam shone in her honey-colored irises; eyes he would never forget.

He wasn't doing this for the greater good. He didn't want to save the world, not all of it.

Just Ava.

Shame and guilt corroded him from inside. The darkness spread across his body and essence, filling his eyes and sharpening his teeth.

"Michael, have mercy," the Archangel begged.

Her mauled, crying face would haunt him to the end of his days.

"Wars were never won with mercy."

He shot his flames forward, turning the Archangel into a shrieking ball of fire.

14

AVA

*T*he first thing Ava noticed when she stepped into the office was that Kevin seemed older. His red hair was sharply cut in a nearly military fashion, and instead of jeans and a black shirt, the "uniform" of every Selfless, he now wore a suit. But it was the eyes that made him look older. They'd gotten heavier since she'd last seen him.

The image of Kevin, bloodied and injured as he tried to walk on his own, swatting away any support Jal offered, flashed in her mind. Kevin had watched Gabriel murder the entire Nine-five, and he had barely escaped alive. He had also heard the Captain's screams as the Archangel plucked her eyes out in her office.

All of that must've changed him into the somber Selfless who now stood before her.

The second thing she noticed was that Kevin had done well for himself. He had his own office in this new precinct. It was an ample space with three black leather chairs, a chrome-and-glass desk flanked by matching bookcases, and a white-tiled floor. The big windows revealed the city outside.

It was clear that as a healer and forensic researcher, Kevin had become a major asset here.

Her attention fell on a framed group picture of the Nine-five, which stood on the left side of the desk. It hurt Ava to see the smiling faces among the crowd, especially Liam, Archibald, and Kevin. The Captain stood in the middle of the group, a mask of seriousness stamped on her face as always, but a hint of a grin twitched at the corner of her lips.

Ava couldn't help but smile at those carefree, happy people.

People Talahel destroyed.

Kevin plopped onto his leather chair and watched Ezra from behind his desk, making no effort to hide the bitterness that wafted from him in a sour fog.

The Messenger frowned in confusion since they had never actually met—at least not during Kevin's current life as a Selfless.

"Of course I can get dirt on Talahel, dove," Kevin told Ava. "It will be bloody hard, though. I tried finding damning proof on him after Gabriel's death, but all evidence pointed back to Gabriel." Kevin's hand closed in a ball over his desk. "The Sword is smart, but that wanker will slip. And when he does, I'll be ready."

She smiled at him. "I know you will, Kev."

He locked his attention on Ezra again, watching the Messenger from the top of his head to his fingertips. "Why is this tosser giving you the cold shoulder, Ava?"

Ezra hadn't acknowledged her presence on their way here. Simply convincing him to come had been a mighty feat.

Ava cleared her throat. "He isn't. We need to discuss certain matters, that's all."

"Hmm." Kevin shrugged. "I suppose I'd be angry too, if I wanted something that will never be mine."

"Do we have a problem?" Ezra crossed his arms and frowned in annoyance.

Kevin grabbed a pencil from his desk and tapped it on the surface. "Depends. Word through the grapevine is you've been filled in."

Ezra stood beside Ava, his focus on Kevin. "Yes," he finally said. "The light is grand, the darkness mighty, but the gray is freeing."

"The gray is freeing," Kevin repeated.

He'd become an agent for the Legion after being nearly killed by Gabriel. That plus Liam's death had birthed an anger and bitterness in Kevin that didn't suit him. Even worse, these emotions were eating him up from the inside. Ava hoped she could help him with that someday, when the world wasn't burning all around them.

Kevin stopped tapping the back of his pencil on the desk. "I saw him yesterday, by the way."

Him. Liam.

Ava's heart tightened, and her breath caught in her lungs.

"I stopped by the Legion to deliver a report to Jal, then passed by Liam's cell." Kevin scratched the back of his neck, avoiding eye contact with both Ava and Ezra. "He's doing well. He's about to go off on a mission with Archie and that ought to do him good." He began tapping the pencil on the desk again. "He'll be himself soon. You just wait."

Despite his words, Kevin wasn't sure that would happen. As a Dominion, Ava could feel it. She wasn't sure either, but she gave him a supportive nod nonetheless.

Ezra still glared sticks and stones at Kevin. "We thank you for your service, Selfless Davies. We'll keep in touch. And be careful not to call any attention to your research."

With that, he went to leave.

"You got nothing on him, angel boy," Kevin grumbled.

Ava gasped. Not only was Kevin at the bottom of the

hierarchy, but he had just insulted the Messenger. Also, Kevin had been a Dominion before being a Selfless, thus under Ezra's command.

The Messenger didn't turn back. "I can't know for sure if you used to be Cassiel, but if you were, you'll regret this when you die. We were once good friends."

"Were we? Do forgive me, my Messenger," he said mockingly. "I lost all the memories from my past life, you see."

Ezra left without a word.

Ava shot Kevin a chiding glare, to which he simply shrugged, and then she was running after the Messenger.

She caught up to him just as he reached the sidewalk.

Ezra's wings spread behind him in a golden flash. Sunlight turned his feathers with golden tips into shimmering jewels.

"I'll fly to the Order if you don't mind," he said quietly.

He clearly wanted to avoid this conversation as much as Ava, but the more they did, the further apart they would grow.

"Fine," she said. "So will I."

Her wings flashed behind her. A few people passed by, but they paid them no attention since Ezra and Ava were masking their essences.

He shook his head. "No, it isn't safe. A fall from a considerable height, even with your shield, could be deadly."

"Well, I'm feeling adventurous today." She focused on the sky, assuring herself she could do this.

Deep in her rift, Ava felt her beasts of light and dark watching, *daring* her. A mix of eagerness and fear took over.

Heavens, this was a terrible idea, but with one deep breath she remembered that flying was no different from moving her fingers. Light and dark, hands and wings, they were all a part of her.

Besides, she was done failing everyone she cared about. Failing at everything she did.

Ava needed a win, and she needed it now.

With one boost, she went up. Her wings flapped in perfect synchrony, once, twice, so many times she lost count.

When she zinged past the tallest skyscraper in the city, a victorious howl erupted from her throat. The air became chillier by the second, but Ava didn't care. She was free and she was flying.

Finally!

There was no world down below, no worries and no hurt, just Ava alone with the deep blue.

"Stabilize!" Ezra shouted from behind, his wings flapping faster than hers.

The weight of the world she'd abandoned crashed upon her. It wasn't just Ava and the sky anymore.

She grudgingly nodded and spun into a lying position, dashing into the horizon. Heavens, this was beautiful.

The city down below never looked so small, the sky above never so blue. At a distance, sunlight reflected on the ocean, turning it into a small sun in itself.

Ezra quickly caught up, gliding beside her. His earlier frustration had morphed into pride that flowed from him in warm puffy waves.

"You're doing well!" he yelled over the breeze that guided them.

Even after all the hurt she caused him, Ezra still encouraged her.

He still cared.

Ava didn't deserve the Messenger. No angel in the entire Order did.

They pierced into a low hanging cumulus. Tiny droplets broke onto Ava's skin, and she reveled on their coolness.

When she and Ezra shot out, remnants of the cloud followed their tracks for a fleeting moment.

"I'm sorry I left you at the Legion," she blurted. "My meeting with Liam didn't go as well as I expected."

Ezra bit his lip and looked away. "I assumed as much. I just wish you would've told me."

"How could I?" she cried. "You've been relentlessly avoiding me!"

He raised one eyebrow at her. "I wasn't avoiding you. I'm a high angel, remember? I sensed you didn't want me around, so I stayed away. But I am sorry I wasn't there for you."

The wish to cry bubbled in her throat. Ezra had kept his distance, not for him but for her. Ava didn't know what kind of angel she was now, but she hoped one day she would be like him.

"Thank you." That was all she could say without bursting into tears.

Ezra winked at her, then turned left, a cue for her to follow.

They crossed the sky freely, the way only birds do, sometimes plunging in synchrony only to rise again in a swift, fast-paced dance that left Ava breathless.

Her back began to ache because she wasn't used to flying. Her wings flapped with a lag from left to right, and Ava couldn't stabilize her course anymore.

She pointed to a nearby skyscraper. "I think I need to land!"

Without warning, Ezra swiveled toward her and took her firmly in his arms. His attention remained locked on her as her wings disappeared in a flash.

"I've got you," he muttered.

Ava kept gazing at those consuming kind eyes as she wrapped her arms around his neck. "You do."

The Messenger looped and plunged. Ava's stomach flew up to her throat, but by now she was used to the sensation.

Soon enough, Ezra landed smoothly atop the building.

Still in his arms, she smiled. "This was fun."

His fingers dug deeper on her skin. "It was. We should do it more often."

A red and velvety sensation flowed from him in warm waves.

Lust.

All too quickly Ezra tucked it back inside his essence, fear and embarrassment mingling in his features.

Ava faked innocence, hiding the fact that she'd noticed. She also ignored the tendrils of lust that spiraled inside her, wanting, *needing* to connect to Ezra's.

They were simply a memory of how she used to feel about him, nothing more. This wasn't how she felt right now.

It couldn't be.

Inside her rift, her darkness and light chuckled. Perhaps they also knew that ignoring her feelings for the Messenger was pointless.

Ezra pressed his forehead against hers. "I'll always look after you, Ava."

His words cut through her because she'd once told Liam the same. Ava had been his Guardian, his lover, and now here she was in another man's arms after breaking his heart.

Liam's voice echoed in her mind, *"You loved him for what? A hundred years? I can't compete with that."*

Ava jumped from Ezra's strong grip and left, ignoring the simple truth that craved her attention.

Even after the Messenger called out her name, she kept walking. Away from her feelings and her duties.

Away from him.

15

AVA

*C*ongregation happened every Sunday in a vast room located below the last floor of the Order.

White marbled pews lined the space, and a beige carpet led the way into the chancel. Light poured through towering arched windows made of stained glass engraved with the story of the Gods. The colors fit well against the white, almost as if under the right light the windows were painting the space with their rainbow colors.

A dais with a tribune stood at the chancel where the high angel in charge would lead the day's sermon.

Coming here didn't feel much different from when Ava went to church with her mother. It had always made her uncomfortable, though she never admitted it aloud.

Drones with cameras and beamers hovered near the ceiling. They projected blue holo-screens on the walls, showcasing the seven branches of the Order throughout the seven continents. Each branch had specific country subsidiaries and those had divisions which, in turn, had sections.

In many ways, the Order's structure resembled that of a tree. The main trunk—this building—spread into worldwide branches, and those branches spread into twigs. The twigs then gave way to leaves, such as the Selfless departments.

Ava squirmed in her seat as she watched the angels in the pews. The room was filled with second-tiers only. The broadcast would be delivered exclusively to ascended angels across the world.

Lower angels were not allowed to congregate with the ascended, which was an unfair and appalling rule. But so was the way of the Order.

Last week, Ezra had presided over the Congregation. He'd went on about how the Order must be merciful, and how angels shouldn't condemn the In-Betweens. He said they were starved and being drugged—at which point one angel in the crowd yelled, "Allegedly!"

Never mind that every In-Between's testimony stated the same, even if their word was worthless to the Order. Never mind that they begged for help and received none, mostly because Talahel silenced their voices. And never mind that the Order didn't bother to simply look their way.

So much for angelic mercy.

Ever since Lothar and Lilith's attack, the desire for retribution had grown strong in angelic hearts, blinding eyes that should've been able to see.

Revenge might not be the way of the Gods, but it sat remarkably well with angels. The fact that Talahel and his goons fueled this anger en masse didn't help.

Today, he stood proudly behind the tribune, ready to throw gasoline on a burning fire. The Sword grasped both sides of his marbled stand and peered at the full room. He found Ava in the crowd, and his attention lingered on her. He smirked discretely and then straightened his stance.

"Brothers and sisters," he began. "Let us thank the Gods for the week of fortuitous work behind us, and pray for the week that's to come. Let us pray for strength to protect and guide the Gods' greatest creation: mankind. And let us pray for strength to slaughter any force that defies our mighty, blessed goal." At that he closed his fists as if he were squashing a bug in his palm.

For the first time ever, clapping echoed in the Congregation. It was discrete and only lasted a moment, but it had been there.

Shrill red tendrils wafted from angelic essences, filling the room. Dominions, Virtues, Archangels, it didn't matter. They all hated the In-Betweens, even though only lower angels had died in the attack. The same angels who were not allowed in here.

The hypocrisy made her stomach twist.

At least they *felt* the loss. Better than nothing, she supposed.

Ava wanted to be anywhere else. Hells, a bed of nails would be better than this. But she was Ezra's mate, and it was her duty to attend Congregation under all circumstances. Especially when he couldn't be present.

Officially, the Messenger had a meeting with Vera regarding the task force, but in truth he was at the Legion with Jophiel.

When Ava tried to explain why she'd left him on that rooftop, Ezra merely hugged her and said, "I understand."

He was so kind, so good to her, and she only made him suffer. It was far from fair, and yet she couldn't do anything to change it.

Well, she could ... but never mind.

She'd asked if she could preside over the Congregation for lower angels, and Ezra told her he would think about it. Vera had presided two weeks before, so Ava couldn't see why not. It seemed a worthier use of her time.

"You might start a revolution if you do," Ezra had whispered in her ear. "And we need that, we truly do, but not right now."

Fair point.

From the tribune, Talahel spewed words of hate and revenge, his wild eyes showcasing madness, and yet no one seemed to notice.

No one seemed to care.

"My request for more weapons was denied by the Messenger," Talahel went on, and the attention from the entire room fell upon Ava. She shrunk in her seat. "Our brother Ezraphael and his mate are too kind for this world. Too pure. They say we must be merciful to the In-Betweens, the same creatures who gutted and beheaded our brothers and sisters."

The anger in the space turned into something bitter on Ava's tongue. She tried to ignore the boulder of resentment and outrage threatening to smash her.

"The children of the Goddess of Life and Love know nothing of battle," Talahel said. "Full moon is coming, and so are the wolves. Make no mistake, brothers and sisters, we *are* at war."

More like leading a slaughter, but no one would believe her because somehow all proof indicated that the In-Betweens attacked Talahel's angels without mercy. Some Archangels had even perished by their hands, such as Archangel Firma, who was found as a pile of ashes and burnt bones on a sidewalk.

Never mind that her death matched a demonic attack through and through. The autopsy claimed her throat had been clawed by a werewolf who then set her on fire. And no one defied the results, partly because angels were trusting creatures, and partly because they didn't want to see what was right in front of them.

Let Talahel worry about that.

All it took was one curious Virtue or Erudite, one Dominion or Guardian, one Archangel or Warrior … all breath fled her lungs. Maybe Talahel had gotten rid of them. He was capable of such atrocity.

Maybe that's what had happened to Firma. Maybe the arm of the Order had begun taking over the body. Or maybe Ava was losing her mind.

"Without weapons," Talahel continued, "my army cannot ensure the safety of the men and women in this city and the angels within the Order. It's the reason why the Throne has overruled the Messenger's decision and approved the shipment I need to keep us safe." He pointed to the world outside the windows. "All of *them* safe!"

The crowd erupted in cheers.

From the holo-screens, angels in other branches simply watched. Some nodded in support, others peered at Talahel with curiosity if not a bit of confusion. And yet none said a word. No one opposed him.

The room spun around Ava.

She had tried to stop Talahel through the legal ways, the official ways, and they'd failed her. They might've failed a lot of others, too.

The Legion had to hurry, and so did she and Ezra. Soon, there would be no In-Betweens left in the city.

Suther's wolves wouldn't be able to hide for much longer, and Lilith's vampires, the ones who fought for the Legion, were already dropping like flies.

Ava remembered a time when the numbers of In-Betweens were mightier than the numbers of the Order. When angels and demons actually feared their growth.

That time had perhaps long passed. And according to Gabriel—before she beheaded him—humans would be next.

Ava had to do something. Sitting and waiting wasn't an option anymore.

If she was going to defeat Talahel, she would have to play by the rules of his wicked game.

～

WHEN AVA WAS A GUARDIAN, her charges always took priority, which was quite perfect considering she hated being the center of attention. But now, as she stepped into the lower angels' cafeteria, the attention of the room crashed upon her.

She blushed and hurried to the buffet counter, where she took a tray and ordered eggs and bacon.

The cafeteria angel—Guardian Zuli, if Ava recalled correctly—observed her with complete adoration as if Ava was one of the three Gods herself.

She and Zuli were both angels, one no better or worse than the other, and yet Zuli herself would deny that.

A knot tightened in Ava's throat.

The woman served her breakfast and said, "Thank you for gracing us with your presence today, Dominion Lightway."

"My presence graces no one," Ava countered, then nodded up to where ascended angels lived and worked, to where she should be now according to the moronic rules of the Order. "We're all angels."

Zuli frowned in a way that said she doubted Ava's sanity. She attempted an awkward grin. "Indeed, Dominion Lightway. May the Gods be with you."

"With you as well." Ava grabbed her tray.

After Talahel's Congregation, resentment and disappointment fell upon her with the wrath of a mighty avalanche. As a Dominion, she could feel their anger and disgust as clearly as one could smell a flower or hear a sound.

She had to leave the upper floors of the Order, at least for a while.

Ava looked for Justine in the crowded cafeteria and found her friend waving at her from a secluded table at the back of the room.

She stared at her own feet as she made her way to Justine, avoiding eye contact with the angels around her. Regardless, those she passed turned her way. Their awe and adoration slipped into her skin, settling in her bones. A stark contrast against the hate that came from above.

"I hear her wings are white as snow," said an Erudite to her right.

"It's because she's so pure," a Guardian next to the Erudite explained. "No wonder she became a Dominion so quickly."

"She was there that day, you know," someone else whispered from the left. "Unlike the ascended, she fought for us."

Ava tried to ignore the whispers and murmurs all the way to Justine.

Once she reached the table and dropped on her seat, her friend smiled. "Now that was an entrance."

"Not funny." She watched the space, shifting uncomfortably in her seat. "Next time, we're having breakfast outside."

"I think your presence is good for them." Justine took a piece of melon from her fruit bowl and chewed. "You help them think for themselves."

Ava frowned as she watched the lower angels in the cafeteria. *Unlike the ascended, she fought for us.*

"Anyway." Justine shrugged. "How's Olympus?"

"Frustrating." Ava leaned back in her chair and sighed deeply. "I could use some good news."

"How about a distraction instead?" Justine wiggled her brow. "I was reading the old parchments the other day, and do you know what they say?"

"Do tell." Ava forked her eggs and chewed slowly.

"When the soulmate bond snaps into place, both lovers go into mating overdrive to seal it. Can you imagine? All that angelic power consumed in a frenzy of hot, dirty sex?" She fanned herself with her hand. "Oh la la."

"Gods, Justine. Our world is ending, and that's all you can think about?"

"Hey, excuse me for indulging in some light-hearted discussion with my best friend." She raised her palms and looked up as if she was asking the Gods for patience. "We could both use the distraction, you know."

Ava rolled her eyes. Thinking about soulmates didn't raise her spirits in the slightest.

"There's no such thing as soulmates," she said, taking one more bite of her food. "Liam and I are proof, don't you think?"

"Maybe he isn't your soulmate." Justine popped a grape into her mouth. "Or maybe he is. Maybe the bond only forms once you two find yourselves or something equally cliché."

Ava puffed out an annoyed breath. "How convenient and also scientifically accurate of you, *Erudite* Dubois."

Justine showed Ava her tongue. "I might be a child of knowledge and logic, but passion is my favorite subject."

"Clearly."

She threw a grape at Ava. "You must admit that being taken by a territorial male has its appeal." Justine traced the rim of the bowl with her finger. "I hope that happens when my bond with Kevin snaps into place."

"And yet it hasn't." Ava narrowed her eyes. "Because there are no soulmates. The parchments are fantasies and folklore, nothing more."

Justine chewed on another piece of melon. "I have a theory."

Ava buried her forehead in her palms. "Gods, help me."

Her friend went on anyway. "What if the bond only forms if the angelic powers are aligned? What if it depends on an angel's ascendancy?"

"Now that's silly."

"Ugh!" She crossed her arms. "Whatever, you grumpy hag."

Ava chuckled and shook her head. Gods bless Justine for bringing a bit of joy to her life. She then looked around the cafeteria, making sure no one could hear them.

"I found a way to slow down Talahel," she whispered. "But Ezra can't help me. He's the Messenger, and he has enough on his plate. Besides, your set of skills would be perfect for what I have in mind."

"Sweetie, I'm honored." Justine's eyes twinkled, and she rubbed her hands the way a squirrel does when finding a nut. "Are we about to do something mischievous?"

Ava grinned. "Absolutely."

16

LIAM

*G*hosts weren't real. Liam had never feared specters in the movies, maybe because he knew worse things came hunting at night.

Yes, ghosts weren't real, and yet the Archangel he'd murdered stayed with him. A memory of guilt and regret, she haunted his nightmares non-stop.

Good thing he always slept like shit anyway.

"What are we doing here?" he asked Jal, who led him to an abandoned building with a cracked façade. The entrance's broken wooden door balanced on one hinge.

The night was old. Liam could always tell by the silence on the empty streets. It muffled the air around him, sucking all sound.

Liam hated this kind of silence. It always preceded a shit ton of trouble.

Beside him, Jal watched the building, a certain longing in the way he did it. "You've faced the Gorge's demons, so I figured I should show you that not all of us are bad." He nodded to the broken door. "It'll be good for you."

Liam shoved his hands in his black jeans pockets. "I know you're—" He cleared his throat. *"We're* not all bad."

"Hmm." The demon didn't seem to believe him. "Archie told me the Archangel was the first innocent you killed."

His words were blades and axes. Liam shrugged, pretending it was no big deal. "Michael killed humans, right? I'll get over it eventually."

"From what I hear, those humans weren't exactly innocent. Besides, you're not Michael anymore."

Could he drop it?

"I'm fine," Liam snapped. "I can take a rough day at the job."

"Her name was Firma," Jal continued as he scanned the façade. "Remember her when you kill Hauk and this Master of his. That way, her death won't have been in vain."

Liam's throat suddenly tightened. "Is that what you do?"

"More often than you'd think." His voice was a dry sound that oozed sorrow. "My daadi always said that as long as we don't forget those who are gone, they still live."

The thought brought joy to Liam's heart. So did avenging Firma—preferably by slamming a blade into Hauk's chest— even if it wouldn't change the nightmares where the Archangel's charred corpse stretched her hands toward him, begging for mercy.

But he would take what he could get.

Jal tapped his shoulder and led the way into the decrepit building.

The place reeked of old moss and leaking pipes. It was cold as fuck, too. Liam's fire rumbled inside him, burning underneath his skin to keep him warm.

The house was pitch-dark, but Liam could see perfectly. Well, more like *feel* it perfectly. The darkness showed him chipping walls and leaks that created dark blotches near the ceiling. Most planks on the wooden floor stood like sinking ships in his way, so Liam walked around them.

Had he been human, he would have tripped a long time ago.

"Night vision, if you can call it that," Jal explained from ahead, guessing why he moved so slowly. "One of the benefits from being a child of the dark."

"No shit." Liam picked up the pace. "It's just ... I'd never noticed how accurate it could be."

They went on for an eternity until they arrived at a huge dining room. Moonlight swam through a skylight in the ceiling, painting the walls with a melancholic silver.

Some thirty demons gathered on a long table near the end, eating roasted meat with their bare hands.

"This is Blood and Dagger," Jal said. "I used to be a part of this gang. They made me who I am today."

"So, they're good demons?"

"That's pushing it," Jal snorted. "Let's say they're good enough. By the way, we won't use your real name. News travels fast, and we have to keep your cover in the Gorge safe, yes?"

Liam nodded.

A big demon who sat at the center of the table raised his head and looked back at them. He shot Liam and Jal a wide smile as he stood. His eyes were slightly narrowed and gray, the same color of his long hair tied in a topknot.

He approached them with open arms and trapped Jal in a brutal hug that took the demon's feet off the ground. "I'm so glad to see you, old friend!"

Jal tapped his back starkly. "So am I."

The big demon put him back on his feet. Jal turned to Liam with a smile so wide and pure it looked misplaced on a grownup face. "*Barry*, this is my mentor, Eizo. He taught me everything I know."

"Pleasure, Barry." He shook his hand.

"Likewise."

"I was hoping we could discuss a strategy to make some alliances with the wolves," Jal whispered close to Eizo's ear. "I hear the Order just got a new weapons shipment. Word on the street is that soon they'll eradicate any In-Betweens who are left."

Eizo eyed Liam up and down, clearly not trusting him.

Jal chortled. "Don't worry about Barry. He owes me a favor," he said, as if this was enough.

Perhaps it was.

Eizo watched Jal with a curious frown. "Why would I risk my life helping Suther? That stupid boy isn't half the wolf his father was."

Jal's eyes widened. "But he'll need help, even if he's too proud to take it."

"I can't help him." The demon crossed his arms. "I can't help anyone, not after that madman took twenty of my pack. They left to follow him as if all the centuries in Blood and Dagger meant nothing to them."

"What?" Jal shook his head, his mouth hanging slightly open. "Bill? Eirik? What about Takeshi?"

Eizo's face crumpled with a mix of fear and sorrow. "Eirik is still here, but he's not in a good shape." He laid a heavy hand on Jal's shoulder. "We'll have to sit this one out, old friend."

"Are you serious? You're the demon who took ten holy blasts for your werewolf wife! You never abandoned the In-Betweens, and you won't start now." Jal's breaths were becoming uneven. "Where's Gemma? She needs to talk some sense into you."

"Haven't you noticed, old friend?" Eizo growled and pushed his chest against Jal's with the fury of a bison. "Where's her scent?"

Jal sniffed, but by his puzzled glare, he couldn't find it. "What happened?" he asked, his tone shrunken. Fearful.

Eizo pressed forward. "She's dead!"

Liam's hand went to the gun strapped under his jacket. The demons at the table stopped eating and watched them with a warning.

"Hells, I …" Jal attempted, but his voice disappeared.

"He killed her right in front of me." Eizo's eyes glinted with tears. "He took my people, and he took Gemma! You haven't *seen* him, Jal!"

Him.

Eizo was talking about Master.

Jal's throat bobbed up and down in a hard swallow. He stepped back. "I'm so sorry. I didn't know Gemma was gone."

"You have no idea—" Eizo's voice broke, and he sniffed back tears. "I have to protect my crew. They're all I have left." He gave him his hand. "Join us, Jal."

"I can't. I have people of my own to look after now." He glanced at Liam, then ran a hand through his silky black hair. "Eizo, listen to me—"

"No."

"Listen!" Jal grabbed him by the lapel of his shirt, but the bulky demon didn't move one inch. "What do you think Master will do when he kills the In-Betweens, angels, and all humans? Do you think he won't come after you?"

"Gemma defied him. She was a warning, Jal. He could've killed all of us, but he was merciful. He'll be merciful again."

Liam probably shouldn't interfere, but he had to say something. "You don't seriously believe that, right?"

Eizo bared his teeth. "Stay out of it, Barry." He pushed Jal away. "Master is darkness, and he'll bring the Hells upon Earth. Everything that's going on with the Order and the In-Betweens is nothing compared to what's coming. Nothing!"

"Eizo," Jal's voice broke. "I've looked up to you my entire life."

"You didn't see *how* he killed Gemma, Jal. If you had, you would be scared, too." His hand closed into a fist, and a tear slid down his cheek. "I want to live. So should you."

With that, he went to join the demons at the table.

Liam turned to leave but Jal stood there, frozen in shock. He walked back and took Jal's arm. "Come on, buddy."

Jal didn't move. His muscles were stone under Liam's grip, his breathing ragged. "Eizo is the bravest demon I've ever known. And he's terrified."

The pain embedded in his words sent a bitter taste down Liam's throat. "Jal, there's nothing for us here."

The demon blinked, only now turning to Liam. His eyes glistened. He opened his mouth to say something but couldn't.

"No matter what you do, you'll kneel before him," Eizo shouted from the table without turning to them, his strong back highlighted by moonlight. "So will the entire world."

LIAM

*H*ells Gorge never stole large quantities of blood from the banks of the Order. Instead, they spread out the robberies, which made them harder to track.

Liam and Archie warned Jophiel, and in turn he warned his contacts at the Order. But when they searched the system, there was nothing wrong.

Talahel's goons must've hacked into the files because the robbed amounts showed as delivered to covens that were actually starving. There were fake forms, signatures, everything.

Talahel knew how to cover the demon's tracks.

The Order had proof that blood was being delivered, and yet vampires still fed illegally on humans. Which meant that when the bloodsuckers claimed they were being starved, no one believed them. The system never lied.

It was cruel and genius, really.

Selling tampered wolfsugar to force the shift on werewolves had been harder. Suther's dogs weren't buying anymore. They weren't stupid. But without pure wolfsugar to help his packs tame the wolf, especially during the full moon, there would be an army of raging beasts in the city in no time.

And Talahel would be waiting for them.

Days passed too quickly. Liam and Archie weren't even close to meeting with Master, and meanwhile, a genocide loomed on the horizon.

Eizo's words rang in his mind frequently. *"The In-Betweens are only a distraction."*

So, what was the end game?

"Caralho, Liam," Pedro, one of the Gorge's demons, whispered beside him, jarring Liam from his thoughts. "You sleeping with your eyes open or what?"

They both sat atop a pile of scrap at the corner of the warehouse, watching a white van drive into the vast space.

Late night wrapped the warehouse in darkness. The few lamps hanging on the walls added an eerie ambiance.

Liam clicked his tongue, dismissing Pedro's remark. "You know why Hauk summoned all of us here?"

"No. And I know better than to ask." He snorted. "Just smile and nod, man. It makes everyone's life easier, right?" He went to punch Liam playfully on the shoulder, but Liam grabbed Pedro's hand in the air the way a python snatches its prey.

Liam raised one eyebrow and observed him.

The man resembled a mouse, both in stature and semblance—his nose was too big, his front teeth protruding. This was the darkness shaping the demon like it had tried to shape Liam. Or perhaps, Pedro had been ugly his whole life.

Who the fuck knew.

Liam was much taller and stronger than him, not only in size but also in his essence. Overpowering Pedro was too easy.

"Careful, *babaca*," he said as he squeezed Pedro's wrist harder, crushing tendons under his grip. *"Quer morrer?"*

Pedro winced and hissed through his teeth. *"Porra!* Let me go, asshole!"

Liam watched him for a moment longer before releasing his wrist. Hells, he had thoroughly enjoyed that.

Pedro rubbed his reddened wrist, his entire face a shade of purple. "Since when do you speak Portuguese?"

"None of your business."

Pedro eyed him up and down, not with anger or resentment, but with respect. He gave him a small nod. "You're a badass motherfucker, Liam."

Good.

He needed his fame to grow in the Gorge. It was the only way to get closer to Hauk, and in turn, to Master himself.

Archie parked the vehicle in the middle of the warehouse and got out. Hauk followed from the passenger's seat.

From the looks of it, this was just a routine blood theft. But Hauk had requested all fifty members of the Gorge to be here tonight, so there had to be a reason.

Liam's gut warned him no good could come out of this, and his gut was rarely wrong.

Hauk and Archie headed to the back of the van and opened the tailgate. A group of ten humans walked out: four women, six men.

Archie did his best to hide his shock under a mask of disinterest, but Liam easily caught it. He could only hope Hauk wouldn't.

Before the old man had left at sundown, he'd told Liam that Hauk ordered him to drive some blood supplies, and that he would be right back. Archie had no clue he would be transporting humans.

This must have been a hard blow, but his father had been playing the game for a while. The shock that had been there only a moment ago disappeared.

"What will you do with them?" Archie asked casually, hands in his pockets.

Hauk glared at him. "Are you questioning me, Archibald?"

"Of course not. Just curious."

The demon's mouth curved in annoyance. "Curiosity killed the cat."

Hauk's attention then went to Liam, who returned Hauk's gaze with cold, calculating eyes. The demon grinned, clearly pleased. He beckoned him, Pedro, and all of the Gorge's demons to come closer until they formed a half-circle around the van and the humans.

"Change of plans," Hauk said. "The Order is doing a fine job at eliminating the In-Betweens. Our association with them is over."

Talahel wouldn't be pleased. Without demons, no one would tamper with wolfsugar or steal blood from the records. A smile twitched in Liam's lips.

Hauk went on. "It's time for phase two, brothers and sisters."

"Phase two?" Pedro asked.

As if on cue, a tall, slim figure broke the mantle of night outside and entered the warehouse. The temperature dropped so fast Liam thought he might freeze.

"Is that a Possessor?" he asked Pedro quietly, focusing on heating his own core.

Pedro clanked his teeth. "Nasty motherfuckers."

When Liam was a Selfless, he never ran from a battle with an Obsessor—though many in the precinct called him crazy for it. After all, human flesh tended to be weak and young demons could be powerful.

Most of the time, however, he let Obsessors do their own thing, since they enjoyed cozy human bodies as hosts. Killing their "home" made little sense. After a while, they just jumped onto the next human and that was that.

But Possessors, their evolution, were an entirely different animal. These bastards could not only possess someone, but they could change their host's form, often swallowing the human and adding them to their own bodies.

The thing stopped beside Hauk, its entire body hidden underneath a long black robe that pooled at its feet. Only darkness glanced back at Liam from under the hood.

Hauk bowed his head slightly at the Possessor, then strolled lazily along the row of humans. He stopped before a man in a suit. "We drugged a co-worker who would've gotten the promotion you deserved."

The man stared back at the demon, unafraid.

Hauk disregarded his petulance. He approached a young woman who wore a green sweater. "We faked a test note so you could graduate."

She lowered her head and whimpered, but he had already gone to the next man.

"We beat up the lab technician in charge of the paternity test so he would change the results." A pleased laugh rolled in his chest. "All of that does not come for free." He spun around, hands behind his back. "You all agreed to a contract. We granted you the favors you sought, and now it's time to pay up. Tonight, you will give your souls to the dark."

Shit.

Higher demons could close deals with humans in exchange for their souls, so when the mortals died they were stripped of the choice. According to Jal, the demon's darkness infected the human's essence and created a link between both.

It was a skill fairly easy to learn, or at least that's what Jal said. Weaker demons—*"Like you, Liam,"*—could do it too, but the bond was frailer.

Jal used to make deals to send the worthy to the Heavens and the evil to the Hells, because only the demon who had cursed the soul could choose the person's fate upon their death.

Who knows, maybe the girl in the green sweater could've become an angel when she died—Liam sensed she had potential. But since she had struck a deal with Hauk, she had given her final choice to him.

Hellsdamned, the girl had doomed her immortal soul for a stupid grade. How old was she? Twenty, twenty-two?

The Possessor raised a bony hand with skin the color of milk. The creature pointed at the man in the suit, then hissed words that rang ancient and rusted under its breath.

A black fog burst from the Possessor's fingertip and penetrated the man's nostrils, ears, and mouth. He thrashed as the fog entered him, but it only lasted a moment. The black cloud dissipated, and the man took a deep breath.

"Is that it?" he asked.

The Possessor nodded, a pitch-black void underneath its hood. Then it focused on the girl with the green sweater.

Was that thing *sealing* the deals? Hauk might have closed the contracts, but the Possessor was the one signing them.

Did this mean these souls now belonged to it?

Hauk approached Liam from behind while watching the scene ahead. "Your partner has a light stomach." The demon pointed at Archie, whose skin paled as he watched the poor girl be damned.

He shrugged. "Still stronger than most."

"Indeed." Hauk watched the Possessor perform its task. "I will take some of my most trusted members to meet Master in a few days. You mentioned how much you'd like to see him. You're off to a great start, Liam Striker. Keep up the good work, and you might be one of them."

Liam bowed his head, faking gratitude and awe. "It'll be my honor. You won't regret this."

"You're not in yet," Hauk spat, his mouth twisting in a

C.S. WILDE

bitter way. "But keep doing as you're told, and you'll be rewarded."

"Right." Liam nodded to the humans. There was a reason why Hauk was here. "What do you want me to do with them?"

His stomach twisted, and his skin felt clammy and cold. Liam had only prayed once in his life, but he prayed again now. He prayed Hauk wouldn't order these innocents to die.

And yet, those lives were already lost.

"Once the Possessor is done, you'll drive them to their homes," he said.

Liam frowned, trying to hide the relief that washed over him. "We're not killing them so they can become demons?"

"So dedicated to our cause." A sense of pride filled Hauk's scrawny features. "We've marked them. That's enough for now."

An earthquake shook Liam's core.

Marked them for what?

18

AVA

*E*zra returned from the Legion with bad news.

The priests of the Gray fed as many vampires as they could, but their efforts came up short. The hunger often took over and sent vampires hunting in the open, leaving them vulnerable to the Order's attacks.

Danger also surrounded Suther's werewolves. A full moon approached, and without wolfsugar, many wouldn't be able to control the beast. The moment they roamed the streets or parks, Talahel's soldiers would smite them.

Now Ava understood why the Sword had ordered so many weapons. He was preparing to eradicate the wolves, who, according to Ezra, were the only ones still capable of making a dent in his forces.

She hoped, *prayed*, that these were all the bad news, but Ezra wasn't finished.

The number of deals between humans and demons had suddenly skyrocketed. The Legion had to fight Talahel's goons, keep its army fed and safe, and now they also had to save unaware humans from dooming their souls.

Impossible tasks, especially with their shrinking

numbers.

"You should go train with Jophiel," Ezra said quietly, fear imbedded in his tone. "Just in case."

The message was clear: Prepare for the worst.

So she did.

At the Legion, Jophiel showed her battle stances and techniques, and he nearly broke Ava with endless exercises to make her stronger and faster. But when it came to moving blocks of stone with her mind, Ava failed spectacularly.

Every. Single. Time.

Even so, Jophiel made her try until her brain stabbed her skull and every muscle in her body hurt. Until Ava fell numb on the floor, bordering on consciousness.

One day during their training, the Seraph's unbreakable mental wall caved only a little, enough for her to sense how exhausted he was. *Hopeless.* As if he carried the weight of the world on his shoulders, and it was always on the verge of falling.

When Jophiel noticed she had peered into his essence, he put up his wall and pointed to the stone blocks. "Again, Ava. You can do this."

No, she couldn't. Just like the Legion couldn't protect the In-Betweens and fight demons at the same time. It couldn't save the Order, either.

Jophiel would never admit that he—*they*—were failing, but it was the truth.

And Ava was done with it.

~

"I DON'T KNOW how much longer I can take!" Justine shouted. A vein popped out on her forehead as she used her telekinesis to keep the vampire in place.

Ava trapped the creature from behind in a sleeper hold

that wasn't working at all. "Just a little more!"

She pushed herself up and wrapped her legs around the vampire's waist, trying to tilt him forward and onto the floor. Instead, she felt like a backpack.

Heavens, this vampire must be taller and bulkier than Liam, who was a strong man to begin with. If not for Justine's help, Ava might have lost this battle already.

When a vampire went into bloodlust or when a werewolf turned without control, they poured chaos and madness. As a Dominion, Ava could track their emotions; she only needed to be close enough to the raging, murdering beast.

Vampires could walk under the sun, but they preferred places with shadow. So did werewolves—hunters didn't choose open spaces where they could easily be found. Which meant dark alleys were often a direct hit, and also how she'd gotten in this mess.

"Calm down!" she yelled, her words turning into wisps of light that sunk into the vampire's skin.

Ava's empathy worked wonders in humans, but the In-Betweens were much stronger.

The vampire roared out all his fury and broke through Justine's mind hold. Before Ava could jump off him, he slammed his back against the alley's brick wall.

If her golden shield hadn't gone up in time, Ava would be healing organs and broken bones right now.

She kept a firm hold on the vampire, even if her lungs felt like they'd been squashed—quite literally. Her golden shield might be strong, but it wasn't impenetrable.

"We're trying to help you!"

The vampire stopped and glared at Justine as if only now realizing she was here. His focus went to the blue backpack strapped over her shoulder.

Justine swallowed and clutched the strap. "He caught the blood's scent, didn't he?"

The vampire breathed loudly, every up and down of his back taking Ava along. Up, down … no sound in the alley apart from his breathing.

Justine carefully stepped back. The vampire stepped forward. She stepped back again.

He sprinted toward her.

"Control the hunger!" Ava yelled.

Wisps of light and flecks of black snow burst from Ava's skin, penetrating deep into the creature's body. The vampire stopped midway and slowly, his muscles relaxed.

Ava gaped at him. This wasn't her ordinary empathy, but she had no time to figure it out.

"We're on your side," she continued, black snow and golden shine swimming from her pores into his. *A mix of light and dark.* "We want to help."

The creature's shoulders dropped. His frantic breaths evened, and he shook his head.

"We fight everything and everyone," he growled before heaving a deep breath. "We're tired."

"I know."

If the vampire could form coherent sentences, he probably wouldn't lose control and attack them. Ava tentatively let him go and stepped on the ground.

She motioned to the blue backpack strapped over Justine's shoulder. Her friend took the cue and removed a bag of blood from inside, then shot it at the vampire.

He grabbed it midair with a sniper's precision and promptly poured its contents down his throat, smearing the sides of his lips with ruby-red lines.

Once he was done, his constricted pupils dilated and his predatory white irises changed into a deep black. His sharp fangs retracted only a little.

He glared at them as if he couldn't believe angelic hands had been kind to him. "Thank you."

Ava smiled. "We do what we can."

"Fancy seeing you here, angel girl." A sultry voice came from the mouth of the alley.

Ava cringed.

Gods, not her.

She turned to see Lilith, who looked spectacular as always. Today, her hair was tied in a high ponytail, her red lipstick matching her tresses perfectly. The vampire queen wore a black bodysuit with a low-cut neckline that almost put her plump breasts fully on display.

"I see you've already gotten help, Cristopher." Lilith nodded to the street behind her. "Go aid your brothers."

"Yes, my queen." The vampire gave Ava and Justine one last grateful glance before leaving.

Ava crossed her arms. "What do you want, *bloodsucker*?"

"Word on the street is that you're helping my children." Lilith pointed a red manicured nail at Ava as she walked into the alley. "I suppose I should thank you."

"I'm not doing this for you," Ava spat. "If you and Lothar hadn't attacked the Order, things would be different. Maybe the council would have listened to your pleas."

"You know that's not true, angel girl." Lilith's irises bordered on neon blue as she walked closer. Predatory, merciless … beastly. "Our voices aren't holy enough."

Ava scoffed, but Lilith was right. She couldn't blame the Order's lack of mercy and common sense on anything but the Order itself.

Well, Talahel helped immensely.

Justine stepped beside Ava and eyed Lilith with contempt. "If you'll excuse us, we must find more In-Betweens to help."

"No need." Lilith extended her palm to Justine. "I'll deliver the blood."

"Tough luck, bitch." Her friend clutched the backpack. "It stays with us."

C.S. WILDE

Lilith rolled her eyes and raised her bronze eyebrows at Ava.

As much as she disliked doing what the vampire queen wanted, Ava knew Lilith would do right by her people. Her vampires were her children, and she felt their loss like any mother would.

"Lilith would never let them starve," Ava told Justine.

"Oh, really?" She studied the vampire's sinuous curves. "This bloodsucker looks well fed. Much better than the man we just helped."

"You forget I'm one of the oldest vampires alive. I need less feeding to function, you dimwit." Lilith spoke through gritted teeth, her fangs descending. "And you'll be wise to refrain from insulting me."

"Lilith can also fight an Archangel," Ava added. "Which means that unlike her children, she can risk openly feeding and transporting the blood."

Justine glanced at Ava, then Lilith. With one displeased grunt, she tossed the backpack at the vampire queen. "Whatever."

Lilith smiled as she caught the bag. "Don't worry, angels. You can find cowardly werewolves to assist, so your day isn't over yet."

She was right. Ava had helped three wolves shift back just the other day. Then again, Justine had to fling a fourth one miles away with her telekinesis so they could escape.

It was always a gamble.

Lilith turned to leave, but Ava couldn't hold the question that itched in her tongue. "How's Liam?"

The vampire looked back at her. "Don't worry, *princess*. I'm taking good care of him."

Fury forced Ava forward, her fists closing into balls. She would smack a punch on Lilith's beautiful face, and she would thoroughly enjoy it.

He won't like her if we break her.

The thought had come from her rift, but whether it belonged to light or dark, she couldn't say.

Probably the dark.

Lilith faced her with eagerness, aching for battle as much as she did. But Justine grabbed Ava's shoulder at the last minute, breaking her angry trance.

Her friend scornfully eyed Lilith up and down. "Mr. Hunky would never go for a cheap-ass vamp."

Lilith grinned and licked her bottom lip. "Are you certain?"

Ava saw red but managed to hurry past Lilith and out of the alley before ending the bloodsucker with her bare hands. Justine followed her.

They had just stepped into the sunny sidewalk when Lilith asked, "How do you think Liam found you in the Legion?" She watched them from the penumbra of the alley, her neon blue eyes standing out like precious jewels. "You still have a connection with him. It's weak, but it's a bond nonetheless. Focus on him, and that Dominion power of yours might show you how he's feeling. It might even help you locate him, though I'd advise against it. You don't deserve him." She bared her teeth at Ava, and her pretty face morphed into a devilish scowl with too many wrinkles. The face of a lion about to pounce. "Liam is too good for you."

Ava shattered into a million pieces. "I know."

"It's not all your fault, I suppose." The lion disappeared, giving way to a supernatural beauty that watched her with pity. "You have a knack for making men suffer, Ava Light-way. I can certainly relate."

That hungry, merciless voice from the rift—her own voice—whispered, *not just men. We make everyone suffer.*

We are kind, her voice, soothing and calm this time, countered from the rift. *We care for others.*

We burn them.

We save them.

Justine flipped Lilith her middle finger. "To the Hells with you, bloodsucker." With that, she dragged Ava away.

They walked in silence for a while until Justine huffed, "Lilith is a delight, isn't she?"

"It's strange," Ava muttered, her attention on the concrete but not really. She tried to listen to those voices of her own, but they had silenced. "I feel like I'm hanging between light and dark, and no matter which I choose, both will obliterate me."

Light and dark, Liam and Ezra. It was all connected.

And nothing made sense.

Justine frowned at her. "Now that's just absurd—agh!" She bent over as if taken by immense pain. Screams ripped through her throat.

"Heavens, Justine! What is it?"

"Virtue Lisle!" She glared at Ava, catching her breath. Fear clotted around her in a cold gray mass. "My wall was down. He tracked me!"

Ava's throat dried, and she didn't have time to think before two figures landed in front of them: Virtue Lisle accompanied by Ezra.

The Messenger oozed despair and fear, his skin paler than usual. "I've been looking for you everywhere." He took Ava in his arms, wrapping her so tightly she could barely breathe. "I'm so glad you're safe." His strong body shook against hers.

She listened to the fast beating of his heart, trying to ignore the freezing worry that flowed from him. "Ezra, what's going on?"

"I thought I'd lost you, too." He swallowed and let her go, still watching Ava as if he couldn't believe she was here. "Vera is missing."

19

AVA

*V*irtue Lisle tirelessly led the way from the skies, flying ahead of Ava and Ezra. He focused on finding Vera's telepathic presence down below, which was as easy as finding fur on a rattlesnake.

Justine didn't have wings, so she tried to catch Vera's thoughts from the ground. There were eight million people in this city, however, and her friend was only one. Ava doubted the Throne herself could find someone in this manner.

Still, her friend and Lisle tried until their faces went red. As night stretched ahead, exhaustion overtook Lisle and he nearly fainted in midair, his wings vanishing in the blink of an eye. Before Ava could react, Ezra had already caught him.

"We need to rest," the Messenger said begrudgingly as they took Lisle back to the Order.

Ezra warned Jophiel that same night, and the Seraph employed every scarce resource of the Legion, including himself, to the search. But after two days, no one had a clue where Vera might be.

She had simply vanished.

On day four, Ava returned to the Order at night before her wings caved to exhaustion.

She had visited Vera's favorite spots: pier number seven, the hills, even the hot-dog seller on Eleventh and Fourth where Vera used to grab her Wednesday lunches. Unlike most Dominions who preferred to hide their presence with their essence, Vera only masked what could give her away— her uniform and wings.

The man at the stall told Ava he hadn't seen Vera since Tuesday, which was when she'd last seen the old owl herself.

Another dead end.

A grim sensation settled in Ava's stomach as she cut across the night sky. Either Vera was hiding, or Talahel's men had gotten to her.

The need to cry squeezed her lungs, and it didn't come from the painful stings that accompanied every flap of her worn out wings.

The old owl *had* to be okay. She had to be in hiding for a reason. Yes, Vera would find a way to contact them soon, and she would explain all of it.

Or so Ava kept telling herself.

She landed clumsily on Ezra's open balcony and saw the Messenger pacing around inside. His wings vanished into his light, which meant he hadn't been here for long.

The spherical chandelier that hung from the ceiling drenched the room in daylight. Ava noticed the sky-blue of the walls and the white marbled floor, finding it remarkable that while night engulfed the outside, here it was midday.

"We'll sleep for a couple of hours to regain our strength." Ezra walked in circles, his arms crossed. "Then we start again."

She doubted he would sleep in this state. Vera was important to Ava, but she and Ezra had always shared a special bond.

The Messenger had stopped hiding his despair, at least when Ava was around. Now it thundered inside him, shaking the core of her essence.

Her wings vanished behind her as she laid a hand on the back of his shoulder. He stopped moving.

"I can whisper the words of the Gods to you," she said. "Maybe they will help you sleep."

Ezra turned to her, his features tired and yet loving. *Kind.* "Thank you, but you should rest."

He caressed her cheek and Ava leaned on his palm, rejoicing in its comfort. Ezra stepped forward, now looming over her.

Their eyes locked and time stood still. Ava was exhausted, hurt, and lost.

Lost within Ezra.

"Ava, I ..." he started, then bit his bottom lip. A string of silver hair brushed the side of his face. "We haven't had time to—"

A knock came from the door, breaking whatever trance had taken hold of her. Ava stepped back, half-frustrated and half-grateful for the interruption.

Ezra's hand hung in the air where her cheek had been, begging, waiting, until he finally dropped it. He cleared his throat and said, "Come in."

Sithrael entered. He feigned concern as he bowed to the Messenger and placed a hand over his own heart. "We've heard of Vera's disappearance. The Sword has entrusted me with her rescue. I give you my heavenly word I will not rest until she's found."

Blood thumped under Ava's skull. She was done playing games with Talahel and his men. She bit her teeth and stomped toward the Archangel, trying to control the need for violence that bloomed inside her.

"Touch a hair on her head," she whispered, the wild voices

inside her gathering into one, "and I will give you the death of your nightmares."

Sithrael grinned and bent over so his minted breath struck her face. "A meek little Guardian? I doubt it."

The beasts inside Ava smiled, and so did she. The masks were down.

Finally.

Sithrael went to leave, but Ezra moved the way lightning strikes. He trapped the Archangel in a deadly strong hold, his blade drawn at the villain's neck. If Sithrael moved an inch, the Messenger's holy sword would slash his throat.

"You will stay here until Vera turns up," Ezra barked through gritted teeth.

"Are you disrupting the search for your mentor, my Messenger?" Sithrael asked with a hint of amusement. "That's mighty suspicious. I wonder if you had anything to do with her disappearance."

Oh, that bastard!

The Order belonged more and more to Talahel. Ava and Ezra's hands were tied. Always tied.

Ezra pressed the blade into his neck, opening a line that drooled blood. "Don't you dare—"

"Talahel knows I came here," he said calmly, as if the healing wound on his neck was but a paper cut. "Keep me, and he will have grounds to charge you with obstruction."

Ezra kept holding him, his muscles stone. He was so close to killing Sithrael that Ava saw it happening. The beheading, the pool of blood. And she would let Ezra do it. Gods, the darkness inside her ached for bloodshed—so did her light. She didn't know what to make of it.

"Don't let him go," she told Ezra. "If he finds Vera, he'll kill her."

Sithrael snickered. "What makes you think I haven't already?"

Ava narrowed her eyes, catching the distress and anxiety that tittered in his core. If he had killed Vera, he would be much calmer. Yes, Sithrael was worried. This could only mean one thing. "You're looking for her because she found incriminating evidence against Talahel."

Sithrael's eyes widened, and he lost his playfulness.

Bingo.

Ava gave him a ferocious grin that showcased her teeth. "Don't worry. We'll find her first. And when you fall, Sithrael, it will be glorious."

Disgust with a hint of fear wafted from him.

Hmm, delicious.

"Let me go," he ordered.

"I can't let Ezra kill you," Ava went on, watching Sithrael from head to toe. "Was that your plan all along? To bait him into murder so he would be removed from his duties as Messenger?" A fleck of surprise flashed across the Archangel's eyes. "Ah, that was your boss's plan, not yours. Interesting."

Her voice sounded cold, harsh, and yet it fit her lips all too well. "Ezra won't kill you. He's too valuable to the Order. I, on the other hand …" She shrugged and laid a palm on the hilt of her sword.

"No." Ezra took two deep breaths, then in one quick move, he released Talahel's lackey.

Ava felt like screaming. "What are you doing?"

"We can't kill him without incriminating ourselves. Talahel would pay it back in blood with the full support of the Order." He narrowed his eyes at the Archangel. "There's a reckoning coming for you all, Sithrael. This I promise you."

"You lack a backbone, my Messenger." The Archangel straightened his spine and watched Ezra from above his nose. "Mine is the rightful side in this battle. Choose wisely. There's still time, and Talahel is forgiving."

He cast one last snobby glance upon Ava before leaving. As if she was filth or dirt.

The moment the door closed, Ava rushed outside and climbed on top of the marbled handrail of Ezra's balcony. In a flash of light, her body felt heavier. Snow-white wings flapped behind her, eager to take flight even if they still hurt.

"Where are you going?" Ezra asked.

Wind tousled her hair in a gentle dare, night air chilly on her skin. "The Legion," she said over her shoulder. "I need to keep training if I'm to defeat Sithrael. I can't let him get to Vera."

"Why would I let you fight him?" There was a frown in his tone. "We both know I'm not the kind of angel who sits back and watches."

She rolled her eyes. "If you kill him, you might lose your place in the Order. I can't have that; the Legion can't have that."

He shrugged. "Who said anything about killing?"

She drew an exasperated breath and turned back to him. "Sithrael will find her. He'll find her before we do."

"I know. He's the Order's best tracker, and he has centuries of experience in the art of battle. Something *you* do not have. Don't engage with him unless you absolutely have to." He peered at her from below stern, ashy eyebrows. "That's an order."

"I have to do something!" She threw her hands in the air, but instead of abiding to her urges and flying to the Legion, Ava jumped from the railing and back onto the balcony, perhaps to talk some sense into him.

As she walked closer to Ezra, she noticed a certain peace oozing from his core. "You seem excessively calm about all this."

He went to a side table that stood near the balcony's

entrance and picked up a small tablet from the surface. He handed it to her.

The screen displayed a map of the Order, and a blinking red dot moving inside it.

She gaped at Ezra and the small device. "You put a track on Sithrael!" Ava threw her arms around his neck, slamming into him.

Ezra hugged her back so strongly it seemed he would never let go. "That prick will lead us straight to Vera."

Hope bloomed in her chest, warm and soft. "And when he does, we'll be ready."

They stayed entangled for a while until Ava decided to step away. It felt wrong being this close to Ezra, even if a part of her craved for his touch.

"By the way." He scratched the back of his neck, the muscles on his biceps pushing against the fabric of his body-suit. "We need to help prepare the yearly ball."

An incredulous chuckle escaped her lips. "We have bigger worries, don't you think?"

"Yes, but Agathe is pressing me on this. Until we find incriminating evidence against Talahel, we need to keep things business as usual. Like it or not, this is Talahel's game."

Every year, the Order gathered to celebrate the Gods in an annual ball. It was a festivity of epic proportions, bathed in alcohol and music, and it was also the only occasion when lower and ascended angels united in the same room.

For angels at the bottom of the hierarchy, the ball was an opportunity to party with the ascended whom they worshipped almost as the Gods themselves. Ava remembered. Not long ago, she had been one of them, blind and trusting.

A fool.

"Why doesn't Agathe ask Talahel and his Archangels to help?" she grumbled.

"He says he's too busy defending the Order and humans."

Of course. The head of the Order's army got away with what he wanted.

Ezra set a hand on her shoulder. "Until Sithrael makes a move, we can't do much. Besides, I was looking forward to spending this year's ball with you."

Her wings twitched with a mix of fear and exhilaration.

Fueled by alcohol and loose inhibitions, the ball often became an orgy at the night's latest hours. It was a release many found welcoming, considering the heavy duties that the Order imposed. Besides, angelic power gave angels a lot of energy, which they loved to spend in the woes of the flesh. It was a part of angelic nature, something Ava had ignored for far too long.

Well, she didn't ignore it with Liam.

Ava always left the ball before things got heated, but she often wondered if she had stayed, would she and Ezra have … she shook away the thought.

She remembered seeing him once, tangled in a crowd of lean limbs and smooth curves. Even now, the memory sent an irrational jolt of fiery anger through her veins.

This time, however, Ezra wanted to go to the ball. With her.

Heavens, Ava had waited an entire century for this.

But how could she give herself to Ezra when Liam was out there fighting and suffering? How could she celebrate when the In-Betweens neared extinction and the Order crumbled?

In a pulse, her darkness and light connected with a sensation far away. Lines of star shine and smoke stretched into the night, unseen but felt by her heart.

Heavens, she must be truly exhausted.

"We need this, Ava," Ezra said, his blue eyes beckoning.

They'd been through so much. And she truly needed a

distraction, especially now that they had to sit and wait before corralling Sithrael.

She stepped closer and tucked a loose strand of silver hair behind his ear. *Like caressing the moon.*

How could she not give him this? If there was a chance she could make him feel better …

"I'll help you, of course," she finally said. "And I'll be honored to be your partner at the ball."

For Ezra, she would do anything.

But not everything, the voices inside her whispered.

"Great!" Ezra gave her a shy smile before looking at his own feet. "In other matters …" He went to his work desk, where a sword wrapped in rough cloth waited for them.

He handed it to her, and Ava gasped when she removed the material. It was Michael's sword. Silver, blue, and heavy in her hands.

Waves dashed across the strings of light and dark that connected her to something out there.

Help. It needed help.

An unsettling sensation spread inside her.

Was she losing her mind?

"I stole it from evidence," Ezra said. "Being a demon can't be easy. Maybe having the sword will help Liam remember the angel, and the Selfless, that he used to be."

Ava blinked, shocked at Ezra's unending kindness. "You did this for him?"

"Mostly for you." He shrugged. "You try to hide it, but I know you worry about him."

She set the sword aside on the table as tears stung her eyes. She stepped closer and cupped his cheeks. "You constantly awe me with your kindness. I don't have the words to thank you."

Oh, her dear Ezra. His light was magnificent. No, *he* was.

He kissed her forehead. "I never did it for your gratitude."

Desperation sucker-punched Ava in one brutal strike, a nearly physical force that jerked her away from Ezra. Screams broke through her throat as the sense she was falling within herself took over.

"Ava!" Ezra yelled. "What's wrong?"

The wrecking sensation waned only slightly. She gaped at the city outside, her breathing ringing in her eardrums as horrible bellows echoed in her mind, screams coming from the end of her strings.

The path to darkness. The path to light.

The path to him.

Ava took deep breaths, trying to regain her balance as her wings spread wide behind her.

Inhale. Exhale.

"I'm fine," she lied, making sure to hide her shivering despair as she went to the balcony. "There's somewhere I have to be."

With a mighty swish of her white wings, she boosted into the night.

20

LIAM

*H*auk and the Possessor led the way. Liam and some twenty demons from the Gorge occupied a chunk of the sidewalk as they followed their leader, a dreaded silence filling the space around them.

He studied the slim robed figure beside Hauk, which moved like a person in chains and yet seemed lighter than smoke. The creature's stride suited a living nightmare.

Archie once said that the darkness didn't shape someone; it only freed the worst in them. People could overcome it or give in.

Maybe the Possessor had done both.

Screams rang dimly in the back of Liam's mind, even now while he was awake. Firma's shrieks woke him almost every night as the smoky stench of charred flesh invaded his nostrils. She was always with him. But Liam wasn't a rookie, nor did he have a light stomach. He'd been trained to endure the grits of undercover work, and he would get over this.

Killing an Archangel to stop both a genocide and Master?

Small price to pay, really.

Perhaps being a Terror had started rubbing off on him.

Or maybe fooling himself was the only way he could keep functioning.

"You okay, kid?" Archie asked from beside him.

The chilly night air felt hollow. Everything did. "Yeah," he muttered, the weight of his monumental lie ramming onto his shoulders.

Hauk stopped and climbed on a fire hydrant. "Halt!"

The Possessor turned to him and then back to the demons, a soulless void underneath the hood. It was enforcing Hauk's order.

Their leader smiled at the thing before addressing the Gorge. "Today you closed more deals than ever. Soon we'll reach our quota, and angels across the globe will feel our wrath!"

Normally, the Gorge would've burst into applause after Hauk's speech because they either agreed with him or they were kissing his ass. But this time, the group remained silent.

Pedro raised his hand. "Boss, we can't take on the Order."

The Possessor took one step forward and the demons on the front row jumped back, almost slamming against those on the second row—Liam, Archie, and Pedro included.

The worst creatures in the city feared that thing.

"Massssster believes we can." The Posessor's voice was more snake hiss than human, more last breath than living force. Three yellow eyes with slit pupils shone from the darkness under the hood. "Do you believe Massssster isss wrong?"

Three. Fucking. Eyes.

Pedro gulped. "O-of course not."

The Possessor craned its neck and watched the members of the gang, clearly assessing each and every one. It probably read their minds, a skill most Possessors had.

Liam felt like he'd died. He remembered the sensation well, how time went still, how an eternity ran in a second.

But he had trained with Archie for this since the first day they had seen the creature. So he shoved all memories of the Legion to the back of his head, fueling his mind with hate for Ezraphael and for the Order that failed him. The Order that kept failing every single Selfless out there.

Small truths to hide the lie.

Archie's concentrated glare told Liam he did the same.

When the Possessor's three-eyed attention fell on them, the thing hissed, "When the time comesss, will the Fury Boysss sssmite their preciousss Order?"

"The Order can go fuck itself for all we care." He turned to the old man, who had his arms crossed, his spine straighter than a line. "Right, Archie?"

He gave the Possessor one assuring nod. "Let them burn."

Hells yes, Archie still had it in him.

The Possessor tilted its head left, its breathing a rasping wheezy sound. It lifted a bony finger, but before it could say something, a deep voice from the sky shouted Hauk's name.

An Archangel—his black bodysuit and wine red kilt were a dead ringer—landed near the Possessor. He kept his moss and white-tipped wings on display, a sign he was ready to fight.

"Sithrael." Hauk made a beckoning move with his hand, a silent request for the angel to join them.

He didn't.

"Talahel has a task for you," the Archangel said, disgust oozing from his tone.

The leader of the Gorge looked down at the Possessor with a mocking grin. The thing's three yellow eyes disappeared into the darkness of the hood. Its shoulders heaved with a shrill, cruel snicker.

"Pray tell, Archangel." Hauk wrapped both hands behind his back. "What does your master want me to do?"

185

"Find an angel and kill her. Make it pass for an In-Between attack."

Liam's blood chilled. Another angel would perish.

Ava!

The Possessor's attention snapped toward him, and Liam banished her from his mind. Just like that, she was gone.

At least for now.

The creature seemed content with that—a freaking miracle—and turned back to the Archangel.

Hauk bared his teeth at Sithrael. "We don't do the Order's dirty work anymore. The time for us to part ways has come."

"We had an agreement." The Archangel shook with anger. "If you break it, we will end your gang in a flash."

Hauk laughed loudly and slapped a hand on his leg. Some demons laughed too, even if they didn't seem to understand why they did it. The Gorge's leader wiggled his palms, mimicking fear. "Please don't smite us with your mighty light, oh holy one!"

Sithrael's face twisted into something ugly and perverse. "You find my threat amusing?"

Hauk's playful manner vanished. "Extremely so."

"Do as you're told," the Archangel growled low in his chest. "This is your last chance."

Hauk swooshed him away. "Go now, pigeon. You bore me."

The Archangel stood there, befuddled. "Talahel will not forgive this insult."

Hauk stepped down from the hydrant and approached him. The leader of the Gorge was shorter than Sithrael, but when he stopped in front of the Archangel, glaring up at him, Sithrael seemed smaller. "Be glad I feel merciful tonight. Now go take care of your own dirty work."

The angel swallowed, then observed the Gorge. Demons had begun to gather around, ready for battle.

There was no way he could beat all of them.

"You just started a war, demon."

"Oh, no." Hauk grinned. "I didn't start it. But I *will* win it."

Sithrael snorted with contempt before his wings flapped, lifting him off the ground. Liam watched him disappear into the night sky with a pang of despair.

He hoped Sithrael wouldn't find the angel he sought, and he hoped that angel wasn't Ava. It sucked that hoping was all Liam could do right now.

"What an entertaining evening." Hauk clapped his hands and addressed the Gorge. "Now, brothers and sisters, we celebrate!"

After watching the Possessor damn ten souls today, drinking felt like a good idea. Gods, it really did.

At least he, Archie, and Pedro had closed deals with lowlifes, wife-beaters, and thieves, people who had high chances of going to the dark anyway. Still, the memories of what happened would stick to Liam to the end of his days.

When they were done with the deals, the three of them gathered all the doomed in a group and called the Possessor with a burner phone. In a minute, the thing turned around the corner to meet them. How it had arrived so quickly remained a mystery—Liam suspected teleportation, but he couldn't be sure. The Possessor then cursed the souls, but two drug dealers ran away screaming before it finished.

The thing stopped them in their tracks with its telekinesis. The burner phone rang with another deal to be closed and the Possessor left, taking the two men with it. Their bodies floated stiffly in the air, following the creature. Their eyes screamed even if their tight lips couldn't.

The rest of the victims stared at each other in a mix of fear and confusion. Archie had clapped his hands and said, "Well, folks, you know what will happen if you talk about this." He pointed to the direction the Possessor had taken.

"We'll make sure your deals are done. In the meantime, enjoy your lives."

The little they still had left.

Yes, Liam definitely needed alcohol tonight.

They stopped before O'Malley's, a large pub near Fifteenth and Seventh.

The Possessor had disappeared, and as Liam searched for it, a hand landed on the back of his shoulders.

"It doesn't drink or feed the way we do," Hauk said, then nodded to the entrance.

A weight lifted from Liam's chest. He wouldn't need to hide his thoughts anymore, which was perfect considering he was about to get wasted.

All in all, O'Malley's wasn't a bad choice. The beer wasn't the best, but Liam didn't plan on having beer tonight. He would drown in fucking liquor until he forgot where and who he was.

The stench of sweat and pheromones invaded his nostrils as they crossed the dimly lit space. The pub was packed with men and women who flirted at the bar or gathered in groups in red-padded booths. A great deal ground against each other on a small dance floor.

The air inside was smoky and stuffy, and Hells, it was hot in here. Liam had already started breaking into a sweat.

The pheromones that filled the space slipped under Liam's skin, and Ava's face flashed in his mind followed by his old sword.

Michael's blade.

What in the Hells?

It didn't matter. Ava wasn't here; she wasn't his. She belonged to a good angel like the Messenger, not a cowardly demon. A good angel who better protect her from Sithrael or Gods help him, Liam would end Ezraphael with his bare hands.

We trained her well, his own voice whispered. *She'll be fine.*

Liam shook his head and followed Hauk to the bar. He needed a drink *now*.

Archie and Pedro chased after them. Liam vaguely heard Pedro ask Archie where Liam had learned Portuguese.

"His mother was Brazilian," the old man said. "I told him it would be nice if he learned the language. You know, as a way to honor his roots."

Liam had always found it a dumb-as-fuck idea. His birth parents never wanted him, so he paid the favor back. It was hard in the beginning, especially since his mother was a crack whore who overdosed when he was seven.

Archie always told him she didn't know better, but in the end, she had chosen death over her own son.

Liam's darkness felt Pedro pointing at his back. "I'm Brazilian, but I'm not *that* tall. Don't got green eyes, either. Where does that come from?"

Archie could say Liam's father was German. That's what was on the adoption papers: biological father Günther Striker. Liam never bothered to look him up, though. As he'd told himself several times throughout his life, his human parents didn't matter.

Instead of explaining this to Pedro, Archie just said, "Brazilians can be tall, too. Who knows, *seu puto?*"

Liam snickered. Yeah, he'd taught some bad words to the old man.

As they headed to the bar, he watched the Gorge stealthily spread through the vast space. Most had drinks already in their hands. Some watched the humans dancing, others engaged in conversation, while others like Phil and Lacey made out in front of everyone.

Liam couldn't help but compare those two with a demonic version of Bonnie and Clyde. They had closed deals with innocent teenagers, mostly victims of bullying, and then adults who fought depression. Good people who simply needed guidance but instead, damned their souls.

Liam fisted his hands. It wasn't fair, but then again, nothing was nowadays.

They finally reached the bar. Hauk bought them a round of tequila, which they quickly downed, and then the demon ordered two more rounds for the group.

They leaned back on the counter, observing the crowd. Pedro said he would get some fine piece of ass tonight, to which Archie snorted and asked, "Have you seen your own reflection, dumbass?"

"Idiots," Hauk chuckled before downing another drink.

Right then, that asshole didn't resemble the cruel maniac who wanted to burn the world. Just a normal guy having a drink with his buddies.

After the fourth round, a blissful buzz took over Liam. The mass of guilt and regret he carried over his shoulders felt lighter.

Oh, he could get used to this.

Beside Archie, a teenage girl with curly black hair and amber skin ordered a whisky sour. She pulled a fake ID from her pocket and handed it to the bartender.

The man didn't oppose, but Archie raised his brow. "May I see your ID, young lady?"

The girl frowned at him. "Why? You a cop?"

Hauk was at her side in a flash. He smiled down at her and leaned closer. "You don't need to show him your ID." He lifted one eyebrow at Archie. "Right?"

The old man swallowed, and Liam could swear he'd say something that would piss off Hauk. Instead, Archie managed one tight-lipped, "Yeah. It's fine."

It wasn't, of course.

Across from them, two women with too much make-up and overly short dresses talked to one another. They observed the space with cunning eyes, fake arousal beaming from them.

Prostitutes.

A Selfless was basically a cop, which meant Liam often ran into working girls. Human or not, they had a knack for getting into trouble. Every once in a while though, he handled cases where a dead hooker was found on the street —human, most of the time—with no one to mourn her. No one to care.

His thoughts went back to his mother, and he downed his tequila in one go.

Be that as it may, the call girls were a much better option for Hauk than the teenager who openly flirted with him.

Liam approached the one with brown hair tied in a high ponytail. "Evening, sweetheart."

She caressed his chest. "Evening, baby."

"How much for my friend up there?" He nodded to Hauk.

"I don't think I'm his type." She studied the demon and the girl. "Too old, you see."

"C'mon." He grabbed a Benjamin from his pocket and showed it to her. "Won't you at least try?"

"Fine." She took the money. "But you I would do for free."

He winked at her and then returned to the bar, settling between Pedro and Archie. He suspected the old man had put Pedro there strategically to add some distance between Hauk and himself.

The leader of the Gorge flirted non-stop with the teenager, who gladly accepted his advances. No wonder. Hauk was the cruelest son of a bitch Liam knew, but he looked like he belonged in a boy band.

"Master will be proud!" Pedro shouted before downing another drink.

"He will." Hauk eyed the girl up and down. "*Very* proud."

The girl leaned over the counter to order more drinks

and brushed the side of her hip slightly against Hauk. "You should focus on making *me* proud, babe."

Demons in all the Hells, that kid couldn't be more than seventeen.

What was she doing?

Liam glared at the working girl, who merely shrugged. She couldn't find an opening. The teenager was all over Hauk.

Shit.

"Fucking TV," Archie grumbled under his breath. "Kids are growing up way too fast these days."

This was also a jab at Liam because he'd lost his virginity when he was younger than that girl, and Archie had been far from pleased.

The teenager handed Hauk a drink, then flicked her curly hair over her shoulders. The demon bit his lip, arousal oozing from him.

An agonizing sting pierced Liam's lungs, followed by the sensation of falling into an unending void. He would never forget what his own death felt like, but he had no idea why that cruel dread came back to him now.

Hauk nodded discreetly to some demons around the bar who slowly, carefully, headed to the pub's entrance. They stood there, forming a living wall.

Hauk clinked his glass with the girl's and downed the liquor at once. He slammed the glass on the counter and watched the dance floor. "Want to have some fun, darling?"

"Oh, very much." The girl's words already came out slurred. "You're so hot."

He caressed the curve of her waist. "I know."

The prick of incoming death swirled and thrashed inside Liam, swallowing all of him into a black hole. His darkness pulsed with a warning. *Get out, get out, get out.* But all exits were blocked by second-tier demons who could kick Liam's ass.

"Archie," he muttered, but his partner held still with every muscle clenched. Only then did he notice how pale the old man had grown, even under the pub's dim lights.

"Kid. I'm so sorry for bringing you into this," he croaked.

Liam's throat tightened. He wished he could say something but fear stole all his breath.

A scream broke through the crowd, passing unregistered among the music and the noise. A moment later, a severed head rolled up to Hauk's foot and glared at Liam. The cut on the neck was drenched by the man's own blood. It had left a red path that led to the crowd ahead.

People still danced and talked, barely noticing what had happened. Liam's breathing rushed, and he bit down on his teeth so hard that a jolt of pain swam up his skull.

The call girl with the high ponytail gaped at Hauk and the head before screaming her lungs out.

The music stopped. The moving bodies halted.

People wondered what had happened, and someone even shouted, "Hey, put the music back on!"

The teenage girl stood beside Hauk, glaring at the head. Her lips quivered, but she couldn't form words.

"Time to feast!" Hauk ordered his demons before grabbing the teenage girl by her hair.

Her pleading screams didn't stop him. He bent her forward and lifted her skirt, and then his wings burst from behind him.

Some humans shrieked in horror, others lost their voices to fear.

The second-tiers from the Gorge also unveiled their wings, which meant that they were ready to fight or fuck.

Probably both.

When Liam was eleven, he watched a cow walk into a

piranha-infested river on the Discovery Channel. The water churned and turned red, but soon enough, the cow's bellows silenced as it went underwater.

This was eerily similar. The demons crashed down on all the humans, and the pub became a hellish sight of ripped limbs, flowing red, and horrid screams.

Archie kept his wings tucked inside his essence in a silent sign of rebellion, but Hauk didn't notice. The demon watched the scene with delight, though he still gripped the back of the teenage girl's neck, keeping her bent over before him.

Well, as long as he admired the Gorge's bloody work, he wasn't raping her.

People ran, trying to escape the trap, but there was no way out.

Shock kept Liam standing at the bar, watching in horror as innocents begged for their lives. He tried to ignore their pleas for mercy and the screeches that followed, but they slipped into his skin and settled in his bones.

He was a Selfless, or at least he used to be. His duty was to defend the weak. Kill the monsters, not help them. Yet now, innocent blood flowed on the floor, and he did nothing to stop it.

Liam's right hand hovered over the sword on his belt. His left hand patted the holy—*damned*—gun underneath his jacket. Screw this mission. He would go down killing as many demons as he could.

But then Firma's death would have been for nothing.

Be smart, Liam's own voice rang in his ears.

It had come from inside him, but he couldn't pinpoint where. Definitely not from the darkness, because it still pushed him to leave this place.

Get out, get out!

Ironic that this carnage was too much even for the worst version of himself.

"Help," a voice whispered.

Liam caught the teenage girl's wide eyes brimming with tears. It reminded him of a trapped deer.

She might be okay now that Hauk was distracted, but the demon's attention would return to her soon enough.

Liam nodded discretely. There had to be a way to get her out of this.

His attention fell on the call girl ahead, her back slammed against the wall as she watched the hellish scene around them. Her colleague had disappeared, but a huge smudge of blood painted the wall where she'd stood not a moment ago.

The woman caught Liam's stare and saw through him. She noticed the weeping teenager, and that's all it took. She understood.

The call girl took one deep breath before stepping forward. She swallowed back her tears and focused on Hauk. "Whatever you are, I can make you see stars, baby."

Hauk ignored her.

"Come on, let the kid go." Liam feigned a smirk. "We have enough to play with."

The demon raised a curious brow. "Is that so?"

Liam showed him the room filled by running and screaming humans. They didn't die quickly. Most demons tortured or hunted them, playing with their toys. Pedro himself chased a screaming woman with blood on her forehead.

"There's plenty of adults here to have fun with. Kids are so inexperienced." Liam glanced at the call girl and said, "I bet you can rock his world, right, sweetheart?"

Gods, the words hurt his throat because he was offering one innocent in exchange for another. But the woman understood. She had volunteered for this.

And it gutted him.

Her voice failed but when she focused on the teenage girl, she inhaled deeply. "This little thing doesn't know half the shit I do." She approached and stopped beside Hauk, drawing patterns with her fingers on his chest. "What do you say, baby?"

Hauk rolled his eyes at Liam. "I know what you're doing. Consider this your baptism into the dark. The true dark."

The talons of his wing pierced the woman's body from behind, impaling her like meat on a skewer. He raised her so high her feet dangled in the air. She tried to scream but could only gurgle blood.

"You will thank me later, Liam." Hauk threw her body against the wall.

Liam swallowed the cry that ripped him from inside. As he watched the woman's corpse fall to the floor like a broken doll, her eyes glassy and hollow, he begged for her forgiveness. Not that she would ever give it.

She was dead, and it was his fault.

Kill Hauk, the darkness hissed. *End him now.*

Be smart, his own voice demanded, burning with light. *We've sacrificed so much.*

Liam watched his own hands. He slayed monsters. He wasn't … he couldn't …

He turned to where Archie stood beside him, his rock, his only beam of light right now. The old man just stared ahead as if he wasn't really here.

This was how he coped: by shutting himself off from his surroundings. Liam wished he could do this, but he didn't know how.

He couldn't ignore what was happening.

Hauk caressed the teenage girl's hair. "Fine, Liam. I won't rape her."

He pulled her to him so that she had her back close to his

chest. The demon then took her trembling hand gently, intertwining her fingers with his own. In one quick move, Hauk snapped them all.

The sound of bone cracking went almost imperceptible against the screams in the pub. The girl howled and cried as she bent over in pain.

Hauk would torture her, and he was only beginning. Firma's wounded and swollen face flashed in Liam's mind.

Gods, please, no.

He couldn't go through that again.

The need to hurl built up in him. For the first time in a while, he prayed. *Holy Gods in the Heavens, I am your servant, so long as I exist in your infinite Glory. The Gods are with me, and I'm with the Gods.* The words came from his light, more recorded memory than Liam's own will. They helped him block everything happening around him.

Maybe, just maybe, he could reach that place where Archie had gone.

"I see the beauty of Master's work is too much for your partner," Hauk's voice cracked his focus. He was nodding to a catatonic Archie. "Yet you remain here with us, Liam. For someone who used to be an angel, that's remarkable."

His jaw felt tight, his tongue glued to the ceiling of his mouth.

"Yeah," was all Liam could say.

Someone's arm flew in the air, looping in spirals that dripped blood. Liam noticed a flower tattoo stamped on the bicep.

A laugh rumbled low in Hauk's chest. "Why do you think I'm Master's favorite?"

Liam bit back the remark, but it came out anyway. "Because you're a sick fuck?"

"Yes, I'm a sick fuck." Hauk grinned as he pulled the girl's back against his chest and cupped her breast.

She glared at Liam. "P-please," she cried. "Help me."

Hauk kept watching him, never breaking eye contact. "We're all sick fucks. So are you, Liam. You just don't know it yet."

Kill him now, the darkness roared.

In time, the light countered.

Hauk closed his hand around her throat, and the girl bawled louder, begging him to spare her.

"Will you behave?" the demon whispered in her ear. "I'll be good to you if you behave."

She stilled and didn't utter a single sound.

He nibbled at her earlobe. "Smart little bitch."

Holy Gods in the Heavens, why do you allow this?

But the Gods weren't the ones allowing it.

Liam was.

"Today, you watch," Hauk said through gritted teeth, his eyes feral. "But I'm not merciful, Liam. One day, you and your partner will be forced to act."

He would throw up right here while the girl cried without a sound. Her silence was louder than the symphony of bellows and screeches that rang around the pub.

Red smeared the walls, the floors, the bar, everything.

Liam took a recomposing breath and watched the space ahead. Most humans were dead. He tried to ignore their unblinking stares and the bloody pools on the floor.

Some demons raped the survivors, but the men and women barely screamed now. They had given up, blanked out. The mind could only handle so much, and this … well, this was the Hells.

The demons who were done murdering and raping raided the bar and drank themselves senseless. Liam stood there, frozen with shock and helplessness, his entire body shaking. Angry tears tried to push their way out, but he didn't shed them. He had to remain strong; this war depended on it.

He'd killed that Archangel. *Firma. Her name was Firma; remember that. Always remember that.* He killed her so they could win this war, and if he ended Hauk now, she would've died for nothing.

A choking sound came from beside him. Hauk was squeezing the girl's throat so hard that her tongue stuck out.

"You said you wouldn't hurt her if she was quiet!" Liam cried.

"And?"

It took all of his strength not to wield his sword and cut off Hauk's head.

Firma flashed in his mind, begging Liam for mercy. His flames engulfed her, leaving a charred corpse that pointed at him and said, *"You're one of them."*

No, she was wrong. Liam would prove it. One day, he would make Hauk pay. All these bastards would pay.

"I thought you were a man of your word," Liam spat.

The grin that cut across Hauk's face spoke of madness and cruelty. Still, the demon opened his hand and the girl took a deep breath, coughing and gasping as she desperately sucked in air.

"You thought wrong," Hauk said with amusement. "In fact …" He punched the girl in her ribs and she fell on the ground, crouching over her knees.

This was Liam's punishment for killing Firma; it had to be.

The Gods could be cruel.

Don't listen … Tendrils of light and darkness wrapped around his consciousness in an embrace that was both freezing and boiling.

Let us take you away, they whispered.

Sounds dimmed, and Liam's vision funneled until there was only darkness around him.

Coward. Liam's voice echoed in the void. *I'm a fucking coward.*

So many sacrifices, the words came from the right. He couldn't tell which voice was light and which was darkness.

Wars were never won with mercy, the same voice—*his*—replied from the left.

"I-I kill the monsters," he muttered.

We are the monsters, he countered.

Liam was blind, trapped in complete darkness, but he kept the teenager's face carved in his memory. She joined Firma and the call girl. He collected the innocents he'd failed, keeping them for the day he would settle the score with Hauk.

As for the rest of the pub ... there were too many for him to remember.

"Stay here!" Hauk growled in the distance and Liam blinked, returning to the Hells ahead. "I see your dark, Liam, and it's glorious! Stay and the rewards will be endless."

"This better make me a stronger demon, you asshole," he managed, every word a bitter taste in his tongue.

"It will." Hauk dropped to his knees and grabbed the crawling girl's hips. He dragged her closer to his crotch.

No, no, no!

"You promised you wouldn't!" Bile surged up Liam's throat as he realized how futile the argument was.

"As I've said." Hauk lowered her skirt and panties, then unbuckled his belt, lowering his black jeans to his knees. "I'm not a man of my word."

He spread her legs apart and shoved himself inside the girl.

"You did well today. Better than your partner." Hauk gritted his teeth as he thrust violently. "I won't forget that."

Maybe Liam was going crazy, but he could hear the girl's tears streaming down her cheeks, a soft sound similar to a thin river.

She didn't utter a word; she didn't breathe. She didn't fight or scream.

It was as if the girl was already dead.

This, he figured. This would be his doom.

21

LIAM

*L*iam didn't remember how he'd gotten here, crouched on the sidewalk under a bridge. Holes filled with rainwater peppered the cement on the street—he didn't know why he noticed that. "Fuck the police" was spray-painted on the underside of the concrete above.

Funny. He'd been part of the supernatural police once.

His breathing rushed, and his head spun.

Damning himself was the only way to gain Hauk's trust, and he'd done it. *A victory that tasted like defeat.* Liam already felt the Selfless inside him disappearing into oblivion.

He remembered the young girl's face, her unblinking eyes staring at the ceiling, her back on the bloodied floor as she waited for the Possessor to arrive.

Once Hauk was done with her, he gave her a choice: eternal life or the uncertainty of a normal death. The girl wrinkled her forehead. She didn't understand what he meant, but eternal life had its appeal, especially to a human who had been through the Hells.

She made the obvious choice.

Liam had to leave the pub before the Possessor arrived.

He couldn't keep a contained façade anymore. That thing would see right through him the moment it stepped into the place.

Archie didn't move to follow, even though he was back from his mental shell—or whatever the Hells he called it.

If Liam knew the old man well, he was beating himself up for bringing him to the Gorge.

Well, he shouldn't. Liam was Archie's son, yes, but he was also his partner. This had been *his* choice, even if he regretted it.

He'd hurried to the exit but slipped on the slimy floor, painting himself red. When he tried to get up, he slipped again before gaining some footing—thanks to Archie, who rushed to help him.

Liam left the Gorge behind as fast as he could, but he still heard Archie calling his name and demons laughing their asses off.

"You've been baptized by blood, brother!" Hauk shouted.

Delusional prick!

Now Liam watched his red and shaking palms. Blood was sticky on his clothes, on his hair, on his cheeks, in his damn soul. The teenage girl, the hooker, Firma, their faces flashed in his mind nonstop, bathed by red, always red, red everywhere.

A scream broke from his lips. He rocked back and forward as soul-purging bellows cut through his throat.

He failed them. He failed everyone he wanted to protect.

At some point, Liam wondered if the walls of his throat had turned into raw flesh. It didn't matter. If he kept screaming, maybe all the pain and guilt would leave with his voice.

Michael, the Archangel Liam used to be, had killed humans once. His darkness had taken the best of him and it took the best of Liam too, except for tonight.

Tonight, it urged him out of that pub.

He bent over and threw up, bile burning his already grazed throat. His head thumped and his chest hurt.

Liam's darkness was the same that had consumed Michael once, and yet it hadn't encouraged him to join the carnage back at the pub.

It'd wanted to take him away.

Liam's voice, *Michael's* voice, echoed in his ears. *We chose to become a demon for a reason.*

"Why?" he cried, his voice echoing around him.

No reply.

He slammed both hands on his temples and sobbed.

A swoosh of wings, a brush of wind, and then came her voice, etched with worry. "Liam?"

He kept his eyes shut because Ava couldn't be here. She wasn't real. Hells, he'd lost himself and now he'd lost his mind, too.

He felt her kneeling before him. "You're covered in blood!"

No shit, princess.

He opened his eyes. His Guardian watched him with a mix of joy and sorrow—well, she was a Dominion now. Ava wore the same white bodysuit, but the white Guardian's kilt had been replaced by a light-gray one. Her snowy wings were coiled behind her.

Gods, it was painful to see her this way, an ascended angel when Liam was nothing but a monster. It hurt knowing she was so close and so far from him.

He must be a sight for sore eyes, all clad in blood. He tried to speak, but he shivered so hard that forming words or even coherent thoughts was too much.

"What happened?" Ava asked, a strain in her tone.

He forced the words out, but they got stuck on his tongue.

"Liam …" She sniffed back tears as she assessed him from

top to bottom. "I should've stayed, I should have—" her voice cracked.

"I killed," he managed, his jaw hurting as he tried to speak. "I was supposed to protect them. Instead I just watched."

"Who?"

He couldn't tell her. What would Ava think of him if she knew?

"How did you find me?" he asked, his head feeling awfully light.

Fuck, he was about to pass out.

"I felt your distress." She frowned, almost as if she didn't believe it either. "Lilith said we have a connection and that if I focused on you ... I don't know how to explain it. All I know is I'm here." She leaned closer to touch his face, but he jerked away.

"You'll get blood on you," he muttered, focusing on the cracked sidewalk.

"I don't care." She gently pressed her palm to his cheek. "How are you feeling?"

Jophiel said Liam's darkness and light reacted strangely to Ava's. Right now, however, he felt fine. If anything, his light shone shyly underneath the swarm of hurt and regret thundering inside him. It brushed with Ava's own. His darkness, too.

The forces inside him had once clashed with hers, snarling at each other the way only mad beasts do. Now they tried to connect with Ava's, but for some reason, they couldn't. A pang of frustration swam across him.

Odd.

So Ava was really here; she wasn't a figment of his imagination. She had come for him.

Liam would thank her if his ability to speak hadn't abandoned him again. He glared at his bloodied hands and let out a pitiful sob, the indignity of it not going amiss.

Their faces. Their faces were everywhere.

Air stopped midway in his lungs. Liam wheezed, grasping for oxygen, but he was drowning in his own torment.

Ava jumped to her feet. "Hold on!"

Blissful oblivion swallowed his consciousness from the edges. He'd black out any minute now. And still, their faces would be there, always with him.

Gentle arms wrapped around his shoulders from behind, and then the ground disappeared from underneath him. His feet dangled in the air as the city grew smaller below.

Liam watched the tops of buildings and the streets that had become thin lines. Looking down didn't ease the drop in his stomach, so he turned to Ava. Her fiercely blue irises searched for something.

Only now did he realize how different she looked. Her face seemed harsher, thinner. She resembled more a warrior than the meek Guardian he had met the day Archie died.

Back then, princess had insisted on ignoring this wild, untamed side of her, even though it had always been there, quiet and asleep. But Liam had seen the Valkyrie; he'd found her before Ava did. And it was that Valkyrie who now carried him through the sky.

A sting of longing and sadness pierced his chest.

Was his Guardian gone?

Ava smiled down at him, a hint of the kind angel still there. "Curl into a ball."

The sadness in his chest faded and he smiled back at her. "What?"

She let go of him.

Before he had time to scream, Liam cannonballed into a pool on a building's roof.

He opened his eyes underwater, watching puffy clouds of blood expand around him.

Blood. Surrounded in blood. Forever covered in blood.

When he emerged, most of it had cleared from his skin. He watched faint red rivulets trickle down his palms until there was no red anymore.

"I watched," he muttered to himself, shivers taking hold of his body. Maybe it was the cold water, maybe it was shock; he couldn't tell which.

A body plunged into the pool and when the splash subdued, Ava stood before him.

Her wings made a cocoon around them as she approached. The water reflected on her white feathers, wrapping them both in a shelter walled by dancing blue and white lights.

Only now did he notice Ava's strawberry-blond hair was tied in a braid that cascaded down the right side of her chest. Her wide grin breathed life back into him, her blue eyes nearly matching the color of the pool.

Gods, she was a vision.

"Better?" she asked.

He glared at his shaking hands, then showed them to her. "They're filled with blood."

"Look again." Ava gently grabbed them and presented Liam his clean palms. "Something is eating you from inside, but you must remember you did the best you could. You always do."

How could she say that? Ava never would've watched that girl suffer. She wouldn't have killed Firma, either. His Guardian … she would die for those weaker than her.

Ava was so much better than Liam that his chest hurt.

"I know you're doing undercover work," she continued, "but maybe you should take a step back. We could go somewhere." Her voice failed, and her eyes glistened. "Gods, I'm so sorry for leaving you."

He registered her words slowly, his brain whirring with the effort, trying to overcome shock and despair.

"We both chose duty over our feelings for each other," he finally said. "We can't run away now."

"Liam, please—"

"No. I'm …" He shook his head and took a deep breath. "I can do this. I have to do this. I've given up too much already. So many people …" His focus lingered on her blonde hair, then her rosy lips. He'd lost everything for the greater good, including her. "I have to see this through, Ava."

If he didn't take care of Master, the entire Order would eventually fall and with it the woman he loved.

The Hells he would add Ava's name to the list of people he failed to save.

For her, everything.

"An Archangel named Sithrael tried to put a bounty on another angel," he said quietly. "He asked the demons I'm working with to help, but they refused."

"He's after Vera." Ava gritted her teeth, the Valkyrie taking over. "That coward!"

Liam exhaled a relieved breath. Ava wasn't the one in danger. "You need to be careful, princess."

She stepped closer and cupped his cheeks, tears in her eyes. "I will. You were a great teacher."

Screw it.

Liam leaned forward and kissed her. He probably shouldn't have; they both had work to do, and she was mated to the Messenger. But he didn't care. The storm of guilt and sorrow inside him ceased as he wrapped his arms around her waist and pulled her closer.

Ava kissed him back, her mouth opening to him and her fingers digging onto the back of his neck, tangling with his hair. She still tasted like strawberries and honey; she still smelled like lavender.

With her, he forgot all the Hells he'd gone through.

An eternity passed between them, and it still wasn't enough. Their tongues wrapped in a dance that made Liam forget everything outside their cocoon of feathers. But when he remembered Ava was the best angel he knew and that he had *watched*, he broke their embrace and stepped away.

She belonged with the Messenger, not with a murderous coward. Besides, he had to see this mission through. The people he had carved in his mind didn't need his happiness.

They needed his wrath.

"I have to go," he muttered.

Ava's wings disappeared in a flash of light. "Please don't."

He climbed out of the swimming pool. He had to leave. It was the best for her. For them both.

Ahead was a glass wall that surrounded a fancy loft. He punched the glass, and it cracked into a million pieces— thanks to his supernatural strength. His knuckles bled, but Archie could fix them.

At least this time, it was his own blood on his hands.

Liam crossed the white carpeted living room, leaving a trace of water and red droplets behind. Thank the Gods the place was empty.

He stopped before the wooden door and shot his flames. Demonic heat worked fast, and it charred the door in the blink of an eye. When he kicked the surface, it snapped in half like a twig, raising a small cloud of ashes in the air.

An alarm began to wail, and he cursed under his breath. Liam would have to use the stairs. Emergency exits were usually poorly surveilled, and he had no time for human police bullshit if they caught him breaking in—well, out.

He could've asked Ava to fly him out of here, but his pride was greater than his common sense.

Liam cast one last glance behind to see her standing in the living room. His Guardian was soaking wet. Tears mingled with the water that dripped from her chin.

Peeling his eyes off her was impossible. Her body trembled, and all he wanted to do was hug her and never let go.

"I love you," she muttered.

It knocked all the air out of him.

Ava needed to get away from this mess, to find happiness. And he could never give it to her; he wasn't worthy enough.

This was it. Their last call.

"You love him, too," he said without an inch of bitterness.

Just a simple truth.

Her perfect features crumpled in a silent sob.

Liam forced himself to turn away. He had to be strong now. He didn't look back, even if it ripped him apart.

As he stepped out of the loft, he knew he'd lost his princess.

This time for good.

22

LIAM

*H*e, Archie, and Pedro spent their evenings making deals with humans. Liam had closed so many that he quickly became an expert, even if he was still a lower demon.

His performance pleased Hauk, as he hoped it would. Ever since the pub's carnage, the demon had taken him under his wing. The fact that Liam had the highest number of deals in the Gorge helped. A lot.

Once he had access to Master, he would kill him and Hauk or die trying. It was the least he could do after losing his soul and his heart for this mission.

Every day he fell deeper; every minute he went darker. This was his burden, and his burden alone.

Yesterday, Hauk followed them to one of their assignments because he "wanted to see Liam in action." So off they went, Liam spearheading five of the ten deals he, Archie, and Pedro closed that night.

He'd paid a high price to be here, so close to the end game, and there was no turning back. No redemption for him, either.

Once they were done, they'd gathered the humans in a group and called the Possessor. Everything was going well until one guy regretted his decision and screamed.

Archie quickly punched him senseless, but a night guard had heard him.

"Halt!" the chubby man ordered, pointing his gun at them.

Powdery sugar peppered the sides of his black mustache. He'd probably eaten a doughnut not long ago—the guy was a walking cliché. Liam recognized the type: retired cop who needed to make ends meet.

Hauk snickered and stepped forward.

"I'll shoot!" the guard warned, but the demon didn't stop.

He fired into the ceiling. Hauk kept stomping toward him.

The first blast hit the demon in the chest. Two others hit his forehead, and the last, his thigh. The crumpled bullets dropped to the ground, losing their battle with Hauk's thick skin.

Befuddled, the guard glared at his Glock.

"It's not broken," Hauk explained. "You can't kill me, human." He craned his neck left and eyed the guard up and down. "I wonder what games we could play … How about hanging you with your entrails? That sounds like fun!"

Hauk enjoyed torturing people before damning their souls—it added taste to the process, he'd once said.

Liam nodded to the night guard, who still glared at Hauk's unscathed body. "He's too flabby and weak. Master's soldiers need to be stronger."

He unsheathed his sword from his belt and in a blur of movement, slashed the man's jugular.

A quick death.

Blood sprayed onto Liam as the guard fell limp on the floor, sticky red pooling beneath his light-blue shirt. It stained a picture that had fallen from his pocket: a smiling woman and a kid.

Hauk had laughed and clapped. "You cost me a soul, but I can certainly appreciate bloodlust, brother." He tapped Liam's shoulder. "Just try to contain it next time. I might be your leader, but I too deserve some fun every now and then."

"Yes, boss."

He then ogled Archie from behind his shoulder, annoyance clear in his bleak eyes. "You trained him well, Archibald. I wonder if the student has become the master."

The old man balled his fists. "I'm certainly proud of him, boss."

Later that night, Liam showered. The water purged him from the guard's blood, at least on the surface. He told himself over and over that at least the man's soul was saved, but it wasn't enough.

It would never be enough.

His suffering paid off, though. Hauk had begun to trust him blindly. One day over drinks, he told Liam he kept a hundred pounds of untampered wolfsugar stored in a warehouse not far from sector thirteen.

"Why keep pure wolfsugar?" Liam asked. "Best to get rid of it."

"It's bait for desperate werewolves." Hauk tapped his temple knowingly. "They might not be the focus of Master's plan anymore, but having fewer of them on the streets can't hurt."

His plan became clear to Liam. "Full moon's coming."

"And the dogs are growing reckless. Rogue wolfmen already died by the hands of my guards, but without wolfsugar, they won't survive the Order's wrath." He shrugged easily, as if he wasn't speaking about genocide.

Those wolfmen had come to assess the perimeter. Bad thing is, they never reported back. By running from this war,

Suther might have protected most of his packs—Jal said the number of werewolves tripled those of remaining vamps. But he wouldn't be able to keep them safe for much longer.

The wolf lord's strategy, if one could call it that, would bite him in his tail very soon. Come full moon, the wolves would perish.

Who would be next?

Liam ached to slam his dagger into Hauk's neck, sever his head, and end all of it.

One time, he caught himself stalking toward the Gorge's leader, who chatted with Juniper, the demon's fuck buddy.

Liam's heart beat in his ears, and sweat bloomed on his forehead. He would end that bastard. He was so close … But Master had begun all this. Hauk was just a pawn.

Liam remembered the young girl who'd been raped, and the woman who had tried to save her only to be impaled alive.

One day, he promised them. One day, he would bring them justice.

So Liam went on, never questioning Hauk's orders and always delivering on his assignments.

Naturally, keeping this charade took a toll on him, but it took so much more from Archie.

The old man had lost a lot of weight since the pub; his cheeks were sunken in, the bags under his eyes puffy and dark. Liam often caught him staring into empty space; half of him here, the other somewhere else.

He and his father had crossed lines that would destroy them both; there was no question about that. But Archie perished a lot faster.

When Liam took him outside the warehouse and voiced his concern, the old man trapped him in a tight hug. "You've become so strong, son." He stepped back and watched Liam with glistening eyes. "I'm so proud."

A knot clogged Liam's throat. "I can't do this without you, Archie. Hauk is watching. You have to snap out of it."

"I know." Archie ran a hand over his sand-blond hair and blew out an exasperated sigh. "I'll fix it, okay?"

Could he, though? Hauk had removed the old man from the gang rotation—Master encouraged a good relationship between demonic factions which meant he was smart, whoever he was. Demonic gangs never got along, but Master wanted a unified army and he was getting one.

If Hauk had taken Archie from the rotation, it meant he didn't trust the old man. United or not, the last thing Hauk needed was to show weakness to other factions.

Even if Liam hated to admit it, Archie was way too fragile right now, both physically and mentally. If he'd been in Hauk's place, he would've done the same.

"Hey, Liam!" Pedro called out from the second floor of the warehouse, leaning over a glassless window. "Boss wants to see you."

He glanced at Archie with worry, but the old man nodded. "Go. I'll be fine."

Hauk wasn't known for his patience, so Liam hurried inside and up the cement stairs, then knocked on the steel door.

"Come in," the demon ordered.

Hauk sat at a decaying wooden table as he signed some papers. *Contracts?* Liam tried to read what they said, but he couldn't distinguish the words.

"Curiosity killed the ca-at," Hauk said with a chipper tune, his attention still on the papers.

"Sorry." Liam cleared his throat. "What can I do for you?"

Hauk set down his pen. "Once we reach eight hundred souls, Master will meet with me. I want to take you and Pedro along."

Liam's breathing stopped. According to the Gorge's

ledger, they'd gotten over five hundred souls. Eight hundred was approaching fast.

He could only imagine what the other demonic factions scattered around town had made. Sure, the Gorge was the biggest of them, but Black Dagger ached to please Master. The day he worked there, Liam reckoned they'd gathered at least forty souls in one night.

And now, it had all paid off. Soon, he would meet Master and make him pay. Hauk, too.

"It will be my honor." He bowed slightly, then thought twice about it and figured he should try anyway. "Can we bring Archie along? He would be stoked to—"

"No. Your partner is weak."

"He brought me to you, didn't he?" Liam said. "Archie always has my back. Which means he has the Gorge's back, too."

The demon observed him through narrowed eyes. "Then he goes soul reaping tonight with Phil and Lacey. If he doesn't get me over twenty souls, I'll make you kill him." Liam opened his mouth to argue, but Hauk raised his hand. "You think I don't know you and Pedro are the ones making the deals? That he's just watching?"

Freaking Pedro and his big mouth.

"Tonight Archibald proves himself." Hauk bared his teeth at him. "He proves himself, or he dies."

There was no use in trying to dissuade this asshole.

"He won't let you down," Liam countered without hesitation.

"We'll see." His mobile rang, and he picked it up. "She's ready? Good. I'm on my way."

The demon shoved the device in his jeans' pocket, then raised his index finger. "One chance. That's all he gets."

LATER THAT AFTERNOON, he and Archie met with Jophiel in a back alley in sector three, far from the Gorge's dominance zone.

The Seraph looked fine, if not older than Liam remembered. He wore a dark blue T-shirt with yellow lightning between the letters AC and DC. Say what you will, but Jophiel had great taste in music.

The Seraph gave him a weak smile, then handed him a sword covered in gray rags.

Liam untied the cloth, and his eyes widened when it revealed Michael's sword. His sword. "You found it."

"Ezraphael did," Jophiel corrected. "According to Ava, he hoped it would help you remember who you used to be. And who you are."

He frowned. "The Messenger thought of me?"

"He's good at worrying about others." Jophiel shrugged in a manner that was both wise and carefree. "If circumstances had been different, you might've been good friends."

Liam raised one eyebrow and snorted.

Still, he was happy to have his weapon back. He unsheathed the other sword from his belt and threw it aside. The sheath was the same he'd used back at the Nine-five, so Michael's sword fit perfectly.

He patted the weapon with care. Even if the blade was darker than he remembered, Liam took it without complaint.

"Jal threw a damned coating on it," Jophiel explained. "Should be enough to fool your fellow demons."

Smart.

"Jophiel," Archie said. "We need to do something about the deals the Gorge is closing. They're damning so many souls … either they will send them all to the Hells, or they'll turn them into demons at some point."

"I know, but—"

Archie grabbed him by his shirt and pushed him into a

brick wall. The surface cracked, and a thin cloud of dust puffed around Jophiel. The Seraph glared at him with a mix of surprise and hurt.

"We've given up everything!" Archie bit his teeth and pointed at Liam. "What he had to do! What he witnessed!" His voice failed, and he sniffed back tears. "I brought my son into something far worse than I could imagine. Do you understand that?"

Liam set a hand on the old man's shoulder. "Archie, I'm fine."

He wasn't, of course. The carnage, the cursed souls, the innocents he'd killed, they all haunted him every night. But he had to see this mission through.

So did Archie.

"He's my boy." Tears tracked down the old man's cheeks as he finally let go of the Seraph. He quickly wiped them with the back of his hand. "We gave up everything for your Legion. You failed us, Jophiel."

He'd gone too far. The way Archie glared at his own boots was evidence he knew this too.

Jophiel blinked as pain flashed behind his eyes. "If demons can't do what humans require in exchange for their souls, the deals are automatically voided and the soul is saved. The Gray are trying to get in their way. And they are dying." Archie opened his mouth, either to apologize or to argue, but Jophiel continued. "Lilith's vampires are fighting as many Archangels, Selfless, and demons as they can. They are dying, too. And come full moon, Suther's werewolves will also perish. So you see, my friend," he let out a weary scoff, "you're not the only one I'm failing right now."

The responsibility the Seraph carried on his shoulders was monumental.

Archie sniffed and crossed his arms. "I'm sorry. It's been harder than I'd expected."

"I know." He stepped closer to the old man so they were eye to eye. "You've been strong, but even the strongest of men is allowed to collapse every now and then." He glanced at the brick walls that surrounded them and let out a deep sigh. "It might seem like we're losing the battle on all fronts, but it's not over yet. I still have a few cards up my sleeve. I'm simply trying to find a better way."

Archie stared at the Seraph and gulped. "I don't want you to use those cards. And I'm truly sorry, Jo. I know you're doing your best."

What were they talking about? What cards?

"I do have a plan," the Seraph said.

"You do?"

Jophiel nodded. "Jal's informants said demons are keeping a secret storage of untampered wolfsugar. Does that match the information you have?"

Archie frowned in confusion, but Liam said, "I know where it is. Hauk told me."

"Good." The Seraph turned to the old man. "You must shapeshift into a werewolf tonight, Archibald. This way, you'll be able to maintain your cover in the Gorge. You will then steal the wolfsugar and bring it to Jal at eight. This is our last chance to get werewolves back in the Legion. Only with their help can we move forward in this war."

Exhilaration and resolve shone in Archie's eyes. For the first time in a while, he resembled Liam's fierce hero again; the leader of the Fury Boys. A fucking force of nature.

There was only one tiny problem.

"Archie can't do it," Liam said quietly. "He needs to prove himself to Hauk tonight or that asshole will make me kill him."

"I can come up with an excuse," the old man argued, unfazed by the revelation.

"No, you can't." He stared at his father in a way that said this was not a discussion. "Trust me."

Jophiel's bushy eyebrows knitted. "But it's imperative that we—"

Liam stepped forward and raised his hand. Bones cracked as nails and hair grew until his upper arm had morphed into a werewolf's claw with silky black fur.

Jophiel placed both palms on his waist and shook his head. "You might've been training shapeshifting with Archibald, but you're not a Beast in essence. You're a Terror, Liam. Your specialty is fire and speed. Using a power that isn't yours will take a toll on you."

"I know, but we don't have another choice." He tried to hide his annoyance but failed miserably. What part of his father's life being on the line didn't Jophiel get?

"You've never shapeshifted your entire body," Archie said. "You'll need to keep the cover and fight the guards. I can't let you do this, kid."

"Hey, I'm not a child anymore." With his human hand, he grabbed the back of Archie's neck and pressed his forehead against his father's. "Just focus on getting those twenty souls, all right?"

"I don't like this."

"Me, neither. But it is what it is."

"Oh, son. You better know what you're doing ..." His tone was coated by tears.

"Old man," Liam chortled. "I never do."

23

AVA

*T*he night was dark and rainy, as nights like this should be.

Drops pattered on Ava's hair, her bodysuit, all of her, but she didn't care. Freezing claws of sorrow ripped through her as she watched the scene.

Kevin talked to the human police a few steps ahead. He showed them a fake badge of authority—she guessed Homeland Security, CIA, or the FBI. Humans were fond of acronyms.

His team of Selfless had begun taking over the crime scene, but the detective in charge refused to let them continue.

"The wings were attached to her bones," the detective argued, pointing to the body at Ava's feet. "Don't tell me it's a simple Halloween costume."

The detective couldn't see Ava, and even if he could, all he'd find would be a woman wearing a white bodysuit—her wings were safely tucked into her light.

He had seen Vera's body, though. So had the eight cops surrounding the area.

Beheading might be the easiest way to kill an immortal creature but there were others, such as burning one to ashes or slamming a cursed dagger through their forehead.

Vera's killer had picked the latter.

They would pay for this.

Three officers made the sign of the cross as they watched the body, but most simply shook their heads and claimed it was all a hoax. Kevin had to keep them close until the Virtues, who would erase their memories, arrived.

"They're implants," he argued, turning to where Ava stood. He gave her a grim nod. "The victim had the wings surgically attached."

"That's impossible." The detective shook his head. "That technology doesn't exist."

"It does, and its knowledge needs to stay here, inspector." Kevin removed his badge and showcased it again in a silent warning.

Ava felt the detective's anger flowing in waves, but eventually, he nodded his understanding.

She kneeled on the ground and looked at the blade shoved in Vera's forehead, the clotting blood around the wound, and her unblinking stare at the stormy sky.

Her brown hair, usually fixed in a high bun, now splayed on the floor underneath her head.

Ava's back heaved with a sob. She and Ezra had searched for Vera relentlessly, keeping close tabs on Sithrael day in and out.

In the end, it wasn't enough.

But how had he gotten to her? He hadn't left the Order in days ...

Air swooshed from above, and in one harsh landing that splashed water everywhere, Ezra appeared before Ava.

The moon fallen from the sky.

His majestic wings disappeared as he knelt opposite to

her. He brushed Vera's cheek with the back of his hand and winced with a cry.

"I'm so sorry," he muttered as he took Vera's limp hand. His shoulders shook, and he gulped back tears. "I failed you, esteemed mentor."

"Ezra, I'm—"

He took a device from his belt and showed it to Ava. It was a tiny black pebble that could pass for a black-pearl earring.

The tracker.

"I found it hidden inside a vase back at the Order." His eyes were red, and his body trembled with agony; its sour tang coursed through Ava's essence.

They had followed Sithrael everywhere, but for days all he'd done was walk around the Order. First to meeting rooms, then his chambers.

Well, his tracker had.

"He fooled us," she growled through gritted teeth.

It took her a couple of deep breaths to control the blazing anger that flushed through her veins. She could almost hear Vera saying, "Control that mighty fury of yours, dear."

For you, old owl. Only for you.

Sithrael knew they were tracking him, and he'd played them to his advantage.

"Revenge is not the way of the Gods," Ezra whispered to himself. "I'm not like Talahel, Vera, but it's so hard ... I need you." His tears mingled with the rain. "Give me strength, my mentor," he muttered as he stood up. He watched the old owl one last time. "And forgive me."

He tossed the tracking device in a puddle, and his wings flashed behind him. Before Ava could say a word, he boosted into the night sky, leaving her alone with Vera.

That witty spark was gone from the old owl's bleak,

staring eyes, her soul vanished into oblivion. A thousand blades couldn't hurt more than this.

Vera's voice rang in her mind again. "The Gods aren't known for being fair."

Ava observed the sky and closed her eyes. Rain washed over her, sealing the fury into every cell of her body, every crevice of her existence, until it became a part of who she was.

In her mind, the rain became Sithrael's warm, sticky blood.

"I'll make him pay," she promised the dark sky.

Ava tossed and turned in bed. She must've gotten fifteen minutes of sleep by the time her phone rang.

Outside, dawn painted the horizon in soft blue and orange hues. She watched it for a moment before picking up the device.

"Ava." It was Kevin. "Can you meet me at the morgue in my precinct? It's about Vera."

It shouldn't take her long to fly there. "Yes, of course. I'll be there in five."

She hung up and got into her bodysuit. Maybe she should tell Ezra, but when Ava remembered the pain that had pierced through him, she decided against it.

He needed rest, and if she could spare him from seeing his mentor's body again, she would.

Even if he might hate her for it.

The morgue was a small room walled with lime-colored tiles. A metal autopsy table stood in the middle of the perfectly sterilized space, and atop it lay Vera's body. A white sheet covered her up until the lines of her hair. Brown curls hung from her scalp like an unmoving curtain.

Ava looked away and cleared her throat.

"What did you find?" she asked Kevin, who was accompanied by the coroner—another Selfless.

Kevin eyed Ava, then shot her a sympathetic smile. "Gotten any sleep, dove?"

"Plenty," she jeered, rubbing a hand on her forehead. "What do you have for me?"

The coroner and Kevin exchanged a worried glance. "The case will be passed on to Virtue Suphiel tomorrow at six p.m. Once it's out, Talahel could easily gain access to Vera's body, understand?"

Ava nodded, even though she didn't know why Kevin was telling her this.

He motioned to the coroner, who gently grabbed Vera's wrist and raised it. He beckoned Ava to come closer as he showed her the back of the old owl's lower arm.

Vera had cut a number on her skin. The wounds were half-healed, but the sequence was clear: *3181805.*

"She cut herself with a cursed blade to slow down her healing," Kevin explained. "We think she did this less than twenty-four hours ago."

The coroner laid down Vera's arm with the tenderness of a glass worker. Ava silently thanked him for it. Whoever he was, he seemed to be a kind soul and worthy of Kevin's trust.

"We have no clue what it means." Kevin blew a sigh and ran a hand through his orange hair. "Does this number ring any bells with you?"

"No." She frowned. No matter how hard she tried, there was no sparing the Messenger from this. "But it might mean something to Ezra."

24

AVA

*A*top a skyscraper's roof, Ava watched the city beyond the line of water. Wind slammed against her body, whipping her hair and feathers. It felt strangely freeing.

"Make sure your shield is up," Ezra said as he climbed on the ledge and stepped beside her. "A fall from this height—"

Her body tensed with annoyance. "I'm aware."

Ezra was an overly cautious man by nature, but ever since they lost Vera he'd gone overboard. Ava could almost taste the smoky tang of his worry, always there, never waning.

She understood him, though. Vera's death had been a harsh blow, and he would need time to recover. So she swallowed her irritation. It was the least she owed him.

"I can fly safely now. I'll be fine."

Ezra nodded, but his worry kept pressing on him.

In a flash of light, his magnificent wings spread wide, sharp feathers of silver and gold. He pointed to the city beyond the line of water. "Vera had a storage room where she kept things that were important to her. The number she carved on her arm ..." His jaw tensed, and his voice failed. "The number might be the password to open it."

"How do you know?"

"*3181805*. March 18th 1805. The day I was reborn as an angel," he said quietly, his tone a dry and mournful sound. "The day I met Vera."

Vera loved Ezra like a son, and she had chosen the day they met to keep all that was important to her. A dull ache spread in Ava's chest.

"She brought her killer to sector four on purpose, you know," he said quietly, his eyes watering. "She knew it was an area assigned to a Selfless precinct. She made sure we would get the message before Talahel."

Ava let that sink in, and the sting in her chest increased. Vera knew she would die.

"Revenge might not be the way of the Gods …" Ezra's throat bobbed, and he took a shaky breath. "But you're not alone in wanting retribution."

The Messenger was good and kind, but hatred had nearly destroyed him once. Ava wouldn't let it happen again. Let it taint her, not him.

I'll protect him, old owl.

The rising sun graced Ezra with a soft orange glow, and from this angle it seemed his silver hair was catching fire.

Ava gripped his shoulder. "I'll make sure she didn't die in vain."

With that, she leapt off the roof and boosted into the blue. Once the buildings became small towers below, Ava zinged toward the horizon.

Ezra soon caught up. An aura of pride emanated from him as they flew side by side. His hair was trapped in a high bun, but wind freed thin strands that whirled around his temples.

Heavens, he was too handsome. The loving smile he shot her brought Ava peace and calm.

A realization came to mind all of its own. *She could be happy with him.*

She shook her head and dismissed the thought as fast as it had come. Now was not the time to think about this.

They landed in front of a building with black mildew blotches tainting its blue façade. A bulky iron gate blocked the premises behind them. Ava couldn't explain why seeing the locked gates felt like a dark omen—thank Heavens she didn't believe in such nonsense.

They entered the building, soon crossing empty corridors lined by cold LED lights. Roll-up garage doors bordered their path left and right.

"Which one?" she asked.

Ezra didn't reply; he simply kept checking each door as they passed.

Eventually, he stopped. Before them was a dark-gray door that thrummed against Ava's essence. The metal must've been blessed. Any angel could've done this, but the energy coursing through the door felt different.

It had her taste, her smell. A small piece of Vera left behind.

"This is it," Ezra muttered.

He typed the password on the keypad beside the door and it automatically rolled up, revealing a small cemented room. It was empty save for a square wooden box resting in the back left corner.

They knelt beside it and opened the top. *Case files.* At least eighty of them.

After half an hour scanning through the papers, they found nothing that incriminated Talahel.

Ezra fumbled desperately with the documents. "What was she trying to show us?"

"I have no clue." Ava frowned at the report in her hand. "A

form for demonic activity engagement. Talahel signed it so that Sithrael could contact demons."

She showed it to him.

"That's not forbidden." Ezra shrugged as he read the paper. "Selfless and Archangels have to use demons as confidential informants sometimes. Talahel could easily spin this to his favor." He narrowed his eyes and grabbed the folder from her hand. "Hells' Gorge."

"You know them?"

"They're extremists who preach demonic superiority. The Gorge is also the biggest demonic faction that the Order's aware of." He scratched his chin. "I doubt Sithrael could force information out of them, but this form says that's exactly what he did."

He rummaged through the box and pulled a new folder, then flipped the pages until he found what he wanted. "Last year, Archangels killed thirty demons belonging to the Gorge. This year, none."

"We have to give this to Kevin," Ava said. "He'll find something incriminating. Other than Liam, he's the best detective I know."

"We will. Vera was definitely on to something." Ezra put the folders back into the box and closed the lid. He watched it with care. "Thank you, esteemed mentor."

A silhouette broke through the fake lights from outside, and Ava barely had time to turn before a figure slammed into Ezra.

She spotted moss-colored wings that became white at the bottom walling the Messenger. Ava heard a hollow thud—a punch—and then Ezra fell limp on the floor. She barely registered that her mate had been knocked out when Sithrael swiveled around with a holy gun in his hand.

He fired, but her golden shield covered her body just in time.

The blast flung her outside the storage room and slammed her against the wall. The impact thrummed through her shield and into her bones.

Ava's vision blurred and spun, forming shapes that didn't make sense apart from one: Sithrael grabbing the wooden box.

Her head hurt as her shield faded, slipping underneath her skin. She leaned on the wall and forced herself to stand. "Stop!"

"I feel merciful today," he said mindlessly. "You should run, Guardian."

Ava's pride objected, but her common sense agreed.

She glanced at the room and Ezra's unconscious body near Sithrael's feet. She had to draw the Archangel's attention before he decided to finish the job.

"Gabriel begged for his life." Ava drew her sword and leveled it at him. "This weak little Guardian beheaded your friend, and she'll do the same to you."

A muscle in his jaw ticked, and he carefully put the box down.

"You came here to destroy evidence," she continued, planting her feet and ignoring the instinct to run. "How did you know where to find us?"

"I'm the Order's best tracker." He cracked his neck left then right. "I might've followed you here to destroy evidence, but now the Gods have shown me the true purpose of this encounter." Insanity flashed across his face. "I must end you, sister, so I can pin your murder and Vera's on the Messenger."

He unsheathed his sword, a dark gray beast with two iron bears decorating the cross guard. He charged at once, and the clash of their swords clanged loudly.

Instead of stepping back, he pushed all his weight onto her blade. Ava's arms trembled as she struggled to hold him back, but Sithrael was stronger, and soon he would pierce her defense and cut across her like butter.

The sound of thunder boomed inside her rift. Ava felt as if she were both burning and freezing when golden lightning began to crackle around her. It whipped into Sithrael's skin, but the Archangel's strike didn't waver.

"I'm more resilient than Gabriel ever was," he said, reading the question on her face.

He stepped back all too quickly, finding an opening under her arm. With his free hand, Sithrael jabbed the right side of her ribs, sending her flying through the corridor.

She slammed into the wall near the entrance, which caved with the impact. Ava crashed to her back on the ground outside.

Bones cracked and blood spewed in her organs. She healed all the major injuries—shattered ribs, a broken wing, and the internal hemorrhaging of her lungs. She could heal her dislocated shoulder, but she had to save her energy for Sithrael. Using the powers of the Goddess of Life and Love was less draining than telekinesis, but it was draining none-theless.

She took a deep breath and sat up. Her fingers dug onto her shoulder and with one big pop, she forced it back in place.

Ava didn't scream. She wouldn't give him the pleasure.

From the giant hole she'd pierced through the wall, Sithrael watched her with amusement.

"Your brother Gabriel underestimated me," she said through gritted teeth as she stood. Ava picked up her sword from the ground and gripped the handle so hard her knuckles went white.

Sithrael shrugged, unfazed. "You're a fool, sister. The numbers of In-Betweens were starting to outgrow the holy and the damned. Our mutual agreement with demons ensured our survival. You think we're cruel, but it's simple population control."

"Why aren't you controlling the demonic population then?"

Sithrael chortled. "Those idiots will never coordinate. They are no threat to the Order, and neither are the In-Betweens now." He swung his sword in circles as he approached.

"Surrender yourself," she spat, a certain bitterness crawling up her throat.

The words sounded silly because Sithrael would never do it. But she would give him a chance, if only to honor the merciful Guardian she used to be, the naïve soul who believed in good even underneath evil. The angel Ava barely remembered anymore.

Sithrael laughed. "Your Goddess is weak, and so are you."

He charged, and Ava ducked just in time. Her golden shield covered her body as she spun. Before Sithrael could react, she grabbed him by one arm and slammed her sword into his right shoulder. Her wings propelled her as she pushed him inside the hole she'd made and then zinged up through the floors of the building, using Sithrael's body as a second shield.

Debris rained upon them, but Ava kept thrusting upward, *boom, boom, boom.* The building's structure shook with each hit.

Sithrael bit his teeth when his back cracked. She pushed her sword deeper into his shoulder, and he winced in pain, but she didn't stop.

They broke through the roof and tore into the sky.

Her shield wavered, and her body felt heavy. She kicked his stomach and he bent over, but she didn't let him go. Breathing became harder, and when her shield waned atop her left rib, Sithrael took the cue and punched.

He pushed himself away, and even though Ava yanked her sword from his shoulder with the move, he didn't utter a scream. Instead, he furiously kicked her face, sending her crashing into the roof of a nearby building.

Her skull cracked, as did her spine. Her sword dropped not far from her with a clank.

Drawing on the powers in her essence, she fixed her skull and mended her vertebrae as much as she could. They weren't entirely healed, but it would have to do. Her wings flapped discordantly behind her as she forced herself up.

Meanwhile, Sithrael plummeted from the sky.

Ava fought to steady herself atop both feet as he dove toward her. He had sheathed his sword and now aimed his holy gun at her, swooping in a downward spiral.

He won't make the shot, she thought. *He's too far away.*

He fired. Two blasts pierced her left wing, and Ava shrieked in pain.

Tears and sweat coated her cheeks as she touched the singed area, feeling burnt skin and exposed bone underneath her fingertips. She tried to move her wing but nearly blacked out from the pain.

Sithrael landed before her and threw his empty gun aside. "Let's see how you'll heal from this, sister."

Raw, mad anger took over Ava, forcing the pain out of her mind, locking it somewhere deep inside. A certain calm rushed through her, even though underneath she was lava and bloodlust.

She stretched her palm toward the Archangel and squeezed her fist shut.

Sithrael's arms slammed on the sides of his body. He squirmed and wriggled, trying to break free, but Ava kept her telekinetic hold tightly on him.

Every muscle hurt, and a painful bellow ripped up her

throat. Her body weighed like it was made of lead instead of flesh, iron instead of bones.

"You must be dying inside to keep this hold," the Archangel muttered, eyes wide as she dragged herself closer.

He was right. Ava felt as if she was shattering and burning at the same time. Her teeth snapped so tightly she might pulverize them soon.

Black and golden lightning crackled in the air around her.

"I ripped Gabriel's head off," she grunted in between rushed breaths. "I'll do the same to you."

Sithrael chuckled. "No, you won't." He forced his physical strength against her mental hold, and it cracked too quickly.

He sprinted toward her and smacked a mighty punch on her face that sent her a few steps back. Concrete hit the back of her calf—*the roof's ledge!*

Ava toppled over, free-falling toward the ground. A shriek ripped through her throat so loudly that people down on the ground gasped in awe—she was too weak to mask her essence, especially when pain possessed her like a vise.

Stop, her light and dark ordered.

A telekinetic bubble wrapped around her body, holding Ava midair. She could barely register the pain that clawed at her from everywhere. Her brain might've turned into a thumping puddle inside her skull, but she managed to push herself up.

Her body ached, her essence too, but she kept the bubble around her body until she landed shakily on the roof.

She crouched over, wheezing as she tried to ignore the mountain of pain that crashed upon her.

Sithrael frowned. "How can you use a power that's not yours to such extent, sister?"

We have work to finish, her own voice said, coming from the darkness inside her rift.

Let us take it away, the light added, and the pain dwindled almost immediately, locked somewhere deep inside. Absorbed by the beasts.

Ava felt a sensation akin to leaving her own body as she lifted herself up, balancing on both feet. "I'm not your sister," she spat.

Lightning exploded from her core, engulfing her body, her mind, everything. But this wasn't her normal lightning. Black and golden bolts smashed into Sithrael, and this time his body contorted.

He howled in pain, and the sound was beautiful.

The symphony of lightning pierced his flesh and cracked his bones. Liquid spread underneath his bodysuit, making it a shade darker than black. The pungent stench of urine crossed the air between them, but Ava didn't flinch, didn't give him time to breathe.

Stronger the lightning went, and Sithrael began convulsing. The whiff of burnt flesh overtook the reek of ammonia.

"Ava!" Ezra flew past the seizing Archangel and landed beside her. "We need to interrogate him. We can use Sithrael in our case against the Sword."

"Interrogate him if you must," she said, the words cold on her tongue. "But I won't stop."

Ezra gaped at her in surprise, then turned to the seizing Archangel who bordered on the edge of consciousness.

"Why are you siding with demons?" he asked. "Why did you engage with Hells' Gorge?"

He couldn't answer, of course. His jaw was clinched shut.

Ezra gave Ava with a silent plea, and she rolled her eyes. Her black and golden lightning stopped the attack and rushed back to her, calmly slipping under her skin.

After a few recomposing breaths, Sithrael croaked, "I won't betray ... my commander."

"Answer, or I'll let her loose on you again." Ezra nodded to Ava.

She gave Sithrael an eager grin.

He shivered but still bit his teeth in defiance. Spit covered the sides of his mouth. "You can't stop us. The Order is ours."

Ezra shot anger into Sithrael, then a deep sorrow at things lost; a loneliness that nibbled at Ava's edges, tugging her down into a never-ending fall.

She remembered pushing anguish and misery into Gabriel once. How he had cried and suffered before she'd granted him the mercy of death. For some reason, her throat tightened and a bitter taste invaded her mouth. She preferred hurting her enemies with lightning and blades instead of a flurry of crushing emotions.

It seemed more honorable, somehow.

The Archangel fell on his knees but still managed to speak through Ezra's emotional torture. "I've seen true pain and desperation, my Messenger." He shook as tears flowed down his cheeks. "This is nothing."

Ezra gave Ava a silent "go ahead," so she shot a storm of black and golden lightning into Sithrael, who convulsed furiously with screams trapped in his throat.

When she stopped, he hunched over on his knees, his breaths so shallow Ava could barely hear them.

"We won't ask again," Ezra said, his voice cold and devoid of emotion.

"I'm … not asking you to," the Archangel croaked. "Do your best."

Ezra shook his head. "This is pointless. Let's take him back to the Order. I'm sure we can obtain a permission for a mental scan and have a Virtue look into his mind."

"It won't be admissible in court," Ava countered.

Faking thoughts wasn't hard, even for a human. Any Virtue could be fooled if the subject concentrated hard enough.

"We can try." Ezra pointed at Sithrael. "We could ask for

Agathe herself to peer into his mind. That has to be admissible in court, right?"

"Ezra, we tortured him."

With this single argument, Talahel could destroy their case.

"A world of angels with no demons, no humans, and no In-Betweens is our utopia," Sithrael muttered. "Soon the entire Order will see our way, and I will walk free."

He did have a point. The truth tended to be buried under the Order's blindness and bureaucracy.

"Your utopia strips people of a choice." Ezra's lips curled with disgust. "It annihilates the one in the name of others, when all are equal before the Gods. The Order will never accept it."

Sithrael shot them a wide smile that oozed evil. "Won't it?"

She couldn't tell; she honestly couldn't. Inequalities grew within holy walls with each passing day. Sithrael's utopia might cross a very thick line, but the Order wasn't incapable of getting there.

The Archangel held her gaze as he went on. "I saw your former lover; the demon. He's consumed by darkness, sister. I'll disembowel him in front of you. Yes, that will be the first thing I'll do when I'm set free."

The Order had failed Liam, but Ava wouldn't.

Not again.

She blurred into action before realizing what she was doing. Ava ran to her sword and grabbed it as Ezra screamed for her to stop. Her body felt lighter than air. He tried to grab her shoulder, but his fingers only brushed her back. She dashed through the empty path to Sithrael, raised her blade, and cut across his neck.

His head hit concrete and rolled away slowly, leaving a trail of blood.

Sithrael was smiling. As if he'd won this battle even if it cost him his life.

Ezra glared at her, his mouth half-open. "What have you done?"

Ava's rushed breaths rang in her ears. "He would've walked," she said mindlessly, halfway caught between a nightmare and reality.

"He wouldn't! He played your anger and fear!"

Her lips flatlined. Ezra might be right, but she couldn't run the risk. "I had to kill him. He was going to hurt Liam."

"Gods!" He turned around and ran a hand through his silver hair. "He was our one chance, Ava!"

No. The entire Order had succumbed to Talahel's mad ideas. Agathe would've let Sithrael walk. If the Throne had an ounce of common sense, she wouldn't have overridden Ezra's signature and granted Talahel more weapons.

Ava had to believe this because if she was wrong, killing Sithrael meant she had destroyed the one way out of this war.

"If it wasn't for me, would you have joined Talahel?" she blurted.

The question caught Ezra by surprise. He watched her as if she had slammed a blade in his heart. He grabbed her hand and pressed her palm on his chest, his deep blue gaze locked on hers. "Never."

"But you almost succumbed to Talahel's wickedness," she insisted, her tone sticks and stones.

"Like every angel in the Order," he said, "being fooled into thinking he has everything under control does not mean joining his insanity. Trust me, Ava. Sithrael wouldn't have walked free."

No. Ezra would betray her like Talahel had betrayed the Order. A voice inside her whispered, *we should trust no one.*

Ezra isn't no one.

Ava shook her head. The Messenger was the kindest angel she'd ever met, but the fury inside her was insane and it whispered strange words in her ears, mad words she tried to ignore.

Agathe would have never freed Sithrael. Ava understood this now that she could think straight; now that the red had vanished from her head. The Throne might be a stickler to the rules, but she wasn't completely senseless.

Ezra brushed a lock of hair off her face. "They killed Vera. How can you question ..." he trailed off and blinked back tears, his jaw a tight square.

Guilt filled her completely as her emotions steadied. "I'm so sorry."

"Are you still there?" he asked, his tone broken as he peered into her eyes. "Are you still yourself, Ava?"

"I ..." Her voice failed. The Guardian she used to be turned into a lost memory with each passing day. Someone she used to know a long time ago. Ava was becoming someone else, someone she wasn't proud of. A new version of herself who perhaps had always been there, dooming and freeing her at the same time. She pressed her forehead against Ezra's chest. "I don't know."

25

LIAM

*L*iam walked inside an abandoned house, a crumbling space with one room located four blocks away from the Gorge's main headquarters. The paint on the walls was chipped and mold blotches peppered the ceiling.

He watched his reflection in a cracked mirror near the left corner and grinned. A wolf with sharp teeth smiled back at him. His eyes shone yellow, standing out from the night-black fur that covered his entire body.

Liam licked his teeth with a long wolfish tongue and lingered on his canines. Hells, he'd done a fine job with his fangs.

He looked out the glassless window and into the night ahead, hoping that Archie was reaping the souls he needed to prove himself. But he couldn't worry about the old man now.

Liam's head hurt as if he were hungover.

The clock was ticking.

He moved swiftly under the mantle of night, often hiding behind abandoned cars and piles of rusting appliances and whatnots. It didn't take him long to find the warehouse where they kept the wolfsugar.

Fuck.

Two buildings towered over the place. Taking out Jim and Butch, the third-tiers atop each roof, wouldn't be a problem. But Abrielle guarded the entrance of the warehouse.

A Drakar, like Jal.

Liam studied his own claws, and the pressure under his skull increased. He bit back the pain as his nails grew bigger and sharper.

He hadn't taken his holy guns or sword with him because this had to pass for a werewolf attack. Without weapons, it would be damn hard to win against a second-tier demon. But he would never get the job done by staying here, and now his bones had begun to prickle under his skin.

He had to hurry.

Liam moved swiftly into the first building, climbing up the stairs to the roof.

Taking out the first demon by clawing off his throat was too easy. Jim had barely seen Liam coming.

As the demon's head toppled over what remained of his neck, Liam glared at his own sharp and bloodied claws.

It's not innocent blood, he told himself. These monsters had tortured and raped, so tonight, the grim reaper would come for them with a fury.

A certain relief washed over him as he went on.

Two more to go.

Jumping from the top of this building to the next was a walk in the park. His hind legs boosted him and as he cut through the air, Liam figured being a werewolf wasn't all that bad—even if his brain burned underneath his skull.

He landed with a mighty thud and dodged the blade that slashed the air toward him. One swipe of his claw, and he ripped the demon's face to shreds. Butch's left eye hung from its socket, his mangled jaw evident underneath shredded skin.

The demon gurgled something before falling dead. Had he been a second-tier, he might've been able to heal. Emphasis on might.

"Oh, you're good, wolf."

He turned to Abrielle, who spread her purple wings wide as she unsheathed her sword. That giant psycho—she was at least three heads taller than Liam—smiled pure madness.

He hated fighting a woman, but Abrielle had tortured and murdered plenty of humans back at the pub.

Assholes weren't defined by gender, he supposed.

Liam walked casually to the fallen demon's body and snatched up his sword.

Abrielle let out a shrill, high-pitched laugh. "Wolfmen can't fight with swords. Did they forget to tell you that, puppy?"

The claws were an issue, yes, but fighting with a blade came easily to Liam. Then again, he was a wolf now, and his claws were practically daggers.

His brain pulsed inside his skull, and his vision doubled. His darkness pushed under his skin, so did his light—a faint memory of the angel he used to be. The forces inside him wouldn't be able to hold his wolfish form much longer.

Liam shook his head and took a composing breath. Full moon was coming, and only the wolfsugar in that warehouse could stop thousands of beasts from rushing through the streets, murdering innocents, and getting slaughtered by the Order in return.

He had to get it to Suther. Fuck if Abrielle would stop him.

He watched his own bloodied claws. He was a monster now, and as much as he hated admitting it, the sword would only hinder him. So he dropped it to the ground and howled to the sky.

Abrielle fixed her battle stance and raised her sword.

He charged.

❧

IT WAS quiet here in the woods, but thanks to his demonic hearing, Liam still discerned faint city noises in the distance.

He found Jal waiting for him in a clearing near a rocky wall. "Holy shit, you actually did it," he said, his eyes wide as Liam approached with the black duffel bag containing untampered wolfsugar. "Took you long enough, little Terror. Or should I say little Beast?"

Jal's playfulness disappeared when Liam came closer and the demon spotted the blood sticking to his fur. Jal clutched the strap of the blue backpack he carried. "Whoa! You did a number on those demons."

"Yeah." The word scraped Liam's thick wolfish vocal chords.

He could still taste Abrielle's blood, a metallic, bitter tang which had soon mixed with his own vomit. Liam had never bitten off someone's neck before, and he hoped he would never have to do it again.

Wheezing breaths rasped his throat as his head whirled violently. He took a step back and slammed a claw on his forehead. A thousand needles might be impaling his brain right now. His light and darkness pulsed weakly inside him.

"I'm shifting back," he growled.

"Oh, right." The demon dropped the backpack on the floor and removed some clothes.

Liam's bones cracked, but they didn't hurt. Muscle and flesh shrunk, nails became squared and short, his muzzle flattened, and fur retreated into his skin until Liam looked human again. Human and completely naked.

A giant bloodstain covered his mouth and jaw, going all

the way down his trunk. He resembled a vamp who just had the meal of a lifetime.

"Aren't you a sight for sore eyes?" Jal winked at Liam as he handed him the fresh change of clothes. "There's a river north of here, five minutes on foot."

Finding the river wasn't hard. Unlike the pines that lined the riverbanks, water didn't have any smell. So, he let his demonic senses lead the way into the odorless line that cut through the woods.

Once Liam was clean and dressed, he returned to Jal's side. The demon led him into an abandoned drain pipe that debouched not far from the clearing.

The path reeked of treated shit, which stank like normal shit. Liam had to control his gag reflexes twice. Considering werewolves had sharper senses than his, they must be truly desperate to be hiding here.

Growls came from ahead, and then a group of seven bulky men stepped in their way. If it weren't for Liam's demonic "sixth sense", he probably would've noticed nothing but their shining yellow irises cutting through the pitch-black darkness.

Suther stepped forward from the wall of werewolves and nodded at Liam. "I smell demon blood on you."

"Yeah." He sneered. "You should've seen the other guy."

Well, girl.

"We come for our hearing," Jal said, "and we bring a sign of good faith."

Liam took the cue and dropped the duffel bag before Suther, then quickly came back to Jal's side. Territory and boundaries were key when dealing with wolves.

Suther observed the bag. "I thank you for your offer, but it will not buy your Legion my support."

Jal crossed his arms. "After all we've done, you won't give us a chance?"

"I must think of my packs." Suther stared at his own feet. "Their safety comes first."

Liam saw red. How blind could Suther be? He wasn't just damning his people; he was damning the entire resistance!

"I bit off someone's neck for this?" he blurted. "Look, the 'safety' you have here is fleeting. The wolfsugar might help you through some full moons, but eventually it will run out, and when it does, we won't be here to help. You'll have to face the wrath of the Order and the demons all on your own, and guess what?" He pointed to Suther and his wall of Alphas. "None of you will survive."

The werewolf lord said nothing.

Jal shook his head. "Your father would be ashamed, Suther."

"You don't know how hard it's been." The wolf spun around and released a frustrated bark that echoed through the pipe. "Take the wolfsugar back if it pleases you."

His wolves snarled in protest, but after one glare from their leader, they whined apologetically.

"No, you can keep it," Jal said, disgust coating his words. "I don't fancy seeing the extinction of all werewolves in the city, which is where you're headed if you keep ignoring this war."

Suther shuffled on his feet, still avoiding Liam and Jal. "How's Lilith?" he asked quietly.

"She would be better off if her children could feed on wolf blood," Jal said. "We are fighting the Order and as many demons as we can, but our numbers are dwindling." He blew air through his lips. "Lilith needs help. We all do."

"I …" He gulped and turned his back to them. "I'm sorry."

Jal's jaw set into a grim line. He tapped Liam's shoulder and motioned to the exit. "Let's go. There's nothing here for us."

Liam watched Suther and his wolves leave. "Your father once said that evil wins when good does nothing."

"My father is dead!" Suther roared without turning toward them.

All of this had been for nothing, then.

Fucking great.

26

AVA

*A*va's lightning hadn't killed Sithrael on the spot because of his strong essence. His corpse, however, was nothing but an empty shell.

With his vital energy gone, her light and dark bolts reduced his body to ashes in seconds. Wind blew his remains away, dispersing them throughout the city.

She also had to take care of the blood on the roof—it held Sithrael's genetic code and could constitute evidence of foul play. Ezra said he would clean it with bleach. Ava couldn't tell how or why she knew her lightning would work; she simply did.

When she shot her bolts at the blood, their intensity weaker than before, it quickly became ashes that blew into the wind, leaving the concrete clean and untouched.

This way Sithrael would never be found. He would never be mourned.

Two days passed, and Talahel issued search parties to look for his strongest warrior. He claimed the same demons who had killed Vera might've taken care of Sithrael.

Funny that he had stopped pinning murders on In-

Betweens and now accused demons. Whatever agreement he'd had with them seemed to have fallen apart.

Every time Ava spotted Archangels leaping into the sky and Warriors rushing through the corridors, she rejoiced. The time they wasted looking for Sithrael meant that they weren't smiting vampires and werewolves.

When Talahel passed by Ava in the Order's halls, he paid her no attention. To him, she was a silly little Guardian.

Well, this silly little Guardian had killed Sithrael, and she would kill him, too.

Where remorse should've been, Ava found only relief. Once she would have regretted ending a life, but not this time.

Not ever again.

By day four, the Sword publicly acknowledged that demonic attacks were rising, and he would send his men to investigate. He was absolutely certain demons had taken Sithrael. He was wrong, of course, but at least now the Order focused on the true enemy.

"One angel was murdered and another one is missing." Talahel slammed his fist on the marbled tribune. He had taken over Sunday Congregations by now. "Brothers and sisters, I will make them pay!"

The fools in the audience clapped. It was too much. The wild, untamed angel inside Ava forced her up from her pew.

"You should've done this long ago," she shouted. "Instead, you nearly eradicated the creatures who might've fought with us against them."

She had to leave, otherwise she would attack the Sword and to the Hells with the implications.

"Our sister still mourns Dominion Evestar," Talahel said with fake kindness as she walked out of the room. "It's only understandable. Dominion Lightway is quite frail at the moment."

Frail.

Little Guardian.

Ava slammed the door so hard that the sound blasted through the corridor outside.

Healing her left wing was proving harder than she'd imagined. Ava kept it hidden within her light at all times, otherwise questions would arise—questions she couldn't answer. Not now, when the Order practically belonged to Talahel.

Her wings hurt even when she hid them in her essence. Ezra tried to heal the gaping wounds, but it wasn't enough.

Sithrael's holy gun must've been damned. It was the only explanation for the damage her healing—and Ezra's—failed to fix. The Messenger told her that the mere fact she could function was a miracle.

He sent her to Jophiel, and the Seraph welcomed her with open arms. When he hugged Ava, she sensed his despair and sadness but only for a moment. He was quick to shut down his emotions, and when she asked him if he was all right, he merely said, "The trials of the Gods can be challenging."

That they could.

She pushed her sore wings out from her essence, and the Seraph caressed the pierced and scabbed area that lacked feathers. Warm light shone from his palms, and in a few minutes her left wing was completely healed.

It had taken her and Ezra days to fix only a fraction of the damaged area, and Jophiel had done it as easily as someone would blink or breathe.

He didn't let her rest, though.

Later in the training room, Ava lifted two out of ten stone blocks—which might've equaled her weight. Her telekinetic grip disappeared quicker than she hoped, and the rocks dropped to the ground, shattering into a million pieces.

If she had taken longer to raise herself back to the roof

during her battle with Sithrael, those rocks would've been her body.

Jophiel patted Ava's back and told her this was remarkable progress.

It felt like a remarkable failure.

ON THE MORNING of the ball, Kevin and Justine met with her in the Messenger's office for an update.

The Selfless dropped on Ezra's white couch and rubbed his forehead with his palms. Justine sat on the couch's arm and caressed the back of his neck.

"I got a bunch of dead ends from Vera's files," Kevin said. "At least now Talahel is focusing on demons, so that's a win, I suppose."

"The wolves aren't safe yet." Ava crossed her arms and looked out Ezra's window. A sense of hopelessness took over. "This battle never ends."

"We're doing our best." Justine sighed. "That's all we can do."

And it wasn't enough.

"Things don't look good for the Legion or the Order, love," Kevin said dispiritedly. "We're running out of time and resources."

"That's enough updates for one day." Justine raised her palms. "You party poopers stay away from me. Tonight is all about enjoying ourselves!" She stood and put both hands on her waist. "We've been through so much. We deserve one night of fun." She cast a worried glance at Ava. "Especially you."

"I'm fine." And she truly was.

Maybe she shouldn't be, but Ava couldn't lie to herself.

She had brutally ended lives, and she didn't feel an inch of guilt.

Gabriel and Sithrael had it coming.

Her dark beast gave out a pleased purr. *Sometimes bloodshed is the only solution.*

So are mercy and forgiveness, the light argued.

Ugh. Sometimes, she wanted to punch her own head.

Kevin shrugged and hunched over his knees. "You lot enjoy your party, then."

"It's not fair. You're human, but also an angel." Justine shot a regretful look at him. "The Selfless should've been invited."

"Yeah, maybe one day." He smirked without humor. "I didn't want to go anyway."

A lie. Ava could sense the yellow fog wafting from his essence.

Kevin gave Justine a worried glance. "Will you … hmm … I heard about the sexual tension that can happen later in the night, and—"

"I'm your girlfriend." She bent over and gave him a peck on his lips. Kevin's cheeks flushed as red as his hair. "I only do inappropriate things with you."

He grabbed her chin gently. "It's because of my accent, isn't it?"

Justine giggled. "Pretty much."

A golden, swelling sensation grew in Ava's chest as she watched her friends so happy, so in love. For a moment, she imagined her and Ezra in their place.

Ezra. Not Liam.

A despair she couldn't understand pierced her heart, leaving Ava desolate and cold.

AVA

*I*t was night by the time Ezra knocked on Ava's door and let himself in.

The Messenger was a vision in silver. His white shirt fit him perfectly underneath his tuxedo, which nearly matched the shade of his hair. His tresses were fashioned in a long elegant braid that cascaded down his back.

"You look dapper," she said.

He took her in from head to toe with a certain awe. "And you're stunning."

Ava glanced down to hide her blushing.

Crystal beads trickled down the fabric of her pale blue, one shouldered dress. Justine had picked the outfit, and she had also fixed Ava's hair into strawberry-blond braids that circled the top of her head, then cascaded down her shoulders in soft curls.

Ava wasn't used to dressing up—her bodysuit was practical and enough for her—but she had felt a sense of pride when she watched her own reflection in her room's standing mirror. With the crystal earrings and necklace Justine lent her, Ava resembled a proper *princess*.

A knot clogged her throat, and she swallowed it down.

The only downside of her attire was the uncomfortable shoes—white to match her wings. All ascended angels were required to leave their wings on display when entering the ball. Even Ezra's were politely tucked behind his back.

"They're the crown of your outfit." Justine had said as she handed her the heels. "Your shoes need to match them."

Ava hadn't walked a foot in those shoes, and they already pressed her feet. So she spread her shield's thin golden layer underneath the hard leather.

That should do it.

Ezra gave her his arm and bowed slightly. "Ready?"

He had never looked more charming than right now. Ava hooked her arm with his and they walked out, heading to the grand ball room.

As they went, she smiled at the Messenger. The thought she'd had before rushed back to mind.

She could be happy with him.

Ezra was a wonderful angel; a kind, generous soul and she would be lucky, yes, lucky to have him as a lover. He was water to her fire, the calm to her fury. Funny that once she'd been a pure, good angel like him.

Could Ezra bring that Guardian back?

He laid a gentle hand atop hers and whispered, "We've had a tough couple of weeks. I'm looking forward to a night off."

She leaned her temple on the tip of his shoulder. "I'm tired of worrying and overthinking."

"Then don't," he said simply.

The ballroom was a vast marbled hall filled with golden vines that swirled up the walls to the ceiling. The warm lights turned the white space a dim bronze. The entire setting reminded Ava of the fancy opera houses from the time she was still human, except this felt grander. Cleaner, too—the air was less stuffy, the ambience more modern.

Walking into the pomp and circumstance she'd hated when alive felt odd. Even after one hundred years, Ava hadn't gotten used to it.

From the high ceiling, angels dangled on silky white ribbons in a demonstration of movement and grace that left her speechless. One of them lost his balance and fell, but his teal wings spread quickly behind him before he hit the ground.

The crowd applauded nonetheless.

Soft music rang from the stage at the end of the room where Virtues and Guardians played a mix of classical tunes, a ballet of violins, cellos, and pianos that Ava found sad and remarkably beautiful.

Angels dressed in awe-striking gowns passed by, their wings fully on display. If Ava resembled a princess, most angels here looked like queens, even the third-tiers. And for the first time, Ava saw the Order as it should be: a gathering of angels interacting with each other despite their rank. *Equals.* Guardians strolling alongside Virtues, Erudites talking to Archangels … this was Jophiel's vision, or at least a part of it.

It wasn't fair that the Selfless hadn't been invited. They put their lives at risk every day to keep the peace between the human and supernatural worlds. They deserved to be here.

One battle at a time.

The room silenced as Agathe climbed up the silver and gold stage. Metallic leaves and flowers intertwined with each other to form an arc at the center of the platform where the Throne stood.

Agathe stuck out from the glittering background with her long black hair, black lipstick and eyeliner. Her dress, dark as night just as her raven wings, was a thing to behold.

If Ezra was the moon, Agathe was the night. And Ava …
she glanced at a hanging mirror on the wall which showcased herself and the vast ballroom behind.

Well, Ava didn't know what she was.

Agathe tapped the microphone stand. "Brothers and
sisters." Her voice boomed across the space. "Welcome to our
yearly ball."

Cheers erupted around them and Ezra whooped twice,
bashing his fist in the air. The exhilaration of the evening
was clearly getting to him. Ava could feel the energy thrumming underneath her skin; anticipation and eagerness had
taken over the space.

These angels were ready to let go.

A velvety sensation flowed from Ezra and brushed her
essence in a soft caress. He gave her a lopsided grin. He was
ready to let go, too.

Was she?

Agatha waited for the room to silence. "Let us begin by
praying to the Gods. Let us thank them for their protection,
and let us also mourn for our fallen brothers and sisters."

All angels bowed their heads, and so did Ava. She prayed
for Vera, wherever she was, *if* she was, and she also prayed
for Liam's safety. In the end, Ava begged the Gods for some
guidance, but what was the point if all her prayers remained
unanswered?

"Lastly," Agathe went on, "let us thank our brother, the
Sword, for protecting the Order."

Someone shouted Talahel's name, and the entire room
broke into applause. Ava's stomach twisted in itself, and
blinding fury took over.

Her nails bit her palms, but Ezra held her hand lovingly.
It appeased the fire in her, if only a little.

Vera's words came to mind. *"Always keep you to yourself.
Hiding emotions is the greatest skill a Dominion can have."*

With one deep breath, Ava calmed her nerves and wrapped her emotions inside her essence.

"Thank you, brothers and sisters." Agathe clapped her hands. "Now, let the celebrations begin!"

The ballroom broke into wayward songs that were both beautiful and fast-paced, the mellow tunes replaced by a maddening mix of drums and beats.

Ezra disappeared for a quick moment, only to return with two drinks that tasted sweet and savory. They drank and spoke a world of things, forgetting about demons and Talahel. Tonight, they were simply Ava and Ezra.

Mates. Friends.

More than that, perhaps.

After the second round, Ava's muscles relaxed and smiling became easier. Ezra set their glasses on a small round table and took her hand.

"Come on." He pulled her to the dance floor.

"I can't dance!"

He turned around, and she nearly smacked against him. The thin layer of sweat on his skin had the pleasant tang of lemons mixed with sandalwood. He leaned closer and whispered, "I don't care."

Before she could argue, he was already pulling her to the open circle where angels twirled and swayed sinfully, most of their bodies intertwined in sensual moves.

Ava wasn't the best dancer, but it wasn't hard to shift from one foot to the other. She watched the other females and mimicked them. Her hips swayed in sinuous curves that quickly caught Ezra's hooded gaze.

She enjoyed having his attention, so she lingered on the circles drawn by her waist. He inhaled and bit his lip.

This is good, she told herself. *This is how we could be.*

All at once, Ezra took her in his arms and swirled, once,

twice. Ava threw her head back and laughed as the world spun around her.

Gods, this was fun!

He stopped swirling but didn't let her go. They smiled and danced, so close to each other that she could feel Ezra's heart beating. And below his hips, a part of him grew, eager to fill the space between her thighs.

She could be happy ...

All of Ava's common sense left her, except for one thought. A face.

His face, always.

Liam was suffering and she was here, dancing and grinding against Ezra. Even though she had stopped spinning, her mind whirled.

Sweat coated her skin, and Ava halted. She excused herself, and Ezra motioned to follow, but an angel with narrowed eyes and silky black hair took him in her arms, dragging him back to the dance floor.

The night and the moon.

Ava didn't know how to feel about Agathe's advance on him. Both relieved and annoyed, she guessed.

Ezra strained his neck, looking for her. Ava shrunk amidst the crowd, allowing the strong, towering bodies to conceal her.

She couldn't face Ezra, not when Liam still owned her mind. And yet, she needed to let go of the confusion and angst that haunted her every day. She rushed to the glowing bar, shaped like a white neon halo, and asked for two shots of Heavenly Tears.

Ava didn't usually drink, but tonight she would give herself to Ezra, and this could help.

As soon as the Guardian behind the bar gave her the two shots she had ordered, Ava downed one after the other. The sour liquid burned her throat, and she hissed through her teeth.

"Easy there, angel girl," someone said from her left.

Ava asked for another round before turning to the petite woman sitting on a white barstool. By the curious way her essence thrummed against Ava's, she must be a Virtue.

She looked no older than thirty with her fierce brown eyes and short pixie hair. Ava couldn't tell why, but she liked the woman immediately.

The Guardian bartender laid two shots before Ava, and she handed one glass to the Virtue. "Tonight we celebrate."

The woman analyzed the glass. "Trying to forget?"

Ava leaned back on the counter, observing the packed ballroom. "Always."

"There's only one reason someone downs a drink that fast. Either you want to forget, or you're trying to gain liquid courage." The Virtue downed her Heavenly Tears, then slammed the glass atop the bar.

Ava raised her glass and drank all in one gulp. When the bartender asked if they needed another round, Ava told him, "Keep them coming." She then frowned at the Virtue. "You seem familiar. Do we know each other?"

"From another life, I suppose."

It was the fierce and unrelenting eyes. Ava remembered seeing those eyes once, eyes that had been old and wrinkled. "Gods in the Heavens! Captain?"

The angel chuckled and waved at her own complexion. "Death is the best face lift, don't you agree?"

Ava blinked back tears as she jolted at her, trapping the Captain in a violent hug that nearly toppled both of them over the barstool.

Ava remembered seeing her bloodied corpse and the two empty sockets where her eyes had been. Anger piled up inside her, and she wished she could kill Gabriel all over again. But praise the Gods, the Captain had recovered. She was even out of her room, which had to be a miracle in itself.

They gently broke their embrace, neither really wanting to let go.

"I'm sorry I haven't come to see you." The Captain observed the bottom of her empty glass. "I would say that being brutally tortured and murdered messed with my head, and the centuries of memories that rushed back to mind when I woke as an angel drove me mad. All truths, you see. But—"

"I remind you of Liam."

"Of how I failed him and Archie. The entire precinct, too." She shook her head, her lips pressed tightly. "The Fury Boys are demons now. Gods …" Her tone cracked, and she sniffed back a tear, which showed Ava just how much the Captain was hurting. She had never seen the woman cry.

"You didn't fail them," Ava assured. "And they're okay."

The Captain chortled. "That's what Justine says, too. You're both so certain, but you can't be. No one can."

The bartender set two more shots of Heavenly Tears before them and gave the Captain a pitying stare. "Should I speak the words of the Gods to you, sister?"

"I'm an ascended, Guardian. Your words have no effect on me," she snapped but quickly regretted her harshness. "Thank you for the offer, though. Do keep the drinks coming?"

The Guardian nodded and went away.

"The words of the Gods could help," Ava said.

"I know." She took one glass, handed it to Ava, and then downed hers. "This helps more."

The liquid didn't burn Ava's throat this time. She must be getting used to it.

After a moment of silence, the Captain said, "I deserve the pain. They're probably suffering right now, and so should I."

"Your suffering won't help them." She leaned closer and whispered, "They're okay. I promise."

The Captain's jaw dropped when she caught Ava's meaning. "By the Heavens. They really are?"

"Yes." The word tasted like a lie. As far as Ava knew, Liam wasn't okay. He suffered while she was here drinking her sorrows away.

Or gaining courage.

Her gaze searched for Ezra, who still scanned the room from the dance floor, looking for her. Agathe tried her best to catch his eye, but her attempts failed miserably.

Ava grinned.

The Guardian behind the bar returned with six more shots. She drank two in a row, her attention trapped on the Messenger.

"Are you used to drinking this much?" the Captain asked.

Ava shrugged and hunched over the counter. "Do you care?"

The Captain downed two shots herself and clicked her tongue. "Not particularly."

Ava felt a pressure on her mental wall. She narrowed her eyes at the woman and asked, "What are you looking for?"

The Captain blinked. "Your wall is incredibly strong."

"I had a good teacher."

"But you're a Dominion."

"Yes." Ava wished she could tell her more, but she had no clue why she could tap into different angelic powers.

If Jophiel himself couldn't explain it, how could she?

The Captain studied her a little longer, then turned back to the two drinks left before them. "I'm sorry. I just wanted to see my boys."

Her forlorn tone was a cold blade slammed into Ava's core. But the Legion was in her memories, and she couldn't risk letting the Cap in.

Not yet.

"I can't give you access." She tapped her left temple, then laid her palm gently on the Captain's hand. "But soon."

She handed Ava the first of the remaining glasses, cheered, and then downed her own drink. Ava followed, quickly raising her hand to call for the Guardian.

He must be used to this by now because he soon came with four more drinks.

"Heavens, I might die tonight," Ava grumbled, her words coming out slurred.

The Captain chuckled and patted her on the back. "You and me both, angel girl." Her humor suddenly vanished as she stared ahead. "You know, when I died, all my memories came back. How Archie and I, well, Acheron was his name, how we loved each other …"

"I heard Acheron was a sensible and smart angel."

"Younger than Michael too, who was like an older brother to him." She giggled. "Oh, how the roles reversed."

Ava noticed the tenderness in her words. "I would love to hear more about your adventures with them."

Was there a point in knowing more about Liam's past life, though? Michael and Acheron were gone forever. The Captain seemed to realize this because sorrow took over her features and she downed another drink, motioning for Ava to follow.

She promptly did.

"I remember Vera, too," the Cap said quietly. "She took good care of me when I returned to my angelic form. She saw me at my worst and still, she stayed. I wouldn't be here if not for her and Justine."

Ava raised another glass. "To Vera and Justine."

"Hear, hear." She clinked her glass with Ava's and drank. The Captain made a face as the liquid went down her throat. "Did you know Michael could've been the Sword instead of

Talahel? But he preferred to keep fighting alongside his brothers, so that asshole got the job."

Ava's mind felt fuzzy. "Michael would've been a much better Sword than Talahel. Maybe then Vera would still be alive."

"That she would." The Captain raised her shoulders. "It doesn't matter, does it? Vera's gone. Michael and Acheron are demons now, and they'll never remember. They'll never know." She leaned closer. "He loved you, Ava. I've known Michael for centuries and Liam since he was seven. Neither ever looked at a woman the way they, *he*, looked at you."

Ava's throat tightened and breathing got harder. A tear slipped down her cheek, and she wiped it away with the back of her hand. "I failed him. I keep failing him nonstop."

The Captain glanced at the ceiling and raised one palm as if praying to the Gods for patience. "We've all fucking failed someone at least once in our lives. Don't beat yourself up over it."

Ava clinked her glass with the Captain's. "That's really *fucking* true." She slapped her hand over her own mouth and whispered, "I said *fucking!*"

"I know!" The woman giggled. "I didn't think you were capable of swearing!"

"Shhhhh." Ava put a finger on her lips. "Don't tell anyone."

"Your secret is safe with me." The Captain winked at her, then took another glass.

The bartender was doing an outstanding job at getting them drunk beyond their wits.

A loud, flirty laugh caught Ava's attention, and she looked back at the crowd. The Captain followed her gaze toward Ezra, who talked with Agathe.

The Throne had flushed cheeks and an easy smile on her lips, her body so close to his.

"Justine told me you're his mate now," the Captain said.

"That's right."

The Guardian put four more shots before them, sweat coating his forehead as he worked to attend all the inebriated angels who asked for drinks. Ava made a mental note to thank him later.

The Captain watched her own glass with predatory focus. "Ezraphael isn't Michael, but Michael isn't Liam anyway. Up is down and down is up."

Ava took a swallow, not certain if she followed the Captain's reasoning. Her thoughts mingled with one another, and she had to concentrate to speak. "Ezra needs me. I need him, too."

"Do you?" She handed Ava another shot, and they cheered.

Heavens, Ava could barely feel her feet. Her mind was spinning. Her body felt overly light, but this was good. She had many reasons to feel guilty and frustrated, yet she couldn't remember any of them. Happiness took over angst, bliss overcame sadness.

Ava couldn't remember the last time she felt so fine.

"Your happiness lies with Ezraphael," the Captain said with a long drawl. "You can never be with Liam, not now that he's a demon. Both my boys are gone." She downed her drink and asked for another.

"I …" The words were stuck in Ava's throat.

"You don't love the Messenger like you love Liam, I know." The Captain shrugged. "But you don't have a choice. A demon and an angel, together? When has that ever happened?"

Maybe with the Legion … but even that might be wishful thinking.

Enough about Liam.

Ezra was good to her. He could make her happy. She wouldn't think twice before giving herself to him tonight.

The bartender handed the Captain more drinks.

"Perhaps you and I have more in common than you think." She handed Ava a glass. "We're both here and not with them."

Ava leaned her head back and drank. She could feel liquid bliss pushing down her sadness and worry. No more about demons, Liam, and angels. She wanted to be happy, if only for now.

A hand rested on Ava's shoulder and when she turned, a wide smile spread on her lips. "Ezra!" She threw herself at him, wrapping her arms around his neck. "I'm so glad you could join us!"

He gaped at her with an amused grin, his hands pressing on the curve of her waist. "You're drunk."

She winked at him. "Heavily."

Ava steadied herself on her feet, which proved harder than usual.

"Shelaria!" Justine approached the Captain from behind. Her friend was absolutely gorgeous in a glittering green dress. "There you are!"

"Mom's here," the Captain grumbled as she stood, doing her best to balance on both feet.

Justine took one of her arms and wrapped it over her shoulders. The Captain leaned on her, clearly not able to stand by herself.

"I see you two had your own private party." Justine pouted at Ava. "Next time, you better invite me. You owe me big time now." She began moving away with the Captain. "Come on, dear. You're not fully recovered yet."

The Captain stopped in her tracks and pointed at Ezra. "You treat her right, angel boy. She's special."

A hiccup burst from Ava's throat, and she made a salute. "Oh, Captain, my Captain!"

The woman waved a salute back dismissively, barely able to keep her eyes open.

She and Justine had disappeared into the crowd by the time Ezra's touch hardened on Ava's waist. She didn't understand why he'd done it until she realized she had almost tumbled and fallen to the side.

"My hero," she giggled as she caressed his strong biceps.

"I think it's time to put you to bed," he whispered and nibbled at her earlobe.

His breath bore the taste of Heavenly Tears and other drinks, the same as hers.

"Oops." Ava put a hand on her lips. "Am I in trouble, my Messenger?"

He nudged his nose on her temple. "Perhaps."

Happy. She could be happy with him.

He led her out of the ballroom and into the elevator. Ava felt so light, so carefree. She wanted to feel like this every day.

She hummed the tune of the last song that was playing before they left, something about endless fields of gold.

Ezra laughed, a sweet carefree sound that made her smile too. "You really had too much to drink."

"Why do you love me so?" she blurted through her haze. "It oozes from you. When you let it out, that is." She frowned. "Why are you letting it out now?"

"Because I like that you know. That you feel it."

She tapped the bridge of her nose. "You just want to get in my panties."

"That, too." He smirked and brushed a lock of hair behind her ear. "I care for you, Ava. So much …"

He leaned forward. Ava thought mindlessly that she should've stepped back, but then it was too late, and his lips were on hers.

They were warm and cold at the same time, passionate

but lacking. This wasn't him; it was her. She was the problem. So Ava wrapped her arms around his neck and pulled him closer, deepening their kiss, hoping to find in him what she'd been missing all along.

Ezra took her with thirst. He pivoted around and slammed her against the elevator wall, his palms travelling from her breasts down to her butt cheeks. Excitement pooled in her depths as she rubbed against his bulging crotch.

Their ragged breaths mingled, and their excitement wafted in the cloistered elevator air, building, growing.

It was so warm …

Suddenly, Ava found that thing she'd been looking for. In him.

Finally!

She observed the man before her; the man she loved. His beautiful green eyes, his sharp squared jaw, the smooth olive skin that felt so good under her fingertips; even the prickly three-day stubble was there.

Flocks of dark hair brushed on his forehead as he gave her that perfect wide smile that was half-boy, half-man.

"I love you, Ava," he said with Ezra's voice.

Happy. She was so happy.

"I love you too, Liam."

LIAM

S mall waves crashed on Liam's bare feet. The pebbles on the shore pricked his soles, but he didn't mind. He enjoyed the soothing sensation of water rushing on his skin. He hadn't felt it in a while, and he didn't know if he ever would again.

The city stood ahead like a mountain beyond the line of water. This early in the morning, the buildings resembled a conglomerate of sleeping gray towers. Ship horns rang faintly in the distance as cars crossed the bridge that connected the island to mainland.

He inhaled and closed his eyes, absorbing the salty tang of ocean air.

Her presence pulsed against his essence. Liam knew she stood behind him with her arms crossed.

"Why did you call me here?" Lilith asked.

He spun around and noticed her striking beauty had faded. Lilith looked exhausted and thin. So thin …

She scowled at him. At first he feared she had heard his thoughts, but Lilith wasn't telepathic. The look on his face must've done the trick.

Liam stared at his own feet and shoved his hands in his pockets. "I'll be meeting Master soon. I need you to help me protect my mind. Glamouring is similar to telepathy, right?"

"It's a bit of both but not enough. Glamour stands somewhere between a Guardian's empathy and a Virtue's telepathy." She shrugged. "If you wanted to hide your thoughts, you should've summoned Jophiel."

"You know he and Jal are busy after what happened with the wolves. Look, Master is probably more powerful than a Possessor." He tapped his forehead. "I need to protect what's in here. They can't get access, Lilith. If they do, the Legion is screwed."

"Not exactly. Jophiel blurs the memories of all members," she said as she stepped closer. "They're clear to you, but to anyone peeking into your mind, everything Legion-related will be a disgruntled mess."

That solved his main worry but not the main problem. "I need to get close enough to strike, and Master won't let me if he reads my mind."

She winced before throwing her hands in the air. "Fine. I can try. Maybe it will work, but that's an enormous maybe."

"It'll have to be enough."

She nodded, then crossed her arms, watching the line of water behind him. "How's Archibald?"

Liam scratched the back of his neck. "He's okay."

The old man had gotten the twenty souls he needed to save his life, but he had grown quieter, more distant. Half the time, Liam doubted his mind occupied the same place as his body, but he figured this was Archie's way to cope. Like he was shutting himself down to survive.

"Maybe I can help him," she said.

She meant she could glamour Archie. Help him forget.

No.

The old man would never allow it. He might be

wallowing and damaged, but he would never run from his demons. Literally.

"He'll pull through." Liam rubbed the bridge of his nose. "Let's get this over with; we don't have much time. I have to return to the Gorge soon."

"Well, then. Picture a wall around your brain," Lilith said as she fixed her red curls in a high ponytail that made her look slightly younger.

They stood face-to-face and all too near. Being this close to her made him uncomfortable. There were thoughts in his mind, thoughts that always reverted back to Ava. Thoughts that belonged to him and princess and no one else.

He stepped back and cleared his throat. "I don't want you peeking in there." He pointed to his head.

"I will have to." She frowned. "The point of this exercise is to stop me at best and confuse me at worst. Now, close your eyes."

Reluctantly, he did.

In the darkness, her voice came from everywhere. "You can shapeshift like a Beast which means you can probably mind-block like an Obsessor. So, let's find your essence and see if we can bend it."

Liam snorted. "How am I supposed to do that?"

"Follow the darkness. And the light." He felt her pointing somewhere behind him.

He turned and spotted a mass of darkness standing out from the rest. It beckoned to him, a dark deeper than dark. Liam hadn't actually seen it; he'd *felt* it swirling in his core.

It moved forward, crossing the void that surrounded them. He followed it.

Soon enough, he spotted a beacon in the distance: a tower of golden lava bleeding into the dark. He couldn't see where it started or where it ended.

The mass of darkness that led him here shot forward and spiraled up, wrapping itself around the tower.

"This is your essence, Liam. Dark and light," Lilith said with a certain awe, her voice coming from everywhere and nowhere at the same time.

"Is it?"

He felt her pointing at the golden tower. "Call for them. Bend them to your will."

Them? He frowned at Lilith's voice because she was clearly losing her mind. Then he remembered where he was —inside his own essence.

He let out a deep breath and stretched his hand toward the mass of golden lava and smoky darkness.

As if they were wolves catching a scent, the booming forces halted. The lava stopped bleeding, the darkness stopped swirling around it. They just stopped.

And focused on Liam.

A cold sweat broke through his body. "Shit."

"Don't be afraid," Lilith said right before the mass of light and dark shot at him.

The void around Liam rumbled and roared as the things approached. He kept his hand stretched, the other one protecting his face as if that could save him from the furious storm heading his way.

He closed his eyes. How that was possible he didn't know —closing what was already shut—but he did it.

The rumbling stopped. Liam opened one eye to see golden and dark flames sprouting on his skin. He raised his palm and watched the forces play with each other. They didn't hurt at all.

Why did he think they would hurt?

"Lilith?" he called, only now missing her presence.

She didn't reply. She wasn't here anymore.

A figure of light appeared ahead, cutting through the

darkness. A man with long hair, hard muscles, and a kind smile. Liam saw himself in that man, even though they didn't look much alike.

"Michael," he muttered.

The man stopped before him, all dancing specks of light, as if he was made of fireflies. He was a good head taller than Liam. The Archangel gave him a friendly nod as his glittering wings flashed behind him, mighty as the man himself.

Michael pointed at the distance behind him. "Remember who we are."

Something broke the darkness in a horizontal line. Liam couldn't see it, only feel it.

A wall.

His golden and dark flames pushed him forward, dragging him through the darkness damn close to fucking light speed. When the forces driving him halted, he found himself before a giant wall of obsidian stone.

The golden flames around his arm worked as a torch, and he could see his reflection on the surface. Michael's, too.

Liam turned to the Archangel who stood beside him, his glittering form reflected on the obsidian. His former self watched his own reflection with a certain longing.

"Do you hate me for not being like you?" Liam asked quietly.

Michael chortled. "We're one."

"But I'm a demon now. I let people die, I ... I couldn't save them." Fury possessed him all at once, and he fisted the wall. The impact reverberated down his immaterial bones, but it didn't hurt more than his guilt.

Michael watched him in silence. "There's always a price. If you let it happen, you were willing to pay it."

He stared at Michael, not knowing what to say or do. Tears pricked his eyes.

"And yet," Michael continued, "it all would've happened

without you anyway. Firma would still have been killed, those humans at the pub, and that poor girl … Hauk would've killed the night guard, too." He studied his reflection. "The guilt will always be with you, but sharing the burden with those who are truly guilty might help."

"It's not enough," he muttered.

"It never will be," Michael said. "We're more similar than you think." He observed Liam with love and kindness. "Don't forget who you are. Also, watch over Acheron and Shelaria if you can."

Who?

Images of Archie and the Cap flashed in his mind. A knot swelled in Liam's throat, and breathing got hard.

"I'm trying, but the world keeps crashing around me, and —" The cry was right there, etched into his voice. He swallowed it down.

"It never stops." Michal shrugged. "There's always another mission, always the duty. But she can walk this road with you. And perhaps your feet won't be so sore."

She?

Did he mean Ava? "Is she our soulmate?"

"I could tell you." Michael raised a sparkling eyebrow at him. "But you already know the answer."

"Liam?" Lilith's voice rung in the space around him. "Are you there?"

"I'm fine," he shouted into the darkness. When he turned to Michael, the Archangel had disappeared. "I'm standing before a freaking wall!"

And talking to himself.

"This is insane," he grumbled.

"It's not," she said, her tone still edging on worry. "I can feel the wall. I'll try to pierce it, all right? Try to stop me."

It was the same as trying to stop a car with his bare hands. Lilith broke through easily, and the impact threw Liam backward into the darkness. Breath fled his lungs but he quickly recovered, yet not before wondering how the Hells there could be a floor, and a wall, in his mind.

Mental projections, he guessed.

Lilith's essence thrummed from beyond the pitch-black hole she'd pierced. The endless void around him spread atop the obsidian, and when it retreated, the crater was gone.

"Again," she ordered from the other side.

Liam raised his flaming hand to find the spot's surface as smooth as a black pearl.

"I'm having an acid trip, aren't I?" He'd never actually had an acid trip, but it couldn't be crazier than this.

Lilith went on, crashing through the wall and blasting him away, again and again.

"Fucking bloodsucker," he grunted as he pulled himself back up for the umpteenth time.

He felt her grin from the open crack she'd just made. "I take it as a compliment. But you're getting better. Come on, we don't have all day."

The light and dark in his body shook, growling at the hole—the path to Lilith.

Two beasts ready to prowl.

Liam didn't have time to warn her before his powers shot through the gap and into the vamp, wherever she was.

His wall disappeared, and now Liam was standing inside a giant ballroom with a golden chandelier hanging from the ceiling. Golden sconces cut across the marbled walls, drenching the fancy space in dim lights. Liam peered through the tall arched windows and at the night that swallowed the outside. A full moon shone beyond the glass.

He heard the ruffle of a skirt, and then Lilith passed by him. She wore a green corseted dress, and her hair was up in a loose bun that made her curls cascade down the back of her shoulders.

By her attire and this entire setting, this couldn't be modern time. Liam guessed they must be somewhere in the 16th century.

The vampire queen looked younger somehow, or perhaps she just seemed happier. *Carefree.*

She bowed to a gentleman with amber skin and silky black hair tied in a low pony ... holy shit.

Jal!

He was elegant in a black frock coat and white shirt. The demon bowed slightly to Lilith, gave her his hand, and they began dancing around the ballroom.

Liam had no idea where the mellow tunes that led the pace came from, but he guessed memories weren't famous for being exact.

"Is this the last time?" Jal whispered close to Lilith's ear.

The shine in her features faded, and all her happiness vanished. "I'm afraid so."

He blinked back tears and kissed her forehead. "Then let's make it count, love."

On they went, dancing and turning until Lilith stopped. So did the music. Jal froze in place as his partner scowled at Liam.

"You weren't supposed to see this," Lilith snarled more than said, her fangs in full display.

"I-I ..." He couldn't gather the words.

In the blink of an eye, he was back at his wall, which had reformed itself. No hole pierced it anymore.

"Lilith, I'm so sorry," he finally managed. "I hadn't meant to—"

"It's only natural," she spat with annoyance. "You're a demon, after all."

Her words hurt, but he didn't linger in them. "You and Jal were so happy. What happened?"

A weary chuckle rang from the darkness around him. "Fate ruined it, as it always does."

Liam remembered the first time he met Ava. How beautiful her sky-blue eyes were and how the world stopped when she smiled. The feeling of her soft lips on his, and the warmth of her body as they made love ... Gods. That was an eternity ago.

Yeah, fate could be a bitch.

Energy piled on the other side, a sign that Lilith was about to strike. "Focus, Liam."

He spread his flaming palms on the wall.

The onyx surface thrummed underneath his fingertips, showing him the faces of all those he'd failed. He already knew Firma, but Liam had dug for the others' names—being a detective had its perks.

Madeleine, the working girl. Juarez, the night guard. And Dhalia, the teenager.

Liam collected the names of all those who'd faced violence and cruelty because of this godsdammned war. *Lothar. Archibald. Kevin. The Cap.* He carved them in his mind for the reckoning with Hauk and Master.

His light shot through the obsidian wall, making it shine like the sun. His black flames ran through the surface, half-covering the light with veins of darkness.

This time, Lilith didn't pierce through.

ARCHIE MET Liam outside the warehouse. The old man trapped him in a hug that both warmed his heart and scared the Hells out of him.

"Old man, what's going on?"

Archie let him go. "You know the party planned for today? It's Hauk's wedding."

"What the fuck?" Juniper came to mind, along with all the times she'd gone up to Hauk's office. The entire Gorge had heard their grunts and moans from the second floor. Liam recalled the awkwardness in the air as the demons below tried to ignore the screaming lovebirds. "I assumed he and Juniper weren't serious."

"Me neither. My gut's telling me something's off." For the first time in a while, Archie looked sharp and on edge, once again Liam's fierce partner.

He was glad the old man had gathered his shit, especially now. "Whatever it is, we'll figure it out."

"Always, son." He patted Liam's shoulder. "I won't let you down again."

His nostrils flared, and he slapped Archie's chest. "You never have! We're both doing our best, and you should remember that."

It wasn't enough for his father, it never would be; he could see that. But they had other matters to worry about.

They went inside the warehouse and observed the tables covered with black cloth. They were filled with snacks and drinks. Black ribbons hung from the walls and ceiling but still allowed daylight to venture through the windows. A soft, melodic tune came from the speakers at the back of the room.

He sat with Archie on a large beanbag in the corner. Soon enough, Pedro found them and sat beside Liam.

The fucker followed him like a puppy.

Ahead, Hauk talked with the Possessor as he held a drink in his hand. He seemed happy; no, ecstatic. It was odd seeing that asshole this way.

Liam's attention went to the Possessor, and his blood ran cold in his veins. His throat tightened, and he had to remind himself to breathe.

"I hate those things," Pedro whispered from his left, nodding at the languid figure covered with a long black cloak. Death as in the horror stories. "You think they're fixing the date when we'll meet Master?" He rubbed his hands eagerly. "It's like meeting the devils themselves, you know?"

"We're two lucky sons of bitches." Liam forced a smile. "It means a lot that Hauk trusts us with this."

The Possessor raised a finger at the Gorge's leader, displaying bone-white fingers that could very well be exactly that: bones.

Hauk patted it on the shoulder as old friends do, almost as if he were assuring the Possessor everything would be fine. Liam couldn't catch what "everything" might be, though.

The music grew louder as a girl all clad in black entered the warehouse. The hem of her dress brushed the floor as she moved, and her bouquet was made of black and blue roses. Her curly hair was trapped in a puffy high bun, and her dark beady eyes were contoured by coal eyeliner.

Liam froze, and his stomach dropped to his feet.

Dhalia. The girl from the pub.

This was a nightmare; it had to be.

By her eyes and sharp teeth, she was newly turned. Hauk had raped her, forced a deal on her, then released the poor girl only to come back later and end her life.

There was something wrong with this picture, though. Dhalia smiled, her attention fixed on Hauk, who watched her with adoration. They looked nothing short of an elated bride and groom.

The demon opened his arms and she increased her pace, rushing toward her freaking rapist!

Liam's breakfast sizzled in his stomach.

Dhalia hugged Hauk fiercely, the way only a lover would.

Apparently, she'd forgotten all the unforgivable things he'd done to her.

The Possessor had used his own darkness to seal the deals. Maybe this erased the victim's memory. Maybe it changed them.

Failing to control the rage and desperation thrashing inside, Liam stood and walked to them. He'd let that girl suffer once. He wouldn't do it again.

"What in all the Hells?" he blurted.

"Wonderful, isn't it?" Hauk drew a line with his finger on Dhalia's chin and gave her a peck on the lips. "My bride's darkness is Master's darkness, and it's glorious."

Dhalia grinned at her groom with sharp pointed teeth.

Liam's chest hurt.

Gods, how he had failed her. How he'd failed them all …

He swallowed down the rush of red, roaring wrath, only now remembering he balanced on a tight rope.

"Look, I'm all up for this, but doesn't she remember?" Liam poked Hauk with his elbow. "If I were you, I'd be careful. She might chop off your dick on your honeymoon."

The demon burst in laughs, then patted him starkly on his back. "I appreciate your concern about my dick, but she won't harm me." He tapped the side of his nose knowingly. "Master's gifts are plentiful."

"I remember everything," the girl said, her chin held high. "And I don't care. A part of me even enjoyed it."

Liam's throat might've turned into shards of glass. "Is that so?"

She considered the question for a moment. "I suppose it hurt when my love took me from my home and slammed a dagger in my chest, but when I woke, I was blessed by the dark. I'm immortal now. What a wonderful gift he gave me."

What kind of brainwashed shit was this?

Hauk kissed the girl's temple with the gentleness of a

caring lover. "She's here because she enjoyed being with me. Naughty little thing."

She'd enjoyed being raped and murdered? No chance in all the Hells.

Perhaps the darkness the Possessor imbedded in her tainted Dhalia's mind. Liam's own darkness had been cruel and maddening but not like this.

This was much worse.

He faked nonchalance as he tapped Hauk's shoulder. "Hey man, I'm happy for you." He ogled Dhalia up and down and felt dirty for it. "Maybe one day you can get me a bride, too."

Hauk bared his teeth in a ferocious grin. "All of Master's children will get what they deserve." He stepped aside and clapped his hands, addressing all demons in the warehouse. "It's time!"

They all gathered before the Possessor and the starring couple.

The thing uttered ancient words Liam couldn't understand. Eventually, pitch-black clouds puffed from Hauk's body and mingled with Dhalia's own darkness. After a moment, the clouds disappeared in thin air.

The Possessor hissed, "It issss done."

Hauk kissed her, and the demons around them cheered loudly. Their sick matrimony had been sealed.

Gods, this was torture.

Booming music exploded from the speakers as a rush of demons went to congratulate Hauk and his bride.

Liam stepped back and went to the bean bag. Archie sat there alone, watching the crowd, his expression revealing nothing.

"This won't destroy me, kid," he whispered as he watched Pedro shake Hauk's hand. "I want these bastards' heads more than anything."

The force of nature called Archibald Theodore Brennan was back, and he wouldn't take any prisoners.

"We'll end this, Archie. Even if it's the last thing we do."

Liam's darkness suddenly tingled. Someone was watching.

The Possessor observed him from underneath its hood, three yellow eyes glinting in the darkness.

Liam felt languid, cold fingers caressing his wall, and when he forced his light to the surface, pulsing underneath the veins of darkness, the fingers retreated.

He cleared his mind just in case, fueling his brain with images of a world ruled by demons, and then red pulsing hate. Hate for angels and for Ezraphael. Hate for the Order, too.

The Possessor chuckled and stepped toward him. "Massster will be delighted to meet you," it hissed more than spoke. "Your esssence isss exquisite."

Liam forced pride and gratitude onto himself. "It will be my honor." He glanced at Archie, who watched them with worry. Liam nodded to him. "It will be an honor for us both."

"Hauk sssaid just you and the other." The thing pointed at Archibald. "Thisss one hasss yet to prove himself."

Well, at least he tried.

"Sounds peachy," Liam countered with fake glee. "When will I be meeting Master?"

The thing inhaled deeply. "Tonight, young demon. Tonight you'll face the one we worship."

29

LIAM

*T*he sun was still shining by the time Hauk left the party to consummate his marriage. Well, leaving was an overstatement; he simply went to his room on the second floor.

Knowing how loud Hauk could be, Liam was grateful for the booming music that permeated the ground level.

One hundred demons partied and drank furiously—the Gorge's numbers had increased since he'd joined. Some challenged their peers in arm wrestling, others danced around like maniacs. A group on the left battled playfully and for no reason, while some, such as Phil and Lacey, lost all common sense and had sex in front of everyone.

No surprise. Demons tended to go overboard in everything they did.

It was dark by the time Hauk called Liam and Pedro to his office upstairs.

They entered the space to find the Gorge's leader behind his table, reading some documents. His wife lounged on a wine-colored couch near the corner. She looked blissful and exhausted.

Liam promised himself he would figure out what the Possessor did to that poor girl. Thousands of humans out there would share the same fate if they died, people he and Archie had helped damn.

Hauk raised his head and winked at Dhalia. Pheromones hung heavy between them, their arousal a near physical force. Liam's stomach churned, but he kept his face a mask.

The demon turned to him and Pedro, then propped his elbows on the table. "Now that I have my wife, I can focus on other pressing matters," he said. "As you know, a werewolf stole the wolfsugar we had stored in the warehouse. I did not forget about it. I will not forgive."

"Yeah, we heard," Pedro said. "We want to catch that fucker, too. They killed Abrielle, and she was a fine piece of ass, you know what I'm saying?"

Idiot.

Liam whistled. "A dog doing that much damage? It's nuts. They must be really desperate."

"Yes and no." Hauk raised his index finger. "Someone from the Gorge leaked information to the wolves. They knew exactly where to go and where to find the guards. They had the advantage over Abrielle, and they killed her with one bite. No normal wolf could've done that."

"Maybe it was the werewolf lord," Pedro offered.

"If Lothar was alive, I wouldn't doubt it." Hauk shook his head. "But his son is weak."

Liam tapped Pedro's chest. "We'll find out who it was, boss."

"No need." Hauk peered at them with undecipherable eyes. "I trusted this information to only a few, but any of them could've opened their mouths. Including both of you."

A breath stopped midway in Liam's lungs. "We didn't open our beaks."

"We'll see," he said. "Regardless, someone in this party did."

Liam held the relieved breath that pushed out. Hauk still trusted him, at least for now.

"Finding who did it will be hard," Pedro grumbled. "News travels fast. Tell someone today, tomorrow the entire block knows."

"Ain't that right." Hauk raised one eyebrow. "But I had an idea. See, all our demons are gathered downstairs to celebrate. Let's not forget the Possessor is also here. I find it a great opportunity, don't you?"

A cold sweat broke out on Liam's skin.

"When our friend finds out who did it," Hauk fisted his hand slowly, "I will end them."

Liam pretended not to care about the threat looming over him. "Fine by me, but I assumed we were meeting Master tonight?"

Hauk shrugged. "We can kill two birds with one stone."

What the Hells did that mean?

"Let's go." The demon tapped the table and stood. He then motioned for his wife to come.

Dhalia rushed through the room, her black dress swinging behind her until she snuggled against Hauk's left side. He lay one arm over her shoulders. "The night is young, gentlemen. Let's get this sorted so I can continue enjoying my wife."

The couple led the way, followed by Pedro.

Liam stood there for a moment, his mind spinning as he tried to figure a way out of this. His blood froze solid in his veins as he realized this was the end game.

Even if he could block the Possessor, that thing would still read Archie's mind.

"Hey, *puto*, you coming or not?" Pedro called out.

"Vai se fuder," Liam countered, flipping him the bird as he followed them down the stairs.

His steps drummed through his bones, from his soles up to his skull. His body felt heavy, and a continuous pitch rang in his ears, muffling other sounds.

Why had he tried to help those ungrateful wolves?

They'd doomed him.

From the last row of stairs, Liam found Archie in the crowd and glared at him. The message was clear: *We're beyond fucked.*

The old man pressed his lips together and walked discretely to the base of the stairs, halting on the second step to meet him.

A sea of a hundred demons parted to make way for Hauk and Dhalia, who strolled toward the center of the warehouse. The music faded.

When the couple stopped, the demons around them stepped away, making a round clearing for them amongst the forest of bodies clad in black. They left the way to the circle open, though.

The Possessor stepped out from the crowd and walked the path toward them, its stride slow and labored, almost as if that thing was coming down with a flu.

Pedro placed himself in the crowd and watched. Archie and Liam stayed on the stairs, far from the center but high enough that they could see what happened.

The Possessor halted at the edge of the circle and bowed slightly to Hauk. The demon bowed his head to him in return, as did his wife.

The thing pointed a bony finger at the first row of demons. It touched each of their foreheads and waited a moment or two before going to the next.

It would take a while to examine each demon in this place, so Liam had time to think of a getaway plan.

"You have to run, Archie," he whispered. "I might be able to block the Possessor, but he'll see right through you."

"Might?" He chortled. "Kid, if that thing wants to see into your head, it will."

He glared at his father, his eyes stinging with tears. Liam didn't care what would happen to him; he just wanted Archie out of here. "I lost you once, old man. I can't lose you again."

Archie scowled at him. "I'm not leaving my son to die. That's final." He craned his neck left and right in a preparation for battle. His hand rested on the hilt of his sword. "Before we found out about the wedding, I warned Jophiel something strange was happening today. Hopefully he'll come to the rescue."

"The Legion can't help us." Liam pointed to the crowd ahead, trying to control the anger in his tone. "There are a hundred demons here, most of them second-tiers."

"The Legion won't fail us again, kid. Jophiel is a Seraph."

He blew an exasperated breath. "Archie, you will run, or I swear to the Gods—"

A piercing shriek broke through the warehouse; a hollow, shrill sound that belonged to a dying animal. Liam watched as the Possessor jerked and writhed inside the circle like an invisible force was trying to break it.

Well, snap it in half was more accurate.

Eventually, the attack ceased and the creature hunched over, taking wheezing breaths. All was silent until its hooded face snapped up toward Liam and Archie.

The Possessor walked down the path it had just followed, leaving Hauk and Dhalia behind.

Liam and Archie stepped down from the stairs and waited. When the creature halted before them, two blue orbs shone from the darkness underneath the hood.

"Interesting," the thing said without its normal hiss. It

spoke with a low baritone that belonged to the depths of the Hells; something ancient and beastly.

Blue eyes instead of yellow. Different voice.

Different demon.

Liam frowned. "Master?"

The Possessor craned its neck in a curious manner. "Smart, are we not?"

All demons ahead immediately dropped to their knees, Hauk and his wife included. The hooded figure looked back at the warehouse, surveying the scene.

Holy shit. Master had possessed a fucking Possessor.

Liam swallowed back the mass of fear climbing up his throat.

"You do not bow?" Master asked without turning to him and Archie.

"Forgive us." Liam bowed his head. "We're in awe of you."

The demon pivoted on his heels to face them, wrapping his bony hands behind his back. When his burning blue orbs focused on the old man, Master said, "Defiance is not a habit I appreciate."

Archie bowed his head at once. "Forgive me, Master. We do not defy you."

"A wise decision." He gave out a low chuckle. "When I heard two Archangels had become demons, I couldn't believe it." He nodded back to Hauk. "None of my factions harbor a Fallen, let alone two, but Hauk guaranteed me your obedience, and I trust him. Do tell me, my children. Why did you fall?"

Liam didn't think twice. "The Order betrayed us."

"Their hypocrisy is amusing," Master agreed. "Their blindness will be their doom. It's no wonder you came to my side."

Liam knelt on the floor. "We have proven ourselves over and over, Master. We are with you, now and always."

Megalomaniacs liked thinking they had all the power. Maybe if Liam showed respect, the bastard's ego would swell and he would lose interest.

"You choose them smart, Hauk," he said without turning to the leader of the Gorge.

"Thank you, Master!"

"Not a compliment," he countered curtly, his tone growing deeper.

All demons still bowed at Master as if he were one of the devils himself, their foreheads pressed on the floor.

He spun around and addressed the creatures across the warehouse. "My children, the time is near. The Order will soon fall. Follow my command, and I'll deliver you our promised land! Rise, sons and daughters of the dark!"

"Deliver us!" The demons said in unison before jumping to their feet. The warehouse exploded in cheers and huzzahs.

This asshole had them by their fucking balls.

"Tonight, however, we must celebrate." Master snapped his attention back to Liam, his blue eyes burning. "Also, we must find a traitor."

He felt a piercing pressure into his mental wall and immediately shot his light into it, blocking the rumbling power that pushed from the other side.

"Oh, remarkable." Master licked his own lips. Liam couldn't see it from underneath the hood, but he could feel it. He couldn't sense much else, though. "Your darkness is indeed exquisite."

Was he supposed to be flattered?

"All my children give themselves to me without hesitation, and yet you resist," Master said. "Why?"

If Master were really here, Liam would've drawn him closer and slashed his throat. But if he attacked this thing, he would only kill the puppet, not the monster on the other side.

He had to be smart.

"I'm not the traitor you seek," he stated while his wall did something strange. It retreated and bent in on itself, quickly surrounding only what mattered right now: Ava, Archie, his undercover mission, and the fact that he was the wolf who had betrayed the Gorge.

The wall stood around those pieces of him, uneven but strong as a fortress.

He let Master inside the rest of his mind, his presence a heavy wave of void and dark. "My thoughts are mine to have," Liam said, "but you're always welcome."

Master observed him. "Why do you hide, Liam Striker?"

He analyzed the Possessor from top to bottom. "I could ask you the same."

An amused grin came from underneath the hood; Liam could feel it in his essence. "It seems we're not so different after all, my child."

The heavy presence that washed across his mind faded. Liam let out a relieved breath.

"Thank you, Master."

Flaming cold eyes watched him with a mix of curiosity and surprise. The creature before him laughed loudly, bordering on hysteria. His shoulders heaved as he cackled laughs, and soon enough, some demons chuckled awkwardly after him.

Kiss-asses.

Master's laughter stopped at once. "A long time ago, I met a man who deemed me a fool. So I let him believe it, day in and day out, and when my moment finally came, I opened him up, scooped his entrails like a pumpkin and fed them to him. Do you think he still fancied me a fool then, Liam Striker?"

"Of course not, I—"

"I don't need to break into your wall to read your mind."

He leaned forward, and Liam realized the blue orbs inside the hood had no lids. "A tiny hole does the trick."

Fuck! Liam could feel it now, a microscopic puncture at the base of his uneven wall.

"He was the wolf," Master told the demons in the warehouse. "End him and his father. I'll take care of the Seraph outside."

30

AVA

*A*va knocked on the white wooden door to Ezra's room. Silence replied, so she stood there, stubbornly waiting. She had left twice this morning after no response from him, but she wouldn't budge this time.

"Come in," he finally conceded.

She gingerly pushed the door open and stepped inside. Her head still thumped with the remnants of the greatest migraine of her life, but it felt better now than when she had woken up. Ava could've easily healed her hangover, but she decided she deserved the pain after her monumental screw-up.

Ezra stared out the window as she approached, his arms crossed and his silky hair loose.

"I wanted to talk about what happened yesterday." Her tone was almost a whisper.

He didn't turn to face her. "Later."

"Later will never come, and we need to solve this." She motioned to the space between them. "You're the best angel I know, and you don't deserve—"

"You want to explain? Fine." He pivoted on his heels. His

nostrils flared as he locked eyes with her, their placid blue now consumed with annoyance. "Why did you call me by his name?"

"I was drunk," she said quietly. "I care for Liam, and I care for you as well. You both mean so much to me."

"I know you care for us both," he spat. "I'm the Messenger, Ava. I'm not blind. But love and care are very different things."

"You demand too much from me." She took a deep breath. "I can't give you what you need."

"Yes, you can." He raised one silver eyebrow. "You're confused, I understand. But the best for you isn't him, and deep down you know it."

There was truth to his words, but she ignored it none-theless.

Ava slammed both hands on her waist. "Don't tell me how I'm supposed to feel."

"Never." He bowed and placed an apologetic hand over his heart. "It's logic, Ava. Think back on how you feel when you're with me. Do remember I'm a child of the Goddess of Love and Life and a high angel, so I already know the answer."

"Then why make me say it?" She rolled her eyes, knowing there was no running away from this. "It's peaceful with you."

"Is that why you agreed to become my mate?"

She had to face the truth that had always been there. *Yes.* She'd become Ezra's mate because she needed him as much as he needed her. Once, Ava was kind and pure like the Messenger. As much as she hated to admit it, she wanted to be that Guardian again, or at least meet her halfway.

Only Ezra could show her how.

He smiled, sensing the answer in her emotions. "And how is it with him?"

Ava gulped. Liam was fire, chaos and adrenaline.

Unsettling. Unravelling.

Ezra must've sensed her emotions again because he gave her a proud smirk. "As I said, a matter of logic. You've changed, Ava. You're not the meek, peaceful Guardian you used to be. Now you burn, and so does he. He can't give you the balance you need."

And still, she longed for chaos over peace, fire over water.

Being with Ezra was the wise and the right thing to do. He was good for her. If Ava gave herself to him, she would be happy.

Well, not exactly happy.

Content.

"You ask me to make a decision I simply can't." She cleared her throat. "Not right now."

He gave her a knowing grin. "Later, then?"

"Later." She inhaled deeply. "We must go. Kevin called us for an urgent meeting. He's in your office."

KEVIN WAS SITTING behind Ezra's marbled desk. Atop the table was a single file folder.

On the left side, near the open window, Justine lounged on Ezra's white couch. She basked under the orange hue of sunset, a soft smile stamped on her lips.

"Glad to know you've made yourselves comfortable in my office," Ezra grumbled.

Kevin laid back on Ezra's white leather chair and wrapped both hands behind his head. "Oh yes, it's lovely here."

"You guys will want to hear what Kev has to say." Justine kept her eyes closed as fading sunlight graced her perfect features.

"Then go on already," Ezra urged, impatience swirling in his core.

Kevin looked at Ava. "I was close to giving up. So much so, that I considered asking Agathe to read your mind."

She gasped. "Absolutely not! If she does, she'll find out about the Legion."

"Unlikely, since Jophiel blurs our memories to invasive mental forces. Agathe could still decipher them, though, which would make it an enormous risk." Kevin shrugged. "So, you see how desperate I was."

Ava narrowed her eyes at Justine. Her friend had told her she'd seen the Legion in Ava's mind, but if Kevin was right, that was impossible.

Justine gave her an apologetic smile, a certain fear imbedded in her features.

"Kev was the one who told me about the Legion—with Jophiel's permission, of course," her voice rang in Ava's mind. *"I was so worried, dear. I needed an open channel to you, and I couldn't have it if I faked ignorance about the Legion."*

To her own surprise, Ava wasn't angry. If anything, she appreciated the lengths her friend had gone through to help her.

"I understand," she said through their mind channel.

"Well." Ezra shrugged, having missed their exchange completely. "Agathe would never do it without evidence of misconduct first. So, it wouldn't matter if Ava asked her to read her mind or not."

Justine rolled her eyes. "The Throne is a good leader, but she's such a stickler for the rules."

"I call that blindness," Ava countered.

"You're both right." Kevin tapped the table and stood. He grabbed the folder from the surface. "Are angels allowed to own properties?"

293

Ezra frowned. "No. They may use them, but the owner-ship belongs to the Order."

Kevin strolled in slow circles with hands—and the file folder—behind his back. "Do you know how the police caught Al Capone?"

Ava narrowed her eyes. "The Mafioso? What does he have to do with anything?"

"How did the police catch him?" he insisted.

Ezra raised his shoulders. "He killed someone?"

"Many, actually. But that's not what got him arrested."

The white, taffeta curtains fluttered with a soft breeze. Realization dawned on Ava.

She remembered the reports from when she was still human. It had been everywhere in the papers. 1931, the year the police finally caught him but not because of a murder.

A wide grin spread across her face as Kevin handed her the folder.

"Tax evasion," she said as she read through the pages. "It's also how Kevin caught Talahel."

AGATHE SAT behind the obsidian table in her office, tapping her fingers on the surface. Her long inky nails ticked loudly, making for the only sound in the room.

Ava didn't need her Dominion instincts to notice the Throne's impatience.

Tick, tick, tick.

Twilight had begun by the time Ava and Ezra requested an urgent audience with her, and night had already fallen when they finally got it.

"What is it that couldn't wait until morning?" she asked.

Ezra stepped forward and dropped the folder on her desk. "He fooled us, Agathe. All of us."

She frowned, then fixed the lamp on her desk over the papers. She read through them, and her skeptical demeanor only increased. The Throne flipped the pages back and forth, as if she failed to find an answer in them. "What am I seeking?"

"These documents prove Talahel has properties all around town," Ava said.

The Throne chortled. "That's impossible. Angels are not allowed to have properties."

"We know."

"Look, it says here all these buildings belong to a Peter Miller." Agathe pointed at a page.

After Kevin found the first clue in Vera's papers, it had been too easy. He logged into the Order's system and hacked human real estate databases, seeking properties registered under the name of Peter Miller. In the end, the paper trail was spotless and he had a tight case against the Sword.

"Peter Miller *is* Talahel." Ava walked forward and flipped the pages, stopping at Peter Miller's Selfless ID document which tied him to Talahel's angelic identity. "Talahel was reborn as a Selfless in 1940."

Agathe scanned the pages with a frown, then motioned for Ava to continue.

"At the time, the entire Order believed he was a most honorable high angel, since he left his duties to become human and directly help those in need. Every lower angel loved him for it. How *noble* he was." Ava snorted. "It was also a cover-up. He bought properties under his human name but never gave them back to the Order. He's been profiting from them for decades."

"If I recall correctly, he'd left Michael in charge," Ezra added. "But I doubt he was involved."

"If Michael knew, he would've said something," Agathe mumbled, no doubt in her tone as she scanned the folder.

Finally, she dropped it on the table and leaned back on her chair, slamming both hands on her forehead. "Gods! How have my Virtues missed this?"

"Virtue Locke has been in charge of auditing Selfless lives once they die and return as angels, so I'm guessing he's involved." Ava shrugged. "Talahel has many allies. He's been playing this game for a long time."

"His wealth must be enormous." The Throne hunched over the table and opened the file again, sifting through the pages. "There's at least thirty properties listed in here, all scattered across town."

Ava nodded. "But why would he need the money? And what is he doing with it?"

Agathe peered at her from below thin black eyebrows. "That's what I'll find out once I read his mind." She stood and paced in circles. "Still, we must follow proper protocol. He can't know what we're up to, not until the last minute. Almost the entire Order stands with him." Agathe bit her lips. "We must prepare, Ezra. Our brother has become more powerful than I'd like to admit."

Fear sipped into Ava's chest, a soft sensation at first which grew into lung-crushing terror. She bent over, trying to catch a breath while holding the scream that pushed out.

Something was wrong.

"Ava!" Ezra rushed toward her. "Are you all right?"

The strings of light and dark that connected her to Liam convulsed violently. Sweat beaded on her forehead, and dizziness nearly sent Ava toppling over her knees.

He was in danger!

"Ava?" Ezra called out, but it was too late.

Her wings had already flashed behind her. She bolted through Agathe's open window, following the quivering strings—the path to him.

Chilly night air whipped against her, but Ava didn't slow down. She had to get to Liam.

Hold on, she begged through their connection, hoping that somehow he could listen.

The lines of light and dark suddenly stilled.

31

LIAM

*M*aster had rushed out of the warehouse to find Jophiel, but if there was anyone who could beat that megalomaniacal asshole, it was the Seraph. Liam had to believe this because he couldn't run to his aid, not when an army of bloodthirsty demons closed in on him and Archie.

Monumentally screwed didn't even begin to cover their situation.

Beside him, the old man unsheathed his sword and grabbed the holy gun underneath his jacket. He peered at the oncoming mass with a certain hunger. "You ready for this?"

Liam glanced at the silver wolf claws on the cross guard of his—Michael's—sword and unsheathed the weapon. With his free hand, he grabbed his holy gun from the holster. Well, it wasn't holy anymore. Archie had cursed it, but the bullets could pierce through demonic flesh either way.

Fear coursed through him, but he wore a mask of stone. Liam would die today, this was certain. How many of these fuckers he'd take along was the question.

"Let him come to me!" Hauk bellowed beyond the wall of gnarling demons.

They halted. Once again, the bodies stepped aside, forming a path to the center of the warehouse where Hauk waited for him.

Liam stared right into the demon's furious hazel eyes. A grin spread on his lips.

This was the perfect way to go. He might've failed in his mission, but he wouldn't fail avenging all those innocents.

Hauk unsheathed his sword and pushed his new wife away.

At first Dhalia shook her head and clung to him, but when Hauk grabbed her forcefully by the back of her neck and ordered her to go, she obeyed. The leader of the Gorge didn't tolerate disobedience, and the girl must've learned that quickly.

He bared his teeth at Liam. "You fooled me."

"Wasn't that hard." Liam clicked his tongue as he entered the path walled by demons. "You're really stupid."

Hauk oozed death and cruelty. "I'll enjoy killing you."

With one hand, Liam swung his sword in circles. Fire bloomed from his skin and through his cursed clothes. "Remember what I did to your pretty face? I was a baby demon then. Imagine what I can do now."

"You're still only a Terror." Puffy shadows spread behind the Gorge's leader, soon giving place to gray wings without scales. "And back then, you caught me by surprise. You won't be so lucky this time."

"I burned an Archangel to death." Liam's throat might be walled by splinters. The flames around him intensified, enveloping his body in blazing fury. "I was weaker than her, too."

Hauk snorted. "She was impaired by the cursed cuffs. I gave her to you on a platter, weak little Terror."

C.S. WILDE

"Excuses, excuses." He clicked his tongue. "But don't you worry. I'll avenge her tonight."

In the corner of the warehouse, Hauk's bride curled into a ball as she watched their stand-off with horror. A thorny needle pierced Liam's chest. Yes, tonight he would avenge them all, and then he'd die with a clear conscience.

Not such a bad way to go.

"Son?" Archie called out from behind, his attention on the demons who watched the old man intently. His father moved one step forward, and the wall of demons stepped in his way, blocking him.

Hauk's invitation was for one man only.

Liam turned back, agony squeezing his chest. He would never see Archie again. "Watch out for yourself, Dad."

He moved ahead and toward Hauk, who eagerly waited for him. The demon snarled through clenched teeth, "You're wise to say goodbye to your *papa*."

"I know." Liam stopped in front of him and set his fighting stance, raising his sword.

He was ready.

"You never think strategically. So cocky ..." Hauk smirked, then nodded to a demon in the crowd. "How about we tire you up before our final showdown?"

A bulky Behemoth stepped from the mob into the arena. Hells, that woman was as big as Abrielle.

"Sending others to do your dirty work?" Liam teased. "Are you scared, Hauk?"

The Behemoth bellowed a war cry and rushed to Liam before he got an answer. He kept his attention locked on Hauk, who had stepped aside to watch. He winked at the Gorge's leader, raised his gun, and shot a red blast straight into the woman's forehead.

She fell on the floor with a mighty boom, but she'd

recover soon. Had the bullet been blessed, she probably would have never risen again.

Hauk urged the next in line forward, a Terror with red irises and a long beaky nose that made him resemble a stork. He rushed to Liam, wielding his sword the way one wields a cement block: with effort and no grace.

Liam's blade cut through the air and the demon's neck. His head fell on the ground, and his body toppled forward, almost reaching Liam's foot. Specks of blood splattered on the tips of his boots.

"Is that all you've got?" Liam asked.

A loud grumble rang from above, and he spotted a navy-winged demon with sandy blond hair crossing the air, followed by a Drakar with canary yellow wings.

Archie? What was he doing?

The punch came out of nowhere, sending Liam to the dusty ground. He rolled sideways and jumped to his feet just in time to dodge another punch from Juniper.

"Let's make this interesting," Hauk's fuck buddy said as she stepped back, gaining momentum for an attack. She watched Liam with a mix of lust and anger.

Fire bloomed on her skin as she ran toward him, bellowing her lungs out. He shot at her, again and again, but Juniper dodged the blasts all too quickly.

A Terror's speed was no joke.

"Screw this." He put down his gun and summoned the flames.

From his greatest depths, something else replied. Something wild and furious that had been asleep until now.

Free us, his own voice echoed in his ears.

Well, he didn't have much of a choice.

A black firestorm shot from his arm, engulfing Juniper in roaring onyx flames. Heat blurred the air around them, and most demons stepped back.

Juniper didn't have time to scream; she had already turned into a pile of ashes. The black flames showed her remains to Liam's darkness like a cat showed a dead mouse to its owner, hoping to receive praise.

The demons watched each other with a mix of fear and confusion. Heck, Liam was shocked too, but he didn't have time to dwell on it.

A vein popped on Hauk's forehead. "End him!"

Liam's dark flames spread in a small circle on the ground around him, buying him some time. He grabbed his gun and shot at the demons who dared to come close. His flames gave way to the bullets, otherwise they'd melt when crossing his fire—he didn't have a clue how he knew that, but he did.

We are one.

Three demons went down on the other side, and when he pulled the trigger on the fourth, he heard an empty click.

Fan-fucking-tastic.

He tossed the gun aside and grabbed his sword with both hands. Sweat bloomed on his forehead, and his muscles ached. He hadn't fought much, but using black fire clearly sucked his energy.

Enemies approached from all angles, closing in on him.

This was it. His fire would wane soon—he already felt its intensity dimming by the second—and then Liam would be dead and gone.

He had to find a way to Hauk before that.

Glass cracked from the warehouse's front windows, and a winged figure cut through the air, close enough for Liam to spot wine colored scales that became black at the tips.

Jal!

The onyx flames retreated back into Liam's essence just as his friend landed beside him. Liam glared at his own hands, still not understanding how he could create scorching black flames.

"Hey there, buddy." Jal winked at him. "How about we make this even?"

Either he was overly confident, or he'd lost his mind. How could two demons overpower a small army?

The Gorge was about to charge at them when growls and barks burst from the entrance. The stench of wet fur and old blood overtook Liam's nostrils as a sea of werewolves and vampires crashed into the warehouse, destroying the large door and windows.

Strong arms grabbed Liam from behind and boosted him up, snatching him away from battle. Down below, he spotted Jal punching a demon, and Lilith biting into a second-tier's neck. Not far from them, a big werewolf with caramel fur ripped an enemy's leg to shreds.

Suther.

"I need you safe, kid," Archie shouted, his grip on Liam's shoulders stone-hard.

He thrashed under his father's hold, his feet dangling in the air, but Archie didn't release him. "Come on, old man! I can fight!"

"Those black flames were your hellsfire, Liam! No Terror has ever been able to use them, and only a few Drakars can summon this power."

Maybe he was right. Liam had never seen Jal use black fire. "Then take me back so I can kick their asses!"

"You don't get it! This kind of power consumes you faster. You're not used to it and—" A Drakar caught Archie's foot midflight and flung him against a wall.

The old man smashed on the concrete but not before he dropped Liam, saving him from the impact.

He landed with a thud and damn close to Jal. Liam looked up to see Archie quickly recovering and kicking the Drakar's ass. He smiled with pride. He expected nothing less from his father.

"Back already?" Jal's wings vanished behind him, and he unsheathed an obsidian sword from his belt.

Liam had never seen a blade like that. Like the night and twinkling stars. It was magnificent.

A group of demons approached them. Jal fixed his base and raised his sword. So did Liam, but when he looked at his hand, he wondered how far his hellfire could go. He tried summoning it but couldn't reach that deep void inside him.

Come on!

The incoming demon, a Beast, rushed toward him. Liam shot his normal blazing flames. They might not be hellfire, but they turned the demon's skin into a nasty shade of red peppered by blisters.

Even covered by third-degree burns, the guy didn't stop.

"How do I summon the black flames again?" Liam shouted as he gripped his sword harder.

"You can't. You used a lot of energy," Jal said casually as a sphere of darkness peppered by purple lightning birthed from his palm. "You need to recharge."

He shot the sphere toward the mess of burnt flesh heading toward them, and it pierced a hole through the demon's trunk. The lifeless body fell backward.

"It would be helpful if you ascended sometime soon." Jal's eyes glinted with excitement. "Imagine what you could do as a Drakar with that hellfire of yours."

The dead demon's companions rushed toward them, but Jal shrugged nonchalantly, as if the murderous monsters falling upon them were nothing but harmless children.

Liam's darkness spread underneath his skin, and when he dodged an incoming demon—another Beast—his movements became blurs.

He never felt so light.

The demon watched the empty space where Liam was standing a second ago. Before he could turn around, Liam slashed his blade through the back of the demon's neck, then yanked the sword out and swiveled as the next one charged from behind.

He ducked and slammed the blade through the demon's stomach, pushing it up and cutting through half of his trunk.

Amidst the madness of clashing bodies, he found Hauk, who'd just finished killing a vamp.

Fire burst not only on his skin but inside him. "Time for your reckoning, boss."

Liam jolted toward him, but Jal grabbed him from behind and flung him against a wall.

"He's much more powerful than you," the demon shouted as he rushed toward Hauk. "I'll take care of it!"

"You bastard!" Liam barked, but it was useless. Jal was already neck-deep in battle with the Gorge's leader.

"It ends now, traitor." The voice rang from his left.

Five second-tiers closed in on him. Their draconian wings were splashed with vampire and werewolf blood; he could smell the stench of wet fur and old blood coating the demons' own scent of brimstone.

Anger swirled inside Liam in synchrony with his flames as he sprinted toward the first Behemoth. The demon was caught by surprise, an incredulous look on his face.

Did he expect Liam to cower? He should've know better.

Liam jumped and fire-punched the demon's head, just like he'd once done with Hauk. Liam kept pressing his fist into the demon's skull until he reached his brain. It might not be enough to kill, but it was enough to neutralize him. The tissue charred under his flames, and then the demon slumped on the floor.

Only four remained.

The one on the right snarled and unsheathed his sword as he charged at Liam. He blocked the attack—remarkable, really, since the demon weighed a ton.

A sudden sharp pain bloomed from his back. A second blade had slashed a deep gash in his skin, tearing through muscle.

Unfair game.

Liam fell to his knees, holding back a painful yelp. Warm liquid spread on his back and drenched his shirt.

"You ruined my jacket, asshole," he grumbled to the demon behind him as he gingerly took off what remained of the piece. He let it splay on the ground, a certain ache piercing his chest as if he'd lost a dear friend.

"We don't want you dead yet, traitor." A bald demon stepped closer and punched Liam's head so hard that the ring on his finger cut a line across his forehead. "But when we're done, you'll beg us to end you."

Blood poured down the left side of Liam's face and bloomed in his mouth—he had bit his tongue. His hearing and vision faded only for a moment. "If you were able to kill me, you would've done it already." He spat blood at the demon's feet. "Fucking wuss."

That did it. The demons surrounded him, their blades in hand and murder in their eyes. Flames sprouted from the Drakar's body as the Behemoth on the left shapeshifted into a creature with sharp claws and lizard skin that reminded him of a chimera.

The two other Drakars created the same vacuum sphere Jal had used, only one's lightning was red and the other's green.

Up near the ceiling, Archie fought against the demon with yellow wings, his head coated with blood—like father like son— but when he glanced down at Liam, despair cut through his face.

"No!" he bellowed.

His opponent took advantage of the distraction and punched Archie, shooting him through the ceiling.

A cloud of dust and debris fell down not far from where Liam kneeled.

Watch out for yourself, old man.

He took a deep breath and observed the demons, the four horsemen of his apocalypse. He forced himself up into a fighting stance. His knuckles were white from holding his sword too tight.

This was it.

Liam didn't fear what was coming. But Gods, he wished he could've kissed Ava one last time.

32

AVA

*A*va hurried through the night sky, dodging buildings with glassed surfaces that reflected the city lights.

"Ava!" Ezra screamed from behind as he followed her. "Where are you going?"

She barely registered the question. Liam was out there, and he was in pain.

The city gave way to the darkness of the channel below, and then Ava hovered above sector thirteen.

Liam was somewhere within those abandoned quarters. Even if Ava couldn't feel him anymore, this was where those strings of light and dark had ended.

Darkness fell in a silent mantle over the abandoned buildings and warehouses. Only one construction, a big, bulky cube at least five stories high, had lights flickering inside. No, not lights exactly.

Flames.

He had to be there. And she had to hurry.

Ava swiveled left and descended, soon landing with a big thud. Ezra landed behind her, his presence noted and ignored at the same time.

"Jophiel!" he shouted.

Ava blinked as if woken from a trance. She turned left to see the Seraph crouching on his knees behind a pile of scrap metal. Bulky chains wrapped around his neck, wrists, and ankles; chains that weren't made of iron or silver but a night-black material.

Ezra unsheathed his sword and hit the chains. A spark ignited from where his blade met the metal, leaving a faint scratch on the surface.

These were no ordinary cuffs. If they could hold down a Seraph, they must've been damned by an incredibly powerful demon—or the devils themselves, if that was even possible.

"What happened?" she asked.

"He caught me by surprise," Jophiel said through gritted teeth. Golden veins shone faintly from underneath his ebony skin. "He looked, smelled, even sounded like Liam. Behemoths can impersonate others, but they're never that flawless." A sizzling sound came from where the cuffs touched his skin. He winced and took a shaky breath. "I wasn't expecting to find one of them on Earth."

She would ask who Jophiel was talking about, but screams poured from the warehouse. Silhouettes battled fiercely through the windows and gaping door. Ava sensed the anger that flowed from Jophiel, the fury as he watched what happened inside. It overcame the burns the cursed chains inflicted on his skin.

Whoever trapped him had wanted the Seraph to suffer beyond physical pain.

They'd wanted him to watch.

"Help them," Jophiel ordered, his voice weak.

She didn't want to leave him, not like this.

"Go, Ava." Ezra raised his sword and hit the chains. "I'll free him." He hit them again, and one of the links cracked. "Go!"

She nodded and rushed into the warehouse.

Blood was sprawled on the walls and flowed on the floor. Ava almost slipped in a red pool, but she kept going, dodging the bodies intertwined in battle and jumping over the fallen as she searched for Liam.

The cavernous space amplified the shrieks of horror, pain, and fury; skin-crawling sounds that formed an eerie symphony.

Werewolves and vampires fought against the demons. She found Lilith taken by insatiable bloodlust, and a big werewolf who howled eagerly, urging his packs forward.

The priests of the Gray weren't here, and Ava understood why. The place was peppered by demons with multi-colored wings on full display. Against second-tiers, the Gray would easily perish.

She found Liam near the back of the warehouse and remembered to breathe. He might be alive, but he wouldn't last much longer. Blood painted the left side of his face, and he could barely stand. He was cornered by four demons, all second-tiers.

Despair spread inside as she rushed through the mess of battling bodies, but she wouldn't reach him in time. Her beasts of light and dark, however …

Black and golden lightning birthed from her hands and shot at the winged demons who threatened Liam's life, flinging them across the warehouse.

Liam gaped at the creatures and then at her, his green eyes filled with disbelief and awe.

"Ava?" he muttered as she ran to him.

She wrapped her arms around his chest and pulled him closer. He held in a painful scream because a deep cut slashed across his back, piercing through his shirt, skin and muscle. The wound tainted her hands with his own red.

Warmth took over Ava's body as her light shone,

connecting with his. She never imagined a demon could have light, but then again, she was an angel and her darkness was stronger than she'd like to admit.

Up is down, down is up, the Cap's voice rang in her mind.

Her light penetrated Liam's flesh, mending the deep cuts on his forehead and back. He hugged her with strength, and even when he was completely healed, he didn't let go.

"You're here," he whispered, his voice muffled at the curve of her neck, his fingers digging into her back.

She wanted to kiss him senseless, but there was a time and place for that and this was neither.

She let go of him and tucked her wings inside her light. She then withdrew her sword, swiveled, and slammed her back against his. "Just like old times?"

His body heaved with a chuckle. "Oh Hells yes, princess."

On they went into the crowd of battling bodies, piercing and slashing, burning and electrocuting. She and Liam fought with the coordination of a machine, charging, dodging, and attacking in perfect harmony. Sweat bloomed on her skin, both from the effort and from the heat of Liam's flames as he shot them forward, but she didn't mind.

This was more than like old times; it was better. It felt as if their minds were one. Their hearts, too.

"You've been training," Liam remarked as he slashed across a demon's torso.

She opened her mouth to reply, but someone yanked her away from him—a demon with spiky hair and a mad grin.

Before she could defend herself, the demon slammed a damned dagger in her gut, and a scream ripped through her throat. Ava's legs buckled as blood spurted from the wound. She fell with her back to the ground.

"Ava!" Liam yelled, but battling bodies had already closed the path to her.

The demon dragged her through the warehouse by her foot, leaving a red trail behind.

Gods, she couldn't heal herself, not while the cursed blade was stuck in her stomach.

The pain was blinding, and it sucked all the reason in her. She grabbed the dagger and tried to yank it out, but every move sent a jolt of pain from her gut up to her lungs. If she caused more damage, Ava could die before her healing was strong enough to fix the wound.

She could barely breathe now. The blade's darkness had been built to hurt and kill. It corroded her body, spreading tentacles of pain that curled toward her chest and waist, poisoning her. Ava's mind whirled, and she faintly remarked that the demon had stopped pulling her foot.

He turned back to her, and his smile spoke of madness. The creature kicked her forehead, then her ribs. The attack dislocated the dagger, which dropped tentatively on the ground beside her.

Heal. She needed to heal, but she was so weak and the world was spinning.

The demon spread his charcoal wings and raised his sword. "Now it'll be your head, angel."

Her golden shield swept across her skin. The thin layer wouldn't withstand an attack, not when it was no stronger than a thin coating of glass. The edges of her vision darkened.

The demon laughed. "Let's see how your shield holds against a damned blade." He raised his sword higher.

"Ava!" Liam howled from somewhere, his voice distant.

A blast rang in Ava's ears, but her sight was too blurry. She tried to focus and saw the demon standing still, his mouth agape and soundless. His hand opened, and his sword clanked on the ground.

A hole caked by black lightning consumed the demon's

chest, eating through his flesh. Beyond the gap, Ava spotted Liam rushing toward her. He shot dark spheres of black lightning toward the enemies that stepped between them. Pitch-black flames blazed around his body, turning him into a storm of night and darkness.

Liam's flames sunk under his skin as he pulled the demon's body away. He kneeled beside her, checking her face and stomach. His despair seeped into her core, cold and agonizing. "Are you okay?"

She smiled. "Never better."

"Smartass," he grumbled with amusement. "Can you heal yourself?"

"It's going slowly," she said while trying to ignore the stings of pain that pierced through her body.

"Well, let's give it a try." He spread his hands atop her wound and focused. A fog of darkness unfurled across her skin, diving into her flesh.

"Agh, it's cold!"

"I know."

Ava watched in awe as her wounds began to heal faster than ever before. "I never thought a demon could heal an angel."

"Me neither. But my darkness is connected to yours," he said quietly, his green eyes sharp with focus. "I can't understand why, princess. It just is."

Liam was almost done when he suddenly screamed and crouched over his knees. A horrible bellow burst through his throat as veins popped on his temples. His skin reddened, and he howled as if someone was murdering him from inside.

"Fuck!" he spat, trying to catch a breath.

His bellows caught the attention of a group of demons not far from them. They'd just finished off two wolves and a vampire, and now they were coming.

Ava didn't know what was happening with Liam, but she had to protect him. Her black and gold lightning crackled around them, closing them both in a dome.

The demons stopped outside, watching.

Waiting.

She wouldn't be able to keep this up for long. Already her mind felt fuzzy, pulling her over the edge of unconsciousness. The loss of blood took its toll and still, she managed to fling two demons away with her telekinesis.

Her body felt too heavy to breathe, like a massive stone sat on her chest—the symptom of abusing her abilities in a weakened state.

She would have to be more careful.

Liam kept screaming as talons pierced his back. Bone structures snapped and built atop themselves, forming two ivory trees coated by blood.

Ava's heart stopped. She had never seen how her wings had grown, but it must've been similar to this.

Flesh and muscles spread atop Liam's new bones, the clay of his creation. His naked muscles moved tentatively, accustoming themselves to motion. Skin wrapped over the surface, connecting femurs and ulnas, forming membranes. Finally, scales bloomed over the surface. They were dark as night, but their tips turned emerald green. The color of Liam's eyes.

Heavens, they were magnificent.

"You've ascended," she mumbled.

Or maybe it was descended. She had no idea what the right terminology was.

Her vision darkened for a moment, and then her back hit the floor. The first thing in Ava's mind was the shield—*keep up the shield.* She had to protect Liam; she was his Guardian.

He was her everything.

She blinked lazily, and then Liam was staring down at

her, worry all over him. His labored breaths made her think he was injured, but then she remembered the brand-new wings which had just sprouted from his back.

"I'm fine," she said as he helped her up. "Just a little dizzy."

The dome of lightning still whipped around them. Liam's wings closed them both in a cocoon.

Ava smiled, and so did he. She could almost see her reflection on his magnificent obsidian scales. "How are your wings obeying you? It took me forever to control mine."

"I don't know," he said as he watched her, love and care flowing like a river inside him. He cleared his throat, and the draconian wings coiled behind him. He wiggled them playfully. "They're still sore, but it feels as if I've had them since forever. It's strange."

Not entirely. Liam had been an Archangel for centuries. Some part of him must've remembered having wings.

Around them, demons battled beyond her bolts of light and dark, but that cursed group simply waited eagerly.

Fools.

Ava shot the lightning from the shield forward, flinging the demons away like waves crashing against a rock.

A shriek of pain came from the end of the room. Jal was limping near a scrawny demon with red hair. Their friend wouldn't last long.

"We have to help him!" she said, but Liam held her hand.

"That's Hauk," he growled, his focus on the red-haired demon. "He's mine!"

Hauk punched Jal mightily in his face, and he fell limp to the floor. Liam bellowed a war cry and boosted forward, propelled by his new wings.

Ava yelled after him, but he didn't listen.

A demon approached from behind. She could sense his body moving through her essence, reflected in her light. Ava spun just in time, and her blade clanked against her opponent's.

In the distance, Hauk's form began to change. His bones cracked, and his skin stretched. His muscles swelled until he became a much bigger version of himself. His fingers deformed into claws made to rip the skin off people's bones, and his wings spread behind him, spanning the width of a small airplane.

"Liam!" Ava yelled as she dodged another attack from the demon.

Her relentless, brave Selfless didn't hesitate. Liam jumped and slammed a punch of red, angry flames between Hauk's eyes.

The demon shrieked loudly, his deep, rumbling voice an earthquake in itself. It nearly drowned the rest of the noise in the warehouse.

He grabbed Liam's foot and threw him aside like a rag doll. He then focused on healing the wound between his eyes, which soon closed.

Hauk turned back to Liam to finish him off, but a colossal sphere of black lightning slammed into him, throwing the demon across the room and through a wall.

Ava watched the fight, mindlessly blocking the attacks from the demon who charged at her. When he nearly chopped off her arm, she grabbed him by his neck.

Golden light shone under her skin, but it wasn't her healing light. It came from the lightning that lived inside her rift, the lightning that normally whipped at her enemies. This time, it scorched everything that touched her palm. Like a firestorm raging inside her.

The stench of burnt flesh spread on the air as the demon screamed, but he soon fell unconscious and Ava let go. The skin on his neck was dark and scabbed.

A bright light shone from the entrance of the warehouse,

then zinged through five demons; a merciless bolt that pierced their chests.

The demons stood where they were for a moment, unmoving, before their bodies went down the way ripe apples fall.

Those who remained glanced around in fear and shock, not knowing what had hit their comrades.

From the entrance, Jophiel stepped inside, supported by Ezra. The Messenger had broken the chains, but the collar and cuffs were still locked around Jophiel's neck, wrists, and ankles.

The Seraph's chest heaved up and down in labored breaths. That bolt had clearly come from him, and it must've taken a toll on his already debilitated state.

Bright sickly veins spread further over his body, as if his skin was a cracking vase that kept the sun inside.

Ezra patted Jophiel gently on his shoulder and let him go. "Thank you, my King."

The Messenger then unsheathed his sword and swung it in circles, daring the demons to attack. Blue thunder cracked around his force field, forming a sphere around him.

The remaining demons glared at each other before raising their swords and bellowing a furious war cry.

33

LIAM

*H*auk didn't stay down for long. The asshole walked back through the massive hole his body had punched in the wall, his steps pummeling the ground.

"You may be a second-tier now," the demon spoke with a deformed voice, "but you're still weak!"

He charged at Liam and dodged the two spheres of black lightning he sent his way. The fucker was fast, even with his enormous size.

Before Liam could raise his defense, Hauk smacked his face so hard that he zinged in the air above the battling bodies. He should've spread his wings to slow down, but instinct took over and it wasn't used to them. Not yet. They disappeared into Liam's darkness right when his back hit the ground.

His body dragged on until he lost momentum, and then a freezing cloud spread underneath his skin, attending to the raw flesh on his back, the slight cracks on his skull, and the broken vertebrae on his spine.

Liam forced himself up using his sword as an aid. His

wounds weren't completely healed, but it would have to do. Hauk would be coming for him anytime now.

A scream came from the entrance of the warehouse. *Her* scream. Ava was crouching on the ground, her left arm twisted in an unnatural way.

Nothing mattered but her. Ava was his fuel, his entire existence. Before he could go to her, his princess jumped up and with one swift move cut across the demon who had broken her arm, making his guts rain down on the floor.

Ezraphael rushed to her, and light shone from his palms. He touched the wound.

He's fixing her, Liam's light whispered.

He's touching her, his darkness growled.

"I'll make the one you love suffer!" Hauk bellowed from behind as he rushed toward Liam.

He ducked as the demon's giant claw cut the air where his head had been a minute ago.

"When I'm done with you," Hauk continued as he attacked Liam nonstop, "I'll take her like I took my bride, over and over again!"

"The Hells you will." Black flames engulfed his fist, and Liam punched the left side of Hauk's face, scorching his skin.

The demon stepped back, half of his profile scabbed and deformed. If he felt any pain, Liam couldn't tell. The fucker actually smirked.

"I'll take your love, and then the entire Gorge will have their way with her." The laugh that broke through his throat turned into a cough.

Rage swelled inside Liam. He bolted toward Hauk, smacking a punch so mighty that the demon fell to the ground.

Liam jumped over him, his fists burning with black flames. He punched the demon once, leaving charred skin on the spot. "Her name was Firma!" He punched again, the hollow thud mingling with the hiss of burnt flesh. "Dhalia!" Again and again he punched. "Madeleine! Juarez!" He struck Hauk nonstop. It felt like pounding meat.

He spotted a piece of the demon's skull, blood and scabs already covering most of Hauk's face.

"You'll pay for what you did to them!" He bawled as he punched. Hauk stopped moving, but Liam kept hitting him. "You'll pay for what you made me do!"

The demon's bones cracked, his flesh shrunk, and then Hauk returned to his original size. Still, Liam kept punching. Without realizing, black flames had erupted from his entire body, singing all of Hauk, not just his face.

Liam went on. Hellsdamned if he would let that monster hurt anyone else.

A hand set on his shoulder and he jerked to his feet, expecting a demonic attack. He found Jal instead of the enemy.

The left side of his friend's face was swollen, and he was missing a tooth, but he still gave Liam his typically carefree smile. "Down, boy. We must interrogate Hauk."

Liam glanced at the unconscious demon, a disfigured mess of burnt flesh and broken bones. Hauk barely resembled anything close to human, but the prick was still breathing. "No. I end this tonight."

"We need to get to Master, remember?" Jal sighed despondently. "Hauk's our only link."

Liam's chest heaved up and down. "The things I had to do, Jal …"

"… Will be for nothing if we don't get to the man behind it all."

As much as he hated it, Jal was right.

Liam took one deep breath, then walked away. He had to, otherwise he would finish the job.

Only then did he notice the sounds of battle across the warehouse had ceased. All demons were either dead or gone.

He found Lilith at the corner, helping Jophiel walk. The Seraph looked weak and broken. Light shone from underneath his veins, and for a moment, Liam feared he might dismantle into tiny pieces.

Suther, the werewolf lord, watched them with crossed arms, still in his wolf form. He caught Liam's eye and nodded.

Look at that, he mused. *The dogs came through.*

He soon found Pedro sprawled lifeless on the floor, his black eyes gaping at the ceiling. A holy sword pierced his chest all the way through his heart.

Ezraphael stood beside the corpse, his silver bodysuit ripped and sprinkled with blood. He wiped sweat off his forehead and heaved a worn sigh before yanking the blade out of Pedro's chest.

Pedro deserved to die. He might not have been the worst demon Liam had ever met, but he was an evil bastard like the rest of them.

So, why did he hate Ezraphael for killing the puto?

Archie came forward, limping on one leg, and the Messenger promptly helped him balance. Darkness spread on the old man's calf as he healed himself. His father was hurt, but he would survive.

They all would.

Jal stopped beside Liam and pointed to Ezraphael. "Told you he wasn't bad."

"Jackass," Liam grumbled with a smirk.

He turned back around to see Jal had set a pair of blessed cuffs on Hauk's wrists and ankles.

"He's ready and packed." The demon rubbed his hands as a maleficent grin spread on his lips. "I can't wait to interrogate him back at the Legion. You see, torture used to be a specialty of mine back in the day." He toned down his excitement. "Not that I'm proud of it, of course."

"Of course," Liam chuckled.

He closed his eyes and bent his head back, taking a deep breath.

It was all over. At least for now.

A glint shimmered in his essence, coming from somewhere near the entrance of the warehouse. He opened his eyes to see Ava smiling at him.

He smiled back, ready to take her in his arms and kiss those soft, rosy lips he missed so much. He had almost reached her when an invisible force stole all his breath.

He bent over and watched Ava do the same, her blue stare wide and asking. His chest burned—no, it blazed. The light inside him swelled along with his darkness, aching to explode and connect with the forces inside her.

Thunder boomed everywhere, and the ground shook beneath their feet. At first Liam thought he might be hallucinating, but dust and debris crashed down from the roof.

"Heavens," Jophiel muttered as Lilith helped him balance.

A flash of light and darkness burst from Liam's chest, scorching and relentless, but at the same time soothing and peaceful. It mingled with the storm that rushed from Ava's own heart, a dance of light and dark equal to his.

The forces connected and spread throughout the warehouse, filling it with absolute dark peppered by golden light. Liam didn't know how or why, but he felt complete. As if he was opening a door inside Ava that led to himself.

Ava stared at him as tears slipped down her cheeks. Their light and shadow flickered joyously around the space before sinking back into their chests. The connection remained, though. An invisible line of love and care that bound them together.

Forever.

The warehouse was dead silent. It seemed fitting that Jal was the one to say, "Hellsdamned! Was that what I think it was?"

"No," the Messenger said as he stepped closer to Ava. *Liam's Ava.* He wrapped an arm around her shoulder. "Whatever it was, it meant nothing."

"Ezraphael, no!" Jophiel shouted. "He'll kill anyone who threatens the bond!"

Too late. Fury and bloodthirst engulfed Liam, and he saw red. Common sense slipped away, replaced by something raw and untamed; a primeval force urging him into violence.

She's ours, his darkness whispered. *We're hers,* the light countered.

Kill him, they said in unison.

Liam growled low in his chest, a draconian sound more monster than man. He guessed that's what he was now; what he'd always been. It didn't matter. He would make that asshole pay for touching what was his.

Ezraphael balled his hands; his nostrils flared. "You're not good for her."

The laugh that rolled up Liam's chest was cruel and bitter. "Better than you, asshole."

His wings unfurled from his darkness and spread behind him. Liam flew toward the Messenger, his movements faster than he could register. He had already smacked a punch on Ezraphael's face, then on his stomach. The Messenger barely saw him coming.

Liam grabbed him by his collar and pushed him up, propelled by his brand-new wings. Ezraphael kicked his chest and stomach, but Liam kept thrusting until he smacked the Messenger on the ceiling.

Liam tried to kick him, but the Messenger blocked his attack and jabbed his stomach, sending him on a downward

C.S. WILDE

spiral. Liam grabbed Ezraphael with his wings at the last minute and pulled him along.

They fought as they fell, the Messenger thwacking at his face and Liam kneeing his gut. He pivoted midair so that the angel would be the first to hit the floor. Liam could've flown away, but he wanted to see the job through.

The asshole's golden shield wrapped around him just in time. A cloud of dust rose as they broke a crater on the ground, but they quickly jumped to their feet and kept attacking each other.

Ezraphael's golden jab hurt like a motherfucker, though Liam barely registered the pain. His darkness healed him as he fought and soon enough, the Messenger's shield waned.

"Will you two idiots stop?" Archie yelled, but Liam ignored him.

He nailed a strike on Ezraphael's jaw and rejoiced when blood trickled down the edge of his mouth.

"You bleed easily, angel." His voice was more a growl than a human voice, but Liam didn't mind.

"Fuck you, Michael!" Ezraphael bellowed before punching the side of his face. "You won't take her from me!"

Blood spilled from Liam's lower lip, and he wiped it with his hand. "Oh, I didn't know the perfect Messenger could curse." He clicked his tongue. "You should pray to the Gods for forgiveness."

He took momentum to punch Ezraphael again, but an invisible force pushed him aside. Liam thrust forward, yet the unseen power blocked him.

Ava approached, her expression soft and kind. When Liam pushed against the force that held him in place, his princess winced in pain. Ava was using her telekinesis to stop them, even if it hurt her, so Liam immediately halted.

Ezraphael moved to attack him and smacked against the

same force. When he realized what it did to Ava, he stopped too.

She walked to the Messenger and cupped his cheeks. "I'm so sorry for hurting you."

"Don't." He skipped a breath. "Please don't go with him."

She nudged her nose with his. "You're the best angel I know, and you inspire me to be better every day. But I can't be yours, Ezra."

His fingers dug into her arms as he lowered his head. "Please, Ava ..."

She kissed his forehead, her eyes glinting with tears. "I need to know you'll be okay."

He watched her with a mix of shock and hurt. Finally, he gave her a sad grin.

"You always had such faith in me." She gave him a tight hug. "I have faith in you, too."

Ava gently let him go, then turned to Liam.

Archie approached Ezraphael and laid a supportive hand on his shoulder, pulling him away. "We'll take it from here, kid," he told Liam.

He nodded, then focused on Ava, who now stood before him. He brushed her cheek with the back of his hand. "So, soulmates are real," he whispered. "Who knew?"

She let out that beautiful, perfect smile that always told him everything would be fine. "Deep down, we both did."

He bent over and claimed her mouth, finally his. Forever his.

Liam's arms closed around her waist. Ava pushed herself on the tip of her toes and wrapped her arms around his neck.

Her golden shield spread atop them both. Liam knew exactly what she wanted him to do. Maybe it was because of their bond, or maybe he knew his princess all too well.

With one boost of his wings, they blasted through the ceiling and flew into the night sky.

34

AVA

They broke through the window and crashed into Liam's old apartment. As the golden shield covering their skin sunk back into Ava's core, she noticed her soulmate had pinned her against a wall. Love and warmth coursed through their bond.

Home. He was her home.

Liam cupped Ava's cheek and kissed her the way he used to, gently at first, but his tongue quickly unraveled into her parted lips.

She took all of him, her body aching for his touch. Smashed against one another, Ava felt the volume inside his pants pushing against her entrance. She nearly came undone at the thought of finally having him after so long.

She broke their kisses, her breathing ragged. "I'd always assumed soulmates were folklore, but you're here and you're mine."

Liam kissed her, and that was the only reply she needed. There was nothing outside this room, no world outside these walls, no worries or bloodshed. Just Liam and her.

His hands went to her bottom, and with one jump she

wrapped her legs around his waist, her back still pressed against the wall.

Liam drowned at the curve of her neck, kissing her skin and inhaling her scent. She did the same, catching the musky oak underneath his brimstone.

"I've missed you so much," his words drawled, still half-beast and half-man.

"We're dirty," she hazily said, then gulped. "I mean, we're coated in dirt and blood."

"Hmm …" He gripped her legs tighter and went to the bathroom.

Heavens, he carried her as easily as if she were made of paper.

Liam stopped before the shower, gently put her down, and turned it on. He crossed his arms and arched one eyebrow, his sly grin oozing with mischief.

Slowly, tentatively, Ava unzipped her bodysuit.

She undressed in curvaceous, lazy moves that released a feral snarl deep in Liam's chest. Oh, that sound set fire to her core.

Soon enough, her bodysuit pooled at her feet, and she stepped out of it.

Liam's wings disappeared and he removed his shirt, then unbuckled his belt. She helped him with his pants, then his boxers, and when she was done, Ava kneeled before him and watched his length.

She leaned closer and licked it with the tip of her tongue.

More; she needed more. So, she took him, all of him, in her mouth.

His head snapped back. "Ah, Ava!"

She kept sucking, and his salty oils dripped down her tongue. Her soulmate was so hard that veins thumped across his length and thudded against the walls of her mouth.

Liam stared down at her and caressed her hair. Watching

his hooded eyes love her so completely was almost a release in itself. But in one gentle move he stepped back and lifted Ava by her arms.

"I want that, princess." He nudged his nose with hers. "But I have other priorities at the moment."

He led her to the warm water and underneath it, Liam bathed all the dirt and blood away. All of Ava's worries and fears, too.

She leaned back on his chest and let him work. The soap danced over her skin, then lingered on her most intimate parts. Liam's soft touch drove her to the edge, but once he was satisfied cleaning her, his deft palm went up, toward her breasts. When he rubbed over her nipples, Ava couldn't take it anymore.

They had to hurry if they were to start other things … She faced him and took the soap from his hand.

She washed away the blood on his forehead, then his hair and chest. When she washed *that* part of him, the man gave way to the beast. Liam growled and turned her around, so that she bent over with her palms set on the tile wall.

He kissed her shoulder and neck as Ava spread her legs, opening the path for him.

Liam's touch was frenzied and hurried as he whispered, "I need you, I …" He licked the side of her neck.

She gave him a dizzy, breathless nod, and then he pierced her with a powerful shove. A gasp escaped her lips as she adjusted to his length.

"Hells, Ava!" he barked more than said. "You're so ready."

She tightened around him, and he hissed a curse. Liam rocked into her, each stroke stronger than the last. He drove himself deeper and deeper.

Her fingers dug into the tiles as waves of pleasure swam down her body. This wasn't sweet lovemaking—it was primal and ravenous and desperate. And it was only the appetizer.

Liam kept thrusting, harder, faster and Ava lost her ground, the friction inside her making her head spin. Faintly, she remarked how her inner thighs were soaked. When his hand drifted between her legs and rubbed, an electric wave swam across her, paving the path for the next.

"What you do to me," she rasped in her ecstasy, and then she was gone. Her first orgasm lashed out, making her shiver and lose her ground.

Once she came back to herself, he whispered, "This is just the start, princess."

He stopped thrusting and removed himself from her. Liam turned off the shower, stepped out of the box, and gave her his hand.

Ava scowled at him. "What do you think you're doing?" She nodded at his hard-rock length dripping with her oils. "I need to take care of that."

"Oh, trust me." He smirked. "You will."

She stepped out of the shower begrudgingly. Liam took her in his arms at once, lifting her off the ground. They kissed as he took her to his bed.

Liam laid Ava on her back and hovered atop her, propped on his elbows. Her soulmate drowned her in kisses, his tongue dancing with hers as his hardness brushed against her opening.

Happy. She was so happy.

"I'll never let you go again," Ava muttered as she filled him with kisses. "Forgive me. Forgive me for leaving you."

Liam's forehead crumpled. "You didn't leave me. You did the noble thing like you always do." He brushed a stray lock off her forehead. "You wouldn't be my Ava if you hadn't done what you thought was best for your charge, even if it hurt you."

"But you're not my charge. You've always been so much more." Her throat felt raw and heavy. "I shouldn't have stepped away."

"It was the right thing to do." He bit her lower lip softly. "Now, no more of this."

He trailed a path of blazing kisses down her collarbone, chest, and when he nibbled at her nipple, Ava's mind spun.

He kept kissing the trail down to her navel and only stopped on her most intimate part. His tongue rubbed the pearl between her thighs with hunger, and a moan escaped Ava's mouth.

Underneath his violent kisses, her breaths rushed closer to one another. Ava rose toward a peak so high it might doom her.

"You taste so good," he growled as he suckled and licked with a fury.

Ava's mind spun, and she had no time to breathe or think before she exploded within herself, crying his name twice as she thrashed on the bed. Through her haze, she was barely aware that he'd held her legs tightly in place.

The sadist kept licking.

Ava roared as another wave of maddening pleasure smashed against her. Her body shuddered violently until slowly, her string of orgasms subdued.

Heavens! The entire building must have heard her.

Liam peeked at Ava from between her thighs and gave her a grin that was half innocent, half evil.

He moved up so he could see her eye to eye. His perfect mouth was so close … she kissed him and tasted herself on his wet lips.

With one harsh shove, he filled her to his hilt. Wet sounds came from each slow thrust, his hips moving the way tides strike, once, twice …

"You feel so good," he said, his tone cracking with pleasure.

Propping himself on his left elbow, he took her right breast fully in his hand and tugged at her nipple. His emerald eyes glinted with lust as he watched the pleasure that broke across her face.

Gods, this was a torture she never wanted to end. Each thrust was a punch inside her, but the pain was delirious, wonderful, and it brought her higher and higher, closer to a release that was right there, so close to her fingertips.

And because Liam watched her, he knew she would peak soon. He slowed his rhythm. "Why, princess, so eager for an encore already?"

"Oh, you demon!" She slapped his strong chest. "Don't you dare stop."

He did! His body went still.

"You vile creature!"

Liam raised one tantalizing eyebrow at her. "You lack control, princess."

Oh, she would show him. Ava closed her legs tightly around his waist as her wings flashed free. They propped her to the side so that she turned Liam on his back, pinning him on the bed.

She sat astride his perfectly defined body, his length still locked into her.

He watched her with shock and lust, his hands digging into her thighs. The naughty glint in those green emeralds told her he wanted to turn around and pin her back to bed. Before he could move, Ava began riding him in smooth, calculated strokes.

His back arched, and his features crumpled. "Fuck, Ava. It's too good."

She felt him inside her so fiercely that the edge he'd stolen from her bloomed once again between her thighs.

Liam's beautiful face contorted into something close to pain as he squeezed her bottom. He was holding his release, waiting for hers. But his release was hers to have, and she would have it whenever she wanted.

She struck against him relentlessly, moving her hips in circles as she took him, and when she clenched her belly muscles around him, her own release took her at once.

The tsunami of pleasure that rushed across Ava blinded her. She felt herself shivering but still moving around him in a trance. She faintly heard Liam bellow, "Hells, Ava!" and then his release burst inside her, filling her with delirium.

Still reeling in her orgasm, she vaguely noticed she had stopped moving, barely feeling her own body—it seemed lighter, so her wings must've slipped inside her light.

Gentle arms wrapped around her, and then she was lying on her back. When she came to, Liam was lying atop her. Still inside Ava but watching her, propped on his elbows.

Childlike wonder glimmered in his eyes. "You're everything."

"I can be that and more." She moved her hips sinuously around him.

He kissed her slowly, gently. "Being here with you feels so good. After all I've been through, I …"

"This room, this happiness, is ours." She cupped his cheeks. "Focus on that, not the past."

He nodded and kept kissing her.

Ava's time without Liam had been miserable. She didn't want to remember it, not now. Not ever again.

She caressed his temples, playing with the strings of dark hair that hung over the sides of his perfect, oh so perfect, face.

He looked down at her chest, then at his. "Do you feel this?"

She understood what he meant: the light and dark

connecting them, the balance, the sense of peace that had taken them both.

"Yes. It's strange, but it feels so natural." She brushed her thumb over his bottom lip. "Like this is how we were always supposed to be."

His gaze locked on hers as he moved his hips forward again and again.

She gave him a lazy grin. "Hmm, already?"

He shrugged and kept thrusting, growing inside her. "This soulmate bond is no joke."

He gazed at her breasts, and this time his focus was ravenous. He bent down and took one nipple in his mouth as his thrusts increased.

She felt him, all of him, rubbing against the walls of her intimacy; wet sounds and sensations exploding inside her. When he drowned at the curve of her neck and tilted her hips up, bringing her closer to him, Ava lost her mind.

"Liam, Gods!"

She could feel it coming, the explosion of ecstasy as he mercilessly slammed into her. Liam propped himself on one elbow and lifted his head, watching her with bewilderment as his thrusts increased.

Her rapture hit her so hard she couldn't do much to stop it.

You lack control, princess.

She didn't care. Ava saw white and screamed so loudly her throat felt raw.

Liam smiled ferociously as he kept thrusting. "You coming …" He hissed through his teeth as she tightened her legs around him, closing on his length. "It's too fucking much, Ava!" He hissed again, his face crumpling in frenzied pleasure.

"Hmm," she moaned, still reeling in her surprise release. "Tell me again about control, my love."

His pitch-black wings spread behind him, spanning from almost the windows to the door. If Ava could paint him right now, she would. Liam was night and darkness, and he was loving and he was hers.

"Say that again," he grumbled, edging on his own release.

She nibbled his lips and whispered, "My love."

With one mighty thrust he exploded inside her, a part of him becoming hers. "Ah, Ava!" He kept thrusting as his release slowly subdued.

Still sweating and panting, Liam removed himself from her with a displeased grunt. His wings disappeared in a blur of shadows, and he dropped on the mattress beside her, taking Ava in his arms.

She rested her face on his chest.

Heavens, Justine was right. Sealing the mating bond was a unique, brutal, experience.

"Oh, princess." His tone was a soft caress. "We make this an art."

"We really do," she giggled, the bond between them pulsing, their essences synced. "I've never felt this happy before. Actually, that's not true."

"That time at the Legion?"

She nodded. Their first time.

She should've known he was her soulmate then. Why had the bond taken so long to snap into place?

Liam seemed to guess her thoughts. "Maybe we weren't ready."

"Or maybe we both had to ascend."

She felt him nod. "It's a reasonable explanation. Though I have no idea how this soulmate thing works."

"I think we just found out." She ran a finger down to his navel.

A smooth, feral chuckle rolled up his chest. "That we did." He watched the ceiling, even though it had nothing out of the ordinary to show him. His mood grew somber; she could feel it through their bond. "I've missed you," he said quietly, more a confession than a statement. "Not just as a lover but as a friend. You always stood by me, you always had my back, even if it put you in danger." He held her tighter in his arms as if he were afraid she would break if he let go.

She stamped a kiss on his lips. "Partners?"

He smiled at her as if she had said the most silly and yet beautiful thing in the world. "Forever."

JUSTINE HAD MENTIONED that the mating bond could be consuming, but Ava had never expected it to be this ruthless.

Days passed in a blur of moans and tangled sheets. She did things with Liam she had never imagined, things that stole Ava's sense of self, things that put color in the world.

They made love relentlessly. Gods, they made love on his old couch, atop the kitchen counter and the dining table. They made love on the window sill while masking their essences, and they made love in Liam's shower again—this time they broke the shower head.

Oh, and that thing he did with his tongue …

The muffled air in the apartment reeked of sex and sweat. Ava loved it. She never wanted to leave this nest; *their* nest.

But eventually, they must.

One afternoon, splayed in bed after another furious round of lovemaking, she pressed her face against his chest.

Would he love her less if she told him?

She pondered for a while, listening to his slowing heart-beats. Eventually, Ava figured she would never know if she didn't say it.

"I'm tired of fighting for what's right." Guilt took over the space her words left behind. Vera would be so disappointed, but Ava owed honesty to her soulmate. "We've given up so much, and we almost lost each other because of it. What you told me about the Gorge, what you had to do and endure …" Something shattered in her chest. "I wish we could run from it all."

Liam stilled, and Ava wondered if he thought she was a terrible, selfish person.

He released a pondering breath, then drew invisible patterns with his fingers on her upper arm. "Gods, Ava, I want nothing more than to run away with you." He kissed her forehead and held her tightly. "But we have to go back at some point. Master is still at large, and there's Talahel to deal with."

"Jal phoned you yesterday, didn't he?" she blurted.

Ava was in the shower when she'd heard the line ring. She asked Liam who it was, to which he shrugged and said, "Takeout might be late."

Her soulmate might be a smart detective and a cunning man, but he was also a part of her. Ava knew he'd lied, but her trust in him didn't waver.

It never would.

"I didn't want to worry you," he explained. "Also, I was about to join you in that shower, and talking about Jal would've killed the mood."

She slapped his chest tenderly.

"Anyway, Jal told me he's running out of resources to make Hauk speak," he said. "The asshole finally agreed to reveal where Master is, but only to me."

"That's progress, I suppose." She bit her bottom lip. "I have news, too. Justine sent me a mental message yesterday. Agathe will read Talahel's mind tomorrow in an open session at the Order. I must be there, if only to see him fall."

He gave her a weary sneer. "I can relate."

"Our damned duty ..." She buried her head deeper into his chest.

"Yeah, but when all of this is finished, we'll take some holidays. What do you say? Just the two of us."

She would love to go away with him, but it was wishful thinking. "Even if everything works and our enemies are defeated, the Order will never allow us to be together," she said quietly. "You're a demon, and I'm an angel."

He nuzzled her cheek. "I'll never allow anything or anyone to keep me from you."

She wouldn't, either.

Ava kissed the curve of his neck, gently biting his skin. Liam inhaled sharply before letting out a soft groan akin to a lion's purr.

Her hands drifted down his chest, across his navel, slowly going toward his crotch. She felt how ready he was as her palm closed around him.

She kissed his lips, then crawled down the bed, stopping before his length. "Your stamina amazes me, demon."

Ava had started something on their first day here, and she needed to finish it. So she bent over and took his fullness into her mouth.

Liam clawed the sheets, his head snapping back as she sucked all of him, her lips tightening around his throbbing shaft.

His eyes rolled to the back of his skull and he grumbled, "What you do to me, woman."

A warm and giddy sensation invaded Ava's chest. She didn't care what would happen tomorrow. Today, the world was theirs.

For as long as they would have it.

35

LIAM

*J*al was waiting for him when Liam stepped in the Legion's hall.

The fresh scent of pine wafted from the wooden walls and floor. Liam inhaled deeply as he observed the golden chandelier on the ceiling and the wine-colored carpet with the symbol of the Gods beneath his feet.

It felt as if he hadn't been here in decades.

"Your holiday of fuckery did you good." Jal tapped him on the back. "You look like a new man!"

"I feel good. Really good." A smile creased his lips. "Finally, after the—"

"—humongous shitstorm you went through?"

He gave him a rueful grin. "Always the master of words, *demon*."

Jal shrugged. "It's a gift. *Demon*."

Liam watched the vast foyer. He'd hoped to see Archie today, but the old man had called in earlier and asked if he could accompany Ava to the Order.

Princess had gladly obliged and said, "I would love to spend some time with the man who raised you."

Liam knew the reason behind his father's request, of course. Archie wanted to be near in case things went south at the Order. This way, the old man could watch over Ava while Liam interrogated Hauk.

A pang of anxiety swirled in Liam's chest. What his father thought of Ava meant the world to him, although he had a feeling Archie already approved of her.

Jal led Liam to the wooden door underneath the indoor balcony, which took them to the underground area.

They soon stopped before a training room with a green padded ceiling and floors to match. Inside were Jophiel, Lilith, and a demon with red hair sitting on a metal chair.

Damned cuffs strapped Hauk's wrists and ankles to the seat. The asshole deserved blessed cuffs that would burn his skin, but Liam supposed Jophiel lacked the cruelty to do it.

Pity.

From what he could see through the window, Lilith tried to interrogate Hauk, but the demon kept his head low and unmoving. If he didn't know better, he would say Hauk was either dead or sleeping.

Scabbed patches ran down the demon's arms and left cheek. Hauk was still recovering from the damage Liam's hellsfire had inflicted. He hoped the bastard was in pain.

Jal opened the door, and when they entered the room, Lilith's chest puffed with pride. "I was right. You and angel girl are soulmates." She glanced at Jal with victory stamped on her face.

The demon showed her his tongue, and Liam wondered if they had placed a bet on it.

Scratch that. They absolutely had.

Jophiel smiled at them the way a father did with his children. The Seraph looked tired, but at least golden cracks didn't break through his skin anymore.

Jal had once told Liam that Jophiel felt a great deal of pain when he used his powers. They deteriorated his health too—the price of having Seraph's light trapped in a human body. Using his powers back at the Gorge had clearly taken a toll on him.

A naughty grin spread on Lilith's lips, drawing Liam's attention. "Sooo, I heard the sex is amazing."

He crossed his arms, unfazed. If she expected him to blush, she should've known better. "Mind-blowing."

Jal hooted, but Jophiel shook his head in an exasperated manner. He laid a hand on Liam's shoulder and said, "The soulmate bond is rare and strong, but your connection with Ava goes beyond that."

Liam frowned. "How so?"

"I'm not sure yet. Perhaps the answer lies in your essences, and why the light and dark are so vigorous within both of you. Still, your connection is a beautiful thing that calls for celebration." He clapped his hands and turned to the demon sprawled on the chair. "Everything in due time, however."

Liam nodded and walked to Hauk, then crouched before him. From the floor, he could almost see the demon's face.

"I heard you were asking for me, boss," he mocked.

Hauk's hazel eyes snapped open. "Where's my wife?"

Dhalia.

"She's being taken care of," Jophiel said with a certain defiance. "You should see what a drop of my Seraph's essence does to a poisoned demon. She's recovering from what you did to her."

Relief washed through Liam's core, and he made a mental note to go check on Dhalia later. Not only to make sure she was okay, but also to beg for her forgiveness.

Not that he deserved it.

Hauk bared his teeth at Jophiel. "No! She's Master's gift to me!"

"Not anymore, she isn't," Liam snapped. "Speed this up, will you? Take us to Master so we can finish this."

"Oh, no, you got it all wrong." Hauk's eyes widened, and Liam saw a hint of blue breaking through the hazel. "I'm bringing Master to you."

The demon thrashed wildly in his seat, nearly breaking through the cursed cuffs.

Liam jumped to his feet and stepped back. A cold sweat broke out on his skin as the demon shrieked a raw, desperate sound. Dark throbbing veins spread over Hauk's body.

All at once, the demon's spasms waned and he fell limp on his seat, his labored breaths wheezing through his throat.

"Hauk?" Liam asked.

"He left the building." If evil had a voice, this would be it. A deep, guttural tone that was all levels of wrong. It raised the hairs on Liam's neck.

If he recalled his Selfless lessons correctly, a demon couldn't be possessed by another demon, especially if said demon wasn't nearby.

What if Master was in the Legion?

Despair took over, and Liam gaped at Jophiel. As if guessing his thoughts, the Seraph shook his head. If there had been any hostiles within these walls, he would've sensed them.

Master was far away.

"Hauk gave him permission to be possessed," Jophiel explained before turning to the demon, his expression a mask. "You can't find out where we are, so why possess your henchman? Your theatrics must be taking a toll on you, Wraith."

Liam swallowed dryly, trying his best to hide the fear that ate through his chest. Wraiths were the equivalent of Seraphs, powerful demons who ruled the Hells.

Master laughed. "I simply wanted to say hello. I'm not devoid of social manners, Seraph."

"Playing games is a Wraith's specialty," Jophiel went on, not an ounce of fear or doubt in him. "Forgive me for being overly cautious. Which of the three Wraiths are you? Malachia? Beruben? No, they have a sense of duty, and they absolutely hate Earth." He scowled at the demon. "Ah, Soleigh. You've always been more reckless than your brothers."

Master blew air through his lips. "Soleigh is weak; they all are." He leaned forward, facing Jophiel with unnatural sapphire-blue eyes. "You call me Wraith, but I am so much more. I'm the end of this world. I'm what keeps you up at night. I am—"

"—fucking humble," Liam interrupted, arms crossed to feign nonchalance when all his instincts told him to run from this room and never stop.

Master's attention snapped toward him.

Liam held his gaze and went on. "Look, we'll find you eventually, and we *will* send you back to wherever you came from. Why don't you save us some time and surrender yourself?"

Master observed him with an expression halfway between bored and annoyed. Finally, he asked, "How's Ava, by the way?"

Agony squeezed Liam's lungs. "How do you know about her?"

A playful chuckle rumbled in Master's chest.

"He must've read Hauk's mind," Jal said from the corner with balled fists. "We see through your party tricks, asshole."

"You're wrong, demon," Master countered, amusement coating his voice. "I've been watching her for a while now."

As an experienced detective, Liam could sniff a lie in the air. But there were no lies in Master's words.

Blood ran ice-cold in his veins. His entire body shook, and his muscles turned to stone. The bastard had been watching Ava all this time, and Liam hadn't had a clue.

No, Jophiel was right. This Wraith liked playing games, and Liam shouldn't tag along. He took one recomposing breath and feigned apathy. "Get to the point."

Master leaned back in the chair. "What do you suppose I want, Liam?"

"World domination." He raised his shoulders. "Hells on Earth, the usual megalomaniacal bullshit."

The demon considered his answer. "True, I want all those things. But there's something I want above it all. What I truly want, Liam, is what you took from us."

He couldn't possibly mean ...

Liam cleared his throat, trying hard to feign composure. "Ava was never yours."

"Because she's your soulmate? That's irrelevant." Master sniffed the air as if he were smelling her lavender scent. "We'll have our precious Ava and there's nothing you can do to stop us."

Liam's jaw clinched so hard he could barely form words. But the demon was talking freely now, and he had to take advantage of that. "Who's 'we'?"

"You'll find out, one way or another." Master leaned forward. "She's not quite there yet, you see. Our Ava needs to be darker, crueler. Like a fine wine, she must mature." He smiled delightfully. "Her light is sublime, but we shall squash it."

"You bas—"

"Oh, Ava," Master hummed. "I will rip her from your arms and drown in her lips."

"Over my dead body." Angry tears piled in his eyes. "You won't touch a hair on her head, this I promise you!"

Master clicked his tongue. "Do you stop the sun from

rising or the night from falling? I will have her. It's inevitable. She won't be mine. She already is, Liam."

Screw this.

A sphere of darkness grew in his hand, with black lightning cracking around it. He didn't care that he would kill Hauk and not Master. He just needed to silence this son of a bitch.

Jophiel stepped forward and pushed Liam back. "You die today, Wraith." The Seraph's light shone from his chest and beamed at Master.

Liam narrowed his eyes as scorching golden light engulfed the room, focused on where Hauk was sitting.

Master howled in pain, but soon enough laughter came from the light. He kept laughing, barely catching a breath as the stench of Hauk's burnt skin and hair spread through the room.

"Is this the best you can do?" he bellowed.

A cloud of darkness bloomed from inside the light, a mass of thunder and shadows that broke through the gold and jolted at the Seraph, engulfing him in a storm of rumbling darkness.

Jophiel's light roared from inside and eventually broke through the swarm of shadows, but the damage was done. The Seraph kneeled on the floor, gasping for breath. Golden veins spread on his dark skin as if Jophiel was cracking porcelain.

Jal ran to the kneeling Seraph. "What did you do to him?"

Master bared his browning teeth. His unnaturally blue gaze stood out from skin charred beyond return. All of Hauk's hair was burnt to the roots. The demon barely resembled something human.

"I made it a fair fight." Master's voice rang weak and faded from the blackened remains that occupied the chair. "She needs to mature. And then she'll be mine." He blinked, barely able to keep his eyes open. "Ava will mature, Liam. Rest assured."

Spasms overtook Hauk's body as he thrashed in the chair. Black goo poured out of his mouth and nostrils, covering his burnt chest.

Slowly, his convulsing stopped. The demon exhaled one last time, his irises now hazel. Hauk's head lolled to the left, but his dead gaze still gaped at Liam.

Master had not only weakened Jophiel, but he had also possessed and killed a powerful demon such as Hauk from a distance.

The mere fact this monster existed sent chills down Liam's spine.

"Something bad will happen at the Order," Jophiel rasped. "I saw it in his mind. Leave me!" He waved off Jal. "Take Lilith, take the priests and priestesses, and take Lothar!" Jophiel must be confused because Lothar was dead. He had obviously meant Suther, Lothar's son. The Seraph glared at Liam. "Save Ava!"

"She needs to mature."

The fuck she would.

Liam's wings flashed behind him, and he soared out of the room, breaking the glass walls.

AVA

*A*va and Archibald had plenty of time before the assembly where Agathe would publicly read Talahel's mind, so they strolled leisurely on the sidewalk.

He nodded to the clear blue sky above and said, "If I believed in this kind of stuff, I'd say it's a good omen." He ran a hand through his hair in a very Liam-like manner. Stubborn sand-blond strings waved over his temples in protest.

Archibald may not be Liam's biological father, but the proud swagger in which he moved, his straight posture, they were also Liam's. She found pieces of her soulmate within the man who raised him. The man who was not only Liam's father, but also his partner and friend.

She hoped she could impress him, and that Archibald would approve of her. He was important to Liam, which meant he was important to her.

"Your son has a lot from you, Archie," she said quietly, hoping he wouldn't mind her using his nickname.

"Thank you." A proud smile spread on his lips. He probably didn't hear this kind of compliment often. "So, you're my son's soulmate, huh?"

A slight flush flowed up her cheeks. "I suppose that makes you my father-in-law?"

Archibald smiled down at her and Ava could swear his boyish grin was nearly identical to Liam's. "I suppose it does." He stopped and glanced up at the sky, inhaling the fresh morning air. "The kid's been through the Hells and back. He deserves something good, Ava, and that's you. You're his reward."

"Liam is a piece of me. He always has been, even when I couldn't see it." She raised her shoulders. "He's my reward, too."

Archibald scratched the back of his neck, and Ava noticed the hint of fear that wafted shyly from his core. "I know you two had some rough patches, but—"

"I will never hurt him again," she assured, recognizing the source of his concern. "I love your son, and I would do anything to protect him."

"I know." All too quickly, Archibald trapped Ava in a bear hug that stole all her breath, but she didn't complain. "He told me everything you did for him when I wasn't around. Thank you for looking out for my boy when I couldn't." He choked up and cleared his throat. "I've failed Liam so much …" He let her go and stepped back, sniffing back tears.

Ava had also failed her soulmate—and herself. Yet this was all in the past. Now Liam was hers, and she was his, and the world was right again.

Finally.

"Ah, parental guilt." She turned forward and walked with her hands behind her back. "I've seen it many times in my charges. You constantly think you're failing your children, but you couldn't be more wrong."

"How do you know?"

She looked back at him from her shoulder. "You're doing your best. And more often than you think, that's enough."

Archibald shook his head and pointed a finger at Ava. "Oh, you're good."

She winked as he caught up to her. "I try."

"Well, Mrs. Kid." He shoved his hands in his jacket pockets. "You really are something."

"Thank you, old man."

He frowned playfully, the way a father does when trying to chide a misbehaving child without actually meaning it. "Watch it, kid."

Ava giggled, then let the sun soak her with its warmth as they went.

She had found her peace with Liam. Not only that, but from now on, innocent In-Betweens would be safe. The Legion would grow stronger with the presence of werewolves. Everything was as it should be, and to top it off, Talahel would go to prison today.

The Order's detention center was located on a secret island where no prisoner could escape. The most terrible demons and In-Betweens lived there. She doubted they would receive Talahel and his goons with open arms, which meant the Sword would spend the rest of his endless days in solitary.

A fitting punishment.

When Ava spotted the Messenger walking toward them alongside Justine, her throat knotted and her body felt heavy. Her palms began to sweat.

Archibald leaned closer. "I'm not a Dominion but I can see you're not looking forward to this."

"Perceptive, like your son." She shook her head and muttered, "I don't want to hurt Ezra."

Archie laid a supportive hand on her shoulder. "You owe him respect and care, kid, but don't feel bad for not giving him your heart. It's a gift you owe to no one, not even my boy. You give it willingly, always."

Liam's father could be a wise man.

As they approached, Justine's brown irises focused on Ava. Her friend's voice exploded in her mind. *"Oh my Gods, you have a soulmate! In your face! I was right!"*

Ava held back a giggle. *"Yes, you were."*

"You're telling me EVERYTHING once all of this is over!"

"I will, but first—"

"How was the sex?"

Ava blushed and choked. She slapped her own chest, trying to subside the series of coughs that followed. *"Justine!"*

"Heavens, that good?" Her friend's playful demeanor vanished when she realized Ezra was here. He walked beside her with his attention focused on the floor. *"Er, maybe we'll continue this another time."*

Ezra stopped before them and Heavens, the sadness and sorrow in his face, the purple circles under his eyes ... Ava doubted he had gotten any sleep in the last few days.

Guilt washed through her because Ava wasn't sorry. Maybe she should be, but she loved Liam, and she was happy. She would never apologize for that.

Did that make her a terrible angel?

Ezra briefly glanced at her before giving Archibald a curt nod. "I apologize, but this is where you must stop. You're a demon, and if you approach the Order, I won't be able to guarantee your safety."

Ava remembered how Ezra had helped Archibald back at the warehouse. The old man seemed to share the memory because he watched the Messenger with care. "We knew each other when I was Acheron, didn't we?"

Ezra nodded, his lips in a line.

Archibald lay a hand on his shoulder. "It's a pity I can't remember. I hope you will catch me up one day?"

Ezra gave him a faint smile that broke Ava's heart. "I would like that."

The old man gave him one last tap on the shoulder before turning to Ava. "Thanks for the pep talk, Mrs. Kid." He winked at her and then left, though Ava was certain he would be nearby if needed.

He might not have said it aloud, but Ava knew Archibald had accompanied her for her own protection. He must fear something would go wrong at the Order, even if the chances were slim.

Justine stared at her and then Ezra, the silence between them an awkward veil. "I'll go now, if that's all right." She pointed back to the Order's skyscraper. "Talk to you later?"

Before Ava could reply, Justine had already scurried away.

"That's odd." Ezra scratched the top of his head. "Justine came because she wanted to talk to you, but she left."

"We spoke briefly through our minds." Ava crossed her arms. "I'll catch up with her later. I suppose there are more pressing matters at the moment."

"Ah, of course. So …" He lifted his chin, finally meeting her eyes. "You have a soulmate."

Ava should've said something, but words failed her. What could she tell Ezra without hurting him?

The Messenger tried to smile, but his lips seemed strained. "I never stood a chance, did I?"

Ava stepped forward and cupped his hand, bringing it close to her heart. "You and Vera shaped the angel that I am. Your kindness, your abdication … they are pure and beautiful. You were my role model for a century, Ezra. You still are."

"And I wasn't enough," he countered.

Her heart collapsed on itself. "You are more than enough. I love you, Ezra, but I can't love you the way you want me to."

He gently caressed her cheek. "Timing was never on our side, was it?"

"Even if we had been together, Liam would still be my

soulmate." She raised her shoulders. "Some things, I suppose, are inevitable."

Her words hurt him, so much so that he winced. But eventually, he nodded in agreement. "I suppose you won't be my mate anymore."

"I will keep helping you with the Order, if that's what you need. After all, mates don't need to be romantically involved."

"Yes, but I doubt Liam would be okay with our continued mate status." He inhaled deeply. "Don't worry, Ava. I'll be fine. You're hereby officially released of your duties." He kissed the back of her hand. "Though I would appreciate having you as an advisor."

"It would be an honor." She kissed his hand back. "It always has been."

He took a deep breath before releasing her hand. "So, are you ready to change the Order?"

"Oh." She let out a vicious sneer. "I've been ready for a long time."

They entered the building and took the elevator to the last floor, soon arriving at the courtroom where not long ago, Ava had a hearing about her innocence.

Gods, it felt like forever had passed since then.

She watched the dome that showed the sunny day outside. Light poured through the glass, spilling over the space ahead and highlighting the white marbled floor and rows of seating. Once, the space had felt empty in the way of a cathedral. Today, it was filled to the brim.

Today, it resembled an arena.

The rows formed an audience around the center of the space, where the judge's stand, the defense, and prosecution tables stood.

Voices filled the room. Anticipation and fear thrummed through the air, sinking into Ava's bones.

She and Ezra walked the straight path towered by

marbled seating that led to the center of the courtroom. Drones hovered above with cameras that would broadcast the sentencing to the Order's branches around the world, while also projecting blue holo-screens on the marbled walls. They showed the head angels of each international branch accompanied by their strongest peers.

In the center of the arena, in front of the judge's bench, stood Agathe and Talahel, guarded by two Archangels and two Virtues. A yellow folder containing the evidence rested on the bench.

Ezra motioned discretely to his left as they approached, and two of his strongest Dominions joined him and Ava. The bulky men walked beside them with their hands hovering above the hilt of their swords.

Talahel displayed no emotion. Whatever he felt, he kept hidden inside. Perhaps he didn't wish to show the Dominions in this room how angry he was. Or maybe, there was another reason altogether.

It didn't matter. His sentencing was as good as done.

When they stopped in the center of the space, beside Agathe and her Virtues, his mask broke. Talahel glared at Ava with contempt and red, burning hate.

She smiled.

The Throne raised her palms, and the murmurs and whispers in the courtroom faded.

"Brothers and sisters," she said. "Alarming evidence has come to light, evidence that can shake our Order to its very core. On this day, judgement upon a high angel is required, and you must all be witnesses. The Gods are with us, and we are with the Gods."

The crowd and the angels behind holo-screens repeated the last sentence in a somber encore.

"Naturally, I oppose this assembly," Talahel addressed the room, his voice booming throughout the space. He kept his hands behind his back and his spine straight in typical military fashion. "The Throne will read my mind, but who can make sure her words are true? One of her Virtues? How can one rely on a statement that can very well be filled with lies?"

Most of his Archangels nodded in agreement, so did a good number of other angels in the room. This was Talahel's danger: he used common sense and plausible doubt to protect himself.

A few of his soldiers, however, glared at him with disgust. Archangels and Warriors who didn't agree with his commands.

If Talahel rebelled, no one could predict the outcome. The men and women following him might be the majority between their peers, but they were not the majority in the room. And still, they were skilled fighters with centuries of experience over the other children of the Gods.

A pang of fear swam down Ava's spine.

"I am the Throne, Talahel!" Agathe snapped. "My judgement is fair and honorable. This has been the way since the Order came to be. If you performed no wrong doing, you shall have nothing to fear."

"I did the best for the Order, my Throne," Talahel said more to the room than to her. "Always!"

Agathe narrowed her eyes at him. "You used to trust my judgement. Why the sudden change now, brother?"

Talahel didn't reply. Underneath his mask of honor and innocence, he must know his time was coming. That in the best case scenario he would be imprisoned forever, and in the worst case, he would face his final death.

"You doubt me, sister," he said quietly. "Don't act so surprised when I doubt you in return."

Agathe huffed as she took the folder from the marbled stand. "I doubt you because I have proof! Tell us why you maintained private properties for decades on end, or I will scavenge every bit of information in your brain right now."

He swallowed. "The documents are false."

"They are not!" She pushed the folder against his chest, making him step back. "Why did you betray us?"

His Archangels moved their hands to the hilts of their swords, their shoulders hunched as they watched the interaction intently. The Virtues and Dominions around Ava, Agathe, and Ezra mirrored their stances.

Talahel observed the space with an expression that was both sorrowful and angry. He took a breath to compose himself, then grabbed the folder.

"I did it, sister," he said, leaning closer to her. "Because I had to finance my own army."

The Throne pointed one irate finger at him and turned to her Virtues. "Arrest him at—"

Talahel unsheathed his sword and slashed it across her neck, silencing her mid-sentence.

Agathe's head fell on the floor, and her body collapsed atop it. Her black wings flashed out of her obliterated essence and twitched one final time before they stilled.

Screams of horror and fury cut through the courtroom.

Time passed slower as Ava watched chaos unfold. Most Virtues and Dominions jolted to the center of the arena with vengeance written on their faces. Their high angel had been murdered, and they needed atonement. Some Warriors, the ones against Talahel, followed them.

Other angels led weaker ones, like Erudites and Guardians, to the doors, guiding them to safety. But most lower angels refused to leave. Many—such as Justine— dodged the ascended who tried to get them out of there and hurried to the center of the arena. Screams ripped through their throats, tears in their eyes.

Foolish bravery.

Talahel's Archangels and Warriors surrounded him in a protective circle. So did Ezra's Dominions and Agathe's Virtues, putting themselves between the enemy and the Messenger.

Tears coated the Virtues' eyes because they had failed their high angel—Ava could feel their angst and guilt corroding them from inside. But it wasn't their fault. Ava couldn't have stopped it, either; Talahel had been too fast.

"Treachery!" An angel with a British accent yelled from a holo-screen on the right.

"*Guerre!*" Another bellowed from the screen on the left.

Ava couldn't feel their fury, but it was blatant on their faces. The headquarters of the Order was falling, and there was nothing they could do.

The sound of wings flapping on glass caught her attention, and she looked up. Archangels with black wings and bodysuits peppered the dome from the outside, blocking almost all the sunlight. They punched the glass nonstop.

Ava had never seen those angels before, and she had never seen so many with the same shade of feathers. Almost as if they had been fabricated on a production line.

Liam mentioned a Possessor had tainted human souls to turn them into demons. Could Talahel have done something akin to that?

The Sword shot Ava a wolfish grin just as the dome cracked.

Glass rained upon the courtroom, releasing an army of blood-thirsty creatures upon them.

AVA

*A*va watched the Order fall.

War cries filled the room as brothers and sisters clashed against each other. Swords were drawn, blasts were shot, and blood was spilled.

Children of the Gods turned to enemies.

Ava stood amidst the madness, shock planting her feet. She had meant to save the Order, but never through violence and bloodshed.

Never like this.

The numbers might've been on their side, but that was before those black-winged creatures had crashed upon the room. Their skin was the color of a void, their eyes completely white and matching their sharp teeth.

Even when blades slashed across them, the things kept smiling. Even when life faded from those bright slits, they still grinned.

Ezra flung himself against an Archangel with red and purple wings who attacked a group of Erudites at the far end of the room. Ava should've gone after him, but her feet wouldn't move even if she forced them to.

A pair of Virtues clashed with black-winged creatures not far from her, building a barrier between them and Ava. She couldn't say how long they would endure.

Most holo-screens had blinked out, though others remained, showing horrified angels on the other side. When a Warrior smashed against a drone up above, another screen disappeared.

A blue display on the right showed the empty South American branch. They were the closest to the headquarters and they must've left to help, but they would never arrive in time. A body smashed through another drone, and that screen also blinked out.

Erudites and Guardians fought bravely and fell quickly. Unlike Warriors, they had no experience in battle.

Virtues and Dominions paired with the few Archangels and Warriors who were against Talahel. They tried to fight the fabricated angels, to protect as many third-tiers as they could, but they stood little chance against their former peers and those black-winged things filled with bloodthirst.

Ava heard her name and looked to her left. The Captain was pulling on her arm, her beige wings spread wide behind her.

"Ava!" the Captain yelled as she slammed her sword into a Warrior's gut. "Snap out of it!"

Only now did the clang of metal against metal penetrate Ava's ears, reverberating through her bones. Her body jolted awake. She blinked, unsheathed her sword, and fixed her stance.

The Captain gave her a pleased nod before flying to aid a Guardian who faced one of Talahel's godsless creatures.

Ava's essence thrummed with a warning. A Warrior approached her from behind with his sword raised high. She barely ducked in time, but with one swift countermove, she slashed across his stomach, revealing his entrails.

The Warrior fell on his knees, his essence fading from behind his irises. As a lower angel, he wouldn't be able to heal himself.

We murder, her own voice rang in her mind. *We avenge.*

We also forgive, the same voice countered.

But not today. Her white bodysuit was sprayed with his blood.

A plea for help caught Ava's ear. She followed it to find a group of lower angels cornered by an Archangel—a female with baby-blue wings and violence carved on her face.

She was about to strike them, but a bulky Guardian with ebony skin stood in the woman's way, ready to perish first. He would face his final death with defiance and pride.

A crying Erudite behind him bellowed for help again as she watched the Archangel draw her sword. "Please spare us, sister!"

The Archangel ignored her plea. The blade swung up.

Ava ran and dodged the battling bodies as she held the woman's blade with her mind. The Archangel frowned at her own sword before finding Ava. She then took momentum, knowing that her enhanced strength might break the telekinetic hold.

Almost there.

The sword went down and toward the Guardian.

Ava's invisible hold shattered just in time for her blade to meet the Archangel's with a furious clang. The Guardian jumped back, unscathed.

Her opponent grumbled a curse and charged, but Ava's golden shield covered her own body just in time. The Archangel's sword cut a small line across her chest.

It felt like nothing but a paper cut.

Using her telekinesis, Ava threw the woman toward the ceiling and beyond the sky. Her head immediately hurt, and her bones ached. If she were to survive this, she would have to save her strength.

"Follow me," she told the group.

"It's you!" The brave Guardian's face lit up when he realized who she was. "Dominion Lightway, you saved us during the In-Between attacks, and you save us now."

"Gods be praised," muttered an Erudite who resembled a scared squirrel.

Ava frowned at her. "The Gods aren't here."

A bitter sensation crawled up her throat. Her waning faith left an empty void inside her. Ava wasn't ready to let go; not yet.

Gods, guide me.

"Come on!" she ordered as she led them to the exit.

The doors to the courtroom had been blocked. A team of at least ten black-winged creatures guarded the massive wooden planks and slaughtered those who tried to get out.

Ava cursed under her breath, then looked around the room. Corpses wearing white and light-gray piled on the bloodied floor. The number of black bodysuits had begun winning over the rest.

Air closed around her. There was no way out ... She glanced up to the broken ceiling.

No way out except up.

Ava exchanged one glance with the Guardian, and he nodded. Her wings flashed behind her as she took the terrified Erudite in her arms. The woman shook so hard she might break.

Regardless, Ava boosted to the sky.

She flew past the metal bones of the broken atrium, dodging ascended angels and creatures who battled in the air. Soon enough, she spotted an empty rooftop and gently landed.

She released the Erudite, who took a moment to find her balance—the woman had probably never flown before.

Ava turned toward the broken dome, but the Erudite grabbed her hand.

"We're angels, and we're killing each other," she croaked. "This doesn't make sense."

"I know." It was all Ava could give her before flying back.

Winged figures zinged and clashed in the sky. Ava dodged the rolling, flying bodies as she tried to get back.

Dominions and Virtues carried lower angels out of the battlefield, and some Archangels helped them—Ava spotted a Virtue with navy-blue wings take the ebony-skinned Guardian to a safe rooftop while an Archangel with amber feathers fought a black-winged enemy that tried to smite them.

Ava's beasts of light and dark roared, hungry to join the battle. Gold and black lightning swam underneath her skin, then cracked around her in a sphere.

The lightning pierced through eight black-winged creatures and two evil Archangels who jerked wildly in the air, then fell down to the ground unconscious. They wouldn't wake before hitting the concrete, which meant they would— no, they were—already dead.

Ava shouldn't rejoice in their gruesome ends, but she couldn't help it.

They'd deserved it.

She dashed back into the broken atrium to find Ezra fighting Talahel. A mass of battling bodies stood between her and the Messenger. She couldn't find the Captain or Justine.

Ezra kneeled on the ground as Talahel relentlessly attacked his golden shield until it began sinking back into Ezra's core. She could already spot the white of the Messenger's boots.

Despair and anger filled her chest. "Ezra!"

He found her and gave Ava a faint smile that said good-bye. It was all he could do before Talahel slammed his blade into his stomach.

Blood trickled down the edges of the Messenger's mouth. Talahel lifted his sword and Ezra along with it, his high angel's strength easing his movements. The bastard flung him against a wall.

Ezra's limp body slammed into the surface, and when it slid down the white marble, it left a red trail of blood.

Something inside Ava cracked. Fury scorched her and made her see red.

"Talahel!" she screamed as she unsheathed her sword. "You die today!"

He grinned as he stepped toward her, taking the challenge.

A loud boom blasted from beyond the wooden doors, followed by another. The dark surface shook, and the battle in the courtroom halted. The black-winged creatures that guarded the door stared at each other in confusion.

In one violent surge, the doors burst open and vomited an ocean of In-Betweens that easily swallowed the things guarding the entrance.

Figures in loose light-gray clothing followed the were-wolves and vampires who charged into the enemies. *Priests of the Gray*. The Selfless joined them with Kevin leading the way. They shot at every hostile they could find.

In the mess, Ava spotted Lilith with red shining eyes and blood on her lips. Jal zinged past her, accompanied by Archie.

The old man landed close to Ezra and yelled for assistance.

Thank the Gods.

Ava spotted an olive-skinned demon flying toward her,

his mighty obsidian and green wings glistening under the sunlight.

Liam landed beside her, and she threw herself at him, feeling as if she hadn't taken a breath since this madness started.

"Miss me?" he asked as he shot dark flames into someone behind her.

"Always," she countered as her lightning electrocuted an incoming Warrior. His skin charred, and he jerked violently. When her attack stopped, the Warrior fell dead on the floor.

Had he been ascended, he might've survived.

Only three holo-screens remained stamped on the walls, and they displayed befuddled angels who watched an army of In-Betweens save the Order.

Talahel's men and women stood no chance against the Legion and the Selfless who filled the courtroom. Neither did those strange creatures.

Victory was a matter of time.

The Sword must've reached the same conclusion because he boosted up, flying past the broken atrium.

"He's escaping!" Ava jolted into the sky, chasing after him.

"Wait!" Liam shouted from behind, but she was already gone.

Ava followed Talahel through the city, dodging skyscrapers and the spheres of red lightning he shot at her. Every high angel had a special power, and this was his. Ironic that it was oddly similar to the spheres ascended demons could create.

She evaded four of them, but the fifth slammed into her stomach. Pain blinded her as she plummeted to the ground.

Her left side had become a mess of charred flesh. The fabric of her bodysuit had disintegrated on the spot, and the tips of her ribs poked from the wound. Healing this would take too much energy and time.

She watched Talahel's shrinking figure on the horizon and gritted her teeth. She couldn't let him get away.

Instead of retreating to take care of the wound, Ava used her healing to numb her pain centers. Sure enough, the raving ache subdued and she took a deep invigorating breath.

Her wings lifted her up, higher and higher each time, until she was chasing Talahel from above.

The smug bastard had no idea he was still being followed, so when her black lightning struck, Talahel fell from the sky like a dead fly and crashed into a rooftop garden.

Pain stung Ava's ribcage and stomach as she landed, but she forced her healing toward her pain centers again. The excruciating ache faded.

Sweat coated her skin, and her breathing became ragged. Ava wouldn't be able to keep this up for long. Not to mention she might go into shock any moment now.

All around her, white flowers grew atop curling vines supported by wooden arbors. Lemon and apple trees lined a stone pathway that cut through the green, leading to a small pond ahead. Beside it, Talahel scrambled to his feet.

Ava inhaled the citric scents as she stepped toward him. Her muscles relaxed if only slightly.

This was the end. It felt right to happen in a peaceful place such as this.

"You," Talahel snarled, still recovering from her electric currents as he stood. His hands jerked with a fury. "You'll pay for this."

A sphere of red lightning crackled on his trembling palm, drenching his face in crimson.

Ava ran to him, even if she didn't have the advantage. Time was of the essence.

He shot the sphere, and she dodged it by an inch. Talahel

gaped in shock as her fist crashed into his jaw, sending him to the ground.

Ava unsheathed her sword and attacked, but Talahel blocked her with his own blade just in time. He pushed her back and jumped to his feet.

They walked in circles.

Two prowling beasts.

"Repent," she ordered.

"You've come a long way, Guardian." He clenched his teeth. "Why don't you use that mighty lightning of yours again? Is it because you're getting weaker by the second and need to keep functioning?" He nodded to her wound and shrugged. "Smart move, I suppose."

"I won't ask again," she said.

He charged, and their blades crashed so hard that sparks ignited from the impact. *Clang, clang, clang.* Every strike hit Ava with the power of a wrecking ball, but she stood her ground.

For now.

Talahel was the Sword, leader of all Archangels. His strength remained unmatched in the entire order, his speed, too. Besides, Ava was severely hurt. There was only one way this would end, and it wasn't favorable to her.

He found an opening in her guard and sucker-punched her wound.

Pain raged from the spot, and blood spilled inside her body. Ava bent over, seeing stars. She'd ruptured an organ, that was certain, but the pain quickly faded as she numbed it with her healing.

Ava didn't need to see the blade that cut the air toward her neck; she *felt* it in her essence.

Something mad and starving birthed inside her, and Ava moved faster than she imagined possible. She pivoted out of the blade's way and slashed across his stomach, then his chest. When she punched Talahel's right cheek, the strike sent him crashing into the rooftop's access column, and he dropped his sword.

She walked past it and toward him.

Talahel was panting, and he could barely stand on his own feet. Their fight had weakened him; Ava could still feel the remnants of her black lightning coursing through his body.

"You're a cancer!" She bellowed as she approached, fury taking over her movements, her thoughts, everything. She raised her sword. "Be quick to make your peace!"

"Ava!" Liam yelled from above and landed between her and Talahel.

"Get out of my way!" she ordered.

"You got him." Liam turned back to Talahel, and his muscles tightened in the way of a panther about to strike. "This asshole will serve a very long time."

"Let me finish this, Liam!" Tears stung her eyes. "He needs to pay for what he did!"

"He will." He raised his hands as if she were a wild animal he tried to tame. "If you let hate consume you, princess, you might never come back from the darkness. I've looked into that abyss, and it nearly destroyed me. I can't let that happen to you."

She stood there, frozen midway, her throat tightening as she took in his words. Slowly, Ava lowered her blade, even if every fiber in her being urged her to kill Talahel.

"Fools," the Sword grumbled.

Red lightning flashed behind Liam's back, hitting him with a fury. It shot him past Ava and close to the edge of the rooftop.

Her soulmate crouched on the concrete, his wings burned and tattered. He held gut-wrenching howls in his throat, his body shaking from all the pain.

Ava glared at Talahel as wrath, scorching and unmerciful, took over.

He hurt our Liam, the light whispered.

Make him pay, the dark begged.

She would, pets. She definitely would.

Talahel leaned against the column as he pushed himself up. His red blast had taken a toll on him, and he fell to his knees only to force himself up again. "The Order would've thrived under my command!"

"Thrived?" Ava gnarled through bared teeth. "You nearly destroyed it!"

"Ava, don't!" Liam shouted from behind, but she barely registered his plea.

A certain serenity took over as she raised her sword. With one big swipe, Ava sliced off Talahel's left wing, then his right. They fell in bloodied slumps beside him.

The screams that erupted from his throat were music to her ears.

Yes, Ava would slaughter him, but he must suffer first.

"You whore!" he barked, spit forming on the corners of his mouth. "I'll kill you!"

Pluck his fingernails, then his eyes; pluck him like a grape from the cluster. The idea had come from beyond the darkness; somewhere Ava couldn't find within herself.

A stabbing pain spread over her stomach, and she bent over. Horrid screams pierced the air, and she realized they'd come from her.

Numbing her pain centers had stopped working.

Ava swallowed and tried her best to ignore the maddening ache. Her vision blurred, and she shook her head. Drops of sweat dripped over her eyes.

Not now! She was so close!

She managed one recomposing breath. She didn't have time to play with Talahel, not before she lost consciousness.

Better get to it then.

She raised her sword with difficulty. "Say your prayers."

Someone grabbed her shoulder and yanked her away. Ava crashed with her back to the floor. She forced her head up and through her fuzzy eyesight, she spotted two figures clashing ahead.

Bones snapped, or maybe it was wood cracking; she couldn't tell the difference. Flesh ripped as a body split in two.

Not in equal parts, though.

The remaining figure held a severed head. The spine dangled from where the neck ended.

The figure turned to her, and panic took over. Liam had wings. Where were the shape's wings? They had to be there, they... they weren't.

No. No, no ...

Darkness filled her vision, but Ava forced it away. If Talahel had killed Liam, she would bring the Hells upon the Earth, and she would take her revenge to the Gods themselves.

Curse them! Curse them for all eternity!

"Liam!" His name thrashed through her throat as tears spilled down her cheeks.

Silence replied.

We'll destroy everything, the voice inside her snarled.

The back of her skull hit the floor. She was so weak ...

"Liam, please!" She'd meant to yell, but what came out was a broken croak.

Darkness blinded her for a moment, and when she blinked, he was staring down at her, his green eyes sparkling with humor. "Why, princess, can't you spend five minutes away from me?"

She smiled and cried violently. Her chest convulsed with sobs as she cupped his cheeks and kissed him.

C.S. WILDE

Liam was safe. The Gods were good.

She promised to pray for their forgiveness later.

The blinding pain in her stomach returned without mercy. Ava held a yelp, but soon millions of cold fingers swam underneath her skin, reacting to the darkness in her.

Her wounds began to heal, and her internal organs stopped bleeding. Liam's darkness washed through her as he watched her with love.

"What about your wings?" she asked.

"Tucked them into my darkness. I can worry about them later. Your wounds are way worse than mine." He brushed a stray lock off her forehead. "Sorry I took the killing blow from you."

He wasn't sorry at all. Relief flowed from him in soft clouds.

That strange voice inside her cursed Liam for stealing Talahel's death. But the angel she had once been—and still strived to be—thanked her soulmate with all her might.

"I think you saved me," she said quietly. "In more ways than one."

"I know." He grinned down at her. "Now, how about those holidays we talked about?"

LIAM

$\mathcal{T}$he next morning, the Order's hallway was packed with angels, Selfless, In-Betweens, and priests of the Gray. It made for a nice image: all the supernaturals together in the same room for the first time since, well, ever.

Except for demons. Liam, Jal, and Archie were the only children of the dark there.

They wouldn't have minded, but some of the remaining angels and In-Betweens glared at them with reproach. Those ungrateful idiots had fought with them side by side, and they still didn't trust them.

He rolled his eyes. They had proven themselves again and again.

When would it be enough?

"There aren't many of us left," Ava said from beside him as she observed a group of angels on the right.

Liam squeezed her hand and hated that he *felt* her pain and sorrow through their bond. There was nothing he could do to ease it other than to be here. So he wrapped his arm around Ava's shoulders and brought her to him.

"Most Virtues and Erudites are mind-sweeping an entire

quarter. There are more of you out there." He kissed the top of her head.

Liam guessed there couldn't be more than five hundred angels scattered around the Order, plus some two hundred children of the God of Knowledge and Logic out there, erasing people's memories of the battle.

That was all that remained from the Order. Hells, they used to number thousands.

All angels in the hallway wore white bodysuits with white kilts. There was no difference between them, other than the fact that some had wings and others didn't. Even the few Warriors and Archangels who had fought against Talahel wore white.

Since Ezraphael was the only remaining high angel in the Order, he'd decided to change a few things. From now on, angels could be differentiated by their powers but not by their status. Which meant that an ascended was officially no better than a lower angel—who were now either called third-tiers or young angels. According to Ezraphael, the terminology was demeaning. After all, there was nothing low about them.

The Messenger—if this was still his title—might not be Liam's favorite person, but the guy had principles.

Liam pointed to the winged angels in the crowd. "Why are they showing them off?"

"I suppose it's a way to mourn the fallen. And to show pride," Ava explained.

Odd that she didn't have hers on display.

"Ava!" Justine shouted as she entered the hallway.

Ava gasped, and so did Liam. Justine had wings! Gradient pink and yellow, as if the sun was setting on her feathers.

She ran toward Ava, who hugged her with strength. "You've ascended!"

"I did!" She stepped back and showed her the wings, which wiggled behind her playfully. "Badass bitch that I am."

The two of them talked eagerly as Liam looked around. He remarked something about Justine taking a break from wiping people's minds to come and say hello, but then he zoned out of their conversation entirely.

At first, the groups of supernaturals had gathered in circles around the hall. Wolves and vamps had been standing on the far left, angels, Selfless, and priests of the Gray on the right. Slowly, though, angels walked to the In-Betweens and started conversations. So did the Selfless and the Gray, until the entire hallway had become a mass of creatures who used to hate each other but were now united under the same flag.

Small drones zinged in the air above, carrying cameras that would broadcast Jophiel's speech to all branches of the Order around the world.

"Oy!" Kevin waved from a mixed group of angels and wolves.

He went to Liam and was quickly followed by Archie and Jal, who had been standing in a corner.

Archie held the hand of an angel with short pixie hair. Did he get a girlfriend when Liam wasn't watching?

The woman trapped him in a bear hug that was surprisingly strong considering her petite physique. "I'm so proud of you," she said, her voice hoarse with tears.

Liam frowned and was about to ask who the Hells she was when she let him go.

In the angel's brown eyes, he spotted an old woman with dark gray hair and a lifetime of battle on her shoulders. She had the same button-like nose and haircut as the Cap.

Heavens, she looked so young! And she had her eyes! She had her eyes, and she was okay.

He hugged her back and sniffed back tears to avoid the

indignity of crying in front of everyone. "Hey, Cap," he croaked.

"Hey, kid." She caressed the back of his head the way a mother would. She then stepped back to Archie, who intertwined his fingers with hers.

Liam pointed to the two of them. "I always knew this was a thing, you know."

They exchanged a giddy glance which reminded Liam of the teenagers they must've been once.

The shuffling of feeble, weak feet on the marbled floor was quiet and yet so loud. All voices in the hall silenced.

Ezraphael helped Jophiel walk. The Seraph was still recovering from Master's attack, but at least the golden veins had disappeared from his skin.

They went slowly, catching the attention of the entire room. The crowd parted and cleared a path to the center of the hall. Finally, they stopped under the round chandelier that resembled a small sun.

Jophiel let out his light. It flowed from him in warm, soothing waves. Like he was a star that shone with peace and love.

Everyone in the room bowed to him. Wolves, humans, angels, demons, vamps—every single one of them. Liam and Ava included.

"Rise," he ordered, and so they did.

The Seraph wore a white tunic that matched his white hair and beard. Liam suspected the days of Jophiel's heavy metal T-shirts and ripped jeans were over. It saddened him in a way, but the Seraph winked at him playfully.

Maybe those days weren't over yet.

Wrinkles cut across night-dark skin that had been flawless only a few days ago. Jophiel looked so much older. If Master had weakened him this much from a distance, what could he do to … Liam gazed at Ava, who stood beside him.

He pulled her closer as a mix of fear and anger overtook him.

Master's deep, unearthly voice echoed in his mind. *"Do you stop the sun from rising or the night from falling?"*

His throat tightened.

Ezraphael stepped away, giving the space to Jophiel. The Seraph forced his spine straight, tied both hands behind his back, and observed all the supernaturals around him.

The drones hovered frantically above, ready to stream Jophiel's speech to the Order's branches. Blue holo-screens blinked to life on the white marbled walls. They showcased angels gathered in rooms all around the world, eager to listen.

"Yesterday, the Order fell," Jophiel's voice boomed across the hall. "Today, it rises again as the Legion. But if we're to strive against the oncoming darkness, we must embrace our brothers and sisters who fight for good, no matter their origin." He nodded gracefully at Lilith and Suther, then bowed his head to the priests of the Gray and the Selfless. He smiled at Liam, Archie, and Jal. "Even if they come from the dark, let us welcome them, for they renounced evil to stand in the light. Good comes in many forms, not only angelic ones. What happened yesterday was proof. We must understand this if we're to grow as a unified front against the surging demonic threat."

The holo-screens showed faces full of doubt. Even in the hallway, some angels stared at each other with apprehension.

"How are we to achieve this goal, my Seraph?" asked an angel not far from Liam.

"We'll bring the leaders of every branch around the world to the headquarters for training. They have been warned and eagerly wait." The Seraph must've sensed the hesitation that poured from the faces in the screens and through the hallway. "The transition won't be easy, but against our unified front, the emerging darkness will fall. I am the King of the first Heaven, and I won't fail you."

He had to remind them of who he was. That's all it took. Applause burst from the screens and the hall, echoing wildly around them.

Jophiel waited for them to fade. "From now on, brothers and sisters, we are equals. Surely, we have different power ranges and different needs, but we're connected by our will to help others regardless of our past or origins."

"Pardon me, my king," an angel said from a screen on the upper right. He had long dark hair and wore a white bodysuit. Liam could see the eye of London in the background. This guy must represent the European branch of the Order. "We're meant to fight a *demonic* threat." He shot Liam, Archie, and Jal a disdainful glance. "We cannot accept demons in our Legion."

"I must agree," said a woman with a shaved head beyond another screen, her thick Swahili accent evident in her words. "Vampires and werewolves can be redeemed. But demons? Never!"

The first angel nodded. "Demonic attacks are growing throughout the world, my king. We cannot be expected to fight the dark by letting it in."

Jophiel and Ezraphael tried to argue, but the angels on the screens had made their decision. The discussion turned into muffled sounds Liam easily dismissed.

He already knew the outcome.

Ava watched him with worry. "Gods, this isn't fair."

He kissed her cheek. "I know."

Archie's face showed no surprise. "Well, that's angelic gratitude for you." He cast a longing glance at the Cap and held her hand tighter. "Guess we'll have to be like Romeo and Juliet, darling."

She winked at him. "Should be fun."

Eeew! Archie was his father, and the Cap the closest thing Liam had to a mother. Could they please avoid flirting in front of him?

Kevin shook his head. "This is rubbish."

"It really is." Justine hugged herself and leaned on his left shoulder.

"I never cared about the Legion anyway." Jal shrugged, but his bitter tone guaranteed the opposite.

"You won't get rid of us so easily, Jal of Jaipur," Lilith's voice came from behind. She stepped closer, accompanied by Suther. "I don't care what those stupid angels say. You will fight with us whether the Legion agrees or not."

The demon gave her an adoring grin, then ran a hand through his loose black hair. "You can't live without me, can you, Lil?"

She tapped him playfully on his chest but didn't deny it.

Liam didn't give a rat's ass about the Legion not accepting him. Master wanted Ava, and the bastard was out there.

Waiting.

He pulled his soulmate aside and grabbed her hands, pressing her palms to his chest. "We always chose duty over ourselves."

The glimmer in her blue eyes told him she understood what he meant. His beautiful, loving soulmate leaned on the tips of her toes and pecked him on the lips. "I think it's time we choose us, don't you think?"

"So that vacation …"

"… starts now."

Oh, his perfect woman. How happy she made him.

The Hells he would let Master ever get to her.

Liam felt bad about keeping his true motivations from her, but he figured getting Ava out of town was more important than his guilt.

"I heard about this little deserted island in the Pacific," he said casually.

With one golden flash, Ava's feathery white wings flapped behind her. A brush of darkness sprouted on Liam's back, and then his obsidian wings spread wide.

"Ready?" Ava's feet left the ground. So did his.

He had seen what Master wanted: the bloodthirsty Valkyrie that lived inside her, next to the kind Guardian.

Fire and ice. Darkness and light.

Liam had to keep her safe, no matter what. He gave her his hand. "Always."

With that, they flew through an open window and soared into the sky.

An Exclusive Gift

Join the Wildlings at subscribepage.com/liam to keep up to date with the latest on C.S. Wilde and participate in amazing giveaways. Also, you'll get an exclusive short-story featuring Liam.

Thanks for reading!

Choose which book you want next!

Ratings help me determine which series I'll prioritize, so if you can't wait for the next book in this series, leave a review and show your love. Production on the third instalment only begins once we reach thirty reviews on *Blessed Fury* or *Cursed Darkness*.

That's right: YOU get to choose which books come next by leaving a review.

Yay!

Another aspect that helps me decide which books come next is sales. So if you acquired this book through piracy, make sure to buy your copy.

Piracy is not only a crime punishable by fines and federal imprisonment, but it also ensures that no more books in this series will be written.

Piracy ruins books. It ruins authors too. And that's not cool at all.

Keep up to date with the latest news and release dates by joining C.S. Wilde's mailing list.

And if you want to discuss all things Blessed Fury, join the Wildlings or follow C.S. Wilde on Facebook!

ALSO BY C.S. WILDE

Angels of Fate Series:
BLESSED FURY *(Angels of Fate book 1)*
CURSED DARKNESS *(Angels of Fate book 2)*

Science Fiction Romance:
FROM THE STARS *(The Dimensions series book 1)*
BEYOND THE STARS *(The Dimensions series book 2)*
ACROSS THE STARS *(The Dimensions series book 3)*
The Dimensions Series Boxset *(Get book 1 for free with the boxset)*

Urban Fantasy Romance:
SWORD WITCH

Paranormal Adventure
A COURTROOM OF ASHES

ABOUT THE AUTHOR

C. S. Wilde wrote her first Fantasy novel when she was eight. That book was absolutely terrible, but her mother told her it was awesome, so she kept writing.

Now a grown up (though many will beg to differ), C. S. Wilde writes about fantastic worlds, love stories larger than life and epic battles.

She also, quite obviously, sucks at writing an author bio. She finds it awkward that she must write this in the third person and hopes you won't notice.

For up to date promotions and release dates of upcoming books, sign up for the latest news at www.cswilde.com. You can also connect on twitter via @thatcswilde or on facebook at C.S. Wilde.

You can also join the Wildlings, C.S. Wilde's exclusive Facebook group.

52740716R00233

Made in the USA
Columbia, SC
06 March 2019